A CRITICAL HUMAN ERROR

When Paternity Is Not a Choice

Barbara A. Glasier

 FriesenPress

Suite 300 - 990 Fort St
Victoria, BC, V8V 3K2
Canada

www.friesenpress.com

Additional Contributor:
Corinne Nowoczin did an initial edit (Editor)

This is a book is fiction. All of the characters are fictional and the storyline is fiction. Character development is a blend of the author's experience and imagination. The names of cities/places used are actual locations in British Columbia and Alberta.

ISBN
978-1-5255-6232-7 (Hardcover)
978-1-5255-6233-4 (Paperback)
978-1-5255-6234-1 (eBook)

1. FICTION, ROMANCE, SUSPENCE

TARGET AUDIENCE: *ADULT READERS WHO ENJOY REALISTIC FICTION WITH STRONG CHARACTERS AND RELATIONSHIPS WILL ENJOY A CRITICAL HUMAN ERROR.*

Distributed to the trade by The Ingram Book Company

To My Family
with Love

A hundred years from now, it won't matter
what my bank account looked like,
what kind of house I lived in,
or what kind of car I drove.
But if I can make a difference in a child's life,
the world may be a better place.

~Author unknown

CONTENTS

PROLOGUE

———

Saturday, April 14, 2007

Andy and Meredith Taylor weren't expecting any visitors. They were planning on a relaxing Saturday, a time to re-charge their dangerously low batteries after another long and hectic week of work and travel. Andy was exhausted and already taking a morning nap in his leather recliner after having gotten up only two hours ago. Meredith was beside him in her recliner, cozied up in her baby-blue fleece pyjamas and trying to catch up with the week's accumulation of daily newspapers. The southeast sun was streaming in through six long, vertical windows in the front of their house, warming the room to a pleasant temperature for napping. Meredith was getting sleepy too; her eyelids half closed as she struggled to read.

The doorbell rang. Meredith looked over at her unresponsive husband—not a single muscle quivered. It was usually he who answered the door and the telephone. She glanced out of one of the living room windows where she could see a silver-colored sedan parked across the street with a woman in the driver's seat. She didn't recognize the car and couldn't identify the woman. Her eyes returned to Andy. His chest was moving up and down rhythmically, mouth slightly ajar. He was oblivious to her unspoken expectation and developing irritation.

Convinced that their unsolicited visitors were probably sales people, she alerted her sluggish brain to prepare for a polite refusal. While garnering all her remaining energy, she struggled to push the footrest of her recliner down, went to the door and opened it. She was shocked to see a young girl standing alone beside two large, new-looking suitcases. *What the heck is this about?* She quickly estimated the girl to be about six years old. "Well, hello there, young lady, what can I do for you?"

The girl looked up at Meredith with pleading eyes and spoke in a hesitant quivering voice. "I've come to stay with you for a while as my mommy is very sick."

Meredith was rendered speechless. She managed what she thought was a half-polite smile while she tried to think of something correct to say.

Then the unexpected visitor added, "I'm your granddaughter."

Meredith's mouth fell agape. Shock enveloped her as her eyes took in this child. Her brain flew into action, thoughts flashing across her grey matter and failing to deliver any useful information. She was aware of her knees becoming weak and a slight stricture developing in her throat.

This lovely, obviously frightened, yet somewhat confident, little girl was impeccably dressed. She had a flawless, creamy complexion with slightly rosy cheeks, large vibrantly blue eyes and very shiny, well-groomed, light-brown hair, with soft curls flowing to her mid-shoulders. Just when Meredith managed to restore a minimal smile, she heard someone running away from behind the ten-foot cedar tree that blocked her view of the driveway. She managed to squeeze between the girl and the cedar tree and ran out onto the driveway to see a young woman scurrying away. Meredith ran after her calling frantically, "Wait, please wait! I need to talk to you."

By the time she had reached the end of the driveway, the woman had jumped into the passenger side of the sedan and it was racing away. From behind her, Meredith heard the little girl pleading in a barely perceptible voice, "Bye Mommy, please get better soon."

Oh my god! License plate. Meredith tried to catch it—273 Y… but the car was too far away. She turned and looked back at the girl, whose neatly groomed curls had been disturbed slightly in the breeze. A stream of frenzied thoughts jumped at Meredith. *Holy shit, what has just happened here? A child abandoned on our doorstep. This can't be happening. I must be dreaming. Good god, what do I do now?* Confusion permeated her as she tried to pull something from her brain that made sense. Nothing came. Momentarily she tried to remember the first three numbers on the license plate while she thought of this little girl whom she had never seen before. The girl's face was sad now, not so confident. Tears were threatening, and her brow was wrinkled with worry, as she struggled to smile for Meredith. She clutched at a teddy bear tucked securely under her left arm.

As Meredith walked toward the child, her thoughts continued to race. *Granddaughter…, impossible, what kind of hoax or inappropriate joke could this be? But this child needs my attention right now.* She gathered some calm from somewhere deep within, maybe it was a residual reaction from her long-ago years of experience as an emergency room nurse, and she managed to say, "Oh my goodness, dear child, you must be frightened. Please come in, we'll have a drink of juice and a visit and see what we can figure out." Meredith put her arm lightly around the girl's shoulder and gently urged her forward toward the open door. "What's your name, dear?"

The girl looked up at Meredith with her deep, iridescent-blue, questioning eyes, now filled to the brim with tears, and shakily said, "My name is Samantha Scott but my mommy and my Auntie Colleen call me Sam Sweetie."

As Meredith looked ahead, she saw Andy standing at the door, looking bewildered, his eyes asking, "What's going on here..., and who is this little girl?"

"Andy, we have a visitor. We're going inside to get to know one another. Sam, this is my sleepy husband, Andy."

Andy hesitantly stepped aside, giving them room to enter.

"Please bring in the young lady's suitcases. Just set them in the entrance for now."

CHAPTER 1

———

Getting to Know Sam
Saturday, April 14

Directing Sam into the living room, Meredith spoke gently, "Sam, you can sit right here on the loveseat, and what would you prefer, some orange juice or grape juice?"

"I'll have some orange juice, please," she replied in an unsure, shaky voice as she climbed into the corner of the loveseat.

"Okay, I think I'll keep you company and have some too. What about you, Andy?" Meredith was making a valiant effort to sound cheerful, hoping it would help Sam relax. The child's eyes were brimming with tears. They started to spill down her cheeks so Meredith handed her a tissue.

"Sure, alright," Andy responded reluctantly, still clearly wanting to know what was happening. He had returned to his recliner across from Sam.

Meredith retreated to the kitchen for a few precious moments of thought. Her brain was in shock and logical thinking was still eluding her. She noticed that her hands were shaking slightly as she poured the juice.

It was quiet in the living room. In Andy's sleepy confused state, he wasn't able to initiate any conversation with Sam. He did give her a bit of a smile but she couldn't reciprocate. She clutched her teddy bear tighter.

Meredith quickly returned to the living room with three glasses of juice, setting two of them on the side table between the recliners for her and Andy and one beside the love seat for Sam. Then she settled herself on the tip of her recliner. "Sam, do you know who we are, do you know our names?"

Sam hesitated and blinked, her tear-filled eyes still spilling down her cheeks. Her tissue was all used up, so she wiped her eyes with her teddy bear's arm and hugged him to her with both hands, her little, perfectly white sock feet dangling over the edge of the loveseat. She had removed her shoes at the entry with no prompting.

Meredith's heart softened and she didn't know what to do next. But the question seemed to perk Sam up and she answered. "Yes, I know that you are Mr. and Mrs. Taylor, my gramma and grampa. Mommy has some pictures of you so I sort of knew what you would look like."

Good grief, does this mean we've been researched and photographed? The thought sent Meredith's mind spinning again.

Sam's words apparently put Andy into a state of shock, but he managed to interrupt. "Excuse me, but just who is this young guest of ours?" He moved forward to the edge of his chair and looked like he was ready to jump out of his skin.

"That's what I'm trying to find out, Andy. Sam told me that she has come to stay with us for a while as her mom is very sick." Turning back to Sam, Meredith asked, "Sam, was it your Auntie Colleen and your mommy that dropped you off?" Meredith glanced over at Andy, who was looking edgy, like a cat facing an angry dog. She was sure the hair on his arms was standing up higher than usual. Over the past thirty-eight years of marriage, her awareness of Andy's emotions had become fine-tuned.

"Yes, my mommy was in the backseat with me. She has to go to the hospital again for more treatments."

Meredith hadn't noticed a third passenger in the backseat. *Treatments, huh, I wonder what that's about.* Her mind whirled with possibilities. "Who was driving the car, Sam?"

"Oh, that was my Auntie Colleen's friend, Michelle. She drove us all the way here from Kelowna yesterday."

"Hmm, I see you have a teddy bear with you. Does he have a name?"

"Yes, this is Buddy. He's my very best friend." She held him up for Meredith and Andy to see but quickly clutched him tightly to her chest again. Sam's teddy bear was a bit tattered but very clean. His brown fur was soft and matted and he was adorned in a sky-blue sweater that seemed to match Sam's strikingly blue eyes.

"So… do you live in Kelowna, Sam?"

"Yes," she replied more confidently, her tears subsiding to a shiny residue.

Meredith was killing time while trying to gather her wits about her. Her thoughts were roaring through her head like a fast-moving train with no brakes, giving her a dizzy headache. It felt like her gray matter was in spasm. *This child has been very well cared for! She's intelligent, well spoken, definitely not a typical abandoned child. Just what the heck is going on here?* She looked over at Andy again who appeared panic-stricken now. His mouth was slightly ajar and his eyes were big and bulging like Meredith had never seen them before. He was speechless and her thoughts were muddled. *Police, Children's Services, our son..., oh my god, our son.* That jolted Meredith to her senses. "Sam, did your mommy say how long you might be staying here?"

"She said she didn't know for sure. She wanted me to tell you I'm in grade one and I need to go to school." Sam was answering questions quite matter of fact now.

Grade 1, school, oh dear, Sam could be with us for a while..., our son, ...oh no..., what was he doing six or seven years ago, where was he? Whoa, back to Sam, she needs my attention right now. "Sam, don't you worry, you're safe with us and we'll take care of you for now." *My god, what are we getting ourselves into? But this child needs some kind of reassurance about where she's at.*

She glanced over at Andy again who was looking right at her and mouthing the words, "No way! Are you crazy?"

Meredith looked back at Sam who, thankfully, had not seen or read Andy's lips. "Yes, maybe," she responded out loud. "Grandmother's usually are." She could feel herself already warming up to this lovely little girl who was so very well-mannered and becoming quite poised now, given her dubious situation. She was unintentionally making her way into Meredith's heart at the speed of rapid transit. *Did I actually call myself "grandmother" in relation to this child? Maybe I am crazy. I better not use that term again.*

Sam was looking questioningly at her.

"Sam, my name is Meredith but you can call me Mrs. T for now and you can call Andy Mr. T. Will that be alright?"

"Okay... I'll try to remember."

"So you stayed overnight in Dawson Creek last night, did you?" "Yes."

"Where did you stay?"

"At the Best Western," Sam replied with increasing enthusiasm. "We ate at Tony Roma's. I had the ribs...I liked them but I didn't like the green beans. I don't like vegetables very much but Mommy says I need to eat them to stay healthy or I might get sick like her."

Hmm, this child is quite the little conversationalist. Meredith's interview with Sam continued while Andy sat and listened, impatiently shifting in his chair with his right knee bouncing up and down nervously at times. Meredith discovered that Sam thought their son was her father and she was under the impression that he was dead and up in Heaven." Meredith didn't tell her otherwise. Auntie Colleen had been living with Sam and her mom for a while as her mom was too sick to look after her. Colleen gave Sam rides to school and cooked the meals and helped her with her bath and her homework. From Sam's demeanour, Meredith deduced that she loved her mom and Auntie Colleen very much and was happy with her past living arrangements. But, according to Sam, Auntie Colleen was getting a new job and had to move away. By now, Sam was talking easily and seemed to be very comfortable in Meredith and Andy's company but she was starting to squirm a bit.

"Sam, do you need to go to the bathroom?"

"Um, yes, I think so."

Getting out of her chair, Meredith directed Sam up the stairs to the bathroom. This gave Andy and her a much needed opportunity to talk.

Andy was livid. "We can't keep this child here, Meredith; she's an abandoned child. We need to turn her over to Children's Services or the police right now before she gets attached to us. She's under the illusion that we're her grandparents and we know nothing about her. We certainly don't know she's our grandchild."

"But what if she is? We can't be asking what if she isn't our grandchild, Andy. We have to ask, what if she is?" Meredith spoke with determination but underneath her words were the same worries that Andy had.

"If we find that out later, then we can decide what to do about it. Right now we should take her to Children's Services. Who knows, maybe she was kidnapped some time ago and we were picked randomly as a place to drop her off. We could be harbouring a child on the Missing Children's List." Andy's imagination was travelling rapidly, Mach one.

"Andy, it's Saturday, they won't be open. Don't be unreasonable."

"Unreasonable? Meredith, think about it, you have just taken in a child you know nothing about. She could even be part of a scheme to rob us. Who knows? Maybe she's a child con artist or something. Remember the home invasion and theft we had a few years ago. We were certain that was random so why couldn't this be? Maybe this is another one of those cagey schemes to take advantage of seniors."

"Don't be so paranoid, Andy, she's a harmless little child. Right now she needs some security and comfort. Don't you see, we're over a barrel here? What if she is our grandchild? We can't risk that and take her to Children's Services. She's not a stray puppy that we can take to the SPCA. My god, just yesterday I read in the paper about a child that was sexually and physically abused in a foster home and ended up in hospital with shaken baby syndrome and permanent spasticity due to brain stem injury. Who knows where she could end up? We've been duped, Andy, we're over a barrel."

Andy thought for a moment, obviously trying to find a way to convince Meredith he was right. "But why on earth would Sam's mother choose to leave her daughter on our doorstep with absolutely no explanation for us, even if we are her grandparents? It makes no sense."

"I don't know. Maybe she had no other options—we don't know what's going on in her life. Don't you think it's a bit odd that Sam is feeling so comfortable with us already? Either she's a very confident little girl or her mom has been preparing her for this for a while.

Good grief, she's seen pictures of us, Andy. I wonder what else her mother knows about us. This is spooky."

"It's not only spooky, Meredith, it's unbelievable. If Sam is our granddaughter, and that's a big if, this is going to be a gigantic shock for Aaron. We just can't assume anything and we have to notify the police now."

"No, Andy, we can't yet. We can't risk her safety. Think of her. This is traumatizing enough to be dropped off here with us let alone being taken to the police or Children's Services. We have to talk to Aaron first before we do anything. He's at that conference today so we have to wait until tonight. We need some time..., time to..." Meredith couldn't finish. They both heard the bathroom door open.

Andy threw up his arms in defeat. His brain was telling him one thing but his heart was faltering. Leaving Meredith standing there, he turned and left the room with his hands on his head, looking like he was going to pull out the remaining ring of silvery-grey hair that he had left. He desperately wanted to get away from this crazy situation. He stomped into the computer room and robotically opened up a "Gap Tours" site. He had been planning an "Around the World" tour for them when they retired in just a few months. He sat there staring for a while and then shook his head almost violently trying to extricate his devastating thoughts. Finally realizing Meredith had a point, he returned to the living room wishing he could escape from this earthly dilemma.

Meredith's thoughts and emotions were being pulled in two different directions; thinking of this abandoned child and thinking of their only son, Aaron. *Could this possibly be his child?* Sam came around the corner and back into the living room. Andy entered right behind her. Meredith knew she had grilled Sam enough for a while. She wondered how they should spend a day with a six-year old that they didn't know. "Sam, it's almost noon, are you hungry?"

"Yes, maybe a little," Sam said hesitantly."

"What do you like best, Dairy Queen, A & W or McDonalds?"

"Oh, I like Dairy Queen best, I love ice cream."

Meredith looked up at Andy and noticed his face was ashen, his expression worried. Ignoring this, she said, "Okay then, Andy, what do you think, can you take us two ladies out to the Dairy Queen for lunch?"

"Uh, what did you say?" he asked absent-mindedly.

Upping the pitch of her voice, Meredith asked again, "Sam and I were wondering if you could take us ladies out to the Dairy Queen for lunch?"

"Uh... oh, okay. Yeah, I guess I could do that," he responded reticently. "Alright then, let's go."

Meredith and Andy discovered a number of things over lunch. Sam was indeed six years old and her birthday was July 6th. She had a great appetite and she loved Dairy Queen hamburgers and fries but she especially liked chocolate chip Blizzards. She did say, though, that her mommy and Auntie Colleen only took her to Dairy Queen once a month and they ate most of their meals at home. She said her mother's name was Leanna.

Meredith concentrated on remembering that. When she asked Sam what was wrong with her mother, Sam only knew that she was very sick.

****

After lunch, against his better judgement, Andy was gently coerced by Meredith into driving them to Tumbler Ridge, about ninety kilometres from Dawson Creek, to see where the dinosaurs once lived. They had to do something to pass the time. With the beginnings of spring, the water was running freely in the ditches and the creeks were full to capacity, water roaring through their narrow passages, sometimes overflowing into the fields and trees along their disappearing banks.

The snow was melting fast and there was no end to the new and varying displays of Mother Nature's wonders in the pristine wilderness of the Peace Country.

Dark-blue water bubbled from beneath the unstable glistening snow banks, finding unexpected pathways, and moving in an ever-changing pattern down the ditches. It was travelling with them on the downhill slopes, away from them on the uphill slopes, seemingly not knowing where it was going; water moving everywhere, creating a glorious pattern as it hurriedly searched for a new home. Sam was unexpectedly quiet and attentive, mesmerized by the incessant flows. Finally, she voiced her thoughts. "Mrs. T, the snow is turning itself into water so it can run away and hide from the sun."

Meredith turned to the back seat and smiled, caught up in Sam's wondrous snow and water story. "So it is, Sam. By the time winter returns, the water will be up in the dark grey clouds and return to us again as snow. Pretty clever hey?"

"Yeah, pretty clever!" Sam repeated.

****

Andy was quiet, trying to keep his mind on the driving while enjoying the unfolding scenes around him and listening to Meredith and Sam chat about spring. But his thoughts permeated his mind. *If this really is Aaron's child, he must not know anything about her either. This could send gigantic shockwaves into many avenues of his life and ours. And what about Jessica? They've been married for less than a year. What will she think? This is an incredible mess.*

The drive took them from the rolling hills of Dawson Creek's agricultural land to the Rocky Mountain ranges surrounding Tumbler Ridge. On the way, they discovered that Sam loved dinosaurs and had visited the *Royal Tyrell Museum* in Drumheller, Alberta, a world heritage site of dinosaur fossils and exhibits of prehistoric life. At least, Andy was quite sure that was what Sam was describing.

The Peace Region Palaeontology Museum in Tumbler Ridge is where Andy finally began to shed his armour. He, too, loved dinosaurs and had become quite intrigued by the recent finds in Tumbler Ridge. Andy was a Rotarian and the local Rotary Club had donated funds to the development of this relatively new museum. As he watched Sam, his heart began to melt. This little girl had the same resolute interest in dinosaurs that he did. He couldn't help himself. He was soon describing to Sam the intricate details of how the dinosaur tracks at Tumbler Ridge were discovered by two young boys not much older than she was.

The boys had been tubing down Flatbed Creek and decided to stop for a rest. As they sat on the rocks at the edge of the creek, one boy looked down beside him and said to his friend, "Hey, this looks like a dinosaur footprint." The other boy looked and excitedly agreed. They started combing the rocks for more, and much to their delight, they found what they thought were eight more tracks. Driven by their excitement, they hurried home to tell the one boy's father. He was skeptical but decided to humour the boys and go with them to check it out. When he saw the trackway, he couldn't help but believe the boys might be right.

Sam was enthralled by the story and she won over a new and devoted friend and accomplice, at least until Andy had time to think again. However hesitant and cautious he would be over the next few days and weeks, it was obvious his heart had been captured by this incredible little girl who called herself their granddaughter.

****

When they arrived home, it was past supper time. Meredith took out some leftovers and prepared a meal of roast elk, mashed potatoes, gravy, cabbage salad, carrots, and broccoli. Despite Sam saying she didn't like vegetables, she ate everything on her plate. They had some Dairy Queen ice cream left in the fridge from the past weekend when their three-year old twin grandsons had visited and Meredith served it with some chocolate sauce. Sam remained her overly mature gracious self and thanked Meredith for supper.

After cleaning up supper, they watched one of the movies that their daughter, Wendy, had left behind for their grandsons. Sam had difficulty deciding between *Tarzan* and *Harry Potter and the Philosopher's Stone* but she finally settled on *Tarzan*. Loving children's movies, Meredith and Andy had watched this one before and had not noticed how scary and violent some of the scenes were. Sam cuddled tightly into Meredith's side, clutching Buddy through the scary parts.

While Meredith returned her cuddle by tightening her arm around Sam's shoulder, she wondered how watching the violence would affect Sam, especially in her uncertain situation. "Sam, you know this stuff isn't real, don't you?"

"Yes, I know it's just a story, Mrs. T, but it still scares me."

"I don't like it either, Sam." The violence was quickly over and they were quiet again, happy to watch the pleasant parts.

When the movie finished, Meredith asked, "Sam, what time do you usually go to bed?"

"Mommy says I should be in bed by 8:30 but it's usually 9:00 by the time I get there."

"That sounds like an honest answer and, I guess, since it's almost nine, it's time to be heading there," Meredith replied, while trying to hide her sense of relief. It had been a very long and stressful day and she had been having difficulty keeping her mind focused while thinking of all the possible ramifications of Sam's arrival. She took Sam's hand and led her upstairs. "Andy, will you please bring Sam's suitcases up for us?"

He was up like a scared cat. "You bet I will!"

Meredith offered Sam a choice between their two spare bedrooms. Not surprisingly, she chose the one they had decorated for their daughter many years ago. Sam loved dinosaurs but she was definitely a little girl.

When they had moved to Dawson Creek fourteen years ago, they had brought the decor with them. Andy, who never paid attention to this sort of thing, uncharacteristically suggested that they get new furniture for the spare rooms. Meredith declined, saying she wanted to preserve the feeling of belonging for Wendy and Aaron when they came home from university. But the real reason was she couldn't part with her children's belongings. She needed to retain whatever she could of them.

Wendy's room had a new double bed but the furniture remained from her childhood. There was a small double dresser with two banks of drawers, a night table with one drawer at the top and an open shelf at the bottom, a child's desk with one bank of drawers, and a matching chair. All the pieces were made of pine with a natural wood stain. The duvet and shams were a soft green with flowers, butterflies, and leaves scattered on some irregularly placed squares. Meredith had pictures of Wendy from her school days and more pictures of Wendy and her family scattered on the furniture and the walls. There were two pictures of a kitten and a puppy with wide gold frames at the head of the bed. Over the desk was an idyllic Robert Batemen print of three little girls and one boy playing in some ankle-deep water at the edge of a pond. The room really did need redecorating but it was perfect for Sam.

"Mrs. T, who are the people in all these pictures?"

"This is our daughter, Wendy, Sam. This is her husband, Ian, and the little guys are their twin boys, Colby and Dylan." They were looking at a family picture on the dresser. "The boys were only two in this picture but they're three now," Meredith elaborated.

"They sure do look alike. How do you tell them apart?"

"Well, I guess I just know. This is Colby and this is Dylan." Sam looked around the room at the other pictures and they chatted about them. So far, she had not asked about the family pictures in the living room with Aaron and his wife Jessica in them but Meredith knew that was coming. What she didn't know was what or how she would tell Sam about Aaron.

Meredith opened Sam's suitcases and hung a few of her clothes in the closet. She thought it would give Sam a feeling of some permanence or stability. She noticed that most of her clothes had been purchased at The Children's Place, Roots, and Gymboree, three upscale children's clothing stores. Then she saw an envelope. "What's this, Sam?"

"I don't know, maybe it's a note for you from my mommy."

Meredith tore open the envelope expectantly but was disappointed to see that the paper inside was only a record of Sam's childhood immunizations. She turned the paper over desperate for more but it was blank.

"What does it say, Mrs. T?"

"Oh, it's only a record of all the needles you had as a baby and before school, Sam."

"Oh yes, I forgot, my mommy said she was putting that in so that I wouldn't have to have them all over again."

Meredith's thoughts were off on the run again as she continued to unpack Sam's suitcase. *This little girl was well cared for and her mother was definitely organized. Everything required for Sam's care is here, including a toothbrush, flosses, brush and comb, hats and sunscreen. This drop-off was not a spur of the moment plan. It seems that Sam's mom is not short of money so she must have a few resources at her disposal. So why drop her off here? Dammit, she has covered all the details for her care except for the 'why.'* As Meredith turned back to Sam, she asked, "Now, dear, do you have a bath every night before bed?"

"No, I bathed this morning so I don't need one tonight. Auntie Colleen washes my hair for me."

"Okay, so I guess you can just wash up at the sink tonight. Here's your toiletries bag. I see your toothbrush is in it. Do you brush and floss by yourself?"

"I brush my own teeth and Auntie Colleen flosses them for me."

"Then, if you like, I will floss for you. You can get into your pyjamas, wash up and brush your teeth and let me know when you're ready, okay?"

"Okay."

"Here's your towels. We'll hang them on the rack over here. See you in a bit."

Sam was in bed by 9:30 PM. Meredith tucked her and Buddy in, kissed both of them on the forehead and wished them pleasant dreams.

"Thank you, Mrs. T, Mommy was right, you are a nice lady. I like it here... Mr. T is pretty nice too."

"And you, Sam, are a very sweet and polite little girl. We've had an amazingly good first day together. Good night, dear." Meredith touched her forefinger to Sam's button nose, turned and left, shutting off the light and pulling the bedroom door almost closed behind her. She left a night light on so Sam would know where she was if she awoke during the night.

****

Sam lay in bed thinking about what she and her mom had been talking about in the car on the trip to Dawson Creek. "*Sam, there is just one thing you have to remember. Your last name is Scott. Always tell everyone your last name is Scott, Samantha Scott. Okay, Sam?*"

"*Okay, but why don't you want them to know where you are, Mommy?*"

"*I don't want them to find me until I'm better, Sam. When I'm better, I will come and get you, okay? We need to practise this so you can remember. Tell me your name.*"

"Samantha Scott. Can I tell them you call me Sam Sweetie?"

"*Yes, dear, you can tell them that.*"

Sam was drifting off to sleep, thinking of her mommy's warm embrace, her soft caring voice... Momentarily, she also thought of Mr. and Mrs. T. and smiled to herself. Sleep took her comfortably away from a day she would never forget.

****

Meredith returned to the bathroom to tend to her own overdue physical needs. She lingered there, thinking for a while and wondering about her growing affection for Sam. *Is it misplaced? Should I be listening to Andy and taking his advice...dammit, he's usually right when we disagree. But Sam does resemble Aaron; her blue eyes, her smile... and her sweet demeanour, oh, it's so much like Wendy when she was this age.*

Meredith's mothering instincts had been deeply influenced as a young girl watching her own mother take in and care for two little neighbourhood girls. She recalled her father saying, "Isn't it time you sent these kids home? I think we have enough mouths to feed around here."

Her mother responded definitively, "Send them home to what, a filthy house with no food and nobody to watch over them? They will go home when their mother sobers up and comes for them."

Meredith knew she was right. Her heart was leading her in the right direction. Sam needed her and it was her turn in this crazy mixed up world to love and protect an innocent child.

As Meredith sat there, her thoughts continued. *Why was Sam's mother so desperate that she would make the drastic decision to leave her daughter on our doorstep? Did she think she knew enough about us, about our characters, our morals and our values, to make the staggering assumption that we would take Sam in and care for her? What about Auntie Colleen? Why doesn't she continue to look after Sam? What's wrong with Sam's mother? Why is she so sick? Will she really get better and come back for her?* Meredith's nursing background led her mind through a maze of possibilities.

CHAPTER 2

———

Telling Aaron About Sam
Saturday, April 14

By the time Meredith hit the bottom stair, Andy was there. He'd had some time to think while Meredith was getting Sam ready for bed and his thoughts had put him back into a pit of worry. "We've got some serious talking to do, Meredith."

"Yes, dear, I know, this is going to be a complicated situation."

"Complicated? How about a monumental disaster!"

"Well, let's not get too wound up until we know more. I guess the first thing we need to do is call Aaron. I'm not looking forward to talking to him about his sex life but I guess we have to. Shall I call him right now?

"Yes, let's hear what he has to say about this mess."

"Andy, you sound angry."

"I am angry! Do you realize how this could change our lives for a very long time? Here we are, about to retire and go on our Around the World Tour and now what?"

"Who are you angry at, Andy, at Sam? At Aaron?"

"No, I'm not angry at Sam, this certainly isn't her fault."

"Does that mean you're angry at Aaron?"

"Oh, I don't know, we don't even know if he's involved in this. I'm just angry."

"Okay, but when we talk to him, you better not let him know you're angry."

"Yeah... I guess not, you better do the talking."

"Okay." Meredith punched in the numbers. "I sure hope he's home, it is Saturday night."

He picked up after the first ring. "Aaron, I'm so glad you're there."

"Why, Mom, what's up?"

There was nervous hesitation in Meredith's voice. "Oh dear... where will I start? Your dad and I have had quite a day."

"What's wrong, Mom?"

"Well, we received an unexpected visitor this morning...a six-year old girl who

says she's our granddaughter."

Aaron hesitated. It took him a few seconds to digest what this meant. "Mom, if she's your granddaughter, I must be her father and that's not possible. That's absurd."

"I hope you're right, dear, but you need to think carefully about this. Her name is Samantha Scott and she's going to be seven on July 6th. This means she must have been conceived seven years ago in mid to late October. What were you doing then? Wasn't that your last year of university?"

"Seven years ago...yeah...that's right, and I had that broken leg, remember?" Aaron had broken his leg in late August while wrestling with his buddy Jason. He and Jason had been working for Jason's dad for the summer in a business called "Techno Rigging." They were servicing flare stacks and communication towers used in the oil, gas, and communications industry. He had to climb upwards of four hundred feet for servicing igniters at the top of the stacks. As most mothers would, Meredith had spent more than enough time worrying about his safety. But, oddly enough, he had broken his leg wrestling with Jason in the Saskatoon Berry patch while waiting to do his next climb. When Aaron returned to school for the final year of his Bachelor's Degree in Information Systems, he was in a cast and on crutches.

"That's right, this should help you remember what you were doing then, who you were hanging out with."

"Yes, and I do remember very clearly. I broke up with Marcia just before I left school for the summer. When I went back in the fall, I didn't start dating until I got rid of my cast and those wretched crutches. Jason and Shelly tried to set me up a couple of times, very unsuccessfully, as I recall." Aaron laughed, a short quick laugh. "A cast and crutches is not very conducive to dating, Mom, certainly not for sex."

"When did you get your cast off, dear?"

"Not until November, I remember that clearly too because I still had it for my midterm exams. Does this kid look... anything like me?" he asked hesitantly.

"That's a good question that I have been trying to figure out since she arrived. I look at her and think, yes, she does. Then I look at her again and think, no, it can't be. I just don't know, dear."

"Well, it doesn't matter. I didn't even have a date let alone a girlfriend at the time. She can't possibly be my child. Where did she come from? How did she get there?"

Meredith explained how Sam had arrived and how she'd had no chance to see the three women that dropped her off.

"That's just weird, Mom. Who would drop their kid off like that?"

"Good question—it makes no sense. I'm glad to hear you feel certain, Aaron, but please think about this some more, please make sure there are no other possibilities. After all, it was seven years ago and, if Sam was born a bit premature, I suppose she could have been conceived later in November too. If you think of anything else, give us a call right away." Meredith wasn't sure why but she didn't tell Aaron that Sam had said her mother's name was Leanna. It seemed almost instinctive to withhold that fact unless Aaron could come up with the name himself.

"Yes, I will, but I am telling you now for certain, it just can't be. Mom, this is awful for you and Dad, even if she isn't your grandchild. What are you going to do?"

"Dad says we need to report Sam's arrival to the police and Children's Services. I guess he's right. But I sure hate to turn her over to Children's Services, Aaron. She is the sweetest, well-mannered child."

"What else can you do?"

"Nothing, I guess," she responded, feeling defeated.

"Let me know if there is anything I can do to help."

"Okay, dear...is Jessica home?" Meredith wondered if she had been listening to this conversation.

"No, she's at her yoga class. She should be home shortly."

Meredith breathed a sigh of relief.

Jessica, Aaron's wife, was becoming very involved with yoga. She had taken several instructors' courses and was presently taking one on prenatal yoga. She was one of the most physically fit people Meredith and Andy knew. She had long, dark-auburn, naturally curly hair that she wore in a multitude of styles from loose and flowing to upswept with unruly small curls escaping to adorn her face and the back of her neck. On the weekends, she often wore it in a ponytail or she braided it to suit her active lifestyle of mountain biking, hiking, or playing volleyball. Her gorgeous hazel-brown eyes twinkled with energy and enthusiasm. She was about five foot seven, just a couple of inches shorter than Aaron, and weighed in at a solid one hundred forty-five pounds. Her muscles were very well defined and her figure was movie-star perfect. How Meredith envied her "oh so flat" abdominal wall. Meredith worked hard at keeping fit too but she could never achieve a flat abdomen like Jessica's. She was plagued by a familial round little belly.

"Alright then, we'll call you again tomorrow night to give you an update. We love you, Aaron."

"Luv you too, Mom, I'll be thinking of you. I hope you can sleep okay."

Andy had been listening to Meredith's side of the conversation and wanted to know the details. She filled him in and he seemed immensely relieved. They were exhausted and decided to get ready for bed and then they'd talk some more. Tomorrow would be Sunday. They guessed they wouldn't get too far with resolving anything until Monday but they agreed they should report the incident. Andy would go to the police first thing in the morning to report Sam's arrival and ask their advice.

Once they had the beginning of a plan, Andy found sleep first and was snoring softly beside Meredith, emitting his amazing body heat, which usually relaxed her quickly. But she couldn't turn off her thoughts and she felt like her bowels were tied in a million knots. She lay awake for what seemed like hours, trying to relax on one side, and then the other, a wild river of thoughts and emotions twisting and churning through her head and winding their way to her gut.

She finally got up and went downstairs to call the Children's Help Line. She pretended she was writing a book and she wanted to know what would happen in a situation such as theirs. They said they would send out a child-care worker immediately. Just to be sure, Meredith inquired if they would do this on the weekend. They said, yes, they would, they always had someone on call.

After she hung up, she wondered if they were suspicious of the legitimacy of her inquiry and worried that they may have recorded her call. She also wondered what she would do with the information she had gleaned from the helpline. Should she and Andy call Children's Services in the morning as well as the police?

Meredith had been examining Sam's features all day. She wondered if Sam had been cognisant of her periodic staring. When Sam caught her doing so, Meredith had smiled and usually managed to utter something appropriate.

She went back to bed but Sam's image was ever present in her head and she reviewed the comparisons she had already made. She knew there was an incredible similarity but she hadn't specifically identified it yet. When her daughter, Wendy, was six and in grade one, she'd had much shorter, very light-brown hair with soft curls and deep brown eyes, unlike her brother's sky-blue eyes. Wendy's facial features closely resembled her brother's but her coloring was very different. Aaron was blonde and blue eyed through and through, and his skin tone was fair. Wendy was a brunette and she had gorgeous brown eyes with a darker complexion. What was it then...the button nose, the sweet personality, the shy demeanour, the lively blue eyes? All of these features were suspect but they didn't strike Meredith as a true match. The sparkling blue eyes definitely were like Aaron's but that wasn't enough.

Then it hit her like a hammer on the side of her head—their mouths and teeth were all the same. All three of them had the same lip and mouth shape, the same sweet smile, the same teeth. Sam had not yet lost her front teeth and Meredith could easily remember her children's mouths and teeth, exactly how they looked when they were Sam's age—beautiful teeth that were too close together for baby teeth. Right now, Sam's teeth looked perfect. After her years as a Public Health Nurse, she was somewhat of an expert on child development and she knew that, if there was no extra room between the baby teeth, the adult teeth would likely be too crowded. Sam would need braces just as Aaron and Wendy had.

Meredith knew a bond had already formed between her and Sam and it frightened her. Her thoughts continued to whirl. *This is ridiculous. Here I am looking for characteristics that will prove Sam is our grandchild. I should be looking for characteristics that would indicate Sam is not our grandchild, that this is all a terrible mistake. Besides, probably fifty percent of kids need braces these days. This means nothing.*

Despite Aaron's certainty about there being no possibility that Sam could be his child, Meredith's grandmother intuition still told her she might be. If Sam was Aaron's child, she couldn't help but be far more concerned about him than about Andy and herself, as Sam would ultimately be Aaron's responsibility, not theirs. If, on the other hand, she was not Aaron's child, then who was she and why had she landed on their doorstep? Her thoughts vacillated from one scenario to the other. There was another possibility lurking in the depths of Meredith's subconscious mind. She knew it was there but she wouldn't let it surface. She could feel her resistance to something—to letting an idea escape and take shape.

She tried again to put Sam's features out of her mind. As she did, she thought of how she would tell Sam that they would have to talk to the police and Children's Services. *Sam won't understand this at all and will begin to think we don't want her.* She ruminated about this dilemma for at least an hour.

Then, just as she was almost asleep, an outrageous thought slithered out of her grey matter and hit her like a lead balloon; the idea she had previously been trying to prevent from surfacing. *If Aaron is so certain that this child can't be his, could Andy possibly be Sam's father? No... I have never once doubted Andy's steadfast devotion and faithfulness to me—to his family. Yet, I do think that Sam is carrying the Taylor genes from somewhere. Could the impossible be possible? But if this is the case, Sam would be calling herself our daughter, not our granddaughter. No, it couldn't possibly be. Unless...whoever dropped Sam off thought that a granddaughter would be easier to accept than a wayward husband and daughter, especially at our age.*

She was wide awake again, stewing about this preposterous idea. She chastised herself for thinking such a deleterious thought because she knew Andy's love was unwavering. Her head began to ache from all corners, converging behind her eyes. She got up and took two extra-strength Tylenol and went to her favourite chair to read the newspapers, attempting to blot out her torturing thoughts. At 2:30, she began to feel overwhelmed with impending sleep and crawled back into bed. Instead of cuddling close to Andy like she always did, to absorb the warmth emanating from his body, she stayed carefully on her own side of the bed and eventually succumbed to a restless sleep.

CHAPTER 3

Aaron Remembers
Sunday April 15

Meredith was not certain when she fell asleep but she felt terrible when the alarm went off at 7:00 AM. She crawled out into the unwanted day, the memories of last night still vivid in her messed up mind, and she headed for the bathroom. Sam's room was quiet; she was still asleep. Meredith went downstairs to join Andy who had already made coffee. She said nothing about the wild accusatory thoughts she had conjured up from the recesses of her mind in the darkness of the night.

Golden morning sunbeams were drenching the front lawn, encouraging the new luscious green shoots that dappled last year's brown grass. Usually that was all it took for Meredith to greet the day optimistically. But, this morning, she couldn't quite rise to the occasion. Both she and Andy were lacking exuberance as they quickly reviewed their plans for the day. Meredith purposely did not mention her late-night call to the Children's Help Line.

Within a few minutes, they heard Sam coming down the stairs. Meredith had decided to wait until after breakfast to explain their plans to her. She wanted an opportunity to set the stage with some friendly chit chat first. "Good morning Sam, did you sleep well?"

As usual, Sam had her teddy bear tucked tightly under her left arm. "Yes, but I miss my mommy." Her bright blue eyes were down-cast and her bottom lip was protruding slightly.

"I see you have Buddy with you this morning. Is he hungry?"

"Oh yes, Buddy never misses breakfast."

"Sam, do you like Honey Nut Cheerios?" Meredith had them on hand from when her grandsons, Colby and Dylan visited.

"Yes," she answered with a bit of a quiver in her small voice. "Buddy does too."

"Well then, come and sit right up here beside Mr. T and he will help you."

"Okay." As she came toward the table, Sam's gait perked up and she smiled a little for Andy. She was soon chatting with him about yesterday's dinosaur adventures.

Oh, to be young and resilient again, Meredith thought.

With thoughts of her missing mother pushed back into her sub-conscious mind, Sam ate the Honey Nut Cheerios and some cherry yogurt with enthusiasm.

When she was done, Meredith knew she had to address their morning plans. "Sam, I want you to listen carefully. We need to talk to you about our plans for today."

Looking attentive, Sam turned toward Meredith.

"When you came to our door yesterday, we had never seen you before. Your mother and your Auntie Colleen left you here and we don't know them either. Because we don't know you or your mother, we have to tell the police that you're here."

Sam's face went very serious and her little voice was almost businesslike. "Why do the police need to know about me?"

"Because your mommy and your Auntie Colleen have disappeared and the police may want to look for them."

Sam was quiet, her bright little face became expressionless.

"Mr. T. will go to the police this morning. They may want to come here and talk to you." Sam frowned and Meredith could see the concern in her eyes. *Oh dear, this lovely child, what is to become of her if we don't or can't keep her.*

It was Andy's turn. "Sam, don't you worry. If they do come to talk to you, Mrs. T and I will stay with you. Okay?"

Meredith wondered if they should be promising that; but, after his initial negative reaction to Sam's arrival yesterday, she was pleasantly startled by Andy's quick desire to support her today.

"I guess so." One tear started to run down Sam's pink cheek. She wiped it away with Buddy's arm. "But I don't think Mommy will want them to find her. She says she needs time by herself to get better so she can come and get me."

"Is that what she told you, Sam?"

"Yes."

"All right then, we'll just have to tell the police that too." *Why am I not surprised that Sam's mother doesn't want to be found?*

This triggered a whole new line of speculation for Meredith. *When Sam said her mom had to go to the hospital for more treatments, I wondered about the possibility of terminal cancer. That would be why she needs to find a safe, secure place for Sam. Still, it's taking quite a chance to leave your child on the doorstep of someone you've never met. Undoubtedly, it was a very desperate measure. Maybe Sam's mother is in a drug rehabilitation program? Just another possibility. That would help to explain what appears to be an implausible and most irrational decision.*

When Andy left to make a report to the police, Meredith got Sam to help her with the breakfast dishes. Sam placed the dishes in the dishwasher as if she had done this many times before. She was a competent helper for a six-year old. She had obviously been expected to help her mom and her Auntie Colleen. Then they went upstairs to get dressed and ready for the day. Sam picked out her own clothes and expertly matched a pink lightweight, short-sleeved sweater and pink socks with a pair of blue jeans with pink butterflies embroidered on both back pockets. She washed her face and brushed her teeth efficiently. When they were both ready, Meredith took Sam to the basement to look for a good book to read to her. She still had all of her own children's books boxed up in cardboard boxes. When Meredith saw *Charlotte's Web*, she exclaimed, "This is the one, Sam. I remember reading this to Wendy when she was about your age. She loved it! It's a wonderful story about a pig and a spider."

"I think I might like it too, Mrs. T."

"Okay then, let's go." They walked hand in hand up the stairs.

As Meredith began to read, Sam curled up very close with Buddy under her arm. *Ooo, this girl knows how to win my heart.* She realized that Sam's vulnerability was key to her maternal instincts to love and protect her. But she could literally feel the bond between them growing stronger. This simultaneously conjured up some mixed feelings of pleasure and dread that Meredith was acutely aware of as she continued to read.

Andy got back about 10:30. He looked frustrated but Meredith didn't have time to talk to him. The phone rang as he was coming in the door. "Andy, I have to take this call, can you stay here with Sam for a bit?" Meredith went upstairs and closed the bedroom door to talk. Aaron sounded choked up. "Mom, I'm at work but I have to talk to you. I hardly slept all night worrying about this unbelievable situation. Even though I felt so certain this kid couldn't be mine, my brain was agitated with thoughts.

"What kind of thoughts, dear?"

"I went to the couch so I wouldn't disturb Jessica and turned on the television for distraction. I finally fell asleep and when I woke up from a dream, I started remembering something...something that happened to me in the fall of my final year."

"What happened, Aaron, you sound really upset?" Meredith wondered why he was at work on Sunday but, considering the urgency in his voice, she didn't ask.

He hesitated and took deep breath, "Oh god, Mom, I can't believe I'm going to tell my mother about this. It's so... damn embarrassing. But under the circumstances, I think I better. I haven't even told Jess yet." He hesitated again, sighed deeply, and started to tell his story. "Remember, Mom..., because I broke my leg and was on crutches, I had to go to Student Health Services to get a Disabled Parking Permit so I could park right close to the buildings that my classes were in."

She could hear the anguish in his voice. "Yes, I remember."

"I had to check in every week to let them know my progress and confirm that I still needed the parking permit. I saw the same nurse each time... She was very friendly and we talked a bit at each visit. We just seemed to click; you know, conversation was very easy." He sighed and breathed deeply again. "Well... when I went in the last time to return my parking pass, she said since I wouldn't be coming in anymore, maybe we could have coffee some time. I was quite surprised by her offer, but I agreed to meet her at the student lounge the next night after my last class. God, why did I do that? It was sooo stupid."

"Aaron, what on earth happened?"

"Mom, I had two more casual meetings with her. Her name was Leanna."

Leanna, oh my god, Sam said her mother's name was Leanna.
Meredith said nothing but noticed her heart starting to pound.

"We talked casually about life and she seemed to be quite inter-ested in me as a person. Or so I thought," he grumbled. "I think she was about thirty-two but she wouldn't tell me how old she was. I remember joking with her about younger guys dating older women."

Meredith didn't know what to say so she waited for him to continue.

"The last time I met her…, it was a Friday night and she invited me to her apartment for a drink. Very foolishly, I took her up on the offer, thinking I knew her fairly well by then. Stupid… dumb!"

"Aaron, please tell me what happened."

Desperation in his voice, he continued. "She drove and I didn't even pay much attention to where her apartment was located."

Meredith thought it was totally out of character for Aaron to not pay close attention to where he was going, but she continued to listen, her anxious heart pounding faster.

"I can't believe I was so stupid, so naive, Mom… Anyway, we had a drink and this is what was so weird about it. I woke up the next morning in her bed and couldn't remember what had happened."

Meredith's heart went into high gear. "Oh my dear son, that must have been scary"

"Oh yeah…, and Mom…, she left me a note indicating she had to leave early as she was preparing to move to a new job." Aaron hesitated and sighed deeply again. "I was dumbfounded and far too embarrassed to tell another soul what had happened…well, I didn't even know what had happened! I couldn't remember anything after she poured me that drink… and I can't believe I'm talking to my mother about this stuff."

"It's alright, dear, I'm very glad you are." Meredith's dizziness from yesterday was returning along with a queasy stomach. Her mind was reeling with possibilities.

"There's more, Mom." Aaron took another deep breath. "I was so groggy all weekend." His voice began to crack but he managed to continue. "I tried to work on an assignment but my head felt so fuzzy, I couldn't concentrate. By Monday morning, I was feeling better. I went to Student Health Services after class and asked for Leanna. They told me they didn't have anyone working there by that name. When I asked if they knew where she had moved to, they looked at me strange. Mom, they never did have anyone working there by that name. Do you think... could I have... oh I don't know, it's just too crazy."

"I agree. Aaron, it does sound crazy. What happened next?"

He hesitated, swallowed the lump in his throat, and then continued. "Sometime in the middle of the week, I managed to find my way to her apartment and another girl answered the door. She too said she didn't know anyone by that name. I guess Leanna hadn't told me her real name. It was just so weird. I decided to forget about it, chalk it all up to a bad experience. And *that* is exactly what I did. I forgot all about this until now, put it right out of my mind. Mom, do you think this Leanna person could have gotten pregnant that night?" Aaron's voice was desperate. "Why in God's name would she risk it? And what would be the chances from one contact anyway. It can't be very likely, can it?"

"I don't know Aaron, it does sound unlikely but..." Meredith hesitated, she just couldn't tell him yet that Sam's mother's name was Leanna. Her mind was reeling. *Could Aaron have been drugged and date raped? Does this even happen to guys?*

"I hope you aren't mad at me, Mom."

"Mad at you? Absolutely not, Aaron," she replied emphatically. "Right now, I am more concerned about you than anything. I think, from what you're telling me, you were the victim of a crime. I think you may have been drugged and..." She hesitated wondering if she should say it... "Date raped."

"Date raped. God, I didn't think that could even happen to guys! I've heard of women drugging guys but it's just to get their money and credit cards. She didn't take anything, Mom. She left me fifty bucks and said in her note that it was for a cab ride home if I needed it. Can you believe it? I was so groggy but I did manage to pay attention to where I was on the way home. Mom, I can't believe I could let something like this happen. It was so stu…pid!"

"No Aaron, you weren't stupid, this woman was deceitful and she took advantage of you."

"But surely she wouldn't want to get pregnant in a situation like this. If we did actually have sex, you'd think she would have used protection."

"Meredith could hear his distress building as she searched for comforting words. "Yes, you would think so, but Aaron, please, whatever you do, don't blame yourself. You were the victim here!" Meredith's thoughts about her son being date raped were overwhelming her. She didn't know what to think or say to him. She still couldn't tell him that Sam's mother's name was Leanna. It just wouldn't come out of her mouth.

"I just feel so dumb, so damn dumb... and I'm so tired!"

"Aaron, I'm so sorry this happened to you. But please, son, understand that you are definitely not responsible for whatever happened. And we certainly don't know if this horrible event ended in a pregnancy."

"But what are you and Dad going to do about Sam? What if she is my kid?"

"Your dad and I have been working out a plan as to what we need to do. Sam arrived on our doorstep out of the blue. She's only six years old and she is, literally, an abandoned child. Dad was out to see the police first thing this morning and he just got back when you called. I haven't had time to talk to him about what he found out. We also need to be in touch with Children's Services first thing tomorrow morning. I have no idea what their processes will be. Aaron, Sam is very sweet, she has already won our hearts, even your dad's. She is a beautiful little girl, extremely well mannered, obviously very well cared for, just not typical of an abandoned child. It's a real puzzle! But please remember, we are far from proving one way or the other that this bad experience you had resulted in a pregnancy." As Meredith spoke the words, she doubted them. She did not want to believe that Sam's existence could be the result of a date rape. The thought made her insides crawl.

"Okay, Mom, I better go. I have to get to work. Things are so damn busy here right now."

"Okay, my dear son. We'll talk again tonight. We love you."

"I love you too, Mom, and I'm so… sorry and so... embarrassed."

As Meredith put down the phone, her heart was quivering inside and threatening to stop. *My god, was Aaron really date raped? What did he go through? How could a beautiful thing like Sam come from such a heinous crime? It just doesn't seem possible. And how could this woman vanish into thin air afterwards. Nothing makes sense.*

When Meredith came downstairs, Andy looked up at her momentarily as he continued to read. She felt dizzy. Sitting down on the chair across from him and Sam, she shook her head to clear the dizziness and wondered if she might vomit. She could hear their voices but they seemed so far away. They were talking dinosaurs again. Andy had dug out the book they had purchased at Tumbler Ridge.

Sam looked up at Meredith with concern. "What's the matter Mrs. T.? You look sick."

Oh God, this child is definitely too mature and too perceptive for her age. And so like Wendy. "I'm okay, Sam. I just need a minute. Maybe a glass of cold water will help."

Meredith was addressing Andy but Sam jumped up and said, "I'll get you one." Andy went with her to help reach the glass.

The rest of the day dragged. Once Meredith recovered, they had lunch. When Sam went to the bathroom, Andy asked Meredith what was wrong but she knew she didn't have enough time to tell him and there would be far too much emotion to deal with. They both might fall apart. With all her strength, she pushed her thoughts away and said, "Later, Andy, we can't talk yet, it's complicated." As the day progressed, they caught desperate glimpses of each other, saying with their eyes, "We need to talk." But there just wasn't enough time available without Sam.

All three of them walked to the park and Sam played on the playground equipment for a while. Andy pushed her on the swing, doing run-unders, Sam giggling with each push. Meredith went grocery shopping while Andy and Sam worked on putting together some puzzles and played a memory card game. Meredith got out her daughter's old dolls for Sam. They were very dated but she didn't seem to care. She played with them for quite a while. This finally gave Meredith and Andy a few minutes to talk. Andy was reading when she interrupted him and motioned for him to come to the kitchen. She spoke quietly to be sure Sam would not hear her. "Andy, Sam is quite involved with Wendy's dolls at the moment, please tell me what the police said."

"When I talked to Sergeant Willis this morning, I told him I was quite certain that Sam was not our grandchild. My guess is, he didn't believe it. He asked me if we were willing to keep Sam until tomorrow morning when the Children's Services Office opened. When I said we were, he said that was fine with him. I think his perspective was that Sam was safe, so no action was necessary on his part. He did open a file and ran her name and ours through his computer, and of course, nothing showed up. Then he told me we should report the matter to Children's Services first thing in the morning."

"Wow, I thought they would be way more concerned."

"Yeah, me too, he was definitely laid back about it. Maybe because he knows us and had no worries about Sam's present safety."

"But an abandoned child, that's a serious offense. You'd think he would at least want to see her, photograph her for his file."

"Yep, maybe they had more serious things to deal with this weekend."

"Well, as usual, I guess I worried way too much about that." Meredith sighed and got up to leave.

"Hey, wait a minute." Andy stopped her. "What about your conversation with Aaron this morning?"

"Oh, Andy, I just can't go into that yet. Please wait until we have Sam in bed."

"But Meredith…"

"No, Andy, we have to wait."

He threw her a perplexed look but she turned her back to him and started running water in the sink. She knew their emotions would be explosive and they had to get through the rest of the day with Sam. She swallowed hard and started cleaning the counter and wiping the appliances. She needed to stay focused on mindless tasks.

When it was time to make supper, Meredith asked Sam to help her with the salad. Sam stood on a stool at the sink, washed the tomato, the celery sticks, and the cucumber and dried them with a paper towel while Meredith washed and tore the lettuce. Sam asked if she could set the table. Her enthusiasm for her job was evident as she independently placed the forks and knives correctly, tucked a napkin under each knife and lined up the glasses correctly on the top right side of each plate. Meredith marvelled at her attention to detail.

After supper, Sam had a bath and Meredith shampooed her hair. Meredith noticed her nails were recently and expertly trimmed. When Sam was ready for bed, Meredith read two more chapters of *Charlotte's Web* to her. Sam was intrigued by the story line and asked multitudes of questions. At 8:30, Meredith tucked her into bed and wished her pleasant dreams.

"I love you, Mrs. T. Thank you for being so kind to me. Mommy said you would be but I wasn't sure I believed it. Now I know she was right."

It was all Meredith could do to stop her tears from welling up. It made her wonder again just how thoroughly they had been checked out—obviously more than just with pictures. *Just how much does Sam's mother know? Does she know what kind of people Andy and I are? Does she know we already have some grandchildren whose lives we are very involved in?* She managed to say, "Sam, you are easy to be kind to. Goodnight, dear." She kissed Sam's forehead, forced a smile, and quickly left the room while her emotions were still in check.

****

Hitting the bottom of the stairs and being greeted by her husband who was anxious to talk was getting to be a habit. Once again they were exhausted, but they had to get through this. As Meredith began to tell Andy about Aaron's call and the recollection of what had happened to him, she started to cry. Andy got up, handed her some tissues and pulled her out of her chair for a hug. She recovered and continued.

"Andy, when he woke up in her bed, she was gone, and he couldn't remember what happened."

By this time, Andy's face was bright red and he looked furious. Meredith was afraid his anger might spill over to Sam; but, if he was thinking it, he didn't mention it. All of his anger was directed at this Leanna person who had turned their lives upside down and inside out.

"Meredith, this is just disgusting. And Sam, our granddaughter, a product of this horrible...act." He didn't express his feelings for his son. Meredith guessed he didn't know what to feel, let alone how to express it.

"You're right, Andy, it's disgusting, but we don't know for sure yet that Sam is our granddaughter. We don't know that she was conceived through this incident."

"Come on, honey, if Leanna didn't know we were Sam's grandparents, how and why would she have picked us out of the blue to leave her child with? Sam said her mother's name was Leanna and Aaron said the woman who drugged him was Leanna."

"I know…, but I don't think we should assume anything at this point. The whole situation is just too bizarre." Meredith was struggling to set her emotions aside and trying to put on her investigator's cap, something that nurses frequently need to do. She found it surprising, though, that Andy was calling Sam their granddaughter—Andy, the paranoid skeptic from yesterday. As she processed her thoughts, she began to verbalize them. "Andy, there are still more possibilities. If Leanna did not get pregnant that night, she could have already been pregnant or got pregnant shortly after that with another partner. Maybe she didn't want to leave Sam with her real father or his family so she picked our family thinking Sam would be in better hands."

"Slim hope, Meredith!"

"Yeah, but it's still possible." They were both silent for a moment. "What do we do next, Andy?"

"I don't know but we will certainly need a paternity test!"

"Yes, we will, but I think there are some more urgent things to think about right now."

"What do you mean?"

"I think we…our family needs to have a strategy for what we are telling people about Sam. We've been very lucky so far. We have not run into anybody this weekend that has asked us any questions about her. If she is actually our granddaughter, and possibly the product of date rape, can you imagine what the press might do with this information if they found out? Date rape committed by an older woman on a young college student could be exciting fodder for the press. It's not the usual way for it to occur. And think of the gossip if this gets out."

"God, Meredith, I hadn't even thought of that."

"Well, we need to because, above all else, we have to protect Aaron. I didn't think to say anything to him this morning about this and the time probably wasn't right anyway."

"So what do we tell people? What is our plan going to be?"

"For now, I think we should tell them that Sam is staying with us for a while because her mother, an acquaintance of ours, is very sick. I think we shouldn't even mention the granddaughter part and we certainly can't tell them about what happened to Aaron. If it turns out that Sam is Aaron's daughter, we will have to accept that; but we don't have to tell anyone about the circumstances of her conception. What do you think?"

"Makes sense to me."

"My other question that has been haunting me is, should we be trying to find Sam's mother?"

"God only knows. What can we gain by finding her and how would we try? Sergeant Willis certainly wasn't interested in the case."

"Yeah, well, he might be if he knew the circumstances; but we don't want him to know that. I suppose if we thought we had something to gain, we would have to hire a private detective. Good grief, this is beginning to sound like a suspense novel. Let's look at what we know about Sam so far." Meredith got up and found some paper and a pen and they prepared some notes:

1. *Sam knew who we were, knew our names, had seen a picture of us and knew we were nice kind people.*
2. *Sam's proper name is Samantha Scott????.*
3. *She is six years old and in grade one.*

4. *She used to live in Kelowna with her mother and her Auntie Colleen.*

5. *Sam's mother's name is Leanna.*

6. *She thinks our son is her father and she believes he is dead.*

7. *They stayed overnight at the Best Western and ate at Tony Roma's.*

8. *Her birthday is July 6th. She may have been conceived in November, about the same time of Aaron's frightening experience with a woman named Leanna.*

9. *The people where Leanna worked didn't know anyone by that name????*

10. *Sam has been well cared for and seems to have strong coping skills.*

11. *Her wardrobe is expensive and complete.*

12. *She is well nourished and exceptionally well mannered.*

13. *Her mom is very sick and needs to go to the hospital again for more treatments.*

14. *Auntie Colleen has been living with them and helping to look after Sam because her mom is too sick.*

15. *Maybe Sam's mother has cancer, maybe she is going into drug rehab?*

16. *According to Sam, her mom doesn't want to be found. Small wonder!*

17. *The car Sam arrived in was a new model silver sedan and had a BC license plate starting with 273 Y.*

This still wasn't much to go on. Neither Meredith nor Andy felt very creative; their minds were burdened by their concern for Aaron. Any decisions about whether or not they should start looking for Leanna would have to wait.

The phone rang. It was their daughter, Wendy. She usually phoned them at least once a day but she and her family were in Edmonton this weekend visiting friends. "Hi Mom, how's it going?"

"Oh, Wendy, I'm so glad you called. Where are you?"

"We're in the *Suburban* driving home. The boys are sound asleep. What's up, Mom? You sound worried." Just like Sam, Wendy was too perceptive, she could always pick up on Meredith's mood.

"God, where do I begin? Wendy, your dad and I have had a very unusual weekend." Meredith began to fill her in.

When she got to the part about the date rape, Wendy interrupted, "Oh my god, Mom, poor Aaron, this must be awful for him. Whether Sam is his kid or not, date rape—this is terrible."

"I know," Meredith started to cry.

"Oh Mom, I'm so sorry. Aaron must be beside himself. And you and Dad. Are you going to be okay? How can I help?"

Meredith willed herself to be strong. "Oh, Wendy, just being able to tell you is cathartic. Your Dad and I will be okay. We'll get through this but I *am* worried about your brother."

"Should I call him, Mom?" Wendy and her brother were very close and Wendy was good friends with Jessica. Jessica was an only child and she was thrilled to have a sister now. Meredith was confident Wendy would be helpful to both of them. She was an untrained but skilled and actively practising psychologist, that is, with her family and friends. She always knew what to say. And she would understand the potential impact this could have for Aaron and Jessica.

"I'm sure Aaron would love to hear from you, dear. I'm afraid your brother is quite distraught and I don't know how much he has told Jessica yet. So be careful what you say to her. Before I let you go, I need to talk to you about protecting Aaron. Dad and I were just discussing this a few minutes ago." Meredith filled Wendy in on the plan of what to tell people. She knew Wendy and Ian would be very careful. "Let us know how your conversation with Aaron goes."

"Sure, I will, Mom. And you be sure to let me know if there is anything else I can do."

"We're doing okay." Meredith faltered. "Just very tired."

"Okay, Mom, I'll call him right now. Talk to you later, luv you."

"I love you too, dear."

****

"Andy, I'm exhausted but there is one more thing I have to do tonight or I won't be able to sleep thinking about it. I have to do some research on date rape drugs."

"God, Meredith, can't that wait until tomorrow? I'm dead. What a weekend! What happened to our two days of nothing but relaxation?"

"Yeah, that certainly turned out to be wishful thinking, didn't it? We'll both have to call in to work first thing in the morning and tell them we'll be away tomorrow."

"I guess so. And just what is the plan for tomorrow?"

"I think all three of us need to go to the Children's Services Office right after breakfast. I will go in first and explain our dilemma. You and Sam can wait outside. The child care worker will probably want to talk to all of us after I tell her what has happened. You know, they may feel that they have to take custody of Sam; she is an abandoned child, whether she is our granddaughter or not. And someone will need to be assigned as her legal guardian." Meredith knew some of what to expect because of her years as a public health nurse. "I hope we can keep her with us, Andy. She has been through quite enough in a very short time. She really is an amazing little girl."

"Yeah, she seems to be very self-confident. But we have made this very easy for her so far."

"Yes, we have but...everyone she knows is gone from her life including her mother. That's huge for a six-year old."

"I guess so. I've got to go to bed. I'm sacked."

"Okay, you go ahead, dear, but I have to check out these date rape drugs. I have this question in my mind about how this could happen to a guy. How can they 'perform' if they're out cold, Andy?"

"Be damned if I know but I have to hit the bed. I'm sorry, I just can't handle anymore."

"That's okay, I'll be there shortly. This shouldn't take too long."

Meredith selected google.ca from their "favourites" list and typed in "date rape drugs." She learned that most date rape victims are, of course, women; but an estimated three percent are men. Accurate statistics are difficult to collect because men are even more unlikely to report than women. She studied the information on GHB (also known as Ecstasy or the love drug), Rohypnol, and Ketamine. What she discovered was not reassuring. GHB gives users a sense of tranquility and a feeling of enhanced sexuality and lowers inhibitions. Low doses cause pleasant relaxation and euphoria. It takes only fifteen to twenty minutes to react. The drug's effects can be long lasting and lead to a spontaneous and deep sleep. Rohypnol is a tranquilizer much stronger than Valium and is known as the "date rape drug." It can render the user unconscious and cause memory loss. Effects can occur within one half hour and last from eight up to twenty-four hours. In the United States, it's a prescription drug that is sometimes prescribed as a sleep aid. It is not available in Canada as a prescription drug but it can be purchased on the street and is colourless, odourless, and tasteless in a drink. Ketamine is an animal tranquilizer and it can cause hallucinations, disassociation, and memory loss.

It seemed to Meredith that combinations of GHB and Rohypnol could be very effective in male date rape. GHB works faster and could give the desired effects of increased sexual feelings and lowered inhibitions; then Rohypnol could kick in later, render the victim unconscious and cause memory loss. *Could this be what happened to Aaron? I suppose the staff at a college student health services facility would know a fair bit about date rape drugs. Leanna would likely have access to information about doses used for desired effects. Damn her, it was probably easy for her to pull this off.*

Meredith shut down the computer and headed upstairs. While she was getting ready for bed, her thoughts were with Aaron. *How can this possibly feel for him?* She tried to relate it to herself or her daughter being raped but it just didn't compute. *Usually when women are raped, there is a huge element of physical violence involved. That would not have been the case for Aaron. Nevertheless, his personhood was horrifically violated.* Meredith shivered and her stomach tightened into a hard, heavy stone, rolling around at its own will. Her heart ached and felt like it was twisting on its axis, strangulating the blood flow, her legs were weak, her head dizzy. She sat on the toilet with her head down. When she recovered slightly, she hurried to bed and climbed in carefully, trying not to disturb Andy. She gently snuggled up to his warm back and found his soft snore reassuring. Some of her world was still normal. Somehow, she and her family would survive this mess.

Sleep eluded her for a good while but she finally drifted off somewhere past midnight.

CHAPTER 4

———

Children's Services
Monday, April 16

As soon as the office opened at 8:30, Meredith called Children's Services and arranged an appointment at 9:30. Over breakfast, she explained to Sam what they were going to do. "Sam, it will be fine," she reassured. "We just have to let them know that you are with us." Meredith hoped she wasn't making false promises. Sam was particularly quiet but she ate her breakfast well while Andy and Meredith chatted about their work commitments for the week.

When they arrived at Children's Services, they were asked to take a seat in the waiting area. Meredith thought it felt surreal to be sitting there with Sam and Andy. The woman at the reception desk was behind a protective glass wall with a tiny circular opening to talk through. Given the potential risks in the business of child protection and the anger of some parents, Meredith guessed it was a necessary precaution. The waiting room was small and windowless with only six chairs and a small table with children's books scattered on it, no toys in sight. The austere atmosphere did not feel welcoming.

Delores Scobie, the Director of Children's Services, appeared within minutes. All of her workers were busy so she took the appointment. Meredith went in first to explain the details of their situation. She followed Delores through a heavy solid door that automatically locked behind them. When she heard the locking sound, she felt terribly separated from Andy and Sam and the whole process seemed formidable. Delores's office was down and around a labyrinth of hallways, further isolating Meredith. *This place feels more like a jail than a place for children.*

Delores listened intently while Meredith explained the circumstances of how Sam had arrived at their house. She indicated that the situation was indeed unusual and asked if Meredith thought Sam could be her grandchild. "That is the question of the day. We have so little to go on." Meredith didn't mention her son's experience in college. She didn't want to give Delores any reasons to form conclusions.

"Under the circumstances, do you want to keep Sam with you?"

"Yes, definitely." *That was an easy question.*

"Okay but from what you've told me, Sam is an abandoned child. The Ministry must become her legal guardian. Right now, we have to take responsibility for where she is staying. As I am sure you can appreciate, before we give you temporary custody, we must run a check on you and your husband. I will run Sam in our system too and I'll ask the police to do the same. I will also ask them to do a criminal record check on you and your husband. I'll need you to wait outside while I do that." She escorted Meredith back to the heavy locking door and let her back into the waiting room, leaving her to feel like a criminal suspect.

Sam was reading a children's book to Andy. Meredith noticed how easily Sam was reading. Even the flow of her words and her emphasis was too correct for a six-year old. Despite her amazement at Sam's ability to read so well, Meredith's thoughts soon drifted back to Delores. She estimated her to be about thirty-six. She was slim and had a pretty face with fine features and a narrow chin. Her dark brown hair was cut in a modern, zig zag fashion, with bangs covering her eyebrows. She came across as friendly but guarded, definitely and correctly concerned about Sam.

About twenty minutes later, Delores called all of them back in. She wanted to meet Sam and Andy. "All our systems checked out okay. Nothing came up for Sam, no Samantha Scott. So, Andy, how do you feel about keeping Sam for a while?"

Andy looked at Sam with a big grin. "She can definitely stay with us while we figure out where she came from and where her mother is. Sam is a great kid, she's no trouble at all."

Delores dropped her guard and smiled a bit at Andy's enthusiasm. "What have the three of you been doing since Sam arrived on Saturday?"

Good question. This woman knows how to size us up. Meredith started the story and both Sam and Andy interjected at times. Meredith thought it must be obvious that Sam had been having a good time with them; and, despite the situation, they were enjoying Sam's company too. After they were finished, Delores said she wanted to talk to Sam by herself for a few minutes and asked Andy and Meredith to wait in the waiting room. Meredith gave Sam a hug and assured her they would be back shortly.

This gave Meredith and Andy a few precious moments to share their feelings. "Meredith, why am I feeling so jittery? I feel like we are getting into some pretty deep water here."

"Yes, I know what you mean. This is a damn big commitment we are making at our age. But remember our discussions last night. This is the only course of action we can take. We both know we have to request custody for Sam's sake."

"It's not taking care of Sam that worries me, we can do that. It's all of the other possible ramifications of the situation that are worrying me."

"You mean the fallout for Aaron?"

"Yes, he must be just devastated. A brand new marriage, a life together just beginning. How are they going to handle this? How will Jessica react when he tells her what happened? I sure as hell hope she is understanding and supportive."

"I hope so too. Aaron is going to need support and understanding from all of us to get through this. Even if Sam turns out not to be his daughter, dealing with the impact of what happened to him will be horrendous."

Andy reached for Meredith's hand and held it in both of his and they sat in painful silence with their own thoughts.

It seemed like forever but it was only ten minutes before Delores and Sam were back and Delores asked them to join her in her office again. She set Sam up at a play station in the corner of her office. "Under the circumstances, I feel comfortable enough to invoke the "Take Charge" section of the Child, Family & Community Services Act. This will allow you to have temporary custody of Sam for seventy-two hours but we will be her legal guardian. If her mother is not found by then, she will have to be removed for seven days and placed in foster care."

"Oh no! Surely there must be a way to prevent that," Meredith pleaded. She had been expecting some unfavourable rules but this shocked her. "Will we at least be able to visit her if that happens?"

"Yes, definitely, we can arrange that with the foster family. The Act states we must have a court hearing within the seven days. At the hearing, you will be able to apply for custody under what we call "Ex-parte." If the judge sees fit, he or she can grant you an order for custody and guardianship for up to three months. Then there will be a review. I do have to warn you, though, if we can't find a foster family in Dawson Creek for Sam, she may have to go elsewhere in the province."

"The province! You mean she could end up anywhere in the province?" Meredith asked.

"That's correct. Of course, we will do our best to place her in Dawson Creek."

Andy changed the subject. "What about school?"

"Yes, Sam should be registered for school as soon as possible. I will go with you to do that as it will require a legal guardian. We will also apply for a Care Card for her in case she requires any medical care. But in the event she gets sick and has to see a doctor or go to the hospital, you will have to call us so we can sign for her. We have a twenty-four hour Kid's Help Line you can call." She handed Meredith the card.

Meredith didn't tell her she had already called this line yesterday asking for information regarding process while pretending she was writing a book. Right now, she was pleased that they had waited until today to contact Children's Services. The concept of anywhere else in the province scared her.

Delores asked if they had a preference of schools. Having moved to Dawson Creek only eleven years ago, after both of their children were in university, they hadn't used any of the schools. They asked Delores for her advice considering where they lived and picked the closest one, Canalta Elementary. Delores called the principal and briefly explained the situation. By the conversation, Meredith guessed he knew Delores well and was not surprised by the request for a sudden new registration. Delores made an appointment for all of them at 1:30.

They weren't expecting things to move so fast. On the way home, Meredith and Andy were discussing their work schedules and Sam was very quiet. As soon as they were in the house, she asked, "How long is seventy-two hours, Mrs. T?"

That began a heartfelt discussion with Sam as to what had just happened. She didn't cry but tears welled up in her eyes as she said, "But I don't want to go to a foster home... I want to stay here with you and Mr. T. My mommy told me to stay here." She spoke with determination and her lower lip turned out slightly in defiance.

"Sam, we will do the very best we can to keep you here. If you have to go to a foster home, it will only be for a few days and we will visit you often." Meredith gave her a big hug and asked Sam if she would help her make lunch. The activity seemed to help her forget the situation, at least for the time being.

They met Delores at the school and she explained to the principal, Mr. Hallaway, that Meredith and Andy had temporary custody of Sam and the Ministry of Children, Family & Community Services (MCFCS) was her legal guardian. To protect Sam, none of the details of the situation were to be divulged. Mr. Hallaway asked, "I don't suppose you have any immunization records for Sam?"

Meredith replied, "Yes, as a matter of fact we do, her mother sent a photocopied record. I used to be a public health nurse and it looks like her immunizations are complete. I'll bring it for you."

Sam was registered in grade one as Samantha Scott, birth date July 6th. By the time they were done, it was time for the school's mid-afternoon recess. The principal took them down to meet Sam's new teacher. Her name was Mrs. Babcock. Meredith estimated her to be in her late twenties. She was delightful, full of enthusiasm and warmth. She welcomed Sam to her classroom with a pat on her shoulder.

The maintenance man arrived almost immediately with a desk for Sam. It was placed at the front right beside Mrs. Babcock. Andy and Meredith stayed until it was time for class to resume. By then, Mrs. Babcock had introduced Sam to the little girl that was sitting right beside her and they were already chatting happily. Andy and

Meredith had to interrupt to say goodbye. Both of them gave Sam a quick hug and told her they would be back to pick her up right after school was finished, in just one hour. They left thinking Sam was in good hands. Once again, she seemed to be dealing with another new situation amazingly well.

This gave Andy and Meredith one precious hour alone before school would be out. But tomorrow they would have the whole school day to start looking for answers. Andy decided to go to his office to check for any important emails from the deputy minister. Meredith went with him and used an empty office to call her very dear friend, Arlene Cameron. Arlene and her husband, Hugh, had been in Grande Prairie visiting friends for the weekend. She would be at work now.

Before she made her call, Meredith's thoughts shifted to Aaron and his first day of school, six years old and so ready, much more ready than Meredith had been. Her empty nest had quite an impact as she had stayed home for eight years to parent her two children until they started school. She had planned ahead to take a nursing refresher course and return to work but the transition was still daunting. She smiled at her thoughts, thinking that this "déjà vu" experience with Sam, whom she had only known for fewer than three days was totally different. Yet the feelings were so familiar—leaving a vulnerable child in the hands of others.

"Arlene, have you got a minute to talk?"

"Sure, Meredith, what's up?"

"I have some earthshattering news for you." As briefly as she could, she told Arlene what was happening, being careful to leave out the part about the possible date rape. Meredith felt comfortable confiding in Arlene with the rest of the story. She had been her closest and dearest friend since moving to Dawson Creek.

"Meredith, you sound as if you are okay with all this, but... are you?"

"I guess I am as good as can be expected under the circumstances but believe me, I've had my moments. Andy goes from what I think is okay to looking extremely worried. You know that deep furrow he has between his eyes? I think it's just gotten a lot deeper over the last three days. Mostly, I'm concerned about Aaron and Jessica. I think Andy and I can handle this but poor Aaron, if Sam really is his child, this is not going to be easy for him."

"Yes, I can see it could be complicated."

"And Jessica, well, she's definitely a sensible, down-to-earth girl, but this is going to be a crazy situation for her too. Aaron would have told her about Sam the night before last but I haven't talked to her since then. We plan to call them tonight."

"It's a bit of a coincidence, Meredith. Just last week I was watching W5 and they were talking about exactly this kind of thing, it was called "Parents Again." They talked about the growing number of grandparents in Canada that were raising their grandchildren. If you're interested, you could go to the W5 website for the details on the story."

"Thanks Arlene, when I have a minute, I might do that. Maybe there will be something relevant there for Andy and me." Meredith wasn't so sure she appreciated this information at the moment and certainly wasn't comforted by it. Nor did she agree that their situation was "exactly this kind of thing." She knew Arlene was trying to be helpful but a feeling of dread went up her spine, spreading into her heart and lungs, and causing a pressure sensation in her chest. It became hard to speak. "For now, all we are planning to say to people who ask is that Sam is staying with us for a while as her mom is very sick. We thought we wouldn't even mention the granddaughter word until we know more."

"No problem, you know your information is safe with us and if there is anything at all that Hugh and I can do, please, please let us know. You know you can count on us to help wherever you need us."

"Thanks, Arlene. I so appreciate your friendship, especially at times like this. Andy is waiting at the door so I better get going." She checked her watch. "We have to be back to the school in ten minutes."

"Okay, my dear friend, take care. I'll be thinking of you. When you are ready for us to meet Sam, just give us a call."

"Thanks, Arlene, talk later."

****

Meredith and Andy arrived just before school was out and Meredith went in to collect Sam while Andy waited in the car. She was just approaching Sam's classroom door when the bell rang. The door flew open and children began streaming into the hallway, the noise level elevating quickly with children paying no attention to where they were going. Meredith had to step back to avoid being run over by six-year-olds. When the crowd dispersed, she entered the classroom to see Mrs. Babcock quietly talking to Sam, a gentle smile on her face.

"Oh, Mrs. Taylor, good to see you."

"Hi Mrs. T," Sam interrupted.

"I was explaining to Sam that we just started a new reader a few days ago. She would like to take it home and practice reading to catch up to where we are."

"That's great, we can surely help her with that."

"Wonderful! Sam's first afternoon has gone well; she has made a couple of friends already."

"Excellent. Thank you, Mrs. Babcock. Are you ready Sam? Mr. T. is waiting for us outside." Meredith took Sam's hand and gave Mrs. Babcock a friendly wave.

Inside the car, Sam was exuberant about her afternoon, telling about her two friends, Holly and Rilla. They had worked together on a puzzle once they had completed their printing exercise.

After supper, Meredith decided to bake some cookies, thinking that would be a good thing to do with Sam. She remembered fondly how Wendy used to love to cook with her. By the time Wendy was twelve, she could put together an excellent meal for the whole family. The thought made Meredith smile to herself. Wendy still loved to cook and Andy and Meredith loved to visit her to enjoy her meals and other things; more specifically, the company of their daughter, their son-in-law, and their two precious grandsons.

"Sam, how would you like to bake some cookies with me tonight?"

"Sure, Mrs. T," she responded excitedly. "What kind will we make?"

"What kind do you like, Sam?"

"I love chocolate chip cookies," she said with a little smirk.

"Hmm, I should have known, the way you slurped up that Chocolate Chip Blizzard the other day. Are you a chocolate lover, Sam?"

"Yes I am," she giggled and her effervescent blue eyes twinkled with delight.

"Well then, let's get at it so we can get them done before bedtime. We'll have to send Mr. T to the store for chocolate chips. By the time we have the dough ready to add the chips, he'll be back. Let me check to see if we have everything else we need."

Andy did quite a bit of the grocery shopping for Meredith these days because he adamantly did not want to help with the cooking. He was a wonderful and willing helper with many other aspects of the work around the house and yard. But cooking was absolutely not his line of expertise and he had no intention of learning. Meredith knew he would willingly clean up the baking dishes while she was putting Sam to bed.

After Meredith got Sam tucked in for the night, she came downstairs and sat in her recliner beside Andy. He was reading the paper and didn't even look up. He hadn't met Meredith at the bottom of the stairs with a look of urgent fright tonight. It seemed that, after three days, he was getting used to the idea of Sam invading their life;

his profile displayed a look of ease and contentment, at least for now. Reading the paper was a good escape from the latest events in their lives. She smiled to herself at the change in Andy and leaned back, letting mental and physical exhaustion take over for a few minutes while she tried to relax. Her mind was foggy with thoughts of the last three days, one thought drifting into the next with no logical order. Then she thought of what Arlene had said about the *W5* program she had watched a few days ago. Even though the information about this program had unnerved her, curiosity won and she went to the office, sat down at the computer and googled *W5*, an informative CBC television program. She quickly found the synopsis of "Parents Again."

The program indicated that at least sixty-five thousand children were living with their grandparents in Canada today. Emphasis was on the fact that this was creating a huge financial hardship as many grandparents were raising their grandchildren on very small pensions and living below the poverty line. Many of these children had problems related to fetal alcohol syndrome, learning disabilities, and past physical and sexual abuse.

Even though Meredith could see the possibility of Andy and her becoming one of these statistics, the information actually made her feel fortunate. At least Sam appeared to be very well cared for and was adjusting amazingly well to her new reality with them. As far as she could tell, Sam's mental achievement was well advanced beyond her chronological age. Although she and Andy were not wealthy, they had the means to live comfortably, travel a bit, and if necessary, look after a grandchild for a while without hurting financially. This made her look at their situation from a fresh perspective. Her spirit lifted and she felt some energy returning to her brain and her body. Then she remembered she should call Aaron and Jessica. With a renewed sense of well-being, she turned off the computer and returned to her chair, alerting Andy that she was going to make the call.

"Hi Jessica, it's Meredith, how are you doing?"

"Ohhh, I'm so glad you called, Meredith. I wanted to talk to you. Aaron is sick over this thing with... Sam. I know he told you about his incident at college. I have been trying to reassure him that the likelihood of a pregnancy resulting from it is probably non-existent. I'm sure it's just a coincidence that it happened around the same time Sam was likely conceived. But he's convinced otherwise and he's tearing himself inside out over it. He's just beside himself." Meredith's sense of well-being evaporated, replaced again by fear and uncertainty.

"Good grief, poor Aaron. I don't have a clue how to help him, Jessica." *I wish Jessica didn't sound so certain that Sam was not Aaron's daughter. I wonder how she will react if they do find out Sam is indeed Aaron's daughter.*

"And neither do I. One thing is certain though, he is not going to get any sleep until we find out for sure that Sam is not his daughter. You know how he has trouble sleeping at the best of times. The last two nights have really been bad."

"Jessica, why was he working yesterday, on a Sunday?"

"His project is so busy right now, he went in for four hours yesterday to get some stuff ready for this morning."

"Wow, no sleep and lots of pressure at work, not a good combination."

"Nope, not at all, he's dozing in front of the television right now but I just know he will have a hard time again tonight. I think we better get paternity testing done as soon as we can, Meredith."

"Okay, Jessica, I'll research how to do that tonight yet and see what I can come up with."

"Okay, thanks so much...What happened at Children's Services today?"

"Oh, that went well, we have temporary custody of Sam for three days." Meredith told her the rest of the story including the fact that Sam started school today.

"How are you and Andy doing with all this?"

"Oh we're fine, just a bit tired, that's all." *God, if you only knew.* "Sam, she is a lovely little girl, very well mannered, obviously smart. She's no trouble to look after, that's for sure. Don't worry about us. Andy and I are doing fine."

"Okay then, we'll wait to hear from you tomorrow."

"Sure, Jessica, but just one more thing. We wanted you and Aaron to know what Andy and I have decided to tell other people." Meredith filled Jessica in on the plan.

"Okay, that makes perfect sense to me. We haven't told anyone about this yet, not even my parents; but I guess it's more critical for you because you have Sam there with you. People will certainly be curious. Thanks, Meredith, for thinking this through and being so careful. I'll let Aaron know. He'll appreciate it."

"No problem. You and Aaron take care of each other, now."

"Thanks, we will, and thanks for calling."

Despite her anxiety, Meredith felt a strange sense of relief. The family secret of what happened to Aaron would be concealed among the six of them now.

Andy was listening to the conversation and wanted to know everything. Meredith filled him in on Jessica's thoughts about Aaron and Andy looked very concerned. "God, Meredith, I wish I knew how to help him."

"Maybe you should call him tomorrow and have a father/son chat."

"I have no idea what to say. You know I don't do well with this kind of stuff."

"I know you think you don't do well, Andy, but I think Aaron would like to hear from his father. He needs to know how concerned and supportive you are."

"I suppose but right now I have to get to bed. I'll think about that in the morning." Andy always required more sleep than Meredith did. He usually went to bed at least one-half hour sooner than her and got up one hour later.

"Okay but, before you go, I want to tell you about a *W5* program I just read about. Arlene told me about it." Meredith discussed what she had learned with Andy.

"Well, I agree, our situation could certainly be worse but that doesn't make it okay."

"No, of course not, but it does put a better perspective on it, Andy. Tomorrow, Sam will be in school and we will have the whole day to figure out what we're going to do. Maybe we can get our thoughts straightened out."

"Right, that sounds far too optimistic for me. I haven't had my thoughts straight for years. I'm not sure how Sam being in school will help." They both laughed. Andy got up from his chair, went over to Meredith and offered his hand to help her up. At least they still had their sense of humour. "I'm heading for bed, dear." He gave Meredith a lingering full body hug, the kind where they touched tightly from neck to ankle, his legs wrapped around hers and her head snuggled into his neck. Even though they had perfected this many years ago, Meredith thought that tonight it felt extra refreshing. She felt the power of their love merging in both of them, each being strengthened by the mutual transference of positive energy.

Andy backed away, bent slightly forward, held Meredith by her shoulders and gave her a light but lingering kiss on her lips.

"Goodnight, my love," she said smiling, "I'll be there as soon as I find some information on paternity testing." Meredith went back to the office, opened Google again and started her search.

CHAPTER 5

———

Aaron's Flashback
Tuesday, April 17

The next morning, just after Meredith returned home from taking Sam to school, she went upstairs to tidy up and sat down on Sam's unmade bed to think. Andy had gone to work for a couple of hours. He always walked the two miles to his office; and at 9:30, he walked to Hug a Mug to meet his group of morning coffee buddies. He wouldn't be home until 10:30. They had decided to try to keep their routine as normal as possible even if they weren't going to work for a day or two. Meredith went to the window, raised the blind and stood leaning on the windowsill. The back yard faced north and still had quite a bit of snow in it, protected by the house, the shop, the trees and the wooden fence. Andy had built the shop for woodworking; part of his retirement plan. She fondly recalled how hard he had worked the last couple of summers to get it finished.

Staring out at the spruce trees, the winter-bare aspen, birch and shrubs, she reminisced about last summer and all the fun they had in the backyard, barbecues with family and friends, their grandsons running around, their happy voices and laughter pleasantly penetrating the adult conversation. She loved her back yard. Besides being a perfect entertainment spot, it was a reclusive protected place, a sanctuary she used to get in touch with Mother Nature, do some gardening and meditating.

As soon as the soil was dry enough, she would be out there, raking up the spruce cones that fell during the winter, digging in the shrub beds, trimming the old to encourage the new and promising growth. Andy was always there to help her with the heavy work. Meredith loved flowers and she would soon be out purchasing her bedding plants, pansies, petunias, geraniums, sweet peas, marigolds, grasses, and trailing plants to put in her pots and borders.

This spring would be different though. Meredith would likely be taking Sam with her to choose her flowers and help her plant them. She guessed Sam would be just as enthusiastic about gardening as she was about cooking. She had resigned herself to the fact that Sam would likely be with them for a lengthy time, at least after they got past those dreadful seven days in foster care.

When she was tired of standing, she went around to the other side of the bed, sat down, and leaned back, putting her hands behind her on the bed for support and letting her thoughts drift again. She thought about Sam and how happy she had been to be going to school this morning. Meredith had half-expected her to be hesitant but Sam's first impression of Mrs. Babcock was very positive and she was looking forward to seeing her new friends, Holly and Rilla. Meredith marvelled at Sam's ability to cope with her uncertain situation. She wondered if it was just the normal resilience of children or if Sam had an extraordinary capacity to deal with change. She reminded herself that she would have to make a point of meeting Holly's and Rilla's parents.

Meredith and Andy had seventy-two hours, starting yesterday at 10:30, to find Sam's mother or they would lose Sam for at least a week. Their success was unlikely and she wasn't sure if it was even worth trying. Besides, according to Sam, Leanna didn't want to be found and Meredith had no idea where to start.

Her thoughts were interrupted by the phone. She quickly went to her bedroom to answer the call.

It was Aaron. "Hi Mom."

Meredith immediately detected a high level of stress in his voice. "Aaron, how are you doing?"

"Not so good at the moment, I have something I need to tell you. Have you got some time right now?"

"Of course, dear, what is it?"

"I was coming out of the house this morning to leave for work and I had some sort of flashback… I think. I had these images flash before my eyes; I went all dizzy and my eyes were blurry. I staggered to my truck and had to lean on it for a while."

"Oh, Aaron, that sounds awful!"

Yeah, it was spooky, Mom. One of my neighbours stopped and asked if I was alright. I told him, yes, I was fine, and managed to get into my truck so he left. When the images stopped, I felt so light-headed for a while. I must have sat there for about ten minutes."

"Are you feeling okay now, Aaron?"

"Yes, I just feel…disturbed… stressed...or something."

"What were the images, dear?"

"Well, it wasn't very clear but I seemed to be on a bed with a woman and she was telling me everything was okay, just go back to sleep. I was trying to sit up but I couldn't move more than lifting my head a couple of inches off the pillow. I seemed to be paralyzed or something." Aaron's voice was faltering.

Meredith could tell he was close to tears and trying hard to hold back so he could finish his story.

"And, Mom…, I was naked, stark naked! Then another flash came, it was still blurry but I swear I saw her with a used condom and a syringe. Oh god, this is just awful."

"Oh, Aaron…" Meredith didn't know what else to say.

"I was late for my meeting this morning and I couldn't think straight. I had to tell my boss I wasn't feeling well and I left the meeting early. Mom, I think I was remembering something really weird that happened to me at college, the same incident I told you about yesterday. I think the woman in the image I had was Leanna... Oh Mom, I'm so sorry."

"Sorry, my god, Aaron, what are you sorry for? You haven't done anything wrong." Meredith could tell this story was very painful for him. Her brain was starting to spasm again. *Condom, syringe... Aaron paralyzed.* She didn't know what else to say. She still couldn't tell Aaron that Sam had said her mother's name was Leanna. She recognized that this same Leanna was likely Sam's mother, but that still didn't mean Aaron was Sam's father. Meredith had already rationalized this over and over again and she didn't want to dash Aaron's hopes, just in case.

"Remember yesterday, I said she never took anything… I mean money or my credit card... Well, I think she took my sperm, Mom. I can't believe this. She took my sperm and now I have a six-year old daughter. I think I could accept this better if it had been an alien kidnapping. How did I let this happen to me?"

"Aaron, please, as I said before, don't blame yourself, my god, son, you're the victim here." Meredith's thoughts were racing. *Slow down, Meredith, think clearly. Say something intelligent and comforting...* "After what you told me before, I Googled date-rape drugs.

Your description of what happened to you and how you felt meshes perfectly with how these drugs react, my dear son. You can't blame yourself, you *were* drugged."

"What did you find out, Mom, about the drugs?"

"Well, GHB, or Ecstasy, I expect you're more familiar with that name, takes effect in fifteen to twenty minutes. It increases your feelings of sexuality and lowers your inhibitions and eventually causes a deep sleep." Meredith thought she was on the right track here. Both Aaron and his dad responded well to scientific information. She continued. "Rohypnol, also known as the date-rape drug, is a tranquilizer much stronger than Valium. It causes unconsciousness and memory loss. Some people feel dizzy or lightheaded for up to two to three days afterwards, just as you told me you did. It takes longer to work, maybe one-half hour, and the effects can last for up to eight to twenty-four hours. My guess is, this woman, Leanna, gave you some of both, Aaron. Victims of date rape drugs remember feeling lightheaded and intoxicated, and then they wake up after sleeping for several hours, still feeling very drowsy and confused with no recollection of what happened."

"What you say certainly fits the picture, Mom, but she didn't give me anything until I went to her apartment with her. So that does not negate my stupidity."

"Are you sure she didn't give you anything until the drink at her apartment? Did you have a drink of something with her at the college before you left?"

"Yeah...coffee!"

"Well then...she could have spiked your coffee too, maybe with some Ecstasy."

"Okay, I can see your point, but I still should have seen this coming, Mom. I should have known better. And I must have been a willing participant or how else would she have accomplished it?"

"You may have been a willing participant but you were in a drugged state. That's entirely different than agreeing to it. Just how hard are you planning to be on yourself, Aaron? Remember one thing, you were the victim here."

"Yeah, and a stupid one!"

"Okay, my dear son, you are determined aren't you? I think it is critical to have some DNA testing done as soon as possible, especially after what you have just remembered. What do you think?"

"Yes, Mom, for sure, we need to do that. If DNA testing shows she isn't my child; and god, I hope she isn't, then we can all put this behind us, like a terrible nightmare. If she is my child, then I'm going to have to figure out how the hell I'm going to deal with it."

"That's right, Aaron, but remember, however it turns out, Dad and I are here to help you."

"Thanks, Mom."

"How did Jessica react when you told her what you remembered?" Meredith hated to bother him with more but she desperately wanted to know how Jessica had responded to the information. She knew Jessica's reaction would be critical to Aaron getting through this.

"When I told her, she was so quiet at first, it really worried me. But then we talked about it and she was great, especially with where she is at right now. We actually already talked about DNA testing. But I haven't told her about this flashback thing that I had this morning. I don't want to tell her over the phone. We are both home tonight for a change and we're planning a relaxing supper together."

"That's good, Aaron, but what do you mean by especially where Jessica is at right now?" Meredith's antennae were up and her mother instinct had easily picked up on this.

"I can't tell you now, Mom, but Jessica and I, we'll call you and Dad tonight…after supper. Okay?"

She didn't want to press him, he'd been through enough. "Okay, thanks, Aaron, for sharing this with me. I think it's going to be critical to keep in touch and share everything we find out. We're all in this together."

"Yeah, for sure, Mom. I feel a bit better just telling you about this. It seems like a weight has been lifted off my chest, at least a bit. I better get going. I've got to get my work done."

"Okay, Aaron, we can talk more about DNA testing tonight when you call. I did a search for information last night; and remember, whatever happens, you can't blame yourself. We love you, dear."

Even though Aaron expressed that he was feeling a bit better, Meredith remained very concerned about him. *Flashbacks, date rape, good grief, what could possibly be worse for a man to deal with? The psychological ramifications could be huge. Could this woman have only wanted Aaron's sperm to establish a pregnancy? Aaron is right. This is just too weird. He is going to need lots of support. I sure hope Jessica will continue to be supportive, whether Sam turns out to be his child or not. Thank goodness, she took the initial news well.*

Meredith looked at her watch. Andy wouldn't be back for another twenty to thirty minutes. She was reeling with Aaron's latest information and wasn't up to making beds. She wandered downstairs and sat in her chair. Her thoughts were full of questions. *The condom and the syringe, what on earth was Leanna doing? If she actually wanted to establish a pregnancy, why did she use a condom? Maybe Aaron was still alert enough to ask for one. Or could she have wanted to save some sperm to impregnate herself again in a day or two.* She speculated that Leanna could have improved her chances of conceiving if she exposed herself twice. *If she had been planning this for several weeks and had chosen Aaron, she could have been checking her basal body temperature every morning to know when she ovulated. That would certainly have increased her chances of conceiving.*

Meredith used to teach sex education in junior and senior high school and she knew that sperm could stay viable for up to seventy-two hours in the warmth of the human body. *Leanna would have required the perfect place to store the semen, perfect temperature and humidity conditions. Would she have had access to a lab? If not, could she keep the sperm alive by keeping them next to her body for warmth?* She thought her speculations were as crazy as Aaron's memories. She didn't know how to even think about this from a guy's point of view. She asked herself, *what more could I have said to him?*

Meredith remembered spending hours worrying about Wendy when she started going to school dances and then to college. She had cautioned her countless times to be aware of what she was drinking. But she had never worried about Aaron, at least not about being the victim of a rape. Her wild accusatory thoughts about Andy possibly being Sam's father came back to her and made her feel foolish. Then she saw him walking up the driveway.

Andy was smiling. "Hi, dear, how's it going?"

"Well…, sit down and I'll tell you."

"Oh oh, what's going on now?" Andy's smile vanished as he noticed and took in her distress. She filled him in on Aaron's call and her thoughts.

"Meredith, this gets crazier by the minute. What are we going to do?"

"That is what we have to discuss. What the hell do we do? First of all, I think you need to call Aaron, maybe this afternoon, and give him the same assurances I have given him. He needs to hear it from you too Andy."

"Okay, I'll try my best but you know I'm not comfortable with this stuff."

"It doesn't matter, he just needs to hear the concern in your voice."

"Okay, what else do we need to do?"

"I've been wracking my brain about it all morning and I still don't know. Do you think we should somehow be trying to find Sam's mother? My guess is, she has hidden her tracks well. And what would we gain if we actually did find her? Obviously, she doesn't want to or can't parent Sam right now. I'm thinking we should just let the chips fall where they may."

"I think you're right, besides, we have enough on our plates without trying to play detective."

Meredith questioned her own motives. "Andy, I don't know if I want Leanna found. She would make the situation more convoluted than ever. Dealing with Sam, I can handle; dealing with her treacherous mother, I don't know. If we did find her, how would that be for Aaron? It may increase his stress levels even more. Maybe the further out of the picture she is, the better."

"You've got a point there. So what do we need to do for the rest of the day?"

"I don't know, maybe we should just go back to work. I'll pick Sam up at school at three... Oh, this brings up another issue, we are going to need after-school care for her until five. I guess I better look into that but I can do it from work."

"But she may only be with us for two more days and then gone for possibly a week, Meredith. I don't think we should make any arrangements at least until we know that she is going to be with us for a while."

"That's true, maybe I am getting ahead of myself. I could still inquire about availability at least."

The phone rang. It was Wendy doing her usual daily check on her parents. Andy answered. When Meredith realized who was calling, she went upstairs to the bedroom phone. After filling Wendy in on Aaron's flashback, Andy and Meredith discussed the dilemma of looking or not looking for Sam's mother. Wendy agreed about the futility of it and said she thought her parents had enough on their hands already, dealing with Sam and worrying about Aaron. With Wendy's blessing on their decision, they had lunch and went to work.

At 3:00 PM, Meredith picked Sam up from school. At home, she took out some frozen salmon for supper and put it in cold water to thaw. Sam was right by her side, watching and asking questions.

"Mrs. T, how long will it take the salmon to thaw?"

"Oh, only about an hour, Sam. The cold water makes it thaw quicker. Are you hungry?"

"Yes, I'm starved."

"Starved, my goodness, we better get you a snack. What would you like?"

"Banana," she said shyly with her sweet compelling grin.

God, I'm already loving this child too much. Meredith handed her the banana and poured her some orange juice. *She is steadily seeping right into my heart. And Aaron, our son. Sam's mere presence in our lives is hurting him dearly.* Meredith's thoughts about Sam and Aaron kept surfacing and splitting her in two, right down the middle. How could she care so much for Sam without betraying her love for her son? These two diametrically opposed emotions were wreaking havoc with her heart and her mind. Her head started to throb and the familiar ache in her chest returned.

After Sam finished her snack, she disappeared into the living room and started playing with Wendy's dolls. As she started to prepare supper, Meredith had trouble focusing and almost put the salad dressing on the salmon. She laughed at herself and wondered if that might actually make the salmon taste good. She thought about it only momentarily, then quickly smothered the salmon with the salad dressing and put it in the oven.

CHAPTER 6

Aaron & Jessica's News
Tuesday, April 17

Sam was in bed and Meredith and Andy were in their recliners reading the daily newspaper, trying to divert attention from the intense emotion they were both feeling when the phone rang.

Meredith answered it. "Andy, Aaron and Jessica are on the phone. Please pick up in the bedroom. They want to have a group conversation."

"Hi Aaron and Jessica."

"Hi Dad." Meredith thought Aaron sounded much more cheerful than he had in the morning. "Jessica and I have something to tell you. Go ahead Jess, you tell them."

"We just found out yesterday that we're having a baby!"

Meredith heard the enthusiasm in both of their voices. "Oh, oh my goodness, that's incredible news. A new baby! Oh, now this is exciting. Both of you must be delighted," she bubbled inadequately.

"When's the baby due?" Andy asked, matter of fact.

"We're not quite sure, either December 4 or January 5. My periods are fairly irregular but I think it's going to be January 5. We have an ultrasound booked for May 14 so we'll know better then."

"Oh, you guys, this is such good news. I'm so happy for you," Meredith exclaimed excitedly, hiding her uncertainty. *Oh dear, why am I not thrilled about this news?*

"Mom, Dad, this thing with Sam really does complicate things for us right now."

"You know what, Aaron, you and Jessica have huge things to talk about and huge adjusting to do with your coming parenthood. As I said before, your dad and I will deal with the Sam issue. Please try not to worry about this end. You and Jessica concentrate on each other and your pregnancy. Okay?"

"Thanks, Mom and Dad, for making this as easy as you can for us. You two are such gems. We really appreciate it." Jessica's voice rang with sincerity.

"What did your mom and dad think of this, Jessica?" Jessica was an only child and her parents and her grandmother had been waiting impatiently through four years of dating and living together for Jessica and Aaron to get married. Now that they had been married for almost a year, Meredith was sure they would all be thrilled.

"We just got off the phone with them. Mom was crazy with excitement. Dad was his usual cool self but I know he was thrilled too. We're planning to get together for supper on Friday night to celebrate. It was Dad who suggested it." Jessica's parents lived in Calgary too so it was easy to get together. Meredith felt a pang of envy.

"This is so wonderful. You two know how Dad and I feel about our grandsons. Does Wendy know yet? She has been waiting impatiently for some cousins for her boys for three years now."

"Yeah, I know, she's given me enough of a bad time about hurrying it up," Aaron said. "Mom and Dad, we were planning to wait for a while to tell anyone else. But, under the circumstances, we thought you should know. And since we were telling you, we thought we should tell Jessica's mom and dad too. Could you keep our secret for us for a while?'

"Yes, absolutely, this is your special secret to tell the world whenever you are ready; but I'm very glad that you told us, Aaron."

"So…what about the DNA testing, Mom? What did you find out?"

Meredith's heart was fluttering wildly with this new revelation but she took a deep breath and told them what she knew. The Canadian Children's Rights Council is the leading source of information in Canada about DNA Paternity Testing. There is an ISO accredited laboratory in Toronto that does it for $345.00 and they promise 99.99 percent accuracy. The results would be available five to seven days after they receive the samples. All of the DNA tests are analyzed with state of the art genetic identification systems using sixteen different genetic markers.

"Aaron, all they need is a sample of your hair. I called the toll free number and asked them how to send the sample. All you have to do is put your hair in a plastic bag and label it. I will send you a sample of Sam's hair tomorrow morning. I will label it *Child* with her name and birth date. When you get it, you can do the same with your hair, labelling it *Father* with your name and birth date and send the two samples together by express post."

"That sounds easy enough, Mom."

"Yeah, it's pretty straightforward. You need to enclose a letter of request and a certified check for $345.00. The letter just needs to request a DNA comparison of the two samples of hair for purposes of paternity determination. The website is www.easydnacanada.com if you want to check it out." Aaron wrote the site down.

"Mom, Dad, this is one thing I won't forget to do or delay doing. I'll be on it. I'll write the letter tonight and have it ready. God, I hope this will put the whole thing behind us."

"Express post promises a two-day delivery. If I get Sam's hair in the mail tomorrow morning, you should have it by Friday but then it's the weekend. If you get your package in the mail by Monday, the lab will have it by Wednesday and we should have an answer by next Wednesday, May 2."

"Man, that still sounds like a long time to wait. We haven't told Jessica's mom and dad anything about Sam. We want to wait until we have the results of the DNA test. So please don't say anything if you're talking to them about the pregnancy."

"Okay, as you know, I did tell your sister and she has talked to you, Aaron. I also told my dear friend Arlene. But I only told her about Sam, nothing about what happened to you. I expect Jessica told you what I told her last night about what we plan to say to people. Nobody but our family needs to know about this, Aaron."

"Thanks, Mom and Dad, for all you do for us. As Jessica said, we really do appreciate it." Aaron's love for his parents was steadfast but he wasn't near as demonstrative about it as Wendy was.

"No problem, our dear son and daughter-in-law. However we can help, you let us know," Meredith replied emphatically.

"Okay, we better go now. We have some things we have to get done before bed."

"Bye, Aaron and Jessica, we love you both and we're so excited for you."

"Good talking to you," Andy added

"We love you too, Mom and Dad. Thanks again."

Once off the phone, Meredith sighed heavily and her thoughts raced. *Jessica is one of the most sensible young women I have ever met.*

She has her feet on the ground. She's one year older than Aaron, Aaron is thirty, Jessica thirty-one. They both wanted to start a family and it is the perfect time for a pregnancy, except for Sam's arrival. So far, Jessica seems to be handling the situation like a trooper. But early pregnancy could certainly throw her off. Her emotions will be running high. How will she deal with this mess in the long run, especially if Aaron really is Sam's father? I wonder if Aaron has told her yet about his flashback episode. He may not have wanted to spoil the news of their pregnancy with his growing dilemma.

Andy came down the stairs and fell back into his recliner breaking the silence. "Our lives are getting too complicated. How did this happen to us? I don't think I have ever felt so little control over what's happening. This was not how our retirement was supposed to go."

"Yeah, this is something we are really going to have to just wait and see how it all plays out, isn't it, dear?"

"Yes, but I do wonder if you aren't committing us to taking on too much for Aaron and Jessica. Sam should be their problem too, not just ours."

"Yes, you're right, but...right now, the way I see it, she was left on our doorstep, not Aaron's. Aaron has just realized he was raped and may have a daughter because of it. And at the same time, he and Jessica have just found out they're having a baby. What should we be doing, Andy?" Meredith was bristling.

"Oh, so now I'm being selfish?"

"No, Andy, you have every right to your feelings and believe me, I've had the same selfish feelings about my time and our future, but I don't know what else we can do. This is our situation. And you know our son very well, he is already feeling horribly guilty about his part in this. We have to give him time."

"I'm sorry dear." Andy got up and put out his arms for a hug. Meredith responded hesitantly but once she felt Andy's ever secure arms around her, she relaxed into his embrace and they took from each other the strength they needed to face their latest challenge. Together, she knew they would survive this.

"We are both exhausted again for the third night in a row," Meredith said. "I only hope a good night's sleep will get us through another day." Arm in arm, they climbed the stairs. They slipped quietly into Sam's room to check on her. She was sound asleep, breathing rhythmically, a look of contentment on her face. They both marvelled in the angelic beauty of this sleeping child who had arrived on their doorstep only four days ago.

Meredith remembered some of the tough times they had gone through with Aaron as a teenager. She often crept into his room at night after he was asleep to remind herself that he was still her angelic child. Just by watching him sleep, all her anger from the previous day would fade, washed away by her unfailing motherly love. As they walked back to their bathroom, she and Andy smiled at each other and their situation seemed a bit less devouring.

As they entered the bathroom together, Andy had that special gleam in his eye. He pulled Meredith close and she felt a fleeting spark of sexual desire. Then she remembered that she needed some of Sam's hair to send to Aaron. She could snip a few hairs while Sam was sleeping. She explained this to Andy and he released her from his embrace with a disappointed sigh. She picked her scissors out of the bathroom drawer and went to get some of Sam's hair. As she entered the bedroom again, she suddenly felt like the treacherous Delilah who cut Samson's hair and took his strength away while he slept. She rationalized that this was for a good cause, to determine the truth about Sam. Nonetheless, her heart quivered and her stomach tumbled. Somehow this was not the right way. She turned around and left.

Andy laughed when she told him. "Meredith, don't you think you're over-reacting. It's just some hair."

"I couldn't help but think that I was behaving just like Leanna. She took something from Aaron without him giving his permission. I think we need to be up front and very honest with Sam even if she is only six years old. Tomorrow morning, I'm going to explain to her that we need some of her hair to test to see if she truly is our grandchild."

"Okay, dear, I do see your point but I think you're making too much of it." He grinned again and swept her back into his arms.

"Maybe, but I think I'll sleep better for it tonight."

"I think I can help with that," he said as he bent to kiss her. Even though her exhaustion was overwhelming, she let him guide her to the bed. She welcomed his familiar gentle touches and slowly found her desire to respond.

****

Jessica went to bed right after the call to Meredith and Andy. Aaron stayed up just long enough to write his letter of request for the paternity test. He put it into an envelope with a cheque for $345.00 and left it on his desk. Jessica was asleep by the time he crawled in. With nobody to talk to, he began to stew again. He hadn't told Jessica yet about the flashback that he had experienced earlier in the day. He wondered if he should tell her tomorrow. His brain was sending messages that were like little explosions inside his head. He felt like he was getting ready to erupt like a volcano. He wanted to detach himself from everything, just get away.

He thought about how he felt when he first met Jessica. She was a breath of fresh air after his last relationship with a very controlling and emotionally volatile woman. He was so happy to have finally ended it and definitely was not ready for another relationship when he met Jessica. But she was so easy going and accepting of exactly who he was. Despite his hesitancy, he soon found himself feeling very fond of her.

What he began to recognize is that Jessica made his life easier rather than more complicated. He hadn't experienced that before. As time passed, they began to share more and more of the daily chores of life, household jobs, car maintenance, planning for their entertainment and for the future. Life began to fall into place like the pieces of a puzzle, all the pieces fitting together perfectly and effortlessly. They did the things they both enjoyed together and there was still plenty of room for their own activities. He remembered feeling totally amazed at how good a relationship could be.

Just as he was starting to relax with his pleasant thoughts, he began to wonder if their relationship would be able to endure this latest development. He asked himself if any relationship could endure such a strain. *I have to be strong, I have to see my own way through this without burdening Jessica, especially now that she's pregnant. She seems so accepting of the situation with Sam. Like Mom and Dad, she doesn't blame me. But I know this is my fault, I should have seen it coming.* His feelings of guilt soared. His memories of what had happened put a thick, dark cloud over him, seeming to threaten his relationship with his wife and the wellbeing of his parents. The cloud closed in and he couldn't breathe. He got up, went to the family room and turned on the television, hoping to push his morbid thoughts out with mindless activity.

CHAPTER 7

———

Temporary Care for Sam
Wednesday, April 18

After discussing with Sam this morning that she needed a sample of her hair to send to a lab to see if she was truly their granddaughter, Meredith had snipped a few hairs from the back of her head and placed them in a plastic bag.

Sam was very accepting but she commented, "My mommy and I already know that!" This left Meredith with a cold feeling. She was putting doubt in what Sam's mother had told her.

While Andy walked Sam to school, Meredith labeled the sample and sent it express post to Aaron in the morning mail; but they wouldn't know the result of the paternity testing for at least seven to ten days. They couldn't claim Sam as their grandchild without knowing for certain. Meredith knew the statistical chances of a date rape resulting in a pregnancy were very low. Yet, Sam sure did constantly remind her of Wendy and Aaron when they were little. *When Sam smiles and those bright blue eyes light up and assume that sweet, mischievous twinkle, I see Aaron when he was six. Sam's generous personality, her perceptiveness, and her love of chocolate are so like Wendy. But we can't go on whims; our seventy-two hours of temporary custody are up tomorrow and we are going to lose her to the system for seven days.*

Despite feeling some relief over the reprieve this would give them, Meredith felt like she was being torn to shreds. She knew that as much as she needed some rest, she would continually be filled to the brim with angst about how Sam was faring in foster care. Andy seemed a bit more pragmatic about it but Meredith knew he was concerned too. As she was getting ready for work, she thought about the constantly occurring news stories of children in care being abused physically and or sexually. Her stomach did a somersault, leaving bile in her throat.

Delores from Childrens' Services called Meredith at work. "I wanted to check to see if there was any chance that Sam's mother has shown up."

"No, and I'm quite sure that is not going to happen! Her mother told her to tell us she needs to go to school, so I don't think this is going to be a short-term arrangement."

"Okay then, I do have some good news for you. I have managed to find a foster home placement in Dawson Creek for her."

"Thank goodness for small mercies. Thank you for that, Delores."

"I will pick her up at 1:00 PM tomorrow. She will have to miss school in the afternoon but this will give me time to introduce her to her foster parents while the other children are in school."

This worried Meredith. "How many other children are in this home?"

"There are four others. One of the girls is the same age as Sam."

"Oh boy, Sam is not used to a household full of other kids."

"Yes, it will be different for her. Hopefully, she will get along well with Tina."

"Well…, at least we can have lunch with her tomorrow before we have to say goodbye."

Meredith called Andy to tell him what Delores had said. "Oh Andy, this all seems so cruel; what a crazy system."

"Yes, this is going to be tough for Sam. I sure hope she likes her foster parents."

"Me too, but… I have a bad feeling about this. And, apparently, we will not know when the hearing will be until one or two days before-hand. This is going to be a very long week for all of us."

"Yes it will be but at least it will give us a chance to rest a bit. We're both darn tired, Meredith, mentally and physically."

"That's true but I somehow do not think it's going to be restful. Delores did assure me that we will be able to visit Sam. She said Sam could even come to our house for supper once or twice. She also said that if Sam's mother still has not shown up by the end of the seven days, we have a very good chance of being granted temporary custody. Tomorrow she will bring us the papers we need to sign to apply for custody. If the administrator of the Family Services Act has no objections, the judge will likely rule in our favour. Then if the mystery of Sam is still not solved after the three months are up, there will be a review."

"By then we will have long since had the paternity test results."

"That's right and if Sam is Aaron's child, the decision will be easy. We will apply for permanent custody until Aaron and Jessica are ready to parent Sam. But what if she isn't Aaron's child, what then, Andy?"

"Then we will have some soul searching to do. I can't even think about that right now. Either way, I don't think it's going to be easy. We will have to weigh the situation when we find out."

****

It had been Sam's third day in school and she was thoroughly exhausted when she got home. Right after her snack, Meredith had caught her almost drifting off to sleep on the loveseat while reading one of her library books. She quickly woke her thinking that a nap would keep her up too late at bedtime. She thought about telling Sam about what would be happening tomorrow but she decided against it. She knew it would worry Sam and she wanted her to have a good night's sleep.

Sam was in bed extra early and Andy was helping Meredith with the dishes. "You know what scares me, Meredith? What if Aaron and Jessica decide they never do want to parent Sam?

"That won't happen. If Sam is Aaron's child, he will not make that choice."

"I don't think we can be certain of that. What if he can't work through his bad feelings about what happened to him?"

Meredith was certain in her heart that if Sam was Aaron's child, he would not make that choice. She felt she knew her son well enough to predict that he would eventually overcome his emotion and assume responsibility for his daughter. But she also knew assuming responsibility for Sam was very different from genuinely wanting to be her father, very different from loving Sam as his daughter.

Even though she knew in her heart that it was not possible, Meredith was still haunted by the sudden thoughts that had overwhelmed her two nights ago regarding the possibility of Andy being Sam's father. She hadn't been able to talk to him about it and had decided to keep those thoughts to herself, at least until the results of the paternity test were available.

What an about-face their lives had taken. Five very long days ago, they were looking forward to retirement bliss, freedom to travel, freedom to do whatever they wished, within their budget of course. Once they had launched both of their children into their own seemingly secure adult lives, Meredith had assumed her life would continue to be smooth going. She had felt very fortunate to have raised two wonderful children successfully. She knew life never guarantees anything, but this turn of events was overwhelming.

Meredith joined Andy in bed, cuddling up to his dependable body heat in a full-back snuggle. She laid there enjoying the warmth for a few minutes, squirming a bit to find the most comfortable position for her head, shoulder, and hip, while thinking about Sam's future. She was usually fairly good at turning off her mind, absorbing Andy's warmth, and shutting out the world when it was time for sleep. But tonight she couldn't get Sam and the thoughts of losing her tomorrow out of her head. She started shifting from side to side. She could tell Andy was having trouble too. He was doing as much rolling around as she was.

Meredith re-evaluated every possibility again. *What if Aaron can't come to terms with Sam being his daughter? What if he can't bring himself to parent Sam, ever? On the other hand, is it even Aaron's responsibility at all, given how Sam was conceived? Should we even expect it of Aaron? Well, if it's not Aaron's responsibility, it certainly isn't ours. But we have already accepted responsibility. How could we not? And what if Sam's mother does eventually come back? That would create a whole new set of dynamics.* Her thoughts were jumping out in all directions with no cohesiveness—way too many questions and no answers.

Meredith recognized most of her worrying was premature, but the tide kept flowing in. She was unable to stop the waves of useless thought tonight. They were like a tsunami; she was standing on a shore and the water was coming to swallow her up. In her mind's eye, she could see a thirty-foot wall of water coming toward her at great speed.

Suddenly she felt trapped, it was hard to breathe. She got up and went downstairs, and sat in her chair, shaking and staring into the darkness for several minutes, aware that her heart was beating hard, rapidly, irregularly. *Is this what palpitations feel like?* She had used and described the term, probably thousands of times, in the course of her nursing career. But she had never personally felt it before. She tried to slow her breathing. Then she heard Andy coming down the stairs.

"Meredith, are you okay?"

"No… I'm falling apart. I suddenly feel like I'm in too deep, I'm drowning in emotion, Andy."

"What are you thinking about?" The concern in Andy's voice gave Meredith the opening she needed but she started to cry. She was trying to get her scattered thoughts of all the possibilities out but her crying overwhelmed her. Standing in front of her, one hand full of tissues, Andy offered her his hands, lifted her up, wiped her tears, and gave her a whole body hug, holding her tight until she stopped sobbing. They stood together in silence for several minutes.

"Meredith, remember when you told me about the *W5* program and how lucky you felt when you read about other grandparents parenting their troubled grandchildren on meager incomes? It doesn't matter what happens, we are still very lucky, dear. We have each other and Sam is delightful. All the other circumstances are just that, circumstances. We can weather this storm, dear, we'll be okay."

"Oh god, you're so right, I really did let things get out of whack, didn't I? I couldn't help it. My morbid thoughts… just kept… flowing." She was still having trouble talking in between gasps for air.

They sat in silence for another few minutes, Andy waiting for Meredith's breathing to return to normal. Then he helped her to her feet again. "Let's go to bed. One thing is certain, we need to get some sleep."

Good old sensible Andy, I am so lucky to be married to him.

Once she was back in bed, Andy spooning her and radiating his loving body heat, she was able to fall asleep, completely drained of energy and emotion, an empty vessel.

****

Meredith woke up at 6:00 AM, thirty minutes before the alarm was to go off. She tried to sleep again but couldn't. After ten minutes, she turned off the snooze alarm so Andy could sleep in. She looked enviously at him, snoring softly and looking content as a cat basking in the sunshine. She crawled out into another unwanted day and went downstairs to do some stretch and flex. Meredith hadn't done this since Sam arrived six days ago. Several years ago, she had developed what she thought was an exaggerated stiffness in her muscles, at least for her age. Along with the stiffness came the discomfort of moving in most of her joints. Meredith was probably fifty or fifty-one when it first became significant and it got progressively worse over the next five years. One morning when she got out of bed, she couldn't stand on one foot to pull on her jeans. Before that, she had complained to Andy a bit about it, but that morning she'd gotten worried.

She was reluctant but Andy talked her into seeing his chiropractor. After five or six treatments, she was starting to feel better and the chiropractor recommended she start doing some mild stretching. It wasn't long before she could feel the benefits and began to develop her own comprehensive stretch and flex program that she did faithfully three times a week. Before long she was seeing the tremendous benefits of stretch and flex for aging bodies. As her chiropractor said, "mobility is health." Meredith's vitality began to return and she was feeling better than she had for years. She quickly concluded the importance of people taking responsibility for their own health, doing everything they could to keep themselves healthy. What she had been telling her patients for years was actually true.

By the time she had finished her warmup on the treadmill, a few weight lifts for her arms, and her stretch and flex routine, Andy, Sam, and Buddy were up. Andy had made coffee and was reading to Sam. Meredith made breakfast and they ate together at the dining room table.

Meredith waited until Sam was done eating. "Sam, Andy and I need to tell you something very important." Sam looked up with a smile like she was expecting a nice surprise. Meredith's heart cracked wildly like a fragile drinking glass hitting a tile floor. "Do you remember Mrs. Scobie from Children's Services?" Sam nodded. "She's coming to see us today after lunch. Remember, we discussed before that Children's Services has a rule. After three days, children without a mommy or daddy have to be taken into the care of the government until a home is found for them."

Sam's delightful face became very solemn and she spoke with considerable determination for a six-year old. "But this *is* my home, until my Mommy comes to get me. She said I should stay here until she comes back!"

"I know Sam, but Children's Services won't let us keep you for more than three days until we can go to court and have a judge say we can keep you."

Sam was holding back a well of emotion, her eyes filled with tears and they started to spill down her small round cheeks.

"Sam, do you know what a judge is?"

"No," she sobbed, her small, straight shoulders shaking slightly.

Meredith wiped her tears tenderly with some tissues and did her best to explain but she could see she wasn't getting through to Sam. This was beyond the comprehension of a six-year old. She took Sam's hand and invited her and Buddy to come and sit with her on the loveseat. She reassured Sam as best she could that both she and Andy would come and see her every day and that she could come and have supper with them on some of the days. Although Meredith felt fairly certain the judge would give her and Andy temporary custody and Sam would be back with them within a week, she didn't want to make any promises that she couldn't keep. Life had proven itself very unpredictable lately.

****

It wasn't quite time for school yet so Andy attempted to distract Sam by inviting her out to his workshop to help him make some bathroom stools for Colby and Dylan. "Sam, I think I should make you a stool too for standing at the counter in the bathroom and the kitchen. What do you think?"

"Oh yes, Mr. T, I'd like that. I'm pretty little too." Sam was delighted but her mood was subdued by what would be happening to her later.

"What color do you want yours to be?" he asked, trying to cheer her up.

"Maybe...maybe..." Unexpectedly, she started sobbing and couldn't answer Andy.

"Oh my dear child." He picked her up and hugged her and started to cry himself. Carrying her, he headed back into the house.

Meredith was working in the kitchen. When she heard Andy come in, she turned and was surprised to see Sam in his arms. She thought Sam had been hurt.

"Sam, what happened to you?"

Andy answered for her. "We have a very sad little girl here, Meredith."

"Oh, Sam, I'm so sorry, come here, let me cuddle with you for a while." Meredith took Sam from Andy and went to the love seat with her. Andy found Buddy and gave him to Sam.

"Th-thanks, Mr. T," Sam managed through her sobs.

Once Sam's crying subsided, Meredith suggested they take her to the playground for a while before lunch. She was determined that their last few hours with her would be as pleasant as possible. School was definitely not in the picture this morning.

****

Meredith helped Sam pack one suitcase. They had just finished lunch when Delores arrived at 1:10 PM. She chatted carefully with Sam for about five minutes, trying to establish some trust. She asked her what she had been doing since she had seen her last. Sam had a few stories to tell about school, swimming, water slides, dinosaurs, and her favorite book, *The Coyote Who Swallowed a Flea.*

Delores explained to her in a very kind voice that she was taking her to a different home for a few days and there would be another little girl there for Sam to play with.

"But I want to stay here with Mr. and Mrs. T."

"Mr. and Mrs. T can come to visit you and have you over for supper.

"Can Buddy come with me?"

Delores laughed. "Yes, Buddy is welcome to come with you."

Within twenty minutes, Delores was ready to take Sam. Meredith bent down and gave her a big hug and a kiss on her soft little cheek. "I love you, Sam." That was the first time she had said it and it startled her. In that moment, she knew her heart had made a commitment to Sam, granddaughter or not.

"I love you too Mrs. T," she sobbed. Meredith reached for a tissue and gently wiped Sam's tears.

Andy gave her a warm generous hug. "I'll miss you, Sam."

"I love you, Mr. T," she volunteered.

"We'll have you back with us real soon, Sammy." Andy's endearing term for Sam did not go unnoticed by Meredith. Sam's tears welled up again but she managed not to sob anymore. She was one brave little girl.

Delores took her by the hand, her suitcase in the other hand, and they were gone.

Andy and Meredith looked at each other and had a big mutual hug. "God, this is unbelievable, Meredith, the way that little girl has wormed her way into our hearts. She's infectious."

"I know, she has completely captured our hearts!"

CHAPTER 8

Interim Custody for Sam
Thursday, April 26

Sam had been in foster care with Mr. and Mrs. McClosky for four days and she wasn't happy with the arrangement. Meredith and Andy had invited her for supper on Friday. On Sunday they took her swimming and kept her until after supper. As each day passed, she became more and more reluctant to go back. She wouldn't say much about it but she did divulge that the house smelled funny and she didn't like Tina, the little girl who was in grade two. She said Tina was bossy and mean. Meredith asked if Mr. and Mrs. McClosky were nice to her and she said they were but they didn't read to her or play with her. Meredith knew that, with five foster children, even if Mrs. McClosky wanted to read to Sam, she probably didn't have time. Nevertheless, she was getting worried. She was feeling paranoid about sexual abuse and wondered if she should talk to Delores.

After supper, she and Sam sat on the loveseat to read a book. "Sam, is anything happening to you at the McCloskys that you don't like?" Meredith queried.

"No, I just don't like it there; I want to stay here with you and Mr. T." She snuggled closer and squeezed Buddy harder.

Meredith felt only mildly reassured but didn't know what else to ask. "I know Sam, we miss you so much too. But we're over half-way there now, only three more days." She did her best to sound cheerful. *Dear God, this hearing better go right.* She opened the book and started reading. Sam wiggled even closer and Meredith's voice cracked.

However sad Sam was, she did take Meredith and Andy's hands and walk with them up the sidewalk to the McCloskys' front door each time. But it became more and more difficult to break her embrace when they hugged her goodbye. She didn't cry but her compelling blue eyes welled up with tears and broke Meredith and Andy's hearts over and over again.

They visited her after school on Tuesday and invited her for supper again on Wednesday.

****

When Andy picked her up for supper, it was evident she had been crying. "What happened, Sam?"

Mrs. McClosky was quick to explain. "Just a little disagreement between Sam and Tina, Mr. Taylor, nothing to worry about, right Sam?" Sam gave her a disgusted backward glance and said nothing. She was already holding hands with Andy, pushing him towards the door. Before he turned to leave, Andy noticed Tina standing at the entrance to the hall, a look on her face that he was having trouble interpreting. *Hateful, jealous, envious?* Now even Andy was worried.

But he reminded himself that the hearing was tomorrow, only one more night at the McCloskys for Sam.

Andy remembered his discussion with Meredith about Sam's very grown up nature for a six-year old. He recognized that, as an only child, she had probably been around adults a lot; very caring and devoted adults. *Living with four other children is undoubtedly very different and difficult for her.* In the car, he tried to divert Sam's attention. "Mrs. T is making your favorite dessert tonight, Sam."

She was pouting, her lower lip out slightly. She ignored Andy's comment. "I hate her, Mr. T, Tina's mean to me all the time."

"What did she do just now to make you so upset?" Sam started to cry and couldn't answer. *Wow, I wasn't expecting this. What the heck do I do now?* He patted her hand and just kept driving.

****

As soon as Sam entered the Taylors' house, she kicked off her shoes and ran to the kitchen, crashing into Meredith and throwing her arms around her legs. "Mrs. T, I hate it there," she cried.

"Oh, Sam, come here and talk to me. Andy, please watch the potatoes." She led her to the loveseat in the living room. "Sam, what on earth happened to upset you so?"

Sam was full-out sobbing now. Meredith handed her some tissues and had to wait for her to settle down before she could talk. She had never seen her show her anger or cry like this before. Sam had always been so stoic about her situation and her missing mother. Finally, Sam's crying subsided enough for her to talk in between sobs. "Yesterday, Tina grabbed Buddy from me and threw him in the corner and...she said I didn't need that stupid old bear anymore. She said I should grow up. Today, she hid Buddy on me when I went to the bathroom."

"Goodness, Sam, that certainly was a mean thing to do. Did you tell Mrs. McClosky?"

"No, Tina told me that, if I tell, she would beat me up, so I just sat on my bed and cried. Tina closed the door so nobody heard me. I was still crying when Mrs. McClosky came to find me to tell me it was almost time to go."

"What did she do when she found you crying?"

"She asked me what was wrong. I told her Tina hid Buddy on me and she made her go and get him."

"Gosh, Sam, Tina sure wasn't very nice. I know how much you love Buddy." Meredith recognized that Buddy was the one enduring thing in Sam's life. She gathered her up in her arms for a big hug. "Well Sam, by the time you get back there tonight, it will be bedtime. And tomorrow morning, Delores is coming to get you so we can meet at the courthouse. Then, hopefully, there will be no more Tina!" *At least I certainly hope so. Sam doesn't need this ugly bullying stuff in her life right now.*

Meredith was sure she hated it as much as Sam did. Every day she thought about all those awful newspaper stories and cringed. She didn't know if she could stand it any longer. Andy's pragmatism helped him through. He said that Sam would be fine but Meredith could see the stress in his eyes too when they glanced at each other on the way to the car after supper. They didn't want to promise Sam that they would be taking her home just in case the court decision didn't go in their favor. What they did tell her was that she wouldn't be going to school tomorrow morning and they would be seeing her in court to find out if the judge would let her come and stay with them. They reminded her that Mrs. Scobie would pick her up, bring her to the courthouse, and take Sam to another room to play for a while.

Andy and Meredith slept restlessly, off and on, all night, but they were both up before their alarms went off and purposely arrived at the courthouse early to make sure they were there when Delores brought Sam in. They were sitting on a bench just outside the court-room when she arrived. After many hugs and kisses, squishing Buddy between them, Delores took Sam to a back room and returned to the courtroom.

The room was cool and despite wearing a warm cashmere jacket, Meredith shivered when the judge entered. Under the table, Andy took her hand in his. The judge got right down to business and asked the Taylors to explain their situation. They said nothing about Aaron's college experience, accounting only the circumstances of how Sam had arrived at their door and what had happened since.

"Most unusual case," she said. "Never heard of one quite like this before."

They knew Judge Cameron had recently been appointed to the family court and Meredith estimated her age to be about sixty. She had a small, kindly looking face surrounded by short straight salt and pepper hair. She seemed duly concerned about Sam. Meredith whispered to Andy, "I sure hope she has her own grandchildren and can feel what we're feeling."

Judge Cameron was aware that they were expecting the paternity test results in five to seven days and was careful to ask them what they would do if the test was negative. She wanted to know how they would feel about Sam then.

Andy and Meredith had anticipated this and they decided they had to be honest. Andy stood and answered first. "Your Honor, we simply don't know. What we do know is that Sam is very happy living with us and not at all happy living at the McCloskys. At this point, we can't promise to keep her forever if she isn't our granddaughter. The ramifications for us and the rest of our family would be huge, especially at our age. But, right now, we certainly want to take her home with us."

Judge Cameron thanked Andy for his honesty and asked Meredith how she felt, giving her a chance to express her thoughts and feelings too.

"I am in complete agreement with Andy. We do indeed want custody of Sam and believe she will be happy with us. Sam is an easy child to care for; loving and cooperative. During the few days that we did have her with us, we enjoyed her company and managed just fine. As you may imagine, this has been an emotional roller coaster for us and our son but we definitely want to keep Sam."

"Thank you, Mrs. Taylor, I appreciate your candid remarks. And Ms. Scobie, what have you to say in this matter?"

"Your Honor, I believe that Mr. and Mrs. Taylor have Sam's best interests at heart, and in the absence of Sam's mother, I believe Sam will be happier with them than she would be anywhere else. I trust she will be loved and well cared for by the Taylors."

"Okay then, please excuse me for a few minutes while I talk to Sam." Meredith and Andy were expecting this too and waited worriedly for the judge to return. In about ten minutes, she was back in her chair and called for order. Meredith noticed a slight smile on her face. "I am hereby granting temporary custody and guardianship of Samantha Scott to Andy and Meredith Taylor for a period of three months, after which time, there would have to be a review of the case." She added, "In the event the paternity test is negative and Andy and Meredith Taylor want to have the hearing sooner, they may request it." Then, surprisingly, she said, "For Sam's sake, I truly hope the test is positive. This court is adjourned."

Meredith wasn't expecting that and glanced at Andy, who looked slightly surprised too. Both of them could understand why she said it. She didn't want to see this delightful little blue-eyed girl in the care of Children's Services either.

"Whew, what a relief," Meredith sighed.

"Yeah, not sure what we would have done if it had gone any other way."

"Let's not even think about that." They stood up, unsure of what would happen next. Judge Cameron instructed Delores to bring Samantha out to the care of the Taylors. Within two minutes, Delores came out, hand in hand with Sam, both smiling from ear to ear. Sam broke her hand hold and started running toward Andy and Meredith. After two very enthusiastic hugs, the three of them were out the door and heading for the McCloskys' to pick up Sam's suitcase. It was only 9:40 but Andy and Meredith needed a bit of time to celebrate with Sam. They decided they would get her to school by 10:45, the end of morning recess.

On the way home, Andy stopped at Dairy Queen and picked up a chocolate blizzard for Sam and two soft ice cream cones for him and Meredith. Eating and laughing happily at Sam's excitement, they ate their ice cream treats in the car. At home, Andy packed Sam's suitcase up to her bedroom, while Meredith and Sam climbed the steps behind him, hand in hand. After a goodbye hug from both Meredith and Sam, Andy went back to work and Meredith helped Sam put her clothes away. Sam was right, the McCloskys' house did smell funny and so did Sam's clothes; the smell permeated everything. Meredith didn't want to make a big deal about it though so she didn't comment. She knew she would be washing all of it, including Buddy, as quickly as possible.

Meredith packed a lunch of crackers, cheese, apple slices and a peanut butter and honey bun. By then, it was time to drive Sam to school and Meredith was back at work by 11:00. She hadn't told her co-workers everything; but they did know she was attending a court hearing for temporary custody of the little girl who had arrived on her doorstep only twelve days ago, claiming to be her granddaughter. They also knew that she and Andy were waiting for paternity test results.

Deidre, one of the long-term care case managers, was in her office and saw Meredith come in. "Hi, Meredith, how did you make out this morning?" she asked with sincere concern. Just then, Janet the new home care nurse, came in to hear Meredith's story.

Meredith smiled widely at both of them and told them what had happened.

Janet responded, "I just can't believe this has happened to you and Andy, and just when you are about to retire. How can you look so happy?"

"Well, you know, Janet, I'm not happy at all about what has happened." Meredith gave Janet a slight smile. She liked this new nurse and had noticed how friendly she was with all the staff. "This has already had a profound effect on Aaron. But, given the circumstances, how we both feel toward Sam is quite astonishing. This little girl has won our hearts, hands down, even Andy. I can't believe how quickly he has succumbed to her charms. When I think about Aaron, it just breaks my heart. But when I think about Sam, she just makes me smile. My emotions are being pulled in so many directions right now, I'm amazed at how well I seem to be managing everything." She purposely did not mention the meltdown she had experienced a few nights ago.

"How much longer do you expect the result of the paternity test to be?" Deidre inquired.

"We should have it within five to seven days."

"It's a long wait," Janet commented.

"Yes, I think it's driving us all crazy, especially Aaron. Poor kid. I talked to him last night and he sounded pretty distraught. He feels overwhelmed with guilt that he may have created this mess for all of us."

Deidre shook her head. "You know, I couldn't help but think, if this happened to our son... to us, how would we react? I want you to know I'm thinking of you, Meredith, we all are. If there is anything at all that I can do to help, just let me know."

Meredith laughed. "Did you just volunteer to babysit, Deidre?"

But Deidre was serious. "Sure, anything I can do to help, you let me know. I know the impact for you and your family must be enormous. Besides, if Sam won Andy's heart so quickly, I'm sure she'll have no trouble with Vern and I."

"Okay, thanks heaps, Deidre. If we're stuck, I'll keep you in mind. I think I better get to work. It's been a bit hard to concentrate lately."

"I don't doubt it. See you later, Meredith." Deidre and Janet left together, leaving Meredith to her work.

Deidre and her husband, Vern, were between fifty-five and fifty-eight and had three grown children; two daughters and a son, no grandchildren yet. Meredith had suspected Deidre would be able to identify easily with her situation. She was a wonderful co-worker and friend. She had always been so supportive and caring, always there just when Meredith needed her. Countless times, the two of them had confided in each other over office issues and people problems. Managers and consultants seemed to come and go like the seasons and they all had big egos that needed massaging. Both Deidre and Meredith had no patience for these people. They just wanted to do their jobs and serve the people they needed to serve.

****

Andy was having trouble concentrating at work. As pleased as he was with the result of the court hearing, he was terribly disturbed by his thoughts of what it all meant for his pending retirement and for Aaron. He decided to leave early. As soon as he got home, he went downstairs to dig out Wendy's old wooden easel. Andy had made it for her fourth birthday present. One side was a blackboard and the other side had clips at the top to hold up big pieces of paper to paint on. Each side had a ledge; one for chalk, the other for small containers of paint. Meredith had purchased three big cans of tempura watercolor powders in the three primary colors; red, yellow and blue. Andy had shown Wendy how to mix the paints to make different colors; red and yellow for orange, yellow and blue for green, red and blue for purple, green and red for brown. Wendy was thrilled and she had spent hours and hours over the next three to four years mixing colors and painting on her easel.

When Meredith got home from picking Sam up from school, Andy met her at the door with a sheepish grin on his face and gave Meredith and Sam a big hug. Then he wanted to know if Meredith still had any of those tempura powder paints left. She noticed immediately that the easel was standing in the kitchen, covered with an array of brightly spilled colors, a testament to their daughter's early enthusiasm for painting. Meredith went downstairs and found the three cans of paint and the old paint brushes that Wendy and Aaron had used. Andy set up the easel in one corner of their large kitchen beside the pantry. While Meredith was making supper, Andy was showing Sam how to mix the primary colors and she too was thrilled. They were giggling together like two six-year-olds with a juicy secret.

Sam ate her supper quickly, hardly able to wait to get back to her painting. Andy showed her how to make great big streaks of color by swooping her brush across the paper. Then he went and got the camera to take her picture, the first picture they had taken of Sam since her arrival. He went right to the computer to download the picture and called Sam and Meredith to have a look.

Sam was enthralled. "How'd you do that, Mr. T?"

"Easy, Sam, sit here and I'll show you."

While Andy was explaining digital cameras and downloading to Sam, Meredith was in a state of shock after looking at the picture. She went to look in her old photo albums to find a picture she knew Andy had taken of Wendy twenty-nine years ago on her fourth birthday. It was of her standing by her new easel, paint brush in hand, looking back to get her picture taken, big swoops of color on her paper. When Meredith found the picture, she gasped in amazement. The similarities were shocking. Sam had Wendy's hair color and complexion but not the dark-brown eyes. Her eyes were that unmistakable captivating blue like Aaron's. Her light-brown hair was slightly curly like Wendy's and her delightful smile was identical to both Aaron and Wendy's. She looked so much like Wendy in this picture, it was incredible. Meredith closed the album and went back to the dishes.

Later that night, when Sam was in bed, Meredith showed the picture to Andy.

He couldn't deny the astonishing resemblance either. "Good grief, Meredith, you're right!"

"Yes, I think we'd better prepare ourselves for a positive paternity test, Andy. It was startling, when I saw Sam's picture—in the same instant, my mind's eye saw this picture of Wendy and I had to go and search for it."

"This is going to be a huge blow to Aaron. I know he's counting on a negative result. I wonder how he's going to deal with it?"

"Aaron has quite enough to deal with already, with his recollection of what happened to him and a new baby on the way. And now, a six-year-old child. Oh, Andy, poor Aaron. I have so quickly come to love this little girl who has come into our lives, but I fear she is going to be a huge psychological burden for our dear son. I feel so torn apart about my love for Sam and my love for Aaron. It's a horrible, disjointed feeling."

"Maybe we're getting ahead of ourselves, Meredith. Let's wait for the test results." Andy recognized there wasn't much hope for a negative result, but he was trying to find a way to comfort Meredith. They sat in silence, leaning into each other for a few minutes, gazing with wonder in their eyes at the picture of their precious little daughter and thinking about what the future held for them and their family.

Wendy was only four in the picture and now they had six-year old Sam to care for. It felt like they were starting all over again.

Meredith released a huge sigh. "You know Andy, if the test is positive, we may have to keep Sam with us for a good long time. We just can't expect Aaron to take this on. He is going to need some time and space to adjust to this idea and we better not give him any indication that we have certain expectations of him until he is good and ready. That kind of pressure could send him right over the edge."

Andy groaned. "I know, Meredith, I know, and it scares me to death. This is not what I had planned for our retirement."

"Yes, but as I have heard my dear husband say many times, life doesn't always go as planned and we have to make the best of what we have."

"Did I say that?" He had a look of childish innocence.

"Only a multitude of times!"

****

It was 9:15 PM when the phone rang and ended their conversation. Andy got up to answer it.

Aaron knew the court hearing had been scheduled for today and he knew Sam was usually in bed by 9:00 PM.

"How did the court hearing go, Dad?"

When Meredith heard Andy say, "Good, we were granted temporary custody and guardianship," she knew it was Aaron calling. With a sudden burst of new energy, she raced up the stairs to pick up the phone in the bedroom just in time to hear Aaron exclaim, "Three months! The paternity test result will be back in five days, what if it's negative?"

Andy responded, "Don't get excited, Aaron, the judge said if the test is negative and we want another hearing sooner than that, all we have to do is ask."

"Oh, okay, that sounds better."

"Hi, Aaron, how you doing, my dear kid?"

"Okay, Mom, I'm hanging in there for five more days."

"Yeah, it's a tough wait, my son."

"You said it, the next five days can't go fast enough for me. I'd like to go to sleep and wake up five days later. I can't remember ever wishing my life away quite this desperately before."

"Can your dad and I join you in that five-day sleep, Aaron?"

"Sure, let's just all go to sleep for five days." They all laughed a bit; a short guarded laugh—none of them really feeling like laughing.

"And how is Jessica doing?" Meredith asked.

"She's feeling great, no morning sickness or anything."

"Thank goodness for that. I remember how sick I was with your sister."

"Really, how bad was it, Mom?"

"Oh, we were living in Ottawa at the time and it was so hot and humid. The humidex reading was one hundred and ten or more for most of the summer. All our bedrooms were upstairs, which made it worse. I spent the days in the basement eating dry popcorn and trying to keep cool. At night, Dad and I had to go to bed naked with wet towels over us to get to sleep. We had a fan on the dresser blowing air over the towels to get cool with the evaporation. Air conditioning was uncommon then, only for the wealthy, not for newly married couples with university debts."

"I guess Jessica is pretty lucky then."

"She sure is—about that, anyway."

"And what about me, were you sick with me, Mom?"

"No, not so much."

"Well, I'll have to tell Wendy she caused all the problems for you then." His laugh was a bit more unrestrained this time.

"You do that, Aaron, she'll love you for it." Meredith's thoughts drifted. *Thank goodness, we have the pregnancy to focus on, and at least Aaron hasn't lost his sense of humor. He dearly loves to bug his sister.*

"Okay, I just wanted to know how things went for you today. I'll tell Jessica."

"Thanks for calling, Aaron," Andy said.

"Bye, son, we love you," Meredith added.

"Luv you too, Mom and Dad."

Meredith thought Aaron sounded quite grounded tonight but she wondered if he was putting up a good front for them. She and Andy knew he had experienced several more flashbacks and he wasn't sleeping well. Jessica had called Meredith from work a couple of days ago to tell her she was very worried about him. Meredith had discussed the possibility of post-traumatic stress disorder with Jessica and they had agreed that might be what was happening to him. Jessica had suggested counseling but Aaron emphatically refused the idea saying he would deal with it.

Meredith was, once again, exhausted but she headed downstairs to the computer to do some research on PTSD. She had been meaning to do this for a couple of days. Andy met her at the bottom of the stairs again, arms open. She welcomed Andy's hug, both of them unwilling to have it end too quickly. It seemed they needed to let their energies merge these days to keep going, hers into him and his into hers, their two bodies like a permeable membrane, taking from each other what they needed to cope with each day...and each night. This was a habit they had developed years ago to help each other get through the tough times; times that all families encounter from time to time. Times like when Aaron, in grade ten, had decided he didn't want to go to school anymore. Times like when Wendy and Ian had announced they were going to live together when they went to college; Wendy only eighteen and Ian only nineteen. Times like when Aaron got a drunk driving charge and Meredith and Andy had to pick him up at the jail. In comparison, all those times seemed so insignificant at the moment.

Meredith was about five inches shorter than Andy. She stood on her tiptoes to snuggle her head into Andy's neck, their legs entwined and holding on tight. Reluctantly ending their embrace, Meredith continued on her way to the computer room and Andy made his way to bed.

As the computer took its time to boot up, Meredith thought of the tender moments she'd had with Aaron as a child. Layers of images from the past returned to her. She had so many sweet memories from the year Wendy went to grade one and Aaron was still at home. Together, they watched *Mr. Dress Up* and *Sesame Street*, built castles out of blocks, played memory games, went for walks in the woods, went to the library, read endless numbers of stories, did the grocery shopping, and baked cookies. She wished she could fix his troubles like she used to when he was little; bandaging a scraped knee, kissing his little injuries better. Her dear son...hurting so much. Then her feelings for her son collided head on with her feelings for Sam, causing a huge crash in her head and sending the remnants of the thud to her gut. She felt like she was trapped in a cocoon with both of them.

CHAPTER 9

———

Sam meets Colby and Dylan
Saturday, April 28

Across the living room from Meredith and Andy's recliners, Meredith had two large wedding portraits hanging side by side; one of Aaron and Jessica and one of Wendy and Ian. Just to the right of Wendy and Ian was a recent portrait of her two twin grandsons. Meredith spent a fair bit of vegetation time gazing at those portraits with a feeling of pride in her children and a feeling of appreciation that life had granted her a loving and attentive husband; two healthy, successful children; a fantastic son-in-law; an extraordinary daughter-in-law; and two extra-special grandsons.

As she gazed at the portraits of her children and grandchildren while having her morning mug of hot water and lemon, she thought her good fortune in life had been amazingly plentiful. She and Andy had worked hard, made wise financial decisions, and raised their children to be prudent, responsible adults. But she couldn't help but wonder if her blessings were going to be mixed from now on. She realized that no matter how wisely you plan, you cannot control the actions of others who can affect your life dramatically.

Ever since Meredith had told Sam about Wendy's birthday party and about visiting her twin grandchildren, Colby and Dylan, Sam had been asking questions and looking at the pictures around her room with excited enthusiasm. She was enthralled with the twins and wanted to know how Meredith could tell them apart. Meredith wondered why Sam had not asked before about the family pictures that were scattered in abundance about the house. She had only inquired about some of the pictures in her room and she still hadn't asked about any of the pictures of Aaron and Jessica.

It was becoming more and more obvious that Sam's life with her mother and her Auntie Colleen had been quite narrow. She didn't seem to be aware of any extended family members for her mother or for her Auntie Colleen. Sam had explained a few days ago that Auntie Colleen wasn't really her aunt; she was her mother's good friend. At the time, it had crossed Meredith's mind that maybe Leanna and Auntie Colleen were a couple.

After supper last night, Sam helped Meredith make Wendy's birthday cake. Wendy's favorite for years had been Black Forest Cake with cherry pie filling and whipped cream. Sam had a great time helping to put the cherry pie filling and whipping cream on all three layers. She chatted happily throughout the cake-making procedure, asking all sorts of difficult questions that Meredith struggled to answer like, "Why is it called a Black Forest Cake?" and "How come the cream gets thick when you whip it?"

This morning, Sam came to Meredith's chair, a picture of Dylan and Colby in hand, and asked, "I forgot, tell me again how you tell the twins apart, Mrs. T."

"Well, I can tell Colby from the front because his face is a bit smaller around the chin area and his eyes are slightly bigger than Dylan's. I can tell by their voices because Dylan's voice is a bit deeper. I can even tell them from the back because Dylan has a hair swirl called a cowlick exactly in the middle, at the top of his head, and Colby's swirl is on the left side."

Sam was concentrating hard to remember the details. "What's a cowlick, Mrs. T?"

Meredith laughed. "It's a spot from where the hair swirls around. Let me see, Sam, do you have a cowlick too?" Meredith inspected Sam's head which made her giggle. "Yep, you have a cowlick too, Sam, a small one right here on the left."

"Really, I do? Do you have one too, Mrs. T?"

"You bet I do. Mine's on the right side." Meredith leaned down so Sam could find her cowlick.

"Here it is! Yeah, mine is on the left and yours is on the right." Sam skipped off, picture in hand, to put it back in her room.

Wendy's birthday had been on Thursday, the day of the court hearing, but Ian and Meredith had planned to celebrate it today— two days late. Meredith gave herself the luxury of sitting a bit longer, thinking about the day ahead. *It will be Sam's first chance to meet Colby and Dylan. I think they will all get along spectacularly and I know that Wendy will welcome Sam with her usual friendly, expressive gusto.* She smiled to herself and got up to make breakfast.

They were in the car and heading to Grande Prairie by 10:00 AM. Alberta was on Daylight Savings Time so Grande Prairie was an hour ahead of them. They would get there by 11:30, which would be 12:30 Grande Prairie time, just in time for lunch.

On the way to Grande Prairie, Sam and Andy sang all sorts of children's songs including, "There was an Old Lady who Swallowed a Fly," "Insy Weensy Spider," "Old MacDonald's Farm" and "The Wheels on the Bus go Round and Round." If Sam really was their granddaughter, it seemed she had Andy's singing talents. Neither Wendy nor Aaron were lucky enough to have inherited them. Meredith was in the habit of always bringing a book to read on road trips, but today she enjoyed listening to Andy and Sam sing while gazing out at the spring countryside.

Unlike on the trip to Tumbler Ridge, the snow was mostly gone now. Spring was coming fast as usual. The undulating hills were interspersed with natural forests of deciduous and evergreen trees and farm fields. The deciduous trees were not turning green yet and the grass in the ditches was still a dead yellow gray.

The fields were mostly bare, except for the stubble from last year's crops, water accumulating in a few low spots. They were sitting in wait for the spring planting of a wide variety of Peace Country crops; grains, oilseeds, grasses, and legumes. Wheat, barley, rye, oats, canola, peas, corn, flaxseed, fescue, brome, and alfalfa were just some of the wide variety of crops grown in the region. Meredith knew that within three to four weeks, the farmers would have most of the fields seeded and she would be able to see the tiny rows of green sprouts coming through the ground, a promise again of the earth's abundance. In the north, the growing season was short, but the long days of sunshine would make the crops mature quickly. In only two and a half months, they would be ready to harvest.

One of the things she dearly loved about the Peace Country was the distinctiveness of the four seasons and the incredible changes each of them brought. She didn't have a favorite one, she loved them all for the special gifts they delivered; spring for the new and delicate growth; summer for the extremely long and warm days of sunshine; fall for the golden, plentiful harvest and the array of fall colors; and winter for the crisp air, the crunchy snow, and the perfectly clear blue skies.

When Sam and Andy ran out of songs, Meredith played I Spy with Sam for a while. Finally, Sam, as excited as she was, settled down to reading a book. For a grade oner, her reading skills were excellent. After Sam's first week in school, Mrs. Babcock had told Meredith she thought Sam was reading at an "end of grade two" level, another sign that she had received lots of attention from adults.

Meredith had time to think and remembered how pleased she was with herself that she had managed to come up with what she thought was a great present for Wendy. Wendy and Ian treasured the few times they were able to get away on their own since Colby and Dylan had arrived but Wendy was darn fussy about who she would leave her boys with. Meredith had bought her a gift certificate for The Granaries; the Peace Country's Most Unique Bed and Breakfast, a luxurious and unique hide-away located on Bear Mountain, just south of Dawson Creek. She had written in Wendy's card an offer from her and Andy to grandparent the boys for them for a one night get-a-way and tucked the pamphlet into the envelope.

Meredith had shown the pictures on the pamphlet of the B & B to Sam and explained the reason for the gift. "I think Wendy will really like this, Mrs. T," Sam said in such a grown up way. It made Meredith laugh.

When Sam asked her what she was laughing at, Meredith had replied, "At you, Sam, because you're so sweet. You make me laugh with joy." Sam danced away, just as pleased with herself as Meredith was.

****

As soon as Wendy saw Sam, a delighted expression of surprise crossed her face, noticed by both Andy and Meredith. They all did their usual family hugs and Wendy made a special effort to welcome Sam. She took her by the hand into the living room, calling the boys to come and play. All three children were normally shy at first, but it wasn't long before Sam was organizing the boys and they were responding willingly, thinking that this little girl was quite interest-ing. Most adults, except for their parents and grandparents, were not able to tell Colby and Dylan apart. But it only took Sam about five minutes to see and hear the differences, revealing the easy brilliance of children. Sometimes, adults just don't pick up on the subtleties that children do.

Andy and Ian had gone outside to inspect the new deck that Ian had just finished building. Back in the kitchen, Wendy said to Meredith, "Yeah, okay, Mom, that's Aaron's kid. She looks just like the pictures of him when he was that age."

"You think so?" Meredith responded innocently.

"You can't tell me you don't see it too. That's why you've already fallen so hard for her, Mom." Meredith and Andy had tried to keep their hunches to themselves and had not shared them with Wendy and Ian. When Wendy had pressed them about what they thought, they had said they wanted to wait for the test results—they didn't want to make any assumptions.

"Okay, Miss Know-it-all. How can I help with lunch?" Meredith retorted.

During lunch preparation, Wendy and Meredith discussed their mutual concern for Aaron and the complexities of the situation. Wendy was always able to make Meredith feel better. She reassured her that she and Ian would babysit Sam any time Meredith and Andy needed a break. She agreed that if the test result was positive, it would be wrong to press Aaron into taking responsibility for Sam.

Meredith told Wendy what she had learned about post-traumatic stress disorder, and they agreed that it was certainly congruent with what was happening to Aaron. Meredith expressed her concern for him and the seriousness of the situation and Wendy agreed that Aaron's reactions were dire and he needed counseling. "I'll do what I can, Mom, to help you convince him."

Wendy, Ian, Andy, and Meredith had a wonderful visit while Sam and the boys played endlessly inside and out. The day was beautiful, sunny, and warm; about seventeen degrees Celsius, and the yard was dry except for a few puddles. Their wonderful little imaginations took them on safaris, picnics and replays of movies they had all seen. At one point, they were all running around in circles yelling, "Hurry, hurry, the ice is cracking, the ice is cracking [from the movie, *The Polar Express*]. Save Mr. Bear, save Puppy, save Buddy." Colby's bear blanket was "Mr. Bear," Dylan had a puppy blanket that was simply "Puppy."

For supper, Ian had expertly prepared and barbecued steak and an array of fresh vegetables; yellow and orange peppers, broccoli, cauliflower, zucchini, and snap peas. Meredith made a Caesar salad. Ian insisted they eat outside on the new deck. Sam ate well but Colby and Dylan were getting tired and fussy so there was no lingering over supper. Meredith quickly brought out the cake and lit the candles. Andy led everyone in singing "Happy Birthday." All three of the children were allowed to have a turn blowing out the candles.

Meredith asked Sam to give Wendy her gift. "Here you go, Wendy. Happy birthday, you will really, really like this!"

"You think so, Sam?"

Sam smiled confidently from ear to ear, her perfect white teeth lighting up her face with the unrestricted joy that only a child can know. Meredith's thought came suddenly, leaping from her brain and refusing to be held back. *Sam loves to give presents just as Wendy does.* The likeness made her shiver even though she had previously observed so many other examples of family resemblance.

Wendy opened the envelope, read the message, and looked at the pamphlet. Immediately, she jumped up and hugged Sam and Meredith and Andy, thanking each of them profusely.

"I can help with the babysitting, Wendy," Sam volunteered.

"You sure can, Sam. You have entertained the boys famously today." She smiled at Sam. "Thanks again, all of you, this is just fantastic. Right, Ian?"

"Yeah, it's great! Thanks, Sam and Mom and Dad. I'm sure Wendy will be planning that weekend real soon."

While doing the dishes, Meredith asked the question that was bothering her. "Wendy, tell me, you're thirty-four and you should be able to identify with this situation better than I can. If you were single and really wanted a child and you were running out of biological time, would you use the sperm bank?"

"I don't think I can identify very well with this, Mom, remember, I haven't been single since I was sixteen when Ian and I started dating. But using a sperm bank would really queer me out. How would you know what you were going to get? I know they must have descriptions of physical attributes and intelligence, but that wouldn't be enough information for me. No way. Why are you asking, Mom?"

"Oh, I don't know, I'm just trying to explore this crazy situation from all angles. I'm trying to put myself in Sam's mother's shoes. She must have really wanted to have a baby but why would she steal Aaron's sperm? Was she completely crazy or was she just desperate?"

"But Mom, I think you'd have to be more than just desperate to have a child to actually plan to rape a man for his sperm. Wouldn't it be better to try to make a deal with the guy in question?"

"Maybe but then this guy would always know and someday he may come back and want to get to know his child."

"So…why would that be so bad?"

"That may be how some women would feel but if Sam's mother had some bad experiences with men in the past, maybe she simply did not want that to be a possibility. I guess, if the paternity test is positive, I'm just looking for ways to help Aaron feel better about what happened."

"Okay, I see your point, but no matter how we look at this, desperation or not, it's hard to justify what we think may have happened."

"I guess you're right. Have you talked to Ian about what he would do or how he would feel if this happened to him?"

"We've touched on it. Ian said it's really hard for him to put himself in that situation and think about what it would be like. But he said he thinks he would be really angry, both at himself and at the woman, but mostly at himself. He just can't even begin to imagine how he would feel about the child."

"'Mostly at himself.' That's the thought I'm most worried about, Wendy."

Before they knew it, it was bedtime and Meredith, Andy and Sam had to head home. Sam, Colby, and Dylan were all prepared for bed. Sam could sleep in the car on the way home.

It was hard for both Wendy and Meredith to let go of their hug. Wendy whispered in Meredith's ear, "It'll be okay, Mom, we'll all get through this together." Meredith started to cry and had to hold back with all her might in the presence of Sam. Sam was in her pyjamas and bare feet, her curly hair flowing and circling around her face. Andy picked her up with ease and carried her to the car.

After a few questions, Sam was quiet in the backseat, tired after a very busy day with Colby and Dylan. Meredith and Andy were exhausted and quiet too, alone with their thoughts covering the day's events, unable to share them while Sam was awake in the backseat. Meredith remembered Wendy's certain comments about Sam being Aaron's daughter. Initially she smiled to herself, and then, once again, she was overcome with confused feelings. Her delight with Sam and her sense of foreboding for Aaron were so diverse, so incompatible. She didn't know how she could deal with both of them at the same time. It wasn't long before she was lulled to sleep by the car's motor and the smooth movements over the small bumps in the pavement, relieved of her torturing thoughts, at least for a while. She slept most of the way home, waking only once to check on Andy. "How are you doing, dear? Are you sleepy?"

"Yes, I'm going to stop in Beaverlodge and pick up some coffee."

"Okay." The next thing Meredith knew, they were home.

CHAPTER 10

———

The Paternity Test Results
Wednesday, May 2

"Hi Mom." It was Aaron. He was calling Meredith at work and he sounded extremely upset.

"Hi Aaron, what's wrong, dear?"

"We got the paternity test results last night."

Meredith knew immediately and for certain that Sam was his child by how he was sounding. She didn't have to ask but she did. "And…"

"I was scared shitless to open the letter so Jess and I opened it together. It said the test has an accuracy level in excess of 99.99 percent. Without a shadow of doubt, I'm definitely Sam's biological father. But Mom, that doesn't make me responsible for her, does it?"

Meredith heard the anguish in his voice. She had already given a fair bit of thought to this question. "Legally, probably not, considering the circumstances, Aaron. But despite the law, Sam does exist, she is your biological daughter; our granddaughter. I guess the real question is, morally what are we going to do about it?" She didn't want him to feel alone in this predicament.

"Okay, so what am I supposed to do?"

"Aaron, I don't want you to worry about Sam right now. You and Jessica have enough on your plate to think about. You are expecting a baby in a few months. You both deserve this pregnancy so much and I know you will make wonderful parents. But this is a huge adjustment for both of you without worrying about Sam. She's happy staying with us and we're quite willing to keep her until we can figure out a long-term plan."

"But Mom, this is all my fault. I should have known better than to go to this woman's apartment with her."

"Stop right there, Aaron. This is not your fault."

"Yeah, because of me, you and Dad have a six-year-old kid to look after. This is so awful and I'm so sorry."

"No, my dear son, you absolutely have to get your head around the fact that you are not responsible for this situation at all. *Period!*"

"Okay, but I am afraid I can't see it that way. I was so stupid to go to her apartment with her. God, why did I do that?"

"Because she won your trust, Aaron. You thought you could trust her. And perhaps because she had already drugged you with the coffee you had at the college before you decided to go with her. She took advantage of you while you were drugged. How can you be responsible for that?"

"I just should not have let it happen, Mom. Poor Jess, she doesn't need this right now. And neither do you and Dad."

"Aaron, people who have been assaulted usually feel ashamed, shocked, confused, and guilt ridden. They always ask the question, what could I have done to prevent this? And guys have the mistaken belief that they are immune to being victimized, so the idea of being a victim is hard to handle. Maybe you should see a counselor about this."

"Mom, I'm not going to go to some stranger and pour out my sad, disgusting story. Forget that!"

"But, Aaron, this is no easy matter to deal with. It was a huge personal invasion that you have managed to put out of your conscious mind for years and now it has reared its ugly head again. This would be very difficult for anyone to deal with. A counselor would be able to help you look at this from many different angles, help you to come to terms with what has happened to you and move on in a positive way. My guess is you are very angry; angry at yourself, angry at Leanna, angry at the existence of Sam. You need to find a way to deal with that anger or it will eat you up, my dear son." Meredith was hesitant to use the term "post-traumatic stress disorder"; it sounded too ominous. But she knew the flashbacks that Aaron was having were indicative of PTSD.

"I can't... I just can't right now."

"Well... at least think about it, Aaron. I don't know what it is with guys that they are so opposed to counseling. It's not something you do because you're weak, you know. Women who have been raped often seek counseling, and I would think the effects are no less disturbing for men."

"Okay, Mom, I've got to go. I've got to get to work."

Meredith could tell she'd said enough, maybe too much. "Alright, son, but whatever you decide to do, don't you dare shut your Dad and I out. Please promise me you will at least keep talking to us. I love you."

"Luv you too, Mom. Bye."

"Bye, my dear son. We'll talk soon." *Oooh, that was not a good exchange. I didn't handle it well. But what else could I have said? Aaron needs a reality check. How the heck can I get through to him?*

****

Meredith could see that Aaron was at an impossible crossroad and his ability to cope was quickly eroding. He wasn't ready to meet Sam, let alone parent her, and he didn't want to leave his parents with this responsibility either. Somehow he had to get out of this vicious circle of self-deprecating behavior. She thought he must feel completely discombobulated and her heart ached for him.

She started to visualize what must have happened to him. Her tears welled up and started to flow. She grabbed a handful of tissues to catch them and got up to close her office door. The tissues were soaking up her tears but nothing could stop her heart from bleeding. She started to feel dizzy, like she was going to lose consciousness and automatically put her head between her legs, thinking she might faint. It felt like her heart was bleeding into her chest cavity and creating a painful pressure between her breasts.

Meredith sat up again, leaned back in her chair, and took some slow, deep breaths. A morbid thought crossed her mind; could this pain she was feeling for her son actually kill her? She and her fellow nurses had often commented about an older man or woman who had recently lost his or her spouse and subsequently died of a broken heart. She wondered if this is what they felt like before they died.

She continued to breathe slow and easy. Eventually her chest pain began to ease. She checked the clock on her desk. She had no idea how long she had sat there just breathing but it was now 11:45. She got up, put on her sweater and headed home for lunch.

By the time Andy arrived, Meredith had methodically and unthinkingly gone through the motions of warming up some tomato soup and making two salmon sandwiches for lunch. When Andy looked at her, he said, "Meredith, my god, what's wrong? You look terrible."

She laughed an uneasy laugh. "Thanks, honey."

He wrapped his arms around her and she started to cry and shake uncontrollably. He walked her over to the loveseat in the living room where they sat in an embrace for quite a while, Andy patiently waiting for Meredith's emotional upheaval to ease.

Through her gradually slowing sobs, Meredith finally blurted out, "The paternity test was positive. Sam is irrevocably our granddaughter, dear."

Andy hesitated… "But Meredith, we were both expecting that. What else happened?"

"I don't know, Andy, maybe I just forgot to be strong for a while. Aaron was so distraught. I could hear it in his voice. He's suffering big time."

"What did he say?"

"He's so angry at himself."

"But he hasn't done anything wrong."

"Yeah, right, you tell him that. He thinks it's all his fault. And that is a typical male reaction, Andy. Go figure. You guys think you should be able to control everything, and men have the mistaken belief that they're immune to being victimized. If it happens, they totally blame themselves."

"Yeah, we are a strange lot, aren't we?" They both laughed a little.

"I had an overwhelming sense of foreboding when I got off the phone with Aaron. I think he is going to put himself through hell over this, Andy. I'm afraid Aaron is going to do this the hard way."

Meredith and Andy decided not to go to work for the afternoon. While Sam was still in school, they went for a walk along the walking paths beside Dawson Creek. The creek was full to capacity, demonstrating the power of water as it rushed along its banks. The force of the water had taken out some of the trees along the banks and it was washing a cavity into the outside curve of the creek. In a couple of weeks, most of the spring runoff from the mountains would be finished and the creek would be winding its way slowly and easily. Meredith wondered how long it would take for their lives to be winding slowly and easily again. Certainly more than two weeks, she thought. Holding hands, she and Andy discussed the dilemma their family was facing.

Again they wondered, now that they knew for sure that Sam was Aaron's daughter, was there any point in trying to find Leanna? Again, they decided that there could be nothing positive gained by doing so. If they found her, what would they do? They certainly wouldn't insist that she take Sam back. Obviously, that would not be a good situation for Sam, regardless of why Leanna had left her. It had been a desperate move by a desperate mother.

They decided to call Jessica as soon as they got home to see how she was doing and express their concerns for her and Aaron. Jessica would be at work and they could talk to her without Aaron present. And, of course, they would call Wendy to let her know what the results were. They thought they should also tell Delores Scobie from Children's Services.

As they walked, the emotional pressure they were feeling seemed to ease.

Meredith thought about Aaron a few years ago and how she had worried about a pregnancy occurring in a less than stable relationship that he was in. And now, here he was in a wonderful marriage, leaving nothing for her to worry about, and out of the blue, they'd been hit with Sam. "Funny how the expected hits you at the least expected time, Andy."

"What do you mean, dear?"

"Well, I was just thinking about how worried we were when Aaron was dating Cece. Remember Cece, that girl from his second year of college?"

"Oh yes... I remember Cece. I always wondered how he had hooked up with her."

"Good Lord, she worried me. I was so scared she would get pregnant. I even asked Aaron what they were doing to prevent it, and he nonchalantly told me not to worry, Cece was looking after it. I told him he better make sure of that and do his part too. He was less than happy with my interference and told me to butt out—that he was taking care of it. But you know me, I pressed him farther, told him he was playing with fire and better be damn careful or he could ruin his future. Now here he is married to our lovely Jessica and we thought our worries were over. Go figure. Life is just so unpredictable."

"You got that right! I never dreamed we would be where we are. These things happen to other families, not us."

Somehow, they both managed to laugh at the oddity of it even though they knew they were in for a lot of family turmoil.

CHAPTER 11

———

Telling Sam Aaron is Her Father Saturday, May 5

Meredith and Andy had decided to wait until the weekend to tell Sam that they had found out Aaron was indeed her father. How do you explain such a thing to a six-year old? They knew they had to keep it simple, but even so, they were sure they would get some tough questions. They wanted the weekend for it to sink in before she was off to school again. And they needed some time to figure out their strategy, which would probably all go to heck after the first sentence. She had talked to Aaron the day before about telling Sam but he wasn't in much of a mood to discuss anything. He did agree with her that it was the right thing to do. He said, "Just don't give her any hopes of meeting me soon, Mom. I simply can't do it."

She replied, "That's alright, son, we can tell her you live quite far away, have a very busy job with lots of traveling, and can't come to visit us right now. She might be sad about that, but overall, she seems pretty happy to be living with us. I think she'll be okay. We'll make sure we have something fun to do afterwards to distract her."

"Okay, go ahead then, but she is probably going to have lots of questions that may be hard to answer. I'm glad it's you and not me."

"I think Dad and I are ready for at least some of them," Meredith replied.

Once she was off the phone with Aaron, she analyzed his continued reaction, wondering if he would ever be able to get past how his daughter had been conceived. *If a woman is date raped and a pregnancy results, she can have an abortion. In fact, most segments of society would expect and condone it. After all, who could be expected to bear and raise the child of a rapist? But Aaron had no choice in this pregnancy.* Meredith was sure that everyone in the family had their innermost feelings about the situation that they were not voicing. Nevertheless, Sam had been born and now she was here with them, alive and needing love and parenting. That was what they had to concentrate on. They had to move forward— forget the past circumstances. It was the only conceivable path left to take.

Now it was Saturday morning and Meredith and Andy were both dreading their job. They knew in their hearts that Sam deserved to know she had a father and he wasn't dead. It was never going to get easier.

They finished breakfast and Sam was her usual happy self, singing along with a Raffi tape and playing on the table with some Fisher Price Adventure People. Meredith had kept the tapes and the toys from when Wendy and Aaron were kids and they seemed to be as timely as ever. Colby and Dylan loved them too.

"Sam, Mr. T and I have something good to tell you." Sam's ears picked up on the "good" and she looked up, smiling. Meredith took a deep breath and said, "We have just found out for sure that Aaron, our son, is truly your dad."

"My mommy said he was," she responded, implying that was no news to her.

"Well, remember when I cut your hair a couple of weeks ago? We sent it away with some of Aaron's hair to be tested. They can test hair now to see if it matches and it showed that Aaron is definitely your dad."

Sam looked inquisitively at them, still wondering what the good news was.

Meredith continued, "Aaron, our son, is your dad and he's not dead."

Sam took a few seconds to digest this. Then she said, "But my mommy said he was dead."

"Aaron is living and working in a place that's quite far away, Sam."

"Then why did my mommy tell me he was dead? She said he was dead and up in Heaven so we could never see him."

Meredith hesitated to contradict Sam's mother. She glanced over at Andy and back to Sam. Sam's eyes were welled up with tears and she grabbed Buddy and ran upstairs to her room. Meredith and Andy looked at each other and didn't know what to do. "Andy, what do you think is going through her head?"

"I don't know, but I think we should leave her for a while to digest this."

Meredith waited for five minutes until she couldn't stand it any longer. She had to go to Sam. Quietly, she entered the room. Sam was sitting on the bed sobbing, looking dejected and holding on tight to Buddy.

Meredith walked up to the bed cautiously and sat down beside her, leaving a few inches between them. She thought Sam might need some space. "Sam, what are you thinking right now?"

"Why would my mommy lie to me, Mrs. T?"

"I can't answer that, Sam. But she must have thought she had a good reason." Meredith handed her some tissues and waited.

"Why isn't my mommy married to my daddy, and why didn't he live with us?"

"Aaron didn't know about you until you arrived at our house three weeks ago. That's why we had to do the test to see if you really were his daughter."

"I don't understand, Mrs. T."

"Well, it's a hard thing to understand, even for me, Sam. And you are just a little girl." Meredith inched closer and put her arm around Sam's shoulders. "When can I see my daddy?" Sam finally asked through her tears.

"Well, that's the 'not so good' part. Aaron lives quite far away; he has a very busy job and he has to travel a lot. He can't come and see us for a while." Meredith paused. "I think Aaron needs some time to get used to the idea that he has a daughter. You've turned out to be quite a surprise for him. But you will get to meet him sometime; you just have to be patient. Can you do that, Sam?"

"I guess so." She was still sobbing, her face wet and covered with red blotches. "But why didn't he know about me?"

Oh no, here's one of those hard questions. "Well, I guess your mommy didn't tell him." Meredith hugged her closer and waited for another "why" question but it didn't come. Sam's sobbing was slowing down.

"Why don't we go and look at some pictures of your dad? We can do that much right now."

"Okay," she said, quivering through her sobs.

Meredith took Sam's hand and walked down the stairs with her, wondering how she was going to explain who Jessica was without upsetting Sam even more. They headed for the table by the window and Meredith picked up a framed portrait of Aaron and Wendy, taken on Aaron and Jessica's wedding day.

"This is your dad, Sam. And you know his sister, Wendy. Did you know that you look like your dad?"

"I do?"

"Oh yes, look at his eyes. They sparkle with mischief just like yours do."

As Sam stared at the picture, a small smile began to form and she wiped her eyes with her sleeve and gave one last sob.

"Now that we know Aaron is your dad, that makes Wendy and Ian your auntie and uncle and Colby and Dylan are your cousins."

"They are?" Her exuberance was starting to come back.

"Yes, you can call her Aunt Wendy now. And…Mr. T and I want you to call us Gramma and Grampa now too."

"Really, Mrs. T?" She looked at Meredith with a new sense of hope.

"Yes, from now on, Sam, please just call me Gramma…or Gramma T."

She formed a big smile and said, "I like Gramma T."

"I like it too, Sam." Meredith knelt down and gave her a big hug. "We're your family, Sam. Welcome home!"

Andy was still sitting at the table drinking his coffee, reading and listening. He turned in his chair and said, "What about me, Sam, can I be Grampa T?"

"You sure can, Mr. T." She ran toward him for a hug.

"Well then, now that we have our new names settled, I think we should all go for a hike up to the ridge and have a picnic," Andy declared assertively.

"What a perfect idea," Meredith echoed, pretending that it was a sudden and unexpected plan. "It's a gorgeous day out there. What do you think Sam?"

"Yeah, let's go for a picnic."

"Okay, but first, I need your help to make a picnic lunch," Meredith said.

They drove about ten kilometres west of Dawson Creek to the hiking entrance to Tower Ridge, named for the communication towers on it. The ridge overlooked the Kiskatinaw River Valley and surrounding farm land. The grass was just beginning to send up new shoots and the new, lime-green leaves on the aspen trees were starting to emerge sporadically across the landscape. It was incredibly warm for the fifth of May and all three of them had to take off their jackets and tie them to their waists. Andy pointed out to Sam a small patch of crocuses starting to bloom on the south side of the ridge where it gently dropped off. He told her she could pick a few on the way back. Sam was an energetic hiker, keeping right up with them. When they reached the top of the ridge, they found a flat grassy spot to sit down and have their picnic while looking out over the immense farming valley below.

Andy bent down to Sam's level. "See the fields out there. See how they look like a patchwork quilt from here, and look how small the farm buildings and the cows in the pasture look. And see the Kiskatinaw River at the bottom of the valley; that is where all of Dawson Creek's water comes from, the water that comes out of all of our taps."

Sam looked confused. "But how does the water get to Dawson Creek and our house?"

It travels in underground pipes from the river to the city where it's stored in big reservoirs. From the reservoirs, it goes to a treatment plant to be cleaned. Then it is piped out to all the houses."

Meredith thought he was getting a bit too technical for a six-year-old but Sam was as fascinated by this as she was by dinosaurs and *Charlotte's Web*. "Just listen for the sounds of the birds, Sam. I love just sitting quietly and listening to them sing."

"Yes, it sounds like there's a whole bunch of them," she smiled.

Andy tried to identify them for her; robins, whiskey jacks, chickadees, crows, magpies. Then they heard some rustling in the grass and saw a squirrel scurry up a tree. He chattered at them for a few minutes, then disappeared. Sam was intrigued with everything, including the horse and cow droppings on the trail.

Later in the afternoon, Meredith was in the kitchen making supper and she overheard Sam talking to Buddy. She was sitting in the loveseat with the picture of Aaron and Wendy in her hands.

"Buddy, this is my daddy. His name is Aaron. Gramma T says I look like him. What do you think?" She waited. "I think he looks like Grampa T. He looks like he's very kind and lots of fun...he looks happy. Do you think he's happy to be my daddy?" She waited again for Buddy's imaginary answer.

Meredith was quiet in the kitchen so she could eavesdrop. Sam continued her conversation with Buddy. "My daddy is very, very busy but he will come and see us when he can. You have to be patient, Buddy."

Sam sat there, staring at the picture for another minute. Then she got up, left the picture on the love seat and went to the family room to play.

She's going to be okay, Meredith thought.

As she continued to make supper, Meredith's thoughts stayed with Sam. She began thinking about when Sam was a baby, thinking about how she had missed out on so much of her granddaughter's life already. Then she unexpectedly thought about a baby quilt she had made a number of years ago. It had a bright-purple teddy bear appliquéd on a white background print with small green, blue, yellow, and purple transparent bubbles. The teddy bear was floating in the air, hanging onto some bright yellow, green and purple balloons. The quilt was framed with borders of sun-yellow, mint-green and berry-purple with a purple backing. Meredith had made it thinking that she would give it to her first grandchild. When Wendy became pregnant and the ultrasound showed twin boys, she found herself having to make two matching quilts, according to Wendy's specifications, with bunnies on a green leafy background. Meredith thought the teddy bear quilt would be the perfect gift for her newly discovered granddaughter.

Oh my goodness, it was seven years ago when I was making the teddy bear quilt. She remembered easily because it was the same year that her friend Mavis became a grandmother and Mavis' granddaughter was seven years old now. Mavis had been in the quilting course with her. *Sam was conceived in October and I decided to make the baby quilt in February when Sam's mother was about three to four months pregnant.* The idea was too overwhelming. She felt weak and dizzy and had to sit down. Once she recovered, she began to realize her spiritual connection to Sam had begun a very long time ago.

Meredith had noticed throughout her life how serendipity had played its part many times and she did believe in the Law of Attraction. But this coincidence was just too much for her to take in. She remembered Andy saying to her when she had decided to make the baby quilt that she was getting a bit ahead of herself. When she thought about it back then, she really didn't know why she had decided to make a baby quilt. She had explained it away, saying that it was a good way to learn how to quilt. Now, as she realized that she must have made the quilt for Sam, the thought sent wild shivers through her entire body. Could this possibly be? What if Wendy and Ian had not had twins? This quilt would have gone to her first grandchild. But destiny was in control, they did have twins and this quilt was still waiting. She knew it belonged to Sam and she would give it to her tonight.

While Meredith was flossing Sam's teeth, she told her she had a surprise for her.

"What is it, Gramma T?" She had converted easily to the new names in her family.

"Well, if I tell you, it won't be a surprise now, will it?"

"When do I get it?" she giggled.

"Just as soon as we finish flossing so stop talking, Sam."

Meredith went to the linen closet and put her hand on the door. "Sam, I made a little quilt a while ago and I have been wondering who I should give it to. It has a teddy bear and balloons on it. Who do you think would like this quilt?"

"I would, Gramma T, I would!" She was jumping up and down.

"Meredith pulled it out and held it up for Sam to see."

"Oh, I love it, I love it!" She grabbed it and hugged it to her. "It's soft and it smells nice. Buddy will love it too." She lunged forward to hug Meredith, the quilt between them. "Thank you, Gramma T."

"You are very welcome, Sam," Meredith whispered softly into her ear. "Now, let me tuck you in, my dear, sweet granddaughter."

"Okay, but I want to cover up with my new quilt!"

CHAPTER 12

A Visit From Auntie Colleen
Monday, May 7

Sam had been in school for three weeks. She was outside for morning recess, playing with two other girls. Mrs. Babcock was on playground supervision for the day. Teachers on supervision are always on the alert for any strange adults coming onto the school grounds. She noticed a white, mid-sized sedan stop on the street adjacent to the playground. A lone woman got out and headed toward the three girls who were playing on the twirl-a-whirl. Mrs. Babcock did not recognize her as one of the parents. The woman was about 5'4" with very short, curly, dark brown hair and an attractive face. She guessed the woman was about thirty-five to forty years old. Her figure was slender and she was neatly dressed in navy-blue Capri pants, a white polo shirt, and white running shoes. She moved across the playground with an energetic walk, like she was quite fit and in a hurry.

When the woman was within about a hundred yards of Sam, she spoke and Sam turned to look at her. She jumped off the twirl-a-whirl and went rushing toward the woman, who was now bending at her knees with her arms outstretched toward Sam. They hugged enthusiastically. Then, still kneeling, the woman put both hands on Sam's shoulders and backed her away a bit so they could make eye contact. Mrs. Babcock tried inconspicuously to walk closer. She could see their conversation was happy, both of them were smiling. Then Sam spoke and when the woman answered, Sam's happy expression vanished. After not more than four minutes of conversation, the woman directed Sam back to the playground and quickly left, almost on the run. She jumped into the white sedan and drove away. It was too far away for Mrs. Babcock to see the license plate but she thought it was from British Columbia. Sam didn't join the other girls. She stood watching them vacantly, her eyes filled with tears. Mrs. Babcock went over to her and asked if she was okay.

She managed a "Yes" between sniffles.

"Sam, who was your visitor?" Mrs. Babcock asked.

"My Auntie Colleen."

"Did she say something to upset you?"

"She said my Mommy wasn't getting better yet." Sam started to sob, trying to hold back the floodgates of emotion.

Mrs. Babcock bent over and gave her a gentle hug, took her hand and led her over to a double swing where they sat together talking until the bell rang, ending the fifteen-minute recess. She didn't know Sam's history but she did know that Children's Services was involved and Andy and Meredith Taylor were Sam's present guardians. Intuition told her that this visit may have been significant. On the way to her classroom, she reported it to the principal, who called Meredith at work at about 10:45.

"Mrs. Taylor, this is the principal, Mr. Hallaway calling. Sam had a visitor on the playground this morning; she said it was her Auntie Colleen. Do you know this person?"

"Oh my god, yes, I do. No, I mean, I don't know her, I just know about her. What happened? Is Sam okay?"

"Yes, she is back in her classroom now."

"I'm not sure but this Auntie Colleen could be a threat to Sam's safety."

"What kind of threat do you mean?"

"She may want to take Sam away and we can't let her do that."

"Okay, we will watch her closely and, if the woman returns, what then?"

"Please, interrupt her and ask her what she is doing. And, above all, don't let Sam go with her."

After the call, Meredith couldn't get down to any real productive work. She tried to call Andy but he was on a conference call with the deputy minister. Her thoughts wandered, touching on many possibilities as to why this Auntie Colleen would come to visit Sam at school. At noon, she had lunch with Andy and told him what she knew, which was very little. Andy agreed with the principal that they shouldn't go to the school and make a big deal out of this for Sam.

At 2:45, Meredith looked at her watch. She was still edgy and couldn't concentrate, so she left work early and went to the school to pick up Sam. A few days before, she had arranged for Sam to go to after-school care until she could pick her up after work. But today, she met Sam at her classroom at 3:00 PM when classes ended. She noticed that Sam looked sad; but when she saw Meredith, her eyes brightened immediately, making Meredith's heart soar with growing feelings for this special little girl, her granddaughter, who had so suddenly and unexpectedly come into their lives just over three weeks ago.

"How come you're here early, Gramma T?" She gave Meredith her broad winning smile.

"I just felt like leaving work early to come and get you, Sam." They hugged and Meredith took her hand and headed for the car. *Thank goodness I have a flexible schedule and I'm able to leave early at times like this.*

On the way home, they chatted about Sam's school friends and their family plans for the weekend. Meredith never mentioned the visitor Sam had at school. Once they were in the kitchen at home, she made tea, served some milk, whole wheat crackers and cheese to Sam, and sat down to join her at the dining room table.

"Sam, how was your day at school?"

"Okay, I guess, I had fun with Rilla and Holly. Mrs. Babcock taught us about germs today. We had to wash our hands and put them under a funny looking blue light to see how well we had washed. None of us did a very good job," she giggled. "And we all had to go and wash again. This time, we sang the 'Happy Birthday' song while washing. Mrs. Babcock told us that if we washed the whole time it took to sing 'Happy Birthday,' then rinsed and wiped our hands, they would be much cleaner. When we put our hands under the blue light again, they were much better," she said emphatically.

"Good for Mrs. Babcock," Meredith cheered. "It is really important to wash your hands well, Sam, to get all those nasty germs off that can make you sick."

"That's just what Mrs. Babcock said," she replied with certainty.

It seemed Meredith was going to have to ask Sam directly about her visitor at school. But then, finally, Sam volunteered. "Auntie Colleen came to visit me."

"Your Auntie Colleen...what did she have to say?" Meredith tried to sound surprised.

"She said Mommy isn't getting better yet." Tears welled up in Sam's eyes and she started to sob uncontrollably. Meredith gathered her up in her arms and went to the loveseat. She cuddled her close and waited for Sam's sobbing to abate.

"Oh Sam, I'm so sorry. You miss your mom a lot, don't you?"

"Yes," she shuddered.

Meredith didn't know what else to say and hesitated… When Sam's crying slowed, she asked, "What else did Auntie Colleen say?"

Sam thought for a few seconds, her big iridescent blue eyes still glistening with tears. Then she responded shakily. "She wanted to know how I was doing and she asked if I was happy here… I told her you and Grampa T. were nice to me and we have lots of fun." In a bit, she added, "Mommy used to read to me when I was sad."

"Sam, would you like me to read to you?"

"Yes, please, can we read the book about the coyote who swallowed a flea?"

"You bet we can."

"Just a minute," Sam said and ran upstairs. "I'll be right back." She came back down with her new quilt and Buddy in her arms and then cuddled up with Meredith, putting the quilt over both of them. Feeling a warm sensation of satisfaction, Meredith read her the coyote book and they managed to laugh together over the pictures. Next, Meredith read her another chapter of *Charlotte's Web*.

"Sam, it's time to make supper. I have some hamburger thawing. What should we do with it?"

"Let's make meatballs."

She was once again her cheery self. Meredith marveled at her ability to bounce back so quickly.

"Alright but I'll need your help to roll all those little balls.

****

After Sam was in bed, Meredith and Andy talked about Auntie Colleen's visit.

"It really scared me, Andy; I feel like we could lose her as quickly as we found her. She could just disappear one day with this Auntie Colleen. What should we do?"

"I don't know, dear, I'm feeling like a pawn again, like someone is playing chess with our lives."

"I think we better go to the school tomorrow and discuss this Auntie Colleen with the principal and Mrs. Babcock. I already told Mr. Hallaway that this woman could be a threat to Sam's safety, but I think we should talk to him again, and to Mrs. Babcock. Maybe all the teachers should be alerted. And we should also tell Children's Services; after all, we only have temporary guardianship."

"It certainly wouldn't hurt to let everyone know," Andy agreed.

"Good grief, how can this be? Only three weeks ago, we were both so worried about how Sam's arrival would affect our lives, our family, our future. And now, our biggest concern is that we could lose her."

"Yes, Meredith, that little girl has wound her magic spell around us. There is no going back now, is there?"

"Nope, we're in it all the way now."

"Yep, up to our eyeballs." Both of them had bonded to Sam as if she were their own child.

"What do you think the purpose of Auntie Colleen's visit was?" Meredith asked. "She must have come for a fairly important reason. And it was more than somewhat risky—we could have caught her."

"Well, if we take what we know at face value, I'd say she came to check out how Sam was doing, to make sure she was okay. If Sam's mom is really sick, she would be worried about Sam and wanting some reassurance that things are going well for her daughter."

"I suppose, that does makes sense, but I sure don't like her popping up so secretively. It worries me. It makes me wonder again if we should try to find Sam's mother to see if we can figure out what's really going on."

"Yes, but I think our former theory still holds. What could we gain? And how would Aaron react?" Andy questioned.

"Yeah, you're probably right."

After Andy had gone to bed, Meredith was alone with her thoughts. She continued to wonder if they were making a mistake by not trying to find out what was behind Sam's precipitous appearance.

She rolled it over and over in her mind. *Are we behaving like lemmings, letting Leanna lead us over a cliff?* Now that Sam was so much a part of their lives, somewhere deep in her gut Meredith felt a visceral fear of losing her and a frantic need to protect.

She went to the computer, Googled "private detectives" and found a toll-free number for the Canadian Private Investigators' Resource Centre. Meredith hesitated and thought about Aaron again…thought about how finding Leanna would affect him. She guessed that it would only create more trauma for him and she knew she shouldn't proceed. She turned off the computer and headed for bed.

CHAPTER 13

Colleen's Disappointment
Tuesday, May 8

Colleen drove all day and half the night to get back to Vancouver, arriving at 3:00 PM. She stopped once to eat and twice more only for short restroom breaks. She had to be at work in the morning and would be exhausted after her long trip and getting less than four hours of sleep. She had hoped to gather evidence to show Leanna that Sam was not welcome in her grandparents' home and that their anger about Sam's sudden appearance on their doorstep was reflected in their treatment of her. To the contrary, Sam had confirmed that she was very happy there and her grandparents were more than kind. Colleen could lie to Leanna about what she found, but that darn Janet would dispute her lies.

As Colleen prepared for bed, her frustration soared. *Damn, Leanna, why did you have to plant Janet at the Health Unit where Meredith works? She seems to have a direct line on what's going on in the Taylor household and keeps Leanna well informed with phone calls every other day or so. I need to find a believable way to contradict her reports.*

Knowing she would not be able to sleep, Colleen decided to take a sleeping pill even though she knew it would leave her feeling groggy when her alarm went off at 7:00 AM.

CHAPTER 14

Colby's Illness
May 15

The call came to Meredith's office at 10:10 AM. "Mom, I need you right now, Colby's really sick." She was crying.

"Wendy, what's happening?"

"We're at the hospital and they've admitted him to intensive care. They don't know what's wrong, Mom. I'm really scared. Ian's in Japan. I need you to look after Dylan." She was speaking rapidly, urgently. "He's with Baba and Gido right now but they have to leave for Edmonton today. Gido has an appointment with the cardiologist. Can you come?"

Meredith didn't hesitate. "I'll be there as soon as I can, Wendy. Andy's in Victoria so I have to find a sitter for Sam. But I think I

can cover that. I'll be out of here very quick. I love you. Bye dear."
Meredith could tell Wendy didn't want to waste time with details.

Shivering with fear for her grandson, she quickly walked down the
hall to Deidre's office. *Thank God, Deidre's in and not on the phone.*
"Deidre, do you remember when you said, if there's anything you
could do, just ask. I need a big favor *right* now." She was talking as fast
as Wendy and her heart was pounding.

"Oooh, sounds serious, Meredith, what's happening?"

"Colby's in intensive care, we don't know what's wrong. I have to
go right now. Wendy needs me. Ian's in Japan and Andy's in Victoria
until tomorrow. Can you look after Sam?"

Deidre didn't hesitate. "Yes, of course, what do I need to do?"

Meredith was mapping her plan as she talked. "I'm going to go
home and pack her a suitcase. I'll go to the school to tell her you will
be picking her up at 5:00 PM from after school care. Then I'll stop at
the school office to let them know. I'll leave her suitcase at the office."

"Meredith, do you think Sam will be okay with this? She doesn't
know me."

"I think she'll be fine, Deidre. Remember, she arrived on our doorstep a month ago and we didn't know her either; but she's been fine
with us. She's quite an amazing little girl. I've got to go. I'll call you
as soon as I can.... On second thought, can you meet me at Canalta
School in fifteen minutes? I'll introduce you to Sam."

"Yes, you go, I'll be there!"

Meredith met Deidre at the school and pulled Sam out of her
classroom to tell her what was happening. "Sam, Colby is really sick,
he's in the hospital. Wendy needs my help right away." Sam's face filled
with concern. "My friend, Deidre, will take care of you until Andy
gets back from Victoria tomorrow. I know you don't know her, Sam,
but here she is, I have brought her here to meet you. She's a nurse in
my office, she's my good friend and she loves kids. You'll have fun
with her. Okay?"

"Okay," Sam responded apprehensively. Meredith gave her a big hug and told her she had to go. Sam looked frightened but Meredith's thoughts were with Colby and she couldn't take the time for any reassurances. "I love you, Sam, bye, my little sweetheart."

As Meredith was racing down the hall, she could hear Deidre talking to Sam but she couldn't hear what was being said. She had to leave Sam in Deidre's willing and capable hands.

Once she was in the car and driving out of town, she consciously told herself to relax and she could feel her adrenalin rush subsiding. She tried to call Wendy on her cell but Wendy didn't answer. Meredith expected that. Wendy would have her cell turned off in Intensive Care. She dialed Baba and Gido, Ian's parents. "Baba, it's Meredith. I'm on my way to Grande Prairie. Can you fill me in on what's happening?"

"We don't know much," Baba said uncertainly. "Wendy called and asked us to come and stay with Dylan. She was taking Colby to the hospital with a very high fever and difficulty breathing."

"Wendy sounded really upset when she called me. They've admitted him to ICU. She wanted me to come and babysit Dylan because you and Gido are leaving for Edmonton this afternoon. I'll be there as soon as I can but I have to stop at the hospital to see how Colby's doing."

"Okay, Meredith, you drive careful, not too fast, be safe."

Meredith did drive too fast, she couldn't help herself. But she got there safely. Arriving at the *Queen Elizabeth II Hospital*, she quickly found a parking spot and went straight to ICU. When Wendy came out to talk, she looked white and drained with worry. Through their hugs and Wendy's tears, she said, "Mom, they still don't know what's wrong. The doctor is going to do a spinal tap in a few minutes. His fever is very high and he's so lethargic, its scares me to death."

They went to the desk and Wendy asked if her mother could come in for a few minutes. They said yes. Colby was lying prostrate on the bed, wearing only some boxer shorts. They were trying to keep

147

him cool. Meredith picked up his limp little hand and said, "Colby, Gramma's come to check on her boy."

Colby opened his eyes slightly and spoke in a barely audible voice "Gamma." Then he closed his eyes again. He was dreadfully pale and his eyes were glassy. Meredith's trained eye could see he was acutely ill. Her fear for her grandson rose somewhere deep in her gut and spread throughout her body leaving her weak in the knees and slightly nauseated.

She looked at Wendy, whose tears were welling in her eyes. Meredith noticed that Colby had an IV running in his foot and she knew they would have done a cutdown to access a deeper vein for a dependable IV. She tried to turn her attention to the details of his treatment. "What are they giving him, dear?"

"He's on two very strong antibiotics and an antiviral." Meredith automatically checked the drip rate and the drug labels. The IV was running at an appropriate rate for a three-year-old. She knew it was all too easy to fatally overload a small child with IV fluid. "How long has he been sick?"

"Only since this morning. He woke up with a fever and by 9:00 it was way worse, even though I had given him some Motrin. I called Baba and she came over right away so I could bring him to the hospital. It's awful, I can't even cuddle him because it will make him hotter. They're giving him Motrin and Tylenol alternately to control his fever. What could it be, Mom?"

"I don't know, dear, but the spinal tap is a good idea."

"Oh, I wish Ian was here," Wendy whispered, her voice breaking with sobs. "I haven't even been able to reach him yet. Here's his number, Mom. I can't use my cell in here. Can you call him every half hour until he answers? You better go and relieve Baba and Gido. Give Dylan a big hug for me and tell him I love him."

"Okay dear, any other instructions for Dylan?"

"No, you know what to do, Mom. I just hope he doesn't get sick too. You know how they both get everything within one to two days of each other."

"Okay, I'm only a phone call away," she whispered back, ignoring her own thoughts of how these precious twin boys had always shared their colds and fevers in the past. "Stay in touch, my dear. I'll be thinking of both of you." Meredith bent down and gave Colby a quick kiss but there was no response. Holding back her tears, reluctant to leave, she gave Wendy another long tight hug, turned and left.

Dylan was playing happily on the floor with Gido. "Gamma!" Neither of her grandsons had yet mastered the R, S, and L sounds and Meredith found it endearing. He was up and running toward her. She gave him a big hug and he was back to playing. Meredith exchanged some quick information with Baba and Gido, thanked them, and they were on their way.

She sat on the couch close to Dylan and tried to call Ian. No answer. It was 3:00 P.M. She dialed Andy, no answer. He would have his cell turned off if he was in a meeting. She went and made herself some tea and got a snack for Dylan, sat down and dialed Ian again.

"Ian, thank goodness, I got you."

"What's up, Mom?"

Meredith started to tell him what was happening and he stopped her before she could finish. "I'll be on the first flight I can get, Mom. I'll call you." Meredith tried to say more but the line was dead. She had heard the fear in his voice and she knew Ian was a devoted husband and father. Wendy and his boys were his life. He would be back as soon as humanly possible.

At 4:30, Meredith tried Andy again. "Andy, thank goodness, I've been trying to reach you, I'm in Grande Prairie." She filled him in without Andy cutting her off as quickly as Ian did. "He said he'd forget his morning meeting and get the first flight available but it wouldn't be until tomorrow morning." Meredith's tears were streaming down her face when she got off the phone.

"Gamma, what the matta?" Dylan asked, concern written all over his face. He got up from his play and went over to her.

"I'm just thinking about your Mom and Colby, dear."

"Coby ick, Gamma."

"Yes, he is dear. Now let's go get some supper, Dylan, you can help Gramma."

At 6:30, Andy called. His departure time was 11:10 in the morning; he would be home by 3:30 PM.

Meredith called Deidre right after she got off the phone with Andy to let her know.

"Meredith, how's Colby?" She gave her an update, intermittently choking on her emotion.

"You'll let me know as soon as you know anything more, right?"

"Yes, Deidre, I will, thanks for your concern, I really appreciate you. You're such a great friend, always ready to help when I need you."

"No problem, Meredith. How many times have I spilled my guts to you?"

"Yeah, we are good mentors, both ways, aren't we?" Deidre and Meredith had experienced a few adversities in their workplace over the years. "I called to let you know that Andy will be home tomorrow at 3:30 and will pick Sam up at after-school care."

"Oh no, we've had so much fun tonight. What a great kid! She loves my dogs and they love her attention. She's playing ball with Bailey right now."

"That's great. Yeah, she's quite the lovable kid. Thanks again, Deidre, I have to run. Dylan's looking at me as if to say, Gramma, haven't you been on the phone long enough?"

Meredith had just put Dylan in the bathtub when the phone rang. It was Ian. She had no idea what time it had been in Japan when she'd called him. But Andy had quickly figured out for her that it was 5:30

AM. He had probably slept through Wendy's previous calls. "Mom, I just got off the phone with Wendy. She says there's been no change in Colby since you were there. They did the spinal tap but won't have the result until tomorrow afternoon, it takes at least twenty-four hours."

"Oh, Ian, I'm so glad you were able to call Wendy. She needs you right now."

"I know, Mom, it's 8:00 AM here now and I'll be on a flight at 10:45. I have to change planes in Chicago and Edmonton and I'll be in Grande Prairie by 3:00 PM tomorrow. I'll call Wendy between flights. How's Dylan doing?"

"He's just great, in the bathtub right now, no sign of illness. He's as happy as can be, threatening to splash me right now."

"Can you put me on speakerphone so I can say hi?"

"Sure, okay… go ahead."

"Hello Dylan, Daddy misses you. I'll be home tomorrow, okay?"

"Daddy, Gamma here, Coby ick. Mommy at ta hopita wit im."

"Yes, I know, you be good for Gramma, okay?"

"Okay."

"I love you, Dylan."

"Uv you, Daddy."

"Thanks, Gramma."

"No problem. Dylan and I are doing just fine. Travel safe, Ian."

At 9:30 Meredith hadn't heard from Wendy yet. Now that she had Dylan in bed, she couldn't stand the wait. She called the ICU desk. They said there wasn't much change in Colby yet but they were managing to keep his fever at a reasonable level. They would have Wendy call her.

Wendy called at 9:50. Colby had been having some chills in between his fever spikes. Wendy said she liked the chills much better, at least she could cuddle him and he tended to be more awake and responsive. She wanted to know how Dylan was. "Mom, will you check him for fever just before you go to bed?"

"Yes, dear, of course."

"Goodnight, Mom, thanks, I love you."

"I love you too, Wendy, I hope you can get some sleep tonight."

Dylan was at Meredith's bedroom door sometime in the middle of the night. She leapt out of bed and went to him. "What's the matter, honey?"

"I can'd eep, Gamma, can I cudda wit you?" Her hand was on his forehead. *No fever, thank goodness.* "Of course you can cuddle with me, Dylan, come up onto the bed." He jumped up enthusiastically and snuggled in. He was back to sleep in no time but Meredith didn't sleep much for rest of the night.

At 9:10 the next morning, Wendy called to check on Dylan. Meredith could hear her sigh of relief when she told her he was fine. There was still no change in Colby's condition.

Meredith went through the day like a zombie with Dylan, trying her best to be nonchalantly cheerful. He asked a couple of times when Colby and his mommy were coming home. Otherwise, he played happily, oblivious to the critical situation unfolding around him. She thought briefly of Sam a couple of times but her concern for Colby overrode any worries about Sam.

Finally, at 4:30, Ian called. He was at the hospital and they had the results of the spinal tap. They were negative. No bacteria were found and there was no increase in the white blood cell count, so bacterial meningitis could be ruled out. That was good but now they were back to square one and no diagnosis. The doctor had assured Wendy and Ian that with acutely ill children, this is frequently the case. They get very sick, run a high fever for a few days, then start to recover and there never is a specific diagnosis. That was somewhat reassuring but when you're watching your very sick child in a semi-conscious sleep, it's hard to feel optimistic. The doctor reassured them again that he was covering all the bases he could with wide spectrum antibiotics and an antiviral. Colby hadn't eaten for forty-six hours and Wendy could see he had lost a lot of weight already.

At 9:30 Ian called again. "Mom, we think he's finally improving. His fever is down a bit and he said he was hungry. He's had some apple juice and Wendy is giving him some yogurt right now."

"Oh, thank God, Ian, you must be so relieved."

"Yeah, he woke up about an hour ago looking a bit brighter and his muscle tone has improved. Man, that was scary. Is Dylan still okay?"

"Yes, he's been in bed since 8:30. He's just fine."

"Thank God again for small mercies, maybe he won't get it."

In the morning, Wendy called. Meredith could tell immediately by her tone that Colby must be considerably better. "Mom, they're going to move us out of ICU in a few minutes. Colby is so much better but they want to keep him for another day and keep him on his IV antibiotics just to be safe."

"Oh, Wendy, what a relief."

"Yes, Ian is going to go home as soon as we are moved and settled. You'll be able to leave, probably after dinner. Mom, I think I really screwed up your work week."

"Wendy, you know our family always comes first. No big deal."

"Thanks, Mom, what would I do without you?"

"You are very welcome, my dear child."

****

Meredith arrived at home at 3:15 knowing Andy would still be in flight. She was exhausted and flopped into her chair, deciding not to go back to work. Lying back, she tried to relax for a few minutes. On the way home, she had realized she hadn't talked to Aaron or Jessica for four days. She knew Aaron wasn't doing well and he was still refusing to see a counselor. She didn't know if she had the emotional strength to call him. After a few minutes, she dialed Jessica.

"Hi Meredith, how are you doing?"

"Well, I've just come back from two days in Grande Prairie, Jessica. Colby has been very ill; he was in intensive care. He's okay now, though."

"Oh no, what happened?"

While Meredith was explaining about Colby, Jessica picked up that she was tired. "Meredith, you sound exhausted."

Meredith immediately picked up the tempo, admitting she was a bit tired but claiming she was alright. She quickly changed the subject. "How are you and Aaron doing? We haven't talked to you for a few days."

Jessica indicated she was doing just fine but she remained very concerned about Aaron. "He's continuing to have frequent flashbacks that leave him weak and dizzy for at least a half hour afterwards."

"Oh boy, that's not good."

"And Mom, he's becoming quite distant and doesn't want to talk about his problem."

"That makes it hard for anyone to help him."

"Yes, and I can see he's lost weight."

"Lost weight?"

"Yeah, he admits his appetite has vanished. He used to go out with his buddies on Wednesday night after work while I'm teaching my yoga class. Lately, he hasn't even done that. And, Mom, I heard him turning down an opportunity to golf in a tournament next weekend. That is very unusual."

"Jessica, does he have the same self-deprecating conversations with you that he does with me?"

"Oh yeah, he totally blames himself for Sam's existence, no matter how I try to spin it for him."

"It makes him such easy prey to his emotions when he's constantly blaming himself." Meredith felt so tired. She didn't know what else to say. Finally, she added, "I'll talk to a counselor at work to see if he has any ideas as to how to persuade Aaron to seek counseling."

Meredith had looked for information on PTSD over a week ago and discovered Aaron's behavior was classic. She knew he desperately needed counseling but how could she or anyone convince him? She leaned back in her chair, thinking it would soon be time to pick Sam up from after-school care and wondering how she would get through the rest of the week. She felt defeated. When she finally managed to muster up enough energy to call Andy, she caught him at the airport waiting for his luggage. He was glad to hear that Colby was so much better and Meredith was home safe. He volunteered to pick up Sam.

Meredith was sound asleep when they got home. Andy whispered in Sam's ear that they should leave Gramma sleeping and bring home pizza for supper. Sam's azure blue eyes lit up with enthusiasm. They slipped out, quietly closing the door behind them.

After supper, Wendy called. "Colby's doing fine, Mom, feeling much better, tired but smiling and even wanting to play a bit. Did Dad make it home okay?" she asked with her usual concern.

"Oh yes, he's right here, dear, teaching Sam to play checkers. Do you want to talk to him?"

Wendy filled Andy in on some of the details of the scare Colby had given them. Their doctor had just been in for an evening visit and was planning to discharge Colby in the morning.

Meredith had taken over Andy's place with the checkers game and was listening to the conversation. She was so relieved to have Colby's critical incident over but the burden of Aaron's dilemma still weighed heavily on her shoulders. *God, how I wish Aaron could recover as quickly.*

CHAPTER 15

Fishing with Arlene and Hugh
June 8

As the days rolled by, Meredith and Andy's fears of losing Sam subsided. But their worries about Aaron escalated. He was still having flashbacks and refusing counselling and couldn't imagine coming to meet Sam. The counsellor that Meredith had talked to indicated that more often than not, young men like Aaron need to hit a wall before they relent and seek help. The best Meredith and Andy could do was to remain supportive, keep busy themselves, and hope that Aaron would change his mind. Meredith cried for an hour the night she told Andy what the counsellor had said. They considered going to Calgary for a visit but they would have to leave Sam with someone. If they left her with Wendy and Ian, she would have to miss school. They decided they would wait for the school summer holidays starting in July.

Meredith and Andy's friends, Arlene and Huge Cameron, were keen campers and loved to fish, especially Hugh. He loved to fish, hunt, and golf—that was his life, apart from work. The Camerons had a holiday trailer as the Taylors did and they went camping frequently on weekends during the summer. Charlie Lake was a common hangout where they could fish for northern pike and walleye and golf on the waterfront golf course. When Hugh called to say, "Let's go fishing," he seldom got a refusal. Last year they had made an agreement; he would call and say "Fishing," and they would answer "When?"

Hugh called on Monday and said "Fishing." Andy knew the distraction would be good for Meredith. On Friday night after work, the Taylors and the Camerons loaded up their trailers and headed for Charlie Lake. Sam had never camped before and wasn't quite sure about the idea but she soon got into the act. She helped Meredith load up the food, clothes, and other gear and they were on their way by 5:45 PM.

Charlie Lake was an amazing get-a-way for people from Dawson Creek and Fort St. John. It was about ninety kilometres from Dawson Creek so it was easy to get there after work on Friday in time to cook a great barbecue supper. They stopped at the local country store to purchase their live bait, a small plastic bag of earthworms. Sam was a bit worried about the fate of the worms. She couldn't believe Andy was going to put hooks into them for the fish to bite.

"Won't that hurt, Grampa T?"

"No Sam, did you know that you can cut an earthworm in half and he will grow a new tail?"

"Really?"

"But if we cut off your arm, you couldn't grow another one, right?"

"I don't think so." She giggled at the thought of it.,

"Earthworms have amazing powers of regeneration, Sam, they can grow back their missing parts."

"Okay, but I still don't think you should stick hooks into them. That will be mean...and yucky."

"Well, Sam, you'll see how it all works when we start fishing."

While they were descending into the valley, Sam was spellbound by the rich blue color of the lake ahead and the mixed forest of pine, spruce, aspen and birch surrounding the road leading to the lake. It was early summer and the wild roses were just starting their bloom. They rolled down the windows of their truck to take in the full scintillating scent of these native roses. Although they were the official wild flower of Alberta, they grew in abundance in British Columbia too. Without a doubt, they were Meredith's favourite, both for their delicate beauty and their delectable, fresh, light fragrance. These exquisite flowers of varying pinks were everywhere, invading the air with their aromatic welcome to the campground.

After they arrived at their campsite, Sam was kept busy watching Andy set up and stabilize the trailer and put up the full-length awning. The patio table and chairs outside by the trailer, the campfire pit, the closeness of the neighbours in the other camping spots, were all intriguing. She had a million questions. Meredith could hear her and Andy talking it up outside while she prepared the inside of the trailer. She handed out to Sam a table cloth and a candle to put on the table.

They lucked out with the weather, with a high of twenty-four Celsius predicted for Saturday and Sunday. The evening was a pleasant twenty-one degrees as they were cooking their supper. Arlene and Meredith always shared the cooking. Sometimes Meredith would make supper one night, Arlene the next night. The men always did the barbecuing. Often, like tonight, they both contributed to the meal. Meredith and Andy were barbecuing the steak and vegetables and Arlene was bringing the salad and dessert.

Both Arlene and Hugh were great with Sam. They were each about five years younger than Andy and Meredith and had two grandchildren of their own so they were very in tune with young children.

159

After supper, while Arlene and Meredith cleaned up, Andy and Hugh showed Sam the fishing boat and took her down to the lake to check out the condition of the water. She was so excited when she came back, she couldn't contain her exuberance. "Gramma T, Uncle Hugh is going to take us all fishing tomorrow morning in his fishing boat. Do you think I will be able to catch a fish, Gramma T?"

"I don't know for sure, Sam, but I do know that Uncle Hugh sure is good at finding where the fish are. We may get lucky."

"If I catch a fish, Grampa T said he would show me how to clean and cook it and we can eat it for lunch."

"That sounds great, Sam. We'll make a salad to go with it, and, presto, we'll have our lunch."

"Yeah, I can't wait." She was jumping excitedly around the campground, exclaiming, "We're going fishing, we're going fishing."

Andy got her busy with the intricacies of starting a campfire. After roasting a couple of marshmallows, it was Sam's bedtime. Even getting ready for bed in the trailer was a thoroughly interesting experience for Sam. She had never seen such a small bathtub. Obviously, she had never experienced anything like this before; the coming together of two families to eat, camp, play games, and sit around the campfire laughing and singing together. Andy accompanied the singing with his guitar and Sam sang heartily once she had heard the words once. She was enthralled with everything. Meredith wondered how she would sleep but all the fresh air had its effect and she was out cold within ten minutes of going to bed.

After breakfast, they loaded the necessities for a two-hour fishing trip into the boat; warm coats, life jackets, sun screen, snacks, fishing gear, cameras, and live bait and then headed down to the lake. The bait had been kept in Meredith's fridge, which was somewhat worrisome for Sam. She wondered if she would find a worm or two in her breakfast. Andy had teased her saying that a little extra meat would be good for her. It was a perfect morning, the sun was shining, there was no wind, and the lake surface was perfectly calm, clearly reflecting the rocky banks and trees at the far edge of the lake. The morning air was still damp with the fresh sweet dew of the boreal forest and the fragrance from the wild roses.

Hugh backed the boat and trailer down into the water and released the boat while Andy held the rope to control it. They were a very efficient pair at doing this but it scared Sam.

"Be careful, Grampa T, don't fall in."

"It's okay, Sam, Grampa T has done this many times before." Sam's concern warmed Meredith's heart.

Hugh and Arlene's fishing boat was nothing fancy, it was a sixteen-foot aluminum workhorse with a twenty-five-horsepower motor, effective for small lake fishing only. It had four padded benches going across the boat to sit on. Hugh was up front, driving the boat, Arlene and Meredith sat at the back, Sam and Andy were in the middle. Hugh gave them a fairly fast and thrilling ride out to one of his favourite fishing spots, the front of the boat lifting out of the water and an icy cold spray hitting them in the face.

Sam was mesmerized by the boat going through the water. "Grampa T, look what the water is doing behind us."

"Yes, Sam, that's called the wake. It's caused by the propeller on the motor spinning under the water. That's what makes us move forward." The wake was exceptionally dramatic this morning. The sun was behind them reflecting on the glassy lake surface and the white rolling foam caused by the propeller was angling away from the back of the boat, creating a dramatic V formation that glistened like diamonds. Funny how a child's observations make adults look at the ordinary and see the spectacular. Sam was good for all of them.

Hugh stopped the boat and he and Andy helped Arlene, Sam, and Meredith get their fishing rods baited and ready. Then he started up the boat again and let it move very slowly across his favourite dependable spot. Andy showed Sam how to cast her line and, after a couple of tries, she was a miniature expert. Within five minutes, Andy had the first fish, a beautiful little walleye. Once someone had a fish, Hugh shut down the boat and they all had to reel in their bait while Andy and Hugh netted the fish out of the water. Hugh had a measuring marker on the side of the boat to measure the length of the fish. This walleye was just long enough to keep. Sam was right in there watching the measuring. "Yes, Gramma T, it's big enough to keep, it's just big enough. We've got our lunch!"

"Sam, that's a pretty small fish, I think we need at least three of them for our lunch," Hugh laughed.

"Okay, I'll catch another one," she responded optimistically.

Arlene had the next bite so she changed fishing rods with Sam and Andy helped her reel it in. When Hugh caught it in the net, he exclaimed, "Sam, you've got a big one, a beauty, she is. This will do for lunch."

"Wow, I caught a big one! I caught a big one! Let's measure it, Uncle Hugh." This walleye was obviously twice as big as it needed to be to keep, but Hugh indulged Sam and helped her measure it anyway. "We can keep it, Grampa T, we can keep it," she exclaimed.

"Yes, Sam, this one is plenty big enough to keep."

Again, she had made the ordinary seem extraordinary and kept them all laughing at her excitement. Hugh took a picture of Andy and Sam, holding up her catch. Both of them were smiling ear to ear.

Altogether, they caught seven walleye and one northern pike within two hours. Sam never tired of trying, she was a real trooper, re-casting her line after each catch and patiently waiting for a bite. She did catch one small walleye on her line that they had to throw back in but that didn't dissuade her one little bit. When they returned to their campsite, Andy took another picture of Sam holding up her walleye.

They all went fishing again in the late afternoon and the next morning. The rest of the time was spent playing cards, walking, and visiting around the campfire. Arlene and Hugh had brought their granddaughter's bicycle with them for Sam to ride but she had never had a bicycle and didn't know how to ride a two-wheeler. Arlene spent some time with her helping her balance and it wasn't long before she was proudly riding around on her own on the paved roads throughout the campground. Sam met a couple of children in the campsite down a bit from the Taylor's and Cameron's site. She played with them for a while but she was soon back to her own campsite. Arlene played cards with her while Meredith relaxed with her book. Arlene and Meredith liked to read the same books and discuss them but Meredith hadn't had much time to read lately so Arlene was way ahead of her.

Meredith was quite willing to let Arlene take over for a while. She knew she was on the brink of mental and physical exhaustion. Her worries about Aaron were one thing; and even though Sam was delightful, having a six-year-old to look after at the age of sixty-one was physically and mentally gruelling.

Considering everything, the camping and fishing trip was definitely a big hit. Arlene and Hugh had not spent any time with Sam before, at least not beyond brief visits. Sam quickly charmed both of them just as she had done with Andy and Meredith. On the road home, she wanted to know when they could go fishing again.

The next evening, Hugh stopped by to pick up Andy to go for coffee. Andy told Hugh that Sam was asking when they could go fishing again. Hugh laughed and said, "Atta girl, Sammy, you're my kind of girl, we'll go fishing again real soon."

"Okay!" she responded boisterously, smiling from ear to ear.

Hugh bent down, gave her a big hug and replied, "See you later, partner!"

CHAPTER 16

Sam's Birthday
July 6

Andy had planned to take Meredith sailing in the third week of June. Their plans had been made back in February. Andy's cousin rented a sail boat at least twice a year to sail in the Golf Islands between the Lower Mainland Coast and Vancouver Island and she had invited them to come along. She required a crew of six and her husband and another couple were already booked to come. The Taylors would complete the crew. Andy was really looking forward to this as they had never done any sailing before. In early May, he had discussed their commitment with Meredith, and much to his chagrin, they decided they would have to back out of the plan. They didn't want to create any more turmoil for Sam by taking her out of school or having a babysitter for her.

June sped by without incident. Meredith and Andy were settling into the role of parents again. Sam continued to do well in school. Daily routines seemed to have replaced the upheaval of Sam's arrival but concerns over Aaron's well-being continued to leave a dark cloud hanging over the Taylor family. Meredith had not had any more melt-downs but her diverging feelings for Sam and Aaron left her feeling highly stressed most of the time. She hadn't phoned Aaron or Jessica for quite a few days as making contact and hearing Aaron's voice or listening to Jessica's concerns escalated her stress levels. She felt like she was caught in a bear trap, but instead of a painful leg, her head ached relentlessly and there was no way to get out. Calling was nerve-racking, not calling left her feeling neglectful and guilt-ridden.

Meredith fretted over Sam's coming birthday just as she had done over her own children's birthdays. The thought of having several children to entertain was even more unnerving now than it had been when she was younger. She wanted to keep it simple while making it memorable for Sam. She asked her who she wanted to invite and was relieved when Sam indicated Wendy and Ian, Colby and Dylan, Hugh and Arlene. Meredith reluctantly asked about her school friends, but Sam only wanted what she said was her "new family." Meredith mar-velled at this, her fragile heart touched again with love.

When Wendy had called on Monday evening, Meredith told her who Sam wanted to invite to her party.

"Well, I can't help but feel honoured, Mom," she laughed. "When are you having it?"

"Her birthday is on Friday but I thought I would do it for supper on Saturday. I was hoping you and Ian and the boys could come early and stay overnight. It would be nice to go to the pool in the afternoon for family swim time."

"Sounds great, I think that will work. I'll check with Ian and let you know. The boys are finally forty inches tall so they can go on the water slide now. They'll have a blast."

****

Meredith and Andy had decided to get Sam a new bicycle for her birthday and Andy had purchased it at Zellers a couple of weeks ago. They could hardly wait to give it to her. Sam slept in and when she came downstairs, Meredith could tell immediately something was bothering her. She wondered if Sam had been crying.

"Sam, what's wrong? You look sad this morning."

Sam crawled up on the loveseat with Buddy and her blanket but didn't respond. Her eyes were downcast, avoiding Meredith's gaze. *Oh oh, what's the matter now? This is not like our usually happy little girl.* "Sam, what happened to make you so sad?"

"It's my birthday and my mommy isn't going to be here." She started to cry. "I thought she would come for my birthday party."

Meredith moved over to the loveseat beside her and put her hand on Sam's arm. "Sam, I'm so sorry you're missing your mom today. I can understand why you would want her here for your birthday."

Sam looked up at Meredith with her big sad eyes wet with tears. "I thought for sure she would be here for my birthday. Last time she was really sick and in the hospital, she came home for my birthday. But this time, she's not coming, is she?"

"No, I expect not."

"She's forgotten all about me, Gramma T. Why would she do that?"

"Oh Sam, I don't think she has forgotten about you. Mothers never forget about their children, no matter how long they have to be away. I think she just can't come, sweetheart.... I think she would be here if she could."

"She's been away for a really long time. I don't think she's ever coming back."

She looked so dejected, Meredith wanted to cry too. Instead she said, "Sam, come over here, we are going to have a serious cuddle." She swept her up into her arms and put her on her knee, holding her tight for several minutes. "Sam, are you remembering that Aunt Wendy, Uncle Ian, Colby, and Dylan are coming here this afternoon? I have to get ready for your party and I need your help."

"I forgot," she responded with a flat voice.

Meredith lifted Sam's chin up to look at her and said, "Well Miss Forgetful, we have to get busy."

"What do we have to do?" Sam asked with a hint of enthusiasm.

"Well, let's see, we have to have breakfast, make your cake, get supper ready, tidy up the house..."

Sam was perking up and she interrupted, "Can we have scrambled eggs and toast for breakfast, Gramma T? I can help with that."

Thank goodness, a breakthrough. "You bet we can, Sam. Let's go make it."

After breakfast, Andy told Sam he had something to show her in the garage. When she saw the bike, she squealed with delight. Andy adjusted the seat and handle bars for her and she rode it up and down the street all morning, proudly stopping to talk to anyone in the vicinity. She was as much of a socialite as her father was, willing to talk to and be a friend to everyone.

At noon, Sam helped decorate her own cake, chocolate, of course, including the icing, scattered with ample Smarties and seven pink candles. Then she was out riding her bike again.

As soon as Wendy, Ian, and the boys arrived, they all went for a family swim in Dawson Creek's new aquatic centre. Having started swimming lessons two weeks ago, Sam was familiar with the centre's attractions and was thrilled to show Colby and Dylan around. They were just tall enough by a hair to go on the slides. Sam and the boys loved the water and played tirelessly for the whole hour.

Back home, Arlene and Hugh were given a hearty welcome by all and everyone headed to the backyard for the barbecue. The steaks were almost done when a loud scream from Sam turned all eyes to the back corner of the yard where she lay on the grass, holding her arm and whimpering. Meredith flew into action. She was kneeling beside her in an instant, checking out an obviously broken wrist.

"Gramma T, it really hurts," she blurted through her sobs.

"I can see that Sam, I think it's broken. We're going to take you to the hospital right now and you will be just fine." A large swelling had already formed on the inside of her arm just above her wrist and her hand was displaced backward and outward. Meredith suspected a Colle's fracture. She had witnessed several fractures of this type while working in emergency in her early nursing years. The small delicate bones in the wrist are susceptible to fracture when using the hand to break a serious fall, especially in young children and older adults. She sent Wendy in for a bag of ice and a towel to splint Sam's arm and hand.

Meredith looked around, confused, wondering how the fall had happened. Sensing Meredith's confusion, Sam sobbed, "I tripped over Dylan and fell."

"Don't you worry, my sweetheart, you will be just fine," Meredith reassured again, but she wondered why Sam's arm would break from such a normal childhood tumble. There was nothing on the ground that Sam had fallen on, just a soft carpet of grass. And Dylan was just fine.

Meredith carefully wrapped Sam's arm and Andy carried her to the car, leaving the others to have supper. By the time they returned, Sam in a cast, palm to elbow, Hugh and Arlene had gone home and the boys were ready for bed. Meredith got Sam ready too, tucked her in, and propped her cast up on a pillow. Everyone, including Colby and Dylan, came in and gave her a kiss. She had been given some Demerol for pain prior to setting the break so she was very sleepy but she lapped up the affection with grins and thank yous, her eyelids at half-mast.

Downstairs, Wendy asked the first question. "Was the break bad, Mom?"

"No, as I suspected, it's a simple Colle's fracture but Sam has a lesion on one of her wrist bones and that's why it broke so easily."

"What does that mean?"

"We don't know for sure but the doctor assured us that the break will cause new bone growth and the lesion will likely disappear."

"Likely—what if it doesn't?"

"I don't want to think about that, Wendy. We will have to get it x-rayed six months and a year from now to see if it has disappeared for sure. Do you remember when Aaron broke his ankle just above his ski boot when he was ten?"

"Yeah, I do remember something about that."

"He had a lesion on the site of the break that was taking up two thirds of the width of his bone. That's why it broke so easily. But he was fine. Six months later, his bone was as good as new, lesion gone."

"I remember Aaron's friend not believing him that he had broken his leg because he'd had such an easy fall. He laughed at him at first, thinking he had to be kidding."

"That's right. It was darn worrisome until we got that clean x-ray report."

"Mom, is this familial or something?"

"The doctor couldn't say for sure but it sure looks like it, doesn't it?"

"Oh good, one more thing for me to worry about with my boys. What about when Aaron broke his leg when he was in college, did he have a lesion then too?"

"No, he didn't, that was one thing we double checked on to make sure but it was just a normal break. I don't know of anyone else in the family having similar lesions… but Andy, didn't you break your arm from falling off a chair when you were little?"

"That's right, I did, I think I was only two or three at the time."

"Back then, they probably didn't even take an x-ray. So who knows, maybe you had a lesion too? Kids don't usually break their arm from falling off a chair."

"Changing the subject, Mom, you look tired. How are you and Dad doing looking after a six-seven now-year old child?"

"I have to admit, Wendy, it's not easy to keep up. Somehow, I don't have the energy I had when you and Aaron were little."

"Maybe you should take some time off work. You could do that, couldn't you?"

"I suppose I could but I don't like the idea. Remember, I had two months off last summer with my surgery. So I hate to take time off again. But my holidays are starting soon. We'll see how things go after that."

"Okay, but remember, I'm keeping my eye on you, Mom," she laughed. "You need to look after yourself or you won't be any good for looking after Sam."

"I know, dear, I know," Meredith replied wearily. "Speaking of being tired, I think it's time for all of us to hit the hay."

In bed, Meredith reviewed the day. "Well, I did want Sam's birthday to be memorable but..."

"Yeah, she loves her bike and she won't be riding it for a while. And the rest of her swimming lessons are out." Andy replied, sleepily.

"At least, it's not her right arm, but once she gets her cast off, I still won't want her riding her bike until we get that six-month x-ray. What are we going to do with her for the rest of the summer?" Andy was asleep, his soft snore starting to lull Meredith into sleep too. But before she drifted off, she thought of the Dino Camp, a camp for kids at Tumbler Ridge that had been held every summer for the last while. *I remember reading in the paper last year that it was so popular it sold out so they held an extra one. The children are given tools and shown how to dig carefully around a dinosaur bone or other fossil to excavate it. Sam will like that. I'll look into it tomorrow. The reading program at the library will be a good idea too. And she should still be able to cast a fishing rod.* Her thoughts made her smile a bit just before falling asleep.

****

In the morning, the phone rang while everyone was still in bed. Meredith was awake, vegetating, reluctant to get up. She was somewhat shocked to hear Aaron say, "Hello Mom."

"Aaron... good to hear from you. It's early, your dad and I are still in bed."

"Really? You guys are always up so early."

"Yes, well, I guess we had a busy day yesterday."

"What were you doing?" Meredith had purposely not mentioned Sam's birthday to Aaron.

"Wendy and Ian and the boys came over for Sam's birthday..." Meredith wondered if she should be talking about Sam. It always made the conversation strained. "We were up visiting kind of late."

"Man, I didn't know it was her birthday. Sounds like you had a good time."

Meredith felt a twinge of guilt for not telling him but he sounded cheerful so she ventured further. "Yes, well, we did, but Sam broke her arm."

"Oh no, what happened?"

"Nothing much really, she took a tumble over Dylan in the grass. I wondered why her arm had broken so easily with such a gentle tumble but we discovered she had a lesion at the site of the break. That's why it broke so easily."

"Mom, that's what happened to me on the ski hill when I was ten; I had a lesion on my ankle."

"That's right, dear." Meredith thought the conversation was going well so she continued with the story about Andy breaking his arm when he was young.

"Wow, it seems to run in the family, doesn't it? Is Sam okay?" His enquiry about Sam's well-being and his recognition of her "in the family" lifted her spirits.

"She's still sleeping, but when I checked her at 2:00 AM, her fingers looked good, pink and only slightly swollen. She slept well all night so I think she will be just fine."

"That's good." Aaron changed the subject. "I called to let you know that Jessica and I are headed out to the mountains for a week. We have a cabin rented and we'll be back next Friday.

"That sounds superb, dear. Where exactly are you going?

"We had booked a cabin at Canyon Creek back in February. It's a great place for hiking."

That sounds wonderful, Aaron, you two have a great time and thanks for calling to let us know. We appreciate it."

"We'll have our cell with us but I'm not sure how good the reception will be up there, especially when we're hiking.

"Okay, be sure to give us a call when you get back. I'd love to hear about your trip.

"Sure, Mom, I'll do that."

Meredith couldn't help but smile to herself. Aaron had actually been willing to talk about Sam. *Could this be a breakthrough? Maybe Aaron is beginning to absorb his paternal relationship to Sam. Maybe the fact that they share a bone lesion would help him, in some quirky way, to make a connection with her.*

The phone call had woken Colby and Dylan, so everyone was soon up. Meredith and Wendy made two huge frittatas and a big tray of fresh fruit for breakfast. Afterwards they brought out Sam's birthday cake, which, thoughtfully, nobody had touched the night before.

"Cake for breakfast!" Andy exclaimed, faking shock.

Sam's eyes lit up. "Well, yes, Grampa T, we didn't get any last night."

After the cake and ice cream, Wendy brought the birthday presents out to the living room. "C'mon, Sam, it's time for you to open your presents." She handed Sam a long, narrow, brightly-wrapped package. "This one is from Hugh and Arlene."

Sitting on the floor smiling, arm in a sling, Colby and Dylan on each side of her, Sam began to struggle with her one hand. "Help me, boys." They didn't hesitate and started ripping. "It's a fishing rod, my very own fishing rod...wow!"

Grampa T was down beside her, helping her get it out of the package. He was as interested as she was. "I'll help you rig it up, Sam, so you'll be ready to go fishing."

Next she opened Colby and Dylan's present, with their help, of course. Sam wasn't sure what it was at first until Dylan blurted, "It's a fising tacka box, Sam."

They helped her open the box. "Ya, it's for aw your ooks and jigs," Colby added.

Her eyes lit up as she scanned the contents, a colourful assortment of hooks, spoons, jigs and other fishing gear. "Wow, my own fishing tackle box, Grampa T, look, my very own fishing tackle box."

He leaned over and surveyed the contents. "Yep, you've got just about everything you need in there except your worms, Sam." She grimaced at Andy about the worms, then gave Colby and Dylan big individual hugs while thanking them. They both giggled with pleasure.

From Wendy and Ian, she received several puzzles and books. "This is great, Sam," Meredith stated, "What a good idea this present is, with your broken arm."

Sam got up and gave them both a hug. "Thanks Aunt Wendy, thanks Uncle Ian."

Ian, Wendy and the boys packed up right after the present opening and headed home. As soon as they were gone, Sam said, "I have to phone Uncle Hugh and Auntie Arlene to thank them too." Meredith dialled and handed her the phone.

CHAPTER 17

Permanent Guardianship for Sam
July 12

Meredith came down the stairs from tucking Sam into bed and sat in her recliner beside Andy. As usual, at this time in the evening, he was reading. "Andy," she interrupted. "The hearing for Sam's custody renewal is next week. Maybe we should discuss this."

Andy put his *Canadian Business* magazine down on his lap and turned to her. "What do we need to discuss? Obviously, we will be asking for permanent custody and guardianship so we don't have to keep returning for renewals, right?"

"Yes, but how are you feeling about this, dear?"

"Meredith, you know how I feel."

"No, actually I don't. We've been merrily going along now for several weeks and haven't really talked about how we're feeling."

"Well, I don't see that there is any decision to make. Of course, we're going to keep Sam until Aaron is ready to accept her."

"I'm not asking about our decision, Andy. I'm asking you how you feel."

"Trapped, Meredith, trapped. That's how I feel." He sounded angry. Meredith wasn't sure if he was angry because she was pushing him about his feelings or he was just plain angry.

"But you are still enjoying Sam, aren't you?"

"Of course, I'm enjoying her. She's delightful and funny, she constantly challenges me and I love her dearly. What's not to love? But I still feel trapped. I have not made this choice to parent a seven-year old at my age. We had to give up our sailing trip and goodness knows what else in the future."

"So... what will you tell the judge at the hearing next week?"

"Exactly that. I'll be honest. What will you tell her?"

"I don't know. I feel a bit worried about what she will think when she hears that Aaron has not even met his daughter yet. I think she is going to want to know how this is impacting us and how we're coping."

"And how are we coping? We still have not heard from Sam's mother and have no idea what she's up to. Aaron is not doing well. We're tired and stressed and our lives have changed dramatically. That's honest. All we know for sure that we didn't know last time is that Sam is actually our grandchild."

"Yes, that's all true. But her question, if I was her, is going to be, can we see ourselves coping over the long run and continuing to provide a positive, nurturing environment for Sam. Can we, Andy?"

"Legally speaking, Sam needs a guardian for another nine years. Meredith, I'll be... seventy-four by then and you'll be seventy."

"Ouch, that's a scary way to think about it."

"Yep, it sure is. And we cannot predict how long we will be able to do this for Sam. All we can tell the judge is that, right now, we are prepared to continue in our role as Sam's legal guardians."

"I guess you're right there. You always make it sound so simple though. This pending hearing has been weighing heavily on my mind for the last few days and I get so muddled when I think about it. How the heck do we do what's best for Aaron *and* what's best for Sam? I keep coming up with the same inadequate answer. We have to keep Sam until Aaron is ready. And that is, as you make it seem, a simple fact. But you are very right, we are trapped and I think that is why it's so stressful. We need to forget about being trapped and just enjoy Sam; she keeps us young, Andy. For me, the trapped part is not that we have to look after Sam, it's the dichotomy of Sam and Aaron that's so wearing. They are like two opposing forces and we're right in the middle, being pulled apart from both sides. No matter how well we manage with Sam, it's hard to feel like we're doing well because of our concern for Aaron."

"Yes," Andy agreed. "We are literally being pulled apart and we can't let go of either side because they are both too precious. And that's what is so exhausting, much more so than the physical challenges of looking after Sam at our age."

"I suspect the judge will be asking about how Sam broke her arm. I'm glad we shared that with Delores when it happened."

"Yes, we certainly don't want to appear as if we're hiding anything."

"Let's go back to Aaron's having not met Sam yet. Andy, we can't tell the judge why Aaron is so angry. We don't want to bring up the rape thing, even in the courtroom, right?"

"Especially in the courtroom. Who knows what the judge might want to do with that."

"So our plan is, as you say, to be honest in every way, except for the rape. You're right again, Andy, it's simple but it's still not satisfactory." He smiled gently at Meredith and returned to his magazine. She felt much better. At least she knew they would be on the same page at the hearing.

****

Andy, Meredith, and Sam were at the courthouse by 9:00 AM sharp. Delores Scobie met them in the courtroom and took Sam to another room to be with a sitter. Then she returned to the courtroom for the hearing.

Judge Cameron's first question was predictable. "How are you both doing while looking after a seven-year old?"

Andy spoke first. "We're doing okay, considering our circumstances. We have come to love Sam as our own child, but there's no doubt it is exhausting for us at times."

"Tell me more."

"Our son, Aaron, Sam's biological father, is not doing well with this. He feels terribly guilt ridden about his parents having to look after a child but he's far too angry and has not been able to even bring himself to meet Sam yet. What makes this even more difficult for him is he and his wife are expecting their first baby in January."

Judge Cameron spoke with concern written all over her face. "I can see that would add some stress to the family dynamics. What about you, Mrs. Taylor, how are you doing?"

"Sam is a great kid, easy to look after and I love her as my own child. We definitely want to continue in our role as her caregivers and guardians, despite the fact that it is a bit tiring at our age. We have a daughter living in Grande Prairie who is very willing to relieve us whenever we need a break. And I have a couple of friends in town who will look after Sam any time that we need them. So our support systems are good. There is no doubt that we are worried about our son and the difficulty he's having with this, but I do believe he will come around eventually. Andy and I have decided to give him the time and space he needs without pressuring him."

"I must say, I am impressed with your dedication to Sam and your patience with your son." She paused and looked at her papers. "I have received a report from Delores Scobie prior to the hearing, indicating that she has no concerns at all about Sam's well-being while in your care. I am aware that she recently broke her arm for which there was a natural cause." She hesitated again while looking down at her notes. "The report also indicates that Sam's mother has made no contact whatsoever with you since Sam's arrival. Please excuse me for a few minutes while I talk to Sam."

Judge Cameron returned to the courtroom within ten minutes smiling and holding on to Sam's hand. She bent down and whispered in her ear and Sam came running to sit with the Taylors. The judge returned to her chair. "Sam is obviously happy to be living with her grandparents and her grandparents wish to continue in their role as her legal guardians. I hereby grant Meredith and Andy Taylor permanent custody and guardianship of Samantha Scott. This decision can be reviewed at any time at the request of the grandparents or their son, Aaron, Sam's father. This court is adjourned."

.   **********

In the afternoon, Aaron called Meredith while she was still at work. "How did the court hearing go, Mom?"

"Good dear, the judge granted us permanent custody."

"Wow, what did you tell her?"

Meredith hesitated momentarily. She knew she had to be careful even though she thought that Aaron was doing a bit better lately. "Well, we both told her that Sam was delightful, we love her, she is very easy to look after, and we're prepared to keep her for the foreseeable future."

"Mom, I don't get it. You don't seem to be angry at all anymore and you love Sam. I feel like you don't care what happened to me anymore."

At that moment, Meredith realized Aaron was angry at her and probably his dad too. He must be thinking that, somehow, they couldn't possibly love Sam and still care about him. She hadn't let him know her real feelings because she was trying to stay calm and downplay the revulsion she felt about how Sam was conceived. But Aaron needed to know.

She got up and closed her office door. "Oh my god, Aaron, I'm so sorry, I've been holding back my feelings to try to hold together myself. And I thought my false calm would help you. I didn't mean to diminish what happened to you." She was crying now. "Aaron, I love you so much and I'm feeling your pain like crazy. This woman, Leanna, has done the unforgivable to you. There is nothing worse in my mind than a sexual crime committed by someone the victim trusts. I am damn angry and my heart threatens to stop every time I think about it. My bowels knot up and I get a severe pain in my gut. And your Dad, he's beside himself and doesn't even know how to express his feelings." Meredith stopped, giving Aaron a chance to respond.

There was momentary silence... "I'm sorry, Mom, my own thoughts are so mixed up and I'm feeling so damn sorry for myself. I should have known."

"No, Aaron, it was very wrong of us to hold back our feelings. I can see perfectly clearly now how you would begin to feel like this. All we have ever been is positive when we talk to you. How could you have known? But Sam, all I can say is, we met her before we knew about all this and she won our hearts in an instant. Well, maybe it took your Dad a bit longer, maybe half a day." Meredith tried to laugh a bit. "She is so much like you, it's quite unbelievable. You are at a big disadvantage because you didn't have the chance to know her first Aaron. And she really is totally innocent in this mess."

"But I keep thinking about what kind of person she's going to become, Mom. You know what they say, the seed doesn't fall very far from the tree."

"I cannot predict her future but you know what, nobody ever knows what kind of adult their child is going to turn out to be. As parents, we nourish them with food and thought, love them, and hope for the best. Right now, Sam is a delightful child and she needs someone to love, nourish, and care for her. That fact is inevitable. And I can assure you, my heart is big enough for both of you, dear. It's not a case of you or her. But I was very wrong to not let you know how I was feeling."

"God, Mom, I'm having such an awful time getting my head around all of this. I hadn't thought about it for years, didn't even remember most of it. Now it's with me every day, driving me crazy. It seems like I'm on an impassable road, stuck in a deep mud hole and sinking."

Aaron's description gave Meredith an opening. "That is a very visual way to describe your feelings, Aaron. Think about this. What do you think you would need to get out of a deep mud hole?"

"Mom, where are you going with this?"

"Bear with me here, just tell me, Aaron, what would you need to physically get out of a deep mud hole?

"Well, I guess I would need someone with a big tractor to pull me out."

"Exactly, you would need help, someone with the correct tools and knowledge. That is what Jessica and I and Wendy have been trying to tell you."

"But if I had a hell of a big winch and a strong tree, I could get myself out."

"Oh god, Aaron, you are impossible, impossible on an impassable road." They laughed a bit.

"Well, I could." He laughed again. A tight unnatural laugh.

"Yes, and that is what you still want to try to do, isn't it, dear? But I don't know if your winch is big enough. Only you can decide that. There is one thing I want you to remember though. This is not the worst thing that could happen to you and the world is not going to end because of it. You are still the same person you were before this happened and you can and you will get back to feeling like yourself again. That, I am sure of."

"Okay, Mom, thanks for the discussion. At least I can see more clearly where you and Dad are coming from now."

"You're welcome. We love you, Aaron."

"I love you too, Mom. Bye for now."

****

Aaron sat at his desk staring into space. His heavy cloud had lifted a little and he did feel relieved, but he couldn't help but think that everyone was taking care of Sam except him. Even his sister. His guilt weighed him down like a bag of sand sitting on his shoulders. He thought of what his mother had said but he just couldn't imagine himself telling his story to a stranger. He couldn't get past the embarrassment of what had happened to him and his inability to deal with it. His frequent and disturbing flashbacks fuelled his anger and left him feeling trapped in a swirling vortex.

After Aaron's call, Meredith's thoughts continued too. She hoped she'd had a breakthrough with Aaron but she knew how self-sufficient he had always strived to be and wondered if he would ever be able to seek professional help. She thought again about what had happened to him. *When a woman is date raped and a pregnancy results, she can have an abortion. Aaron had no choice to end the pregnancy and Sam is now a part of our lives. She needs to become part of his reality. But, oh, I do understand his anger and his hesitancy to have anything to do with her.*

CHAPTER 18

Colleen's Desperate Wish
Aug 2

Colleen visited her long-time friend in the hospice palliative care unit every day after work. She had been Leanna's friend for sixteen years and had seen her through the sudden deaths of her parents and her last two bad relationships. Despite her disapproval, she had stuck by Leanna during her pregnancy and delivery as a single parent. Even though Leanna had rejected her as a sexual partner, Colleen remained her steadfast friend. They'd had some serious discussions about their arrangement and Colleen had reluctantly agreed to keep it platonic. After Leanna became ill, Colleen started living with her to help care for Sam. She felt that Sam was like her own daughter, the child she could never have.

She had been unwilling to go along with Leanna's plan to take Sam to her grandparents, but at the time, Leanna still had hopes of recovery and she didn't want to dash those hopes. She also knew that Leanna would need a great deal of support over the next while. It would have been hard to adequately care for Sam with her new job and her commitment to helping Leanna.

Yesterday when she'd visited, she could see that Leanna was going downhill quicker than the doctor had predicted. Today she intended to press Leanna again to give her custody. More than anything in the world, she wanted to raise Sam as her own child. She needed Sam to alleviate some of her extreme loneliness, especially after Leanna was gone. Her reasons were selfish but she had convinced herself that it was in Sam's best interests too.

Today, she had to convince Leanna to give her custody. She found her sleeping and decided to wake her. "Leanna, it's Colleen, I've brought you your favourite yogurt."

Leanna roused but barely enough to groggily reply. "Thanks, please put it in the fridge for later, I'm soooo... sleepy right now." She had been eating almost nothing in the last week and was looking dreadfully emaciated. She had refused to have intravenous therapy, thinking that it would only prolong her pain and suffering. She was too weak to do her own personal care, which made her look even worse; her hair not done, her color a dusky yellow-gray, eyes and cheeks sunken, mouth parched, lips cracked.

Despite her pain, up until two weeks ago Leanna had carefully applied her makeup to put some color on her face. She dressed herself in one of her stylish sporty outfits and wore a matching turban to cover her bald head. But for the last four days, she lay in bed twenty-four hours a day in a hospital gown with her head uncovered.

"Okay, but you have to wake up so I can talk to you about Sam."

"Sam, is she okay?" Leanna's level of alertness accelerated.

"Yes, Sam is fine but I still believe she should be with me after you're gone. I'm the only person in her life that she really knows. I should be her mother. Please, please, Leanna, give me custody of Sam. She belongs with me."

Leanna woke up enough to be resolute in what she believed would be best for Sam. "Colleen, please, we've been over and over this." Her voice was weak but Colleen could still hear the determination in it. "Sam needs her other family now. I know you love her but you can't offer her a family, the family she has not known until now."

"That family will never wholly accept Sam," Colleen responded with more than a hint of anger. "Can't you see that by now? Aaron still has not even come to meet her. It's been four months, Leanna."

Leanna sighed weakly. "I know, you keep reminding me, but her grandparents have come to love her and Aaron just needs more time. I know what kind of person he is, Colleen. Remember, that's why I chose him to father Sam. And once he does meet her, she will win him over too, I'm sure of it. He just has to get through the initial shock of having a child he never knew existed."

Colleen's anger was growing. "I don't agree. What you did to him, how can he ever forgive you for that and come to truly love Sam? Leanna, wake up here, any normal guy will always hold a terrible grudge for what you did and that is bound to spill over onto his feelings for Sam no matter how nice of a person he is." Colleen stopped short. Her guilt feelings for pressuring Leanna at this time were fighting with her desperation to become Sam's mother.

"Colleen, I'm so tired, I can't deal with this anymore. I have made up my mind and I have to have faith in Aaron and his family. You have to promise me that you will abide by my wishes when I'm gone. I'm as certain about this as I am about the fact that I'm dying. Aaron is no ordinary guy. He has a heart of gold and a very supportive family. He will come through for Sam. I have to believe he will. Now let it rest...; after I'm gone, you can introduce yourself to the family and I'm certain they will allow you to remain part of Sam's life if that's what you want. They'll do that for Sam's sake, I know they will. And you can't offer her enough by yourself. It's too hard to do this on your own." Leanna's voice was fading as she talked and her heavy tired eyes closed again. Before she fell completely asleep, she thought of how Colleen did not have it in her to be a good parent. She had no patience for children and had very little understanding of human nature, let alone the nature of a child.

Colleen was fuming and left the unit quickly thinking how ungrateful Leanna was for not recognizing and rewarding her lengthy commitment and her love for Sam. Although she loved Leanna, she felt an underlying anger towards her for rejecting her as her true partner. And now Leanna was rejecting her as a parent for Sam. She didn't care about all the money Leanna was willing to her, she only wanted Sam. She could see that it was too late now to change Leanna's mind. She wished that Leanna had never asked her nurse friend, Janet, to apply for a job in the health unit where Meredith worked; and she wondered how much Leanna's lawyer was paying Janet to be an informant. *Janet's weekly calls to Leanna with updates on Sam's progress are undermining my ability to convince Leanna that Sam would never be happy with her grandparents or her father. I will have to figure this out for myself. Somehow, I will get Sam back after Leanna's gone.*

CHAPTER 19

Leanna's Last Request
August 3

Leanna's thoughts floated before her like dandelion fluff, scattered and disconnected. She struggled to find the strength to focus her eyes. Pastor Felix seemed to have a smoky haze surrounding him as she took in his appearance. He was dressed in black with his usual white clerical collar. She could see that he was a handsome man with a round, boyish face. He had dark curly hair, clear blue eyes and a slightly tanned complexion. His demeanor was warm and caring and she appreciated that he always held her hand as they talked. It seemed to establish a connection for her words to flow. She felt sad to think that she had only been able to trust two men in her lifetime; Aaron and this pastor. She had betrayed Aaron's trust and now she was about to use Pastor Felix's trust in a last-ditch attempt to amend, as best she could, what she had done to Aaron.

Leanna recognized she had very little time left and she knew she had to give her directions to Pastor Felix today. Her raspy voice was hesitant, barely there, as she asked him to look in the drawer of her bedside table for a large brown envelope. Once he had the envelope addressed to him in his hands, she said, "Pastor, I simply have to do what I can to make certain that Aaron and his family will take Sam in permanently. I don't have enough time left to see for myself that this will happen. I have one final request of you." She stopped momentarily, struggling to find the energy to continue. Her eyes closed as if she was falling asleep.

"What is it Leanna, what can I do for you?"

His question aroused her. "I want you to deliver the letters inside this envelope in person to Aaron and his family. I know this is beyond what I should expect from you, but I will pay you well for your time and travel to Calgary and I am making a generous donation to your church."

Not for the first time, Felix didn't know what to say and he could feel his anger developing. He sat in stunned silence, a frown forming on his brow. This felt like bribery and he didn't want to be manipulated into anything.

Leanna continued, her voice becoming weaker and more raspy, "My lawyer will arrange this after I'm gone and you have delivered the letters." She stopped and sighed with exhaustion.

Felix's anger moved to the surface, reddening his face and neck as he struggled to find a response to this unusual request. Finally, he took her hand in both of his. "Leanna, I don't think this is the best way to handle this…"

Despite her failing vigor, Leanna cut him off, managed to garner one last bit of strength, and answered him determinedly, "It is the only way. I have no time for anything else." With her last words, her thin yellow eyelids slowly closed as she succumbed to the morphine.

Pastor Felix could see Leanna was unwavering in her decision, so he didn't try to arouse her for any further discussion. He was beginning to learn just how impossible it was to influence people to change their lifelong behaviors. Perhaps it was foolish for him to even try, especially with a person on their deathbed.

He could tell by her slowing breaths, she was drifting deeper into a narcotic sleep. Felix sat for a few minutes, his own eyes closed, praying silently for guidance and compassion while still holding Leanna's cold, thin hand. As he got up from his chair, he noticed that the small bit of urine in her drainage bag was very dark brown. He suspected her kidneys were shutting down and he guessed that death was imminent. He was aware that she hadn't been able to eat for several days, only taking sips of water and receiving high doses of morphine for pain control. Taking the letters with him, Felix left the unit feeling overwhelmed with sadness and anger.

As he was leaving, a nurse was coming in to provide care. Felix greeted her with a forced smile, his mood not in it. "She has just fallen asleep."

The nurse nodded and smiled, talking as she and Felix passed by each other. "Oh no, I was just coming in to turn her."

The nurse noticed that Leanna had a smile on her face, a look of contentment. She spoke quietly, telling her she had come to give her care. With the movement and the voices, Leanna roused slightly. After giving her mouth care with lemon and glycerin sponge tips, the nurse turned her and rubbed her back gently, trying to stimulate whatever circulation was left. She placed several pillows to support Leanna's new position, gave her morphine pump another push, and asked her if she needed anything else.

"No, thank you," Leanna replied in a whisper. "I have just finished my last life's task. I have no further needs. I can die in peace now."

The nurse didn't know what to say so she smiled and touched Leanna's boney arm with a gentle lingering touch. Leanna's eyes closed and she went to sleep with the same smile of contentment on her face, peacefully drifting through dreams of Sam.

****

Felix was a young pastor, twenty-nine years old, and this was his first full-fledged church appointment. Along with his duties to his church, he belonged to the Ecumenical Council that serviced the hospitals and palliative care units in the surrounding area. He had started his new job at the Community Church in North Vancouver only two months ago and had been visiting Leanna's Palliative Care Unit twice a week ever since.

As Leanna's whole story had slowly been revealed to him, it was almost too much for Felix to comprehend. He became more and more uncomfortable with having to hold the information in complete confidence until after her death. He knew there was a family out there somewhere that was suffering from complete lack of information about Sam and her mother. But she had asked him to promise not to disclose her story until after she was gone, and despite his internal struggle, he had reluctantly agreed.

In one of his early visits with Leanna, she had told him about her childhood, living mostly with her nanny and the gardener. Her parents were seldom home and when they did come home, it was for a very short visit of two to five days. She often eavesdropped on her parents while they were talking and learned quickly how their relationship with each other was based on manipulation and self-interest. They were constantly fighting with their words, and as she grew older, she worried that they would soon get a divorce. Their relationship with Leanna was minimal; and, although she believed they loved her, she came to understand that they were not capable of demonstrating that love. This left a huge hole in Leanna's heart, a hole that gave her constant emotional and physical pain. She felt that pain in her head, her chest, her stomach, and her back. Sometimes, it was like a vacuum, threatening to suck out her insides. Other times, it was just a relentless ache that wanted to devour her. She had told Felix that when Sam was born, she couldn't get enough of her. She wanted to hold her all the time and give her the love she never had, the love that overpowered her with emotion until she had to put Sam down and cry herself to sleep.

Felix had also learned about Leanna's failed relationships throughout her adult years. He wasn't aware of any other friends who came to visit her. The only other person in her life, as far as he knew, was her lawyer; so he came to see her as a very lonely person, a person who really needed his support. But this "last request" was very worrisome.

Felix didn't want to deliver anything to Aaron and his family that would cause any more hurt than they were already experiencing. He wished he'd had more time with Leanna to help her work through her guilt in a more productive way, but her time was quickly running out. He had no idea what he was going to do with the letters yet. He didn't give two hoots about the money; in fact, her offer exemplified the fact that he too was being manipulated, just as Leanna was manipulating the Taylor family. *Money, the root of all evil, couldn't be more true than right now. If Leanna didn't have so darn much money at her disposal, she probably would not have been able to contrive and carry out such a deceitful plan. I understand her reasons, her fraught desire for love, but they do not justify the actions she took to get pregnant. Her desperate concerns for her daughter are legitimate, but, all over again, she is following her devious methods to accomplish her goals. She wants to influence these people to take her daughter into their family permanently and she has made me part of her plan, her instrument.*

In the evening, Felix called his mentor, Pastor James McAfee, for advice. Pastor McAfee was astounded by the story, but in no uncertain terms he assured Felix that he could not be expected to honor this "last request" if he felt it might harm anyone else. He suggested that Felix open and read the letters to see if they would, in any way, be caustic to the Taylor family. If Felix thought the letters would be harmful, he could deliver Leanna's message in his own way. They talked at length about the impact of Leanna's childhood on her behavior and her decisions. This helped Felix to find a renewed sense of well-being and purpose in his ability to help Sam and her new family. As their conversation ended, Pastor McAffee reassured him again that he was in no way bound by his duty to carry out Leanna's wishes if there was any potential for causing further harm.

Even though he felt like he was betraying Leanna's faith in him, Felix decided to take Pastor McAfee's advice and read the letters. After all, he had to know if they could be harmful. Inside the envelope, he found a letter addressed to himself with some instructions. Much to his surprise, he was relieved to discover that the letters for Aaron and his family were potent but honest and revealing. *Maybe I did have some positive influence on her after all.* He smiled to himself. It took him a while to digest and assess the information, but he was amazingly comfortable with all of it. Just to be sure, he decided to share the letters with James McAfee in the morning and get his advice again. Pastor McAfee agreed that the letters were insightful and truthful and should bear no harm. They contained information that the family deserved to hear.

As he prayed for direction, Felix's thoughts kept drifting to Sam, the innocent little girl whom he had never met. He tried to imagine her in his mind's eye from the picture Leanna had shown him and from her affectionate description of her daughter. Then he thought of how the consequences of her unusual conception could follow and affect Sam throughout her life. He knew in his heart that the best place for Sam would be with her father and his extended family. He agreed with that part of Leanna's reasoning. What he didn't like was the manipulation and bribery Leanna had used to pull him into her plan. But he reasoned that the family deserved to know everything that Leanna was telling them and anything he might be able to add. If his part in Leanna's plan could help Sam, he would honor Leanna's request. He had to trust that, somehow, God had a hand in this plan and he would be God's instrument, not Leanna's. *I have to trust that God is looking out for Sam and her family.*

****

Three days later, on August 6, when Felix made his next visit to the palliative care unit, Leanna was gone. He was both saddened and relieved, saddened for her tortured soul and her passing, relieved that he could finally reveal some truths to the Taylor family. She had made him promise he would not contact Aaron or his family until after she was gone. She could not deal with meeting them and wanted to die in peace. When he returned to the rectory, he decided he would wait until evening to call, hoping the Taylors would be home and Sam would be in bed.

"Hello, Mrs. Taylor?"

"Yes."

"This is Felix Johnson, an Anglican pastor from Vancouver. You don't know me, but I need to tell you that I have had a very unusual request from a mother on her deathbed while attending to her spiritual needs."

"Pastor Felix Johnson, you say?"

"Yes, that's correct. The woman I had the request from was Sam's mother, Leanna."

"Sam's mother, oh dear… Does this mean Sam's mother is dead?"

"Yes, Leanna died early this morning."

"Oh my goodness… How did she die?"

"She died of breast cancer."

"Oh, that's a relief...oh dear... that must sound awful, Pastor. We knew from Sam that she was very sick. I was imagining all sorts of much more terrible things like AIDS, drug abuse, awful hereditary diseases that would follow Sam. Please forgive me. We just didn't know what to think."

"Yes, I can imagine that you have been going through some distressing times. How are you and your husband doing?"

"Well... I think we're doing pretty good, considering. Sam is such a sweet child, she has made it very easy to take her into our family. But...our son, Aaron, is another matter. He's not doing so well." She stopped short, wondering why she was so willing to talk openly to this stranger.

"I'm sorry to hear that but I'm not surprised. He has had an incredible and most unusual experience. And to be presented with a six-year-old daughter in this manner, well, I just can't imagine the impact."

It sounds like he knows everything. "Yes, Pastor, it's been pretty tough for him." *I wonder what he knows about Sam's conception. Does he really know everything?* "I think he's suffering from post-traumatic stress disorder. He has frequent flashbacks and his guilt is overwhelming him. He blames himself and feels so terrible about the mess he's caused for his whole family." *I wonder, should I be so open with this stranger?* The tone of his voice revealed a very compassionate and understanding man. Saying what she did seemed to release some of the pressure in her head.

"That, I think is not a surprising reaction. Has he had any counseling?"

"No, that's the difficult part; he's refusing to go and, as he puts it, tell his sad story to a total stranger."

"Maybe I can help with that, Mrs. Taylor. Leanna's last request was to have me read four letters to you and your family while you are all together. My guess is, many of your questions will be answered in the letters. If you still have questions after that, I will answer what I can for you. I think the more Aaron knows about what happened and why Leanna did what she did, the easier it will be for him to deal with it. Would it be possible for you to arrange for all of your family, yourself, Andy, Wendy and Ian to be at Aaron's house in Calgary in the near future for this reading?"

"Oh dear, I don't know when we can do that. I will have to talk to everyone." *Good grief, he knows all about us too, at least all of our names and where Aaron lives.* "You said you think this may help Aaron?" she questioned hesitantly.

"Yes, I think it may be of help to his recovery from this shocking series of events he has endured. I can fly to Calgary whenever you are able to arrange this as long as it doesn't interfere with any of my more significant commitments. Sam must not be present, for obvious reasons. Once you have decided on a date and time, you can call me and let me know. Perhaps you could come up with two options, if that's possible, in case I have a major commitment on one of them. But I will do my best to free myself up when all of you can come."

"Okay… just give me a minute. I'll get a pen and write your number down. Pastor, this is going to be very difficult for Aaron, even if you think the outcome may be positive."

"Yes, I can understand that and I will do what I can to be sensitive to his needs. Maybe I can help to persuade him to take some counseling. This is a very unusual circumstance. It may take him a good while to get through it."

"May I ask, why do the letters have to be read to all of us together? Can we not just receive them in the mail?"

"I know this is an imposition, asking you to plan a sudden trip, but I think it will be important for all of you to be together for the letters, for all of you to hear the whole story."

Meredith hesitated. She felt like she had no control of her life again.

"Hello Mrs. Taylor, are you still there?"

"Yes Pastor, I'm just feeling bewildered and worried about Aaron. I will let you know as soon as I can."

"Good, and I have to ask, how is Sam doing?" He sounded caring in a genuine way.

"Sam is doing remarkably well. She seems to be very content staying with us. She is an amazing little girl, very confident and well adjusted.

"That's a relief to hear. I have been concerned about you and your family for some time now as Leanna slowly revealed her story to me. I'll wait for you to talk to everyone and make some arrangements. In the meantime, if there is anything I can do to help, please call me. My number is 604-498-3030."

Meredith was aware of her hand shaking as she wrote the number.

Andy was sitting in his recliner reading the daily newspaper when Meredith took the call in the family room. It was 9:15 PM so Sam was already in bed. Meredith sat, stunned, for a minute, as Pastor Felix's message sunk in. Then she got up and went into the living room. "Andy, I just received the strangest call from a Pastor Felix Johnson in Vancouver."

Andy dropped his paper and his eyebrows went up, waiting in expectation for her to tell him more.

She hesitated.

"Well, what did the man say?" He sounded slightly annoyed at the interruption.

"It was the strangest message and a request. Leanna died this morning."

"She's dead?"

"Yes, and now…" She told him everything.

"Hm, it seems this situation with Sam is full of ongoing surprises, isn't it?"

"It certainly is. At least we don't have to worry about Leanna coming back and taking Sam away."

"No, but it seems she is still managing to control us, even after her death."

"At least Pastor Felix seemed fairly certain that hearing these letters would be helpful to us and Aaron."

"Well, I guess we better plan to go, then." Andy sounded hesitant. "I think I better try to check this pastor guy out via the internet and make sure he's legitimate."

By then, it was 9:30 PM but both of their children lived in Alberta and they were on Daylight Saving Time. For them, it was already 10:30. It was getting late but they decided to call Wendy first to see when she and Ian might be able to go to Calgary. They discussed dates and, after deciding they could cancel a few commitments, finally came up with two. Child-care would have to be arranged for Colby and Dylan. They would take Sam with them and leave her with Meredith's sister in Calgary. They could all free themselves up for next weekend, August tenth. If that didn't work, they could go on August seventeenth.

Next they called Aaron and Jessica. Jessica answered and they asked her to get Aaron on the line too for some important news. When Aaron answered he sounded tired. Meredith thought he may have been asleep already. She instantly felt bad because she knew how little sleep he was getting.

'What's up, Mom?" he asked groggily.

"Aaron, we received a call tonight from a Pastor Felix Johnson in Vancouver."

"Who the heck is he?"

As they started to reveal Pastor Felix's message, they could hear Aaron's breathing getting louder. He and Andy both tended to do that when their stress levels went up. Meredith stopped and asked if he was okay.

"No, Mom, I'm not okay. I feel like this woman is starting to control us from her grave now. Who the heck does she think she is?

Thinking that we will all just fall into place and gather for the reading of her damn letters. It makes me furious."

Jessica interrupted him. "Hon, I think we need to hear what she has to say. Maybe it will answer some important questions for us."

"Yeah, and maybe it will just create more questions.

Meredith could see that his frustrations were getting the best of him. She tried to reassure him. "Aaron, I know this can't be easy but I think we have to do it. We need to know what she has to say and maybe it will help. This Pastor Felix indicated that he thought it would be helpful."

"Yeah, I know, she's got us over a barrel again, Mom. Okay, when did you say you could all come down here?" He was wide awake now and thinking a bit more clearly.

They agreed that they would try for next weekend. Jessica would cancel out of a dinner date with some friends. Meredith said she would call the pastor right away and get back to them about whether or not he could come.

After Meredith confirmed the date with Pastor Felix, she called Wendy to let her know that it was all arranged. They decided they better book their flights right away.

They talked about the need for identification for Sam to fly. Andy answered that question. "It's not necessary for children under twelve to have identification for domestic flights. But Sam's different last name might create some questions. We better take our documentation regarding our permanent custody."

They all managed to book their seats on-line and get the same *West Jet* flight out of Grande Prairie. Thank goodness for small mercies.

After they had the arrangements made for their trip to Calgary and called Jessica and Aaron, Meredith looked at Andy. "We are going to have to tell Sam her mother is dead. How the heck can we do that? What is her understanding of death going to be? God, she's only just seven years old. And she's expecting her mother to get better and come and get her."

In reviewing the fall-out from this strange call, Andy and Meredith both knew they had to tell Sam and they had to tell her soon. Sam seemed to be so accepting of living with them but Meredith knew she had been extremely attached to her mother and she thought the situation was temporary. As they discussed the how and when of telling Sam, they decided to wait until after they had been to Calgary for the reading of the letters. Maybe the information in the letters would help. This would also give Meredith time to do some reading about young children and death, especially the death of a parent. Andy thought he might talk to one of his Rotarian friends who used to be an Anglican pastor and now had a private counseling service.

"Meredith, somehow I think this family saga is not going to end soon, is it?"

"I don't think so, dear."

"It's exhausting! I've got to go to bed. And you better come with me. It's late."

"Yep, I'm right behind you tonight."

Once again, sleep eluded her. Meredith decided to get up and take a Tylenol and soak her feet in some nice hot water and Epsom salts while she tried to iron out her thoughts on this latest development. She reasoned that if her head and her feet felt better, maybe her heart and gut would settle down too. She laid her head back and tried to relax each part of her body, one piece at a time. Within ten minutes she was feeling much less tense. She dried her feet, left the basin of water on the floor and her thoughts in the family room and returned to bed. She cuddled up to Andy's ever dependable warm back.

CHAPTER 20

Andy's Advice
Aug 8

"Hi Meredith, how's it going?"

"Good, Jessica, are you at work?" Meredith checked her watch, it was 8:40 AM. *Jessica almost never calls when she's at work like Wendy does. Wendy usually calls at least once a day just to talk and tell me what antics my crazy grandsons are up to. But not Jessica, when she's at work, it's all business.* Meredith's antennae went up, wondering what was wrong.

"Yeah, I need to talk to you about Aaron. You already know he's not doing well at all and I'm afraid it's getting worse. We did have a pretty good weekend at the mountains but he is so darn stubborn about not seeking counselling. He still thinks he should be able to deal with this himself. I don't know what to do anymore. He's absolutely tortured by his flashbacks, he's getting very little sleep, and not eating well. I thought last week that things were looking up a bit, but that pastor's call about the letters from Leanna has really pushed him over the edge.

"Oh dear, Jessica, is there any way we can help?"

"I wish I knew. His boss, Max, actually called me first thing this morning to ask what is going on with him. Obviously, his work is being affected. Max said he seems to be checking out mentally in meetings and he's starting to make excuses about what he hasn't done. He said this is just not like Aaron at all. Of all his staff, Aaron is the last person he ever checks up on regarding the progress of the project. Aaron is usually way ahead of him in thinking about what has to happen next."

"Oh dear, how did you respond to Max?"

"Well, the call caught me off guard. I stumbled and stammered out something indicating Aaron was dealing with some tough personal matters right now. I didn't elaborate but tried to assure Max that he was working it out. He wanted to know if there was anything he could do to help and wondered if Aaron needed some time off. I told him I would talk to Aaron tonight and ask him. But I think time off would be the wrong thing for him right now; it would just give him more time to ruminate about his problems. I've been thinking, do you think Andy would consider talking to Aaron about this? He has such high regard for his father. Maybe Andy could get through to him where all the rest of us haven't been able to."

"Oh boy, I know that it would be very hard for Andy to do. He is heartbroken and very angry over what Aaron is going through too. But, I think, when he knows the request has come from you, Jessica, he may rise to the challenge. As you know, Andy is one of those guys who always comes through when we need him. I'll ask him tonight. Will Aaron be home?"

"Oh yeah, he never goes anywhere anymore. I used to be annoyed at him for staying out so late on Wednesday night with the guys and now I just wish he would. Funny how your priorities change in tough times. Thanks, Meredith, I really appreciate everything you and Andy are doing for us."

"Jessica, for that you are very welcome, my dear."

****

They had just finished supper when Meredith decided to make Jessica's request known. Sam was in the family room watching one of her favourite television shows. "Andy," she said quietly to get his attention. "Jessica called this morning and...she's very worried about Aaron." As she described the call to Andy, she watched the red color rising in his neck and progressing to his cheeks, like a fire licking its way up the side of a wall.

He started to squirm in his chair. "God, Meredith, when will this thing ever end for Aaron? It's destroying him."

"Jessica wondered if you would talk to him about getting some counselling."

"Why would he listen to me when he has rejected the idea from his mother, his sister, and his wife?"

"Because, as Jessica said, he has such great respect for you, Andy. You know he calls you whenever he has any big decisions to make. He consults you on everything from business and financial decisions to home renovations. You are a very important mentor in his life."

"But what can I say about this awful situation that will help? What can I say that you haven't already said?"

"I don't know but I'll bet that, if you think about it for a while, you'll figure out something."

Andy got up and left the room, went upstairs to the bedroom, and closed the door. Meredith had only seen him do that a couple of times before when they were having a heated argument. So far, he had been keeping a very low profile in this messy affair; it was typical of Andy to shy away from the emotional family stuff and let Meredith deal with it. He was up there for quite a while, maybe forty-five minutes, and then she heard him on the phone. Her ears perked up as she wondered who he was calling. About ten minutes later, she heard the door open and he came downstairs and sat in his favourite chair. Meredith was cleaning up the dishes but her curious concern got the best of her. She went into the living room with a bowl and dish towel in her hand. Andy was staring into space, tears rolling down his face.

"Andy, what's the matter?"

"I just got off the phone with Aaron. I did my best Meredith. Both of us were crying when I was done."

"What did you say, dear?"

Through his tears and nose blowing, he told her what he had said. "I asked him if he was running a business and discovered he lacked the skills to do a certain part, what would he do? He said he would hire it out. I told him that would be the right decision because that is what all good businessmen do. They hire out the skills they need to move their business forward. Then I told him the situation was exactly the same in his personal life right now. He needed some skills that he didn't have to help him get through this rough time and he should hire them out."

"What was Aaron's reaction?"

"Surprisingly, he said, 'Maybe you're right Dad, I'm sure not doing a good job on this myself.' That's when he started to cry."

"Wow, that was a brilliant analogy, Andy, maybe one Aaron can readily relate to with his stubborn dominant right-sided brain. You just may have gotten through to him."

Andy smiled a bit. "Thanks for the vote of confidence but I don't know, only time will tell, I guess." He looked defeated.

Meredith put her bowl and towel down on the loveseat and went over and reached for his hands and pulled him out of the chair. They had a very tight hug and she whispered in his ear. "Andy, I know how hard that was for you. Thanks again for always being there when your family needs you." That made him cry more as he shuddered into her shoulder. She held him for a very long time until he was quiet and still. Then she suggested they go for a long walk. Andy agreed that some fresh air and exercise would be good for them and they needed some time alone. Sam was still watching television and would need a sitter.

"I'll call Sandra to see if she can come over and spend an hour with Sam," Meredith suggested. Sandra was the neighbour's fourteen-year old-daughter who had looked after Sam for short periods of an hour or two before.

The days were already getting noticeably shorter. It was 8:00 PM and the sun was starting its descent in their northern British Columbia community, a light pink color just beginning in the western sky. The evening air was warm and fresh from a recent shower. They walked briskly, hand in hand, along the walking trails beside the Dawson Creek. The damp scent from the natural flora of trees, shrubs, and clover rose up to greet them, clearing their brains of the day's heavy accumulation of cobwebs.

Meredith felt very hopeful that Andy's talk with his son would be a turning point for Aaron. She could hardly wait until the weekend when she could take Aaron in her arms and hug him tightly. It had been too long since they had seen their son. She looked up at Andy with a smile.

"What are you grinning about, dear?"

"I'm just very proud of you, Andy, you did good!"

They increased their pace and started swinging their arms higher, grinning hopefully at each other. Half an hour later, they were walking up their driveway feeling relieved and rejuvenated. It was time to get Sam ready for bed.

CHAPTER 21

———

Letters from Leanna
Aug 10

Ian, Wendy, Andy, Meredith, and Sam arrived about 5:00 PM at Meredith's sister's condo in Calgary to drop Sam off. Cora had agreed to keep Sam overnight and most of Saturday so that Andy and Meredith could visit with Aaron and Jessica and be available for the reading of Leanna's letters. She was one more person that they had taken into their confidence about what was happening. But she did not know about the circumstances around Sam's conception. All she knew was they were having a family meeting about Sam's precipitous arrival.

Sam and Cora hit it off right away. Cora had six grandchildren and was well practiced at interacting with young children. Meredith had explained to Sam on the flight to Calgary that they would leave her with her Great Aunt Cora as they had some adult business to attend to. As usual, Sam adjusted easily to a new situation and was thrilled to learn that she had a great aunt. This had stimulated a lengthy discussion of how people could be related to one another.

After a brief visit, they were on their way to Aaron's house. Jessica was expecting them for supper and Aaron had just arrived home from work. Meredith was overwhelmed with emotion when Aaron opened the door to greet them. He had lost at least ten pounds and looked very pale and tired. He had been skinny as a teenager but had filled out considerably in his twenties and Meredith was used to seeing a healthy, fit young man. Jessica had warned her but she was still shocked to see how his usual robust appearance had diminished. Meredith dropped her purse and gave him a long, tight hug, whispering in his ear how good it was to see him. Her tears welled up and she didn't want to let go for fear she would break down. Aaron loosened his grip and started to pat his mother's back, a sign that he was ready to be released. She had to let go and, without looking up at her son, went directly to Jessica to give her a long hug, trying desperately to regain her control. Meanwhile, Aaron greeted Andy with a quick father/son hug, Wendy with a big bear hug squeeze and Ian with a handshake.

When Aaron, Ian, and Andy went out to the car for the luggage, Wendy, being her effervescent self, broke the short, uncomfortable silence and said, "Thank goodness for the dreadful Leanna or who knows how long it would have taken for us all to get together."

"Yeah, just maybe she is good for something," Jessica replied hesitantly, doubting her own words.

They were all laughing somewhat hysterically when the men came in and wanted to know what was so funny.

Meredith responded, "You don't want to know but thank goodness, Wendy knows how to lighten us up."

At first the supper conversation was friendly but somewhat strained. This usually exuberant, loving family was more subdued than usual. But it was so good to all be together again. Eventually they loosened up. Maybe it was the wine, but they were back to normal, joking and laughing about past family experiences. Even Aaron lightened up. The visit confirmed for him that his family didn't see him as the bad guy he had been feeling he was. Instead of feeling alone and helpless, he started to feel like they really were all in this together. He was finally beginning to internalize his family's support.

Jessica was blossoming in her pregnancy and managed to appear happy, but Meredith could tell she was very worried about Aaron. Her heavy heart had not been relieved with wine like the other hearts in the room. Jessica was starting into her fourth month now and was just starting to show. She was very fit, having practiced yoga for several years. Prior to her pregnancy, she had taken a course for instructors on "Yoga in Pregnancy" and was continuing to teach and practice whenever her otherwise busy schedule as a Human Resources specialist allowed.

Over supper, she told them her plan. "I'm going to quit my job in one month, so I can teach more yoga. My goal is to open my own yoga studio."

Andy initiated a toast, "To new beginnings, a new baby, and a new career." They all joined in to give her their best wishes.

While Wendy and Meredith were helping Jessica clean up after supper, Jessica said, "Guess what, after Andy called last week, Aaron finally relented and agreed to go to counseling."

"Halleluiah," Meredith responded, while giving Jessica a quick hug. "We're on the right track now."

"Yes, I made him an appointment the next day but he doesn't start until Wednesday."

Wendy smiled. "Well, wonders never cease. My brother finally saw the light." They all chuckled.

Everyone had done far too much speculating about what the letters could possibly contain but they didn't talk about them. They stayed carefully away from that topic. It was going to be good to get this behind them so they could move forward with their lives. The unknown was driving them all crazy.

****

Breakfast was over and the girls were just finishing the clean-up of the dishes when Pastor Felix Johnson arrived. Following formal introductions, they gave the lead to the pastor.

Pastor Felix spoke with obvious concern and compassion. "As you all know, I visited Leanna in the palliative care unit several times before she died. After she told me about her transgressions toward you, Aaron, she remained very distraught and it was I who suggested to her that she write letters to all of you. I thought it would be therapeutic for her to put her motivations, her actions, and her feelings down on paper. I never suspected she would want the letters to be delivered."

"I am sure all of you are aware that as a pastor I must hold what people tell me in the utmost confidence. She desperately did not want me to contact you until after she passed. This was very difficult for me because I knew there was a family out there that was suffering from complete lack of information. I was not expecting Leanna to make this most unusual request of me to deliver her letters in person and read them to you. When she asked me to do this, my initial reaction was anger. I thought it was her way of continuing to manipulate you and I wanted no part of it. I would not have followed through with this request if I had thought the letters would do any harm. But after reading them, I agreed with Leanna that it would be good for all of you to be together to hear them and to support each other."

He continued. "Leanna was part of the human condition that results from lack of love. Although her parents did not die until she was in her early twenties, from what she told me, it was obvious that neither of them had any time for their only child. She was shipped off to a private school at the age of eight, and even in the summer months, she was cared for much of the time by a live-in housekeeper. Having grown up without the loving support of her parents, she vowed that when she had her own child, she would be a loving and committed mother. In Leanna's adult life, this lack of love continued in several failed relationships. I'm telling you this only to help you gain insight into her actions, to begin to understand her motives. Just like you and I, she was trying to make her way in a sometimes very unkind world. When human emotions are pushed to the brink, people often make bad decisions."

Felix paused and took an extra deep breath. Aaron squirmed in his chair. "Altogether, there are four letters, a short introductory one for all of you, one for Meredith and Andy, one for Aaron and Jessica, and one for Wendy and Ian. I will read them to you in that order. Please stop me anytime with questions and I will answer them as best I can." He waited for a few seconds, scanning his audience, then he began to read....

Letter to the Whole Family

As I pass my last days in the palliative care unit, I have had many hours to contemplate my actions and my hopes for Sam's future. I am compelled to write the following letters. I humbly ask that all of you; Aaron, Jessica, Andy, Meredith, Wendy, and Ian, be together for the reading of them and I thank you for honoring this request. One positive thought that I have about my demise is that, if I had lived to parent Sam into

her adult years, she may never have known the won-
derful family that she has inherited from her father.
This is what my premature death will give her. For
that, it will be a worthwhile event.

Pastor Felix put the first letter down and looked up. Everyone was quiet and solemn. No one had questions so he continued.

Letter to Andy and Meredith

I have put the future of my cherished child in your
family's hands and entrusted her care to you. I was
confident you would do the right thing and take her
in. I thought that, by leaving her with you, you would
be a buffer for the shock that Aaron would experience.
I have asked Pastor Felix to tell you my story through
these letters. I humbly ask your forgiveness for what
I have done and all the pain I have caused you. The
one thing I can feel good about now, in the last days of
my life, is that I know I am giving you an incredibly
wonderful child to care for and love—my gift to you.
This is the one thing I know for certain.

Aaron interrupted. He couldn't help himself. "Gift, how dare she call this a gift? Dying woman or not, what she did was no gift. I have been through hell, my whole family has been through hell."

Jessica squeezed his hand tighter and whispered something in his ear. By this time, his face was very red and tears filled his eyes. Jessica jumped up for the tissues on the counter. Meredith desperately wanted to go over and hug him but she knew it was better to leave him in Jessica's hands.

Pastor Felix spoke. "Aaron, I can only begin to imagine what this has been like for you. And I recognize that what Leanna is saying is very hard to swallow. But, as you hear the rest of the letters, I think you will begin to see and understand Leanna's position more clearly, not to condone her actions, but to understand them better."

Aaron wiped his eyes, gave a huge sigh and said, "Go ahead then, let's get this over with."

Why did I do what I did? I was thirty-five and I had already experienced two rather lengthy relationships, both of which ended badly. I had no prospects for a new relationship and my biological clock was ticking down. I had no family and was desperate to have a child. As I write this, my thoughts and actions seem trite, simplistic, selfish, but, at the time, it became all-consuming for me. I was an only child and my parents were killed in a car crash when I was twenty-two.

You are probably asking yourselves why I didn't go to a sperm bank, but I had what I thought was an extremely valid reason not to. Sperm banks have a family medical history, a complete description of physical attributes, and some identifiers of intelligence on every donor. What they don't have is what I considered to be the very most important information of all—an accurate description of human character. Above all, I wanted my child to be a good person, a person with a warm and easy-going personality, a loving and caring attitude toward other people.

I had someone else in mind but when Aaron first started coming to Student Health Services, I noticed him right away, his politeness, his sincerity, his laugh.

There seemed to be an innocent charm surrounding him and he changed my mind very quickly.

I chose your son's genes for my child for many reasons; yes, his physical attributes were very appealing and I definitely knew he was intelligent (I had access to his student performance records). But most importantly, I made an effort to get to know him and discovered he had very high levels of integrity and humility and was unbelievably honest. He was the most kind-hearted and genuine person I had ever known but far too young to pursue as a partner. I wished over and over again that he was older or I was younger.

Aaron interrupted again. "Am I supposed to feel good about this? God, Jess, who does she think she's kidding?"

Pastor Felix paused and waited to see if Aaron was done. Aaron waved his hand in the pastor's direction and told him to go ahead.

I also checked you out; Aaron's parents, his sister, his brother-in-law, and received a very positive impression of Aaron's immediate family. I know what I did was very wrong, maybe even unforgiveable, but, at the time, it seemed an insignificant indiscretion to get the set of genes I was looking for to contribute to my child's hereditary makeup.

Aaron just couldn't hold back his feelings. This was bringing all of his emotions that he had tried so hard to push back to a raw surface. "My God, I can't believe this woman. Who would do a thing like this? I still think she had to be deranged." Jessica gave him a handful of tissues and hugged him gently. Through his emotions, Aaron was unable to comprehend the compliments he was receiving or fairly evaluate Leanna's position. Pastor Felix waited momentarily for Aaron to compose himself somewhat and began again.

> *I know I have caused pain for all of you, especially for Aaron. If I had ever thought that my demise would come so early in life and I wouldn't be able to look after my child, I may have made a different choice. My only requiem is the beauty of Sam. I hope you can see it this way and I trust that you will continue to care for her and love her as I have. Coward that I am, I could not face you in person with this request.*

Aaron blurted, "Damn good thing she didn't. I probably would have strangled her... I'm sorry, Pastor, my feelings... I have never before in my life had such little control over them... They just bubble to the surface all the time."

"It's okay Aaron, I think we all recognize the potency of these letters for you, for your whole family... and it's good for you to let your feelings, as you say, bubble to the surface. You can deal with them better when they aren't being suppressed. And your family needs to know exactly how you are feeling. This is a good thing, Aaron, let it out as you feel you need to." Pastor Felix waited again for Aaron's direction. Aaron said nothing more so he proceeded.

> *I needed to die in peace and I didn't want Sam to see me dying. I wanted her to remember me with fondness when I still had some degree of vibrancy for life.*
>
> *My worst fear was that Sam would end up in the Child Welfare System. I had to find a place for her in your family. It was the only good future I could*

*envision for her. Thank you for all that I know you
have already done for Sam and thank you in advance
for all that I know you will continue to do for her.
Your response has allowed me to die knowing that
Sam will be loved and cared for.*

Pastor Felix asked, "Do you have any questions about this letter?"

Meredith looked at Aaron. He was squirming in the love seat beside Jessica. They were holding hands and he let go and rubbed his face in frustration. "Well, I'd say this Leanna person, or whoever she really was, is making some pretty big assumptions about our generosity and the acceptance of her daughter." His voice was unstable but he got his words out between short emotional gasps.

Jessica grabbed his hand back and held it tight, "Aaron, I think we should hear the rest of the letters before we draw any conclusions."

"Whatever, go ahead, Pastor."

Andy interrupted with a question. "How the heck did she check us out so thoroughly and how did she know that we took Sam in and cared for her?"

"That's a good question that I don't have a good answer for, Mr. Taylor. When I asked her how she knew exactly how Sam was doing, because she did know precisely how things were going, she said with a wry grin that she had her ways and means. She did seem to have plenty of financial resources and my guess is she was paying someone who had close access to you for the information. I'm sorry I can't give you a better answer than that."

"It certainly leaves us with an eerie feeling that we are completely transparent and being watched constantly," Meredith responded.

"I can well imagine it's an uncomfortable feeling." Felix waited but there were no further comments.

Letter to Aaron and Jessica

Without a doubt, this is the most difficult letter I have ever written. I never meant for my actions to have such a profound effect on you and your family. Aaron, I simply ask your forgiveness for my deceitful actions toward you. Because of who you are, I know I have caused you great pain. Because of who you are, you may somehow feel responsible for all of this. Believe me, you are not responsible for any little bit of it. I secured your trust and then I broke it. My belief at the time was far too simplistic and I had not thought it though. I knew the drugs I put in your coffee and the two drinks at my apartment would affect your memory and I believed you would soon forget the whole thing and that would be it for you. If I could have imagined it would end like this, maybe my choices would have been different.

This time Meredith interrupted. "I knew it, Aaron, she did spike your coffee. You didn't have a chance, dear!"

"Okay, Mom, at least we know that for sure."

"Yes, and there is something else we know for sure. Leanna recognized her mistakes and she truly loved her daughter, wanted the best for her. She went to great lengths to make it happen, even on her deathbed. She wasn't totally bad."

Aaron relented. "Yeah, I guess that's true."

Felix waited and then continued.

Jessica, I have checked you out too and have found you to be an honorable, hard-working woman with high-level values and a kind-hearted and loving wife.

217

No wonder you and Aaron found each other in this often cold and cruel world. Both of you have made a good life together. I ask your forgiveness too, for throwing this situation headlong into your life.

Aaron and Jessica, you and your family were my only hope for a good life for Sam. I am so sorry for what I have done to you, but know this, I am not at all sorry for bringing Sam into this world. I am certain she will make it a better place. As I have watched her grow and learn, from the very first, I could see that she was pure of heart, full of love for life and love for others. I have no doubt, if you give her a chance, she will win your hearts. She is so much like you, Aaron, not at all like me. Almost every day, as Sam grew, I would notice something that reminded me of you.

I never once doubted my decision until I became ill the second time with cancer and discovered it had returned with a vengeance. The day of my diagnosis, my thoughts were only with Sam. As I reviewed the possibilities for her, it didn't take me long to decide that she needed to be with her father and I had to find a way to make that happen. Yes, I had to be deceitful again to make it happen but I believed in my heart that it was the only solution. This is how I have come to a peaceful place to die, knowing Sam will be loved and cared for and guided carefully into adulthood.

All I have left to contribute now is a trust fund for Sam so that, at least, she will not be a financial burden for you and your family. When you are ready, you can call my lawyer for the details of this fund. Pastor Felix will give you my lawyer's card.

Felix waited again but none of them had questions. This was a lot of information to take in. He surveyed the room and thought they all looked completely subdued so he started to read again.

Critical Information about Sam

> *There is some information about Sam that you will want to know. She has had all her childhood immunizations and has never been sick beyond the normal childhood colds that all children get. Her birth record is at Kelowna General Hospital and Pastor Felix will give you her birth certificate. For my side of Sam's family history, it will be important for you to know that it was breast cancer that I died from, a tubular ductal type believed to be non-hereditary. Other than that, I have had a very healthy medical history and there is no familial disease in my family that I am aware of including no history of breast cancer. I am enclosing one picture of Sam and I from one year ago when I still looked well. I think, at some time, she will want it. You can give it to her when you are ready and you think she is ready.*

Felix handed the picture to Aaron and Jessica along with the birth certificate and a card for Leanna's lawyer. Aarons's face became contorted. "Yeah, that's her alright." He looked at Jessica, "How are you doing with all this, Jess?"

She smiled at him. "I'm okay, Aaron. Go ahead, Pastor."

<u>What I would like Sam to Know</u>

Sam will be asking questions. Please tell her I desperately did not want to leave her and I tried my best to stay but my cancer took me away from her. Tell her I will love her forever.

I recognize that Sam needs to know the truth of her conception at some point. I have left a letter for her with my lawyer and I have asked for it to be delivered to you to share with her when she is eighteen. The letter will reveal the truth to her about what I have done and why I did it. Until then, please spare her the details. I hope when she is eighteen, she will be old enough to understand and deal with it. I know she will need your love and support to see her through the revelation of my transgressions against her father.

Felix paused again, indicating the last letter was to Wendy and Ian. "Shall I continue?" His eyes circled the room and settled on Aaron again.

"Yeah, go ahead, let's hear the rest." He was more composed now as he looked at Jessica. His concern seemed to have switched from himself to her.

Letter to Wendy and Ian

Wendy, you, Ian, and your sons are now part of Sam's family too. I know much less about you than I do about Aaron and Jessica, Meredith and Andy. But I do know that you have twin boys aged three. I also know, Wendy, that you and Aaron are close friends,

*such a wonderful thing to have between a brother
and a sister.*

Now it was Wendy's turn to break down. She started to shake
and sob. Jessica handed her the tissue box. She wiped her tears and
blew her nose. Ian was holding onto her arm in support, looking
at her with his usual love and compassion. When she was settled,
Felix continued.

> *I know that, because of who you are, you will
> support your brother, Jessica and your parents through
> all of what I have caused them. I know, Ian, that you
> are an extremely supportive husband and a dedicated
> father. Aaron, especially, will need your support,
> understanding and counsel. Thank you to both of you
> for who you are, solid, decent, and thoughtful people,
> just like the rest of your family. Please forgive me for
> the impact of what I have done to all of you.*

Felix looked up and his eyes paused on Wendy, then swept over all
of them. His concern was evident.

"Is that it?" Aaron asked, tears in his eyes.

"Yes," Felix answered and his eyes went to Aaron. He looked pale,
shell-shocked, but seemingly more in control. Jessica hugged him
again from their sitting position. Then they stood and hugged for
what seemed a long time, saying nothing.

****

When their hug broke, they turned to Felix and Aaron spoke with tears in his eyes. "Pastor, are we supposed to forgive her because she has died? I don't think I can."

"No, not because she has died, but maybe because she was human and she made a critical human error." He paused and added, "Aaron, can I speak to you in private?"

"Sure, I guess so."

They retreated upstairs to Aaron's office.

"Aaron, you have been through a horrendous experience. Your mother told me that you had put the whole incident out of your mind for years. Now you have been forced to relive it. I can see the pain in your eyes and can only begin to imagine what you could be feeling. Have you received any counseling yet?"

"No, not yet, but I finally relented and Jessica has made an appointment for me, it's coming up on Wednesday."

"That's good, I can only advise you on the importance of counseling when you are going through something like this. Please don't let your pride get in the way of seeking help. My guess is, you will need it for some time. Please take it. It will help to get your head around all the many pitfalls of such an invasive event."

"I think you're right, Pastor, I do need help. My dad has convinced me of that." His tears erupted again and he grabbed the tissue box on his desk.

Felix waited for him to gain some composure. "Have you met and spent some time with Sam yet?"

"God, no, I'm far too angry for that. I have to deal with this overwhelming anger first…" He choked and hesitated… "I know I should only be angry at Leanna, but when I think of Sam, that makes me angry too. Thank God for my parents. They have taken Sam on so willingly… I don't think you are aware that Jess and I are expecting our first child in January."

Meredith had told Felix that but he didn't let on. "Oh dear, as wonderful as that is, I imagine it adds to the complexity of your emotions."

"Yes, Jess has been super and every time I look at her, I know she needs me and I'm not there for her like I should be. It breaks my heart." His tears welled up again but he managed to hold back the sobs. "God, I hate all this emotion. I'm so not used to it."

"Aaron, all I can say is, take the counseling, for yourself, for Jessica, for Sam, for the rest of your family. For now, concentrate on getting well yourself. As your own emotions begin to settle down… and they will… you will be able to be available again for Jessica and your family."

****

The rest of the family was very quiet for a few seconds after Aaron and Pastor Felix left. Meredith looked at Wendy, who finally broke the silence, "Wow, that was pretty intense. She was certainly a prolific writer."

Meredith knew Wendy was trying to make light of the situation. "Yes," she responded, "a dying woman's last plea. But you know, I don't think she is asking anything of us that we aren't already prepared to do…except for Aaron, and he will get through this, he just needs time. I'm so relieved that he has finally accepted the idea of counseling."

"You know what's amazing to me, Mom?" Wendy said.

"What, dear?"

"Before these letters, I was seeing Leanna as this horrible, criminal person for what she did to Aaron. But now, I'm seeing her as a normal woman with strong maternal desires, a woman who did what she had to do to have a child. I know how much Ian and I wanted a child when we were having trouble getting pregnant. Those desires and the emotions around them are very potent. I can see how, in her situation, she could be driven to do what she did. That doesn't mean it was alright, I just mean I can see how it could happen to an otherwise sane person, to be driven to drastic measures to get what you need."

Meredith looked at Jessica, who was nodding in agreement, so she dared to respond. "Yes, Wendy, it does bring a new and softer perspective to this person we once thought of as just plain wicked. Three things came to me through these letters. Leanna was a very loving and devoted parent right to the end. She has recognized the error of her ways and she has asked us for forgiveness. Now we just have to hope that Aaron will begin to see through all the fog of his emotions and start coming to the same conclusions."

"Yes, and she was right about at least two things," Wendy replied. "Aaron's personality and Sam's positivity."

****

Aaron and Pastor Felix returned to the living room. Aaron looked somewhat relieved.

"Well, folks, I have a plane to catch. "I must say, it has been an honor to finally meet all of you, the family I have heard so much about. I want you to know that you can call me anytime if you have any questions that you think I may be able to answer."

Meredith had two immediate burning questions. "Pastor, we believe Leanna was not using her real name. Did you know her by any other name and what was her last name?"

Felix hesitated. Then he remembered. "I believe her last name was Schafer, it should be on the birth certificate. I only knew her as Leanna." He looked curious.

"We wondered because there was no record of a Leanna having worked at the College Student Health Services. She must have given Aaron a different name than the one she used for her job."

"There is no doubt that she knew the art of deception well," Felix replied. "Even as she disclosed her story to me, I was aware that she carefully told me only what she wanted me to know."

"Did she ever say anything about Sam's Auntie Colleen? We think she was a close friend of Leanna's."

"No, I'm afraid she never mentioned a friend at all. I found it strange that she never mentioned any friends or any other visitors.

She did say she had no other family and I have no idea who looked after her remains. When I asked her if she wanted me to be part of her funeral, she said that would not be necessary. For as much as she did tell me, much still remains a mystery."

"Okay, thanks anyway."

****

As Pastor Felix closed the door behind him, he breathed a huge sigh of relief. His job was done. On the way to his rental car, he looked up at the sky and gave thanks to God, who seemed to be guiding this process after all. He got in the car and took a few minutes to pray for the Taylor family. *Please give them the strength and endurance they need to see their way through this and come to a place of comfort with Sam in their midst. And please give Aaron the guidance he needs to recover and take his place as Sam's father. They're in your hands now, I've done what I can.*

****

Meredith called her sister's cell to see how she and Sam were doing. They were getting along fabulously and were at the Calgary Zoo. Cora indicated that Sam's cast certainly didn't slow her down. Meredith told her it should be coming off the following week, depending on the x-ray result.

She returned to the group and said, "All is well with Cora and Sam. I think the rest of us should go out for an early lunch. Since we're all flying home at 5:00 PM, this is our last chance to have some family time and do we ever need it."

Everyone readily agreed. They had been looking at Sam's birth certificate and handed it to Meredith. She read, "Samantha Aries Schaefer. Hmm, interesting, Aries for Aaron, maybe. Aaron was born under the Aries sign."

"That's exactly what I was thinking, Mom," Wendy added.

Before they left, Meredith assured Aaron and Jessica that they were prepared to keep Sam. "Please feel no pressure to take her into your family yet. You and Jessica need to concentrate on each other and your pregnancy. And Aaron, you need time to work through your feelings."

"Don't worry, Aaron, Ian and I will help out and make sure that Mom and Dad get some time to themselves too," Wendy added. "Sam is great around the boys and they love it when she visits. She even reads to them and they are fascinated by her enthusiasm and energy."

"I'm so sorry, I just can't get my head around all this stuff yet. I feel so darn angry and sometimes feel like I'm barely holding together." The tears welled up in his eyes again. He turned to Jessica. "Poor Jess, I'm not much help or support to you right now."

She gave him an encouraging smile and they hugged again. "Aaron, you are doing just fine considering… We will get through this. All of this new information is just another hurdle to get over. You have to give yourself time."

"Well said, Jessica." Meredith thought how lucky they were to have such an incredible daughter-in-law.

"That's what everyone says, including the pastor. But it's already been almost four months and I don't seem to be making progress. I'm just as angry as ever. How dare she say she's giving us a gift?"

"Aaron, you have every right to be angry. But your anger eats away at you unless you deal with it. That's why you need the counseling."

"Yeah, I think you're right there, Mom."

"And one more thing to think about, sometimes gifts come in strange packages with mixed blessings." Meredith didn't give Aaron time for a response. She just wanted to give him something to think about. "Now, let's try to forget all of this morning's revelations for a while and go out for lunch. Let's find some good things to talk about, maybe even laugh at. We need some positive family time before we have to leave," she directed assertively. She and Andy had to be back at Cora's to pick Sam up by 3:00 PM so they could get to the airport by 4:00 PM. Cora lived across the city from Aaron and Jessica but only ten minutes from the airport.

They had a great visit over lunch. For a short time, their family was back to normal, talking and laughing easily. Meredith loved to listen to Andy, Aaron and Ian banter back and forth about vehicles, computers, the oil business, architecture, politics. And listening to Wendy and Jessica talk about pregnancy, having children, and shopping, was soothing to her aching heart. They were so like sisters as they chatted easily. Jessica was an only child and she had told Meredith how delighted she was to inherit a sister like Wendy.

They tried not to talk about the letters, but one thing they did touch on was Leanna's lawyer and the trust fund for Sam. They decided not to worry about that for a while. They could deal with it later although all of them were curious about how much would be in this fund. They talked about how Leanna had learned so much about them and how she had so purposely chosen Aaron and his family for Sam's inherited traits. Meredith said, "You know, it really is a tremendous tribute to Aaron and a compliment to our whole family."

"Yeah, well, Mom, I'd rather receive my compliments in a different way."

"No doubt, dear, but nevertheless, it is a wonderful tribute to you." Aaron smiled faint-heartedly. Meredith thought he would be able see that more clearly once he started working through his anger.

They lingered as long as they could. None of them were ready to call an end to this family gathering. They all knew it might be some time before they could be together again. At 2:15, Andy told Meredith they better get going. Ian and Wendy could stay for a while yet because Jessica and Aaron would take them directly to the airport. It would be good for the four of them to have some time by themselves to just be the kids. Everyone got up and did the family hug thing, not caring what anyone in the restaurant thought. They were oblivious to the crowd. It was unbelievably difficult but Meredith and Andy finally pried themselves away.

When they got to Cora's, she and Sam had just returned from the zoo. Sam was so excited, she could hardly contain herself. "Gramma, you should have been there, the rhinos, they were the best, there was even a baby rhino, he was so cute. Grampa, there was this thing that looked like a little dinosaur, you would have loved him...what was he called, Auntie Cora? Sam had long since dropped the "T" from Gramma and Grampa.

"That was an iguana, Sam."

"Oh, yes, an iguana. Grampa, have you ever seen an iguana?" She didn't wait for an answer. Sam continued with her enthusiastic descriptions and they listened for a short while, not wanting to dampen her spirits. Andy finally interrupted, "We better get going. We'll have to hear the rest of Sam's zoo stories on the plane home."

Meredith thanked Cora profusely.

"It was my pleasure, Sam was so enthralled with everything and it was an absolute delight to spend the day with her." At sixty-eight, Cora was six years older than Meredith but she was vibrant and healthy and always up for it. Meredith hated to leave her so quickly.

She gave her a big hug and promised to call her when they got home. Andy and Sam gave Cora a hug too and they were on their way.

Once they cleared security, they met up with Wendy and Ian and they managed to find a place to all sit together until they boarded the plane. Sam kept all of them entertained by her exuberant tales of the zoo.

On the flight home, Sam fell asleep quickly. It had been a seasonally warm August day, and she and Aunt Cora had walked the whole zoo and seen all the sights. She was exhausted from all the sun and exercise. The plane was not full and Andy and Meredith were able to move to the seats across the aisle from Sam, giving her more room to lie down and them more freedom to talk about all of the day's revelations. They speculated as to whether or not Leanna had paid Pastor Felix to come to Calgary and read her letters, and if so, they wondered how much he may have received. They contemplated how to tell Sam that her mother had died. At seven, her understanding of death would be, at best, very simplistic. After Pastor Felix's phone call, Meredith had borrowed a book about children and death from the South Peace Palliative Care Society and had read most of it. But she still felt unsure of herself, maybe because of all the extenuating circumstances around Leanna.

Wendy came from farther back in the plane and sat beside them for a while, leaving Ian to have a snooze. Their conversation made the flight go quickly and before they knew it, they were landing in Grande Prairie. After quick hugs and goodbyes to Ian and Wendy, they were on the road to Dawson Creek.

CHAPTER 22

────

Aaron Starts Counseling
August 15

Aaron was sitting in a comfortable arm-chair when the psychologist walked in. He noticed the man's warm smile and relaxed just a bit. The doctor walked toward him and put out his hand. "Hello, I'm Doctor Jeffrey and you must be Aaron."

Aaron jumped up to shake his hand. "Yes, hello Dr. Jeffrey."

They both took their seats. "Have you ever had counseling before, Aaron?"

"No, never," Aaron replied definitively.

"Well then, my guess is you're a bit anxious."

"Yes, you could say that," Aaron responded, squirming uncomfortably in his chair.

At fifty-eight years of age, Aaron's counselor was well-experienced. He was about 5'11, close to Aaron's height. His closely cropped hair was a curly medium brown and just starting to grey at the temples. His face was round and he had a kind fatherly look. When he smiled, his laugh lines deepened accentuating his cheek bones and enriching his warm and inviting appearance. He was dressed casually in a light-grey sweater and navy slacks.

"I think you will begin to find it much easier by the end of this session. Aaron, please tell me why you're here."

Aaron laughed uneasily. "Well Doc, my wife, my mother, and my sister have all been telling me I need counseling. But it was my dad that finally made me realize they were probably right. So here I am."

"I'm very glad to hear you have so much family support. Your family will be a great help to you. Please tell me your story from the beginning. What has happened to you?"

Aaron shifted uncomfortably again, hesitated, then started talking about how he met Leanna. As he talked and Dr. Jeffrey responded, listening with interest, it did get easier and his story spilled out. When Aaron was done, he was wiped and it was obvious.

Dr. Jeffrey thought he had seen or heard about every possible human dilemma. During his thirty-three years of experience, he had counseled only two male date rape victims but never one resulting in a child. The first thing he did was validate for Aaron that he had been through a dreadful experience and his reactions were not unexpected. "I've heard you say that you feel anger, guilt, humiliation, and helplessness, Aaron. I want you to know that all these feelings are an expected reaction to such a personal invasion of your body and your life. Given the circumstances, these reactions, including the dreams and flashbacks you are having are completely normal and expected."

"Normal and expected. I thought I was going crazy."

"Far from it, Aaron. You are very sane, just having trouble dealing with a horrendous experience. I expect you have heard of post-traumatic stress disorder or PTSD. This is what you have and it's very treatable; usually within six to eight weeks it can be fully resolved. But you should start feeling better immediately." Dr. Jeffrey could see an instant change come over Aaron's face. The relief he felt made his tense expression loosen. The fear in his eyes melted away and his shoulders relaxed. He shifted in his chair, assuming a more comfortable position.

"The first thing I want to do is find out a bit more about you; who you are and what you do when you're feeling good." As Aaron described his likes and dislikes, his work and his hobbies, Dr. Jeffrey was purposely establishing a connection with Aaron, finding out what made him tick. Aaron surprised himself as he relaxed and chatted easily. He told Dr. Jeffrey about his daily life, his marriage, Jessica, the pregnancy, his job.

Dr. Jeffrey was soon able to see that Aaron was normally a fun-loving young man in a happy unrestrained marriage where he and Jessica respected each other's freedom and spent reasonable amounts of time doing their own activities while always making time for each other. It was therapeutic for Aaron to remember how he had felt before Sam had arrived and turned his world upside down.

Although Jessica was very understanding of him spending time with his "old buddies," his former bachelor life was slowly being left behind. He was caught up in this new life of interdependency and the beginnings of family responsibility. He was just starting to develop the capacity to love deeply and unconditionally, just beginning to learn the responsibilities of married life, commitment, and family.

"Aaron, from what you have told me, it is no wonder that you are having trouble coping. In addition to the huge change in your life with marriage and all the responsibilities that go with that, you have suddenly been confronted with a huge emotional trauma, one that you had successfully pressed into your subconscious for over seven years."

"Yeah, it certainly has turned out to be a bit too much."

"Let me tell you about men versus women, Aaron. I'm sure you've figured out by now that they think and behave differently."

"Oh yes, I've certainly noticed that!"

"When men find themselves in tough, traumatizing situations, they can become emotionally flooded because they don't have the words or the ability to express themselves like women do. Since they don't have the skills to deal with all the emotion, the trauma can become generalized and reliving the event can be triggered by simple, everyday things like smell or loud noises. This causes the emotional flooding again and it becomes a vicious circle. This is when PTSD really settles in. Does this make sense to you?"

"Oh yeah, that sounds like what's been happening to me, all right. I sure haven't been able to talk about it with anyone."

"There's something else you need to consider, Aaron. Men usually try to face their troubles alone, not only because they can't talk about it but also because they think they need to be tough."

Dr. Jeffrey paused. Aaron squirmed in his chair but said nothing.

"But it's okay to be vulnerable, and it's okay to share your burden. In fact, your family, especially your wife, is probably desperately wanting to find a way to help you."

"I think you may be right there, Doc."

"I'd like to make a treatment plan with your input. Would you be able to come to counseling once or twice a week for the next six sessions?"

"Once a week, I think I could manage, but twice, that might get a bit tricky."

"Okay, let's plan for once a week for the next six weeks and then we'll re-evaluate. Do you think Jessica would come to a counseling session with you?"

"Oh yes, I think she would jump at the chance." He laughed a little. "She has been trying to get me to come for several weeks now, but I was too stubborn and embarrassed."

Dr. Jeffery smiled. "Well then, I think it would be good if she could come with you next time, and we will involve her in the plan right from the beginning. I think she could be a great help to you, Aaron."

Dr. Jeffrey explained that he would use a technique called "brief intervention counseling" along with some hypnosis to treat Aaron. "These methods of treatment will give both of us insight into what's been happening to you. Then I will give you some solid strategies on how to deal with it. After six weeks, we will re-evaluate and likely put you on a maintenance program for a while to make sure there are no relapses. How does that sound?"

"That's great, Doc. I was afraid I was such a mess it would take much longer than that to straighten me out." He let out a huge sigh.

"Aaron, there is one thing that I would like you to start doing right now. I want you to start telling Jessica exactly how you are feeling. Don't shut her out like you have been doing. I suspect that you have been trying to spare her your feelings."

"Oh god, yes, I figured she didn't need to be burdened with my crazy thoughts."

"Believe me, that is not what she wants. She wants desperately for you to talk to her. Talk to her, ask her to hold you, seek her out for hugs when you start to feel overwhelmed. The human touch is an amazing healer. It will help both of you tremendously."

"Okay, Doc, I'll try. But…this is not me."

"Like I said earlier, start small, Aaron, and little by little, it will get easier. The first thing you need to do when you get home is tell her about this session and what I have asked you to do. Once you know that she knows what to expect, it will already be easier to do it. I look forward to seeing you next week. It has been a pleasure to start getting to know you, Aaron." He stood and offered his hand.

Aaron readily jumped up and shook it. "Thanks, Doc, for giving me some hope. Amazingly, you seem to have lifted a big load off my shoulders already. I didn't think it would be this easy but just knowing you think I'm normal is a huge relief."

"That's good, that's what is supposed to happen. I'll see you and Jessica next Wednesday."

While Aaron was driving home, he sheepishly thought how incredibly easy this had been. He remembered Jess and his mom trying to convince him that he had PTSD but he didn't want to believe them. It sounded too ominous. His knowledge of PTSD was from the movies where someone coming back from horrific war experiences relived the ghastly events they had witnessed over and over again until it drove them crazy. He thought what happened to him simply didn't warrant such a reaction and he felt terribly inadequate with his lack of ability to deal with it on his own.

Normal and expected, Dr. Jeffrey said. Mom and Jess said that too but I didn't believe what was happening to me could possibly be normal. Maybe it's about time I started paying more attention to the women in my life. Maybe they do know what they're talking about. This thought made him smile and, again, he was amazed at how much better he felt already. He vowed to go home and tell Jess everything he could remember.

When Aaron's dreams woke him that night and he found himself in the usual cold sweat, instead of getting up and going to the family room, he tapped Jessica on her back. "Hold me, Jess, please hold me."

Jessica responded immediately, rolling over to face him and embracing him with her warmth. She wrapped her leg over his and squeezed gently. "I'm here baby. Tell me what's happening."

Aaron loosened up, relaxed into her, and snuggled like a child after a bad dream. He told her he had been dreaming about waking up after the rape and feeling desperately and completely confused, unable to move. "Jess, I couldn't move and my brain was so foggy I couldn't think either. I laid there naked, under this thick blanket of fog, gasping for breath. It felt like I was dying."

She murmured in his ear, "You're here with me now, Aaron, you're safe and I love you." She rubbed his back gently and her soft touch instantaneously started to relax him. In the morning, he woke up still lying in her arms. He didn't remember much more and he couldn't believe he had fallen back to sleep so soon. He reluctantly slipped away and went to the shower.

Aaron's day didn't go quite as well as his night had, despite the fact that it had been his first decent sleep in months. He was sitting at his desk staring into space when Mark, one of his team members, came in to ask a question. "Hi Aaron, we've got serious network problems and I can't find the source. Can you help me?"

Aaron could hear Mark in the distance but his thoughts were far more pervasive than Mark's voice. "Aaron, are you alright?" Mark asked, a bit louder. Aaron jolted and turned in Mark's direction, looking confused. "Hey, man, are you okay?"

Aaron finally responded. "Yeah, yeah, I'm okay, I was just in deep thought." He could feel the familiar cold sweat returning and embarrassment coloring his face. "What was it you wanted?"

Mark asked his question again. "Oh, okay, yeah, I'll be right there." Aaron traced a rogue device to a port coming from a remote area within one of the plant sites and disabled it. He explained to Mark that it probably originated from one of the contractor's laptops that was being used in a trailer at that site.

When he got back to his office, he felt so cold and alone but he remembered Dr. Jeffrey's advice and he shakily picked up the phone and dialed Jessica. "Jess, are you busy?"

"Never too busy for you, my luv, what's up?" She could hear the familiar fear in his voice.

"Can you take a long lunch and meet me at Tomatoes?"

"Sure, it's already 11:30, I'll leave now and meet you there in about a half hour."

"God, I love you, Jess…, see you there."

When Aaron saw Jessica waiting expectantly in a quiet corner booth, she gave him a warm smile and her usual friendly wave. *God, how lucky can I get, having a wife like Jess.* The thought startled him when he realized that he felt lucky for the first time in four months. He smiled and hurried toward her. She jumped up and gave him a big hug. He was a bit embarrassed, but he hugged her back enthusiastically. He could feel her slightly bulging tummy against his abdomen and it sent quivers through his whole body, pleasant quivers. They sat down and held hands while they looked at the menu.

"You hungry, luv?" she inquired.

"Yes, now that you're here, I think I am." He hadn't wanted to go for lunch because he was hungry. He just needed Jess, a feeling he hadn't felt for some time. In an attempt to shut out all of his bad emotions, he had shut out the good ones too. He reminded himself that Dr. Jeffrey had said it was okay to need help. He smiled and looked back down at his menu.

CHAPTER 23

Telling Sam About Her Mother
August 18

Meredith knew she had to tell Sam about her mother. She just didn't know how, even after all her reading and research. Sam was so accepting of living with them, but Meredith thought she must still be very attached to her mother. She and Andy discussed the how and when and they decided they would wait until they returned from Calgary after the reading of Leanna's letters. They had hoped the letters would reveal something that would be helpful. But they had only exemplified the close and loving relationship Sam had with her mother. The good thing was they had given everyone a different and better perspective on Leanna, that is, everyone but Aaron. After returning from Calgary, they decided to wait until the following Saturday to give them time to gather more information about children and the death of a parent.

They wanted to do this on the weekend so they would both be present all day to support her. Now it was Saturday morning and they had no excuses left.

Meredith had talked to two of the home care nurses who had extensive experience in palliative care. Anne was Meredith's age and had worked as a home care nurse for over twenty-three years. She was as solid as people come and an excellent nurse, quite matter-of-fact about most situations but definitely sensitive to her clients' needs. Brita was probably ten years younger but had also worked in home care for over twenty years. She wore her compassion on her shirt sleeve and was sensitive but sensible. Meredith valued both of their thoughts tremendously. If she wasn't ready now, she never would be. Yet she hesitated. *Why do we always decide to have these serious talks right after breakfast? I know right before bed certainly isn't a good idea. It's time to go for it.*

Sam was blissfully looking out the window at the beautiful August day. The sun was streaming in, warming the dining room with its early morning glow. The Mayday tree in the front yard was already starting to lose its crimson red leaves. Sam was watching the leaves float to the ground and tumble away in the slight morning breeze. The neighbor across the street was out walking his dog. He waved enthusiastically to Sam and she waved back, smiling.

"Sam… Grampa and I need to talk to you." Sam looked up expectantly. About three months ago, they had been sitting there telling Sam that Aaron was her father. That had gone far better and easier than they expected. Meredith hoped this would take the same uncomplicated path but she strongly doubted it. "Come over here to the loveseat with me, my dear." She sat facing Sam and reached out to hold both of her hands. Andy was in his recliner reading a magazine. He put it down.

"We received a phone call from a pastor in Vancouver, Sam. Do you know what a pastor is?"

"Yeah, he works in the church. My mommy and my Auntie Colleen used to take me to Sunday School. Pastor Jim was there."

"That's right, Sam." Meredith suddenly felt like she wasn't living up to some bargain she had made, with whom, she wasn't sure. They weren't church- goers so they hadn't taken Sam to church since she arrived. She bit her tongue and continued. "You knew your mommy was very sick …right?" Sam nodded. "The pastor we talked to has been visiting her in the hospital and he called to tell us that your mommy has died." *Darn it, that sounds so harsh but the book said, when telling a child that someone has died, be sure the word "died" is used because children don't understand euphemisms like passed away. So why am I feeling so unsure about this?*

Sam looked curiously excited. "He knows where my mommy is! Can I go visit her?"

"No Sam, she isn't there anymore." *Oh dear, what do I say next?* Meredith hesitated.

"Will she be coming to get me? She said she would." Sam spoke determinedly but she was beginning to sense Meredith's feelings of discomfort and she suddenly looked desperate.

"Sam, when people die, they can't be with us anymore." Meredith felt completely incompetent. She garnered some strength and continued. "Your mommy can't ever come to visit you but you can talk to her anytime you want. She may not be here but you can still talk to her, tell her how you are feeling and tell her how much you miss her."

"I don't understand. Where is Mommy now?" Meredith thought she looked frightened. *Oh God, what now? The book said children under eight are not able to grasp the finality of death.* "Her body is buried in the ground, Sam. That's what we do with people when they die." Sam's face went sullen. "But her love and your memories of her will stay with you forever."

"But she said she would come and get me." The familiar tears were welling up again, hiding that iridescent sparkle behind a wet blanket.

"Sam, this is not your mommy's fault. She was very sick and her sickness made her die. She wanted with all her heart to come and get you but she couldn't. The sickness took her away from us." Meredith leaned over and gave Sam a big hug. She responded instantly and hugged Meredith back fiercely, her body heaving slightly with the beginning of her sobs. Meredith picked her up and put her on her knee, continuing to hold her tight, giving her the time she needed to feel her feelings.

Andy noticed Sam's quilt and Buddy on the floor by the window. He picked them up and gave them to her. Then he headed to the kitchen and began cooking eggs. Meredith thought he didn't know what else to do. He knew Sam loved devilled eggs and he was going to make her some for lunch.

When Sam's sobs were almost stopped, she asked, between heaves, "Gramma, will you be my mommy now?"

"No, Sam, I can never be your mommy; she was a very special person. But I will always be your grandma, my sweetheart."

"But are you going to die too?"

"Sometime, yes, Sam, but not for a very long time, I'm not sick like your mommy was."

"Is Grampa going to die?"

"Yes, but not for a very, very long time. He's as healthy as a horse." Sam smiled slightly between her heaves. Meredith waited through a short silence. "Did you know Grampa is boiling eggs? I just bet he's going to make devilled eggs for lunch. Would you like to help him?"

"Oh yes, I love devilled eggs." Tears still in her eyes, she jumped off Meredith's knee and headed to the kitchen with the determination of a seven-year old thinking of her favorite food. "Grampa, can I help? I want to mix the mayonnaise into the yolks and put them back into the whites."

"Of course, you can help, pull the stool up over here, Sam." She climbed up and approached her task eagerly.

Meredith sat there in amazement, watching how quickly Sam recovered. But she knew that the harder questions were still to come. Sam had not truly comprehended the reality of her mother's death. She had been living with the Taylors for just over four months now and was very much at home and feeling secure. But thoughts about her mother would surely surface later.

Meredith went upstairs to get ready for the day. She figured it might be a good idea to keep Sam busy. She called her daughter, Wendy, to see if they could come over for the afternoon and supper. Wendy and Ian were scheduled to spend the day with friends. Next she called the Petting Zoo at Rolla and tried to make arrangements to go out there for lunch but they were hosting a big birthday party and had no room for more customers. Then she thought of the pool. Sam's cast had been removed on Wednesday and her lesion was healing well. She would still need a follow-up x-ray in another four months and in a year to be sure but her wrist looked good. She called the pool and discovered family swim time was 1-4:00 PM. That is what they would do in the afternoon. She reminded herself that she had to call Delores Scobie after the weekend and let her know about Leanna's demise.

****

When Meredith was tucking Sam into bed, Sam asked, "What does 'died' mean, Gramma?"

Okay, here we go, I was right, Sam still doesn't understand what happened to her mother. "Are you thinking about your mommy?"

"Yes, how come she can't come and get me? She promised."

"Sam, your mommy loved you so much and she desperately wanted to come and get you but her sickness took her away from us, took her life away. Her heart stopped beating and she stopped breathing. That's what happens when you die. The pastor told us when he called that your mommy was very concerned for you when she knew she was dying and couldn't come for you. But she knew that she had made the right decision, leaving you with your grandparents where you would be loved and cared for, sweetie."

"I love you, Gramma." She said it with such seriousness, no smile, just a look of genuine sincerity.

"I love you too, Sam. When you are going to sleep tonight, you can think about all the good times you had with your mommy and tell her how much you love her. Remember the good times, Sam. You have a good sleep now, see you in the morning."

Meredith kissed Sam, turned and left, leaving her with her bewildered thoughts. She knew she would have to be vigilant of Sam's adjustment to the loss of her mother.

CHAPTER 24

Aaron's Progress
August 29

At Aaron's next visit with the psychologist, Jessica joined him. They were holding hands when Dr. Jeffrey walked in. "Hi Aaron... and you must be Jessica, at least I hope you are, the way you two are holding hands." They all laughed. "So tell me, Aaron, how did your week go?"

"Much better, Doc, I actually had some good nights of sleep."

"Excellent. Jessica, as I'm sure Aaron has explained to you, I suggested you come to this session too as I think you can be quite a bit of help to Aaron."

"She already has been," Aaron volunteered. "I didn't realize how much I needed and wanted her help." Aaron and Jessica were smiling at each other.

"What exactly did she do for you, Aaron?" Aaron explained how his week had gone, the good and the bad, and how he had confided in Jessica and called her when he couldn't concentrate because of his pervasive thoughts. He was still having a great deal of trouble concentrating at work.

Aaron had touched on the letters from Leanna at his first visit and Dr. Jeffrey wanted to know more about them and how they had affected him. Aaron and Jessica took turns describing the content of the letters and Aaron interjected his feelings as they swarmed to the surface.

Dr. Jeffrey listened attentively. When they were done, he said, "Aaron, I want to reframe your interpretation of Leanna's letters for you. There is no doubt that what she did was inexcusable and definitely criminal. I heard you saying that she must have been perverted, even insane. As an unbiased observer of what has happened, I heard her coming across as a very lonely, desperate woman. All her life, love had eluded her and she wanted a child to love so much that she was willing to engage in extremely devious measures. The desire for love is a very powerful human emotion, Aaron."

"Oh, I understand that she was lonely and desperate…but what she did…" He couldn't continue.

"She said that, if she had known she was not going to be able to parent Sam until she reached adulthood, she may never have done what she did. She thought that this would have very little impact on you as you would not even remember what had occurred. And that is exactly what happened. You had no memory about it until Sam showed up on your parents' doorstep. Leanna liked you, Aaron, and she certainly did not intend to hurt you. In fact, she liked you so much that she chose you to father her child. But her plan went astray, badly astray, due to her terminal illness." Aaron was squirming in his chair. "You look very uncomfortable, what are you thinking right now?"

"I feel like you're giving her excuses, Doc. And she doesn't deserve to be excused."

"No, not excuses, just a picture of Leanna from my perspective, of who she was and why she did what she did, a picture painted by someone who isn't seeing her through the lens of your emotions."

"Okay, I can accept that. There is no doubt that my emotions are my biggest problem right now, and, secondly, my lack of control of them... and my embarrassment about my lack of control." Aaron looked at Jessica for reassurance.

"That sounds like an honest and accurate assessment, Aaron. This is progress. You are beginning to recognize what is really happening to you. What I would like to do at our next visit is some hypnosis to help you gain control of some of those thoughts that are flooding you and interrupting your concentration. It will also help to flush out any unconscious thoughts that you may not even know are troubling you. What we need to do is look at everything you are thinking, consciously and subconsciously. True emotional healing requires full recognition of all your feelings, the guilt, the hurt and the anger. We'll lay it all out on the table and separate the emotion from the facts so you can see them more clearly. How does that sound to you?"

"Sounds good to me, now that I'm here..., in counselling, I mean..., I may as well try all the tricks you have to offer." They all laughed again.

"Aaron, do you have any plans to meet Sam yet?"

"No, I don't think I can handle that yet, Doc. I know I'm just postponing the inevitable. Maybe you need to hypnotize me about that too." He offered a short chuckle and Dr. Jeffrey gave him a warm smile.

"Yes, we can work on that too, but tell me why you are so concerned about meeting her?"

Aaron hesitated and took a deep breath. Still he didn't say anything. "Can I tell Dr. Jeffrey what you told me last night, dear?" Jessica asked softly, squeezing his hand.

"Sure, I'll just choke up anyway. Go ahead Jess."

"Sam is a complicated issue for Aaron. He is so overwrought with guilt about his parents having to look after a child at their age because of something he did. I think Aaron understands, at least on some level, that he is not responsible for what Leanna did. But he thinks he should have seen it coming, he thinks he was naive to have not seen through her, and therefore, the whole thing is still his fault. He feels he put himself in a compromising position and he should have known better. Stop me, dear, if I say anything that doesn't ring true for you." Jessica looked caringly at Aaron and he nodded.

"Then there is the issue about accepting Sam as his daughter and taking responsibility for her. He hasn't been able to get his head around that for two reasons. Even though he knows it's unreasonable, his anger at Leanna has spilled over to Sam. Every time he thinks of Sam, he thinks of Leanna and his anger escalates. Secondly, he thinks he will be burdening me with a child that is not mine, especially at this time when we are expecting our own child. Aaron is very hard on himself, Dr. Jeffrey."

"Yes, I am coming to understand that. Aaron, do you agree that everything Jessica has said is correct?"

"Yes, that's about it, Doc. It's a pretty lousy situation." Aaron had tears in his eyes and Jessica handed him a tissue from Dr. Jeffrey's desk. "I feel like I'm at an impossible crossroad. I can't parent Sam and I can't leave her with my parents. How can I possibly come to love her like my own child?"

Dr. Jeffrey knew that Aaron needed to fully understand what had happened and why before he could get past the anger and the guilt, forgive Leanna, and put closure to what had happened. "Okay, Aaron, I want you to know right now that these feelings are understandable and not insurmountable. You and I and Jessica will work on them too, and you will be able to free yourself from all this guilt little by little, beginning today. Thanks, Jessica, for being Aaron's voice when he needed you. Now, can you tell Aaron how you feel about the possibility of parenting Sam?"

"I have already told him, I am ready whenever he is. Meredith, Aaron's mother, has told me how incredibly alike Sam is to Aaron and his sister, Wendy. And Leanna confirmed that in her letters. She said Sam was so much like Aaron, not like her at all. From what I hear from Meredith and Andy, Sam will be a joy to assimilate into our family. In fact, I am beginning to think that our biggest problem will be helping Aaron's mom and dad adjust to losing her." She laughed a bit and looked at Aaron again, leaning over and giving him a hug.

"Well, Aaron, it doesn't sound like Sam is a burden at all to your parents and Jessica is looking forward to helping you take care of your daughter. I think you can start wiping away some of that guilt right now."

"Easy for you to say, Doc."

"Yes, that is very true." Dr. Jeffrey laughed. He could see that meeting Sam was untenable for Aaron right now. "But we are going to work on this until you can start to internalize what Jessica has just told you about her feelings around Sam. I think you may be resisting what she has said so you can continue to punish yourself because you still feel so much guilt. Next time you think about Sam and start to get angry, I want you to say out loud but quietly to yourself, 'Sam is not Leanna, Sam is my daughter, Sam is not Leanna, Sam is my daughter.' Then I want you to go to Jessica or phone her and ask her to tell you how she really feels about Sam. Can you do that for the next week, Aaron?"

"Okay, it sounds a bit weird but...I guess I can try that."

"I know this sounds repetitive but it's very important to keep doing it over and over. It's a bit like brainwashing yourself into believing the truth, Aaron. Your anger and guilt are clouding your thoughts and you need to hear the truth more than once or twice before you can internalize it. And remember from last week, keep talking to Jessica about your thoughts and your worries. She wants to help you. People need to be connected to one another, it's a basic human need. This whole event around Leanna and Sam has caused a disconnection between you and Jessica because you thought you shouldn't burden her; but disconnection is what destroys relationships. You need to work at staying closely connected to Jessica and the rest of your family, Aaron. Let all of them help you."

"Okay, Doc," he responded with a very heavy sigh.

"Jessica, if you notice Aaron showing signs of stress, I want you to continue doing what you are already doing. Hold him tight and talk him through it. The strength and warmth of another person can be very reassuring. It will pull him back to reality."

"I can definitely do that." She gave Aaron a warm smile and squeezed his arm.

"So, we'll see you next week at the same time for some hypnosis and thought analysis."

They all stood. "Thanks, Dr. Jeffrey." Jessica shook his hand.

"Yeah, thanks again, see you in a week." Aaron followed suit and shook his hand too.

"Okay, Jess, what do you really think about Dr. Jeffrey?" Aaron was driving and he gave Jessica a sideways glance.

"I think he really cares and I think he makes sense, Aaron. I believe he was right when he said you may be resisting what I'm telling you because of your guilt."

"Huh, maybe, but why would I do that?"

"Because you want your guilt, Aaron, you want to punish yourself."

"Well, if that's true, it's pretty darn crazy."

"Yep, it is, so let it go, Aaron. It happened and it's time to let it go. You are the only one who wants you punished." She smiled encouragingly at him. "I love you, and I want to see you happy again; more than anything, I want to see you happy."

Tears came to his eyes again and his stomach was in his throat. "I love you, Jess," he managed though his tears while trying to concentrate on the road.

"And I love you, Aaron, my dear husband, my best friend, father of my baby, and father of Sam." She was choking up too. They smiled at each other and he reached for her hand.

****

Following his next counselling session and his first experience with hypnosis, Aaron was beginning to feel like his life was coming together again, like the pieces of a puzzle harshly thrown in the corner and now being gathered up by himself, Jessica, and Dr. Jeffrey. Together, they would put them back in place.

He was developing a cautious respect for his counsellor. Dr. Jeffrey seemed to understand where Aaron was at and was able to gently move him forward into new spaces. He was starting to absorb his father relationship to Sam and beginning to feel a peace and calmness he had not felt for a long time. A protective coat was starting to form around Aaron's emotions, not to hide them but to smooth out the sharp edges on them, making them easier to accept. Over time, they would decrease in intensity until he could finally let them go.

Aaron began to respond to Jessica with more concern and affection. She could see the dark veil lifting from his countenance. His interest in the pregnancy increased and they began to make plans for the nursery. His paternal instincts were coming to the surface, no longer being pushed down by all his negative thoughts and emotions. But Jessica knew she shouldn't push him. She knew he needed to find his own way back to his former world of happy, hard-working satisfaction and the family he cared for so much.

CHAPTER 25

Sam Returns to School September 4

To say the least, spring and summer for the Taylors had been more than eventful. As Meredith was helping Sam dress for her first day of school, she wondered what more the fall could possibly bring. *Surely our lives will settle down to normal, whatever normal can be with our new reality.* Meredith had taken July and August off, using all her remaining holidays and four weeks of leave without pay. She was returning to work this morning.

Jessica had reported on the weekend about how much better Aaron was doing and Meredith desperately wanted to suggest to them that they come for a visit so they could meet Sam. But she didn't. She knew it would be best for Aaron to have tight control over how and when this would happen. He'd had no control over Sam's conception and he needed to do this his way in his timeframe. *I know there is no need to hurry, but, darn, I want to see this happen. I wonder if I should send a picture of Sam. I'll take one this morning when Sam is ready for school and ask Jessica if she thinks sending it is a good idea.*

Sam interrupted her thoughts. "Gramma, I hope my teacher will be as nice as Mrs. Babcock."

"Well dear, you will soon find out. Did you know that Colby and Dylan are starting playschool this week too?"

"Wow, really?"

"Yes, but they only go for two hours twice a week. Wendy is planning to use that time to go to an exercise class. It will be good for her to have time to herself. Looking after two little boys can be quite hectic."

"What does hectic mean, Gramma?"

"Hectic means very, very busy and tiring." *I feel like I'm talking to Sam as if she's an adult. She always seems so mature.*

"Is looking after me hectic too?"

Meredith stood in front of Sam, bent down and put her hands on Sam's shoulders. "No, dear, you are my pleasure." Sam smiled with delight. "Now I think you are ready and I want to take your picture to remember your first day of grade two."

"Okay, let's go." She raced down the stairs at full speed.

Sam was dressed in a white blouse with pearl buttons and a pink, white and navy plaid pinafore, pink being the predominant colour. Over her blouse she wore a navy cardigan sweater. It was a chilly fall day so she had on some white tights and silvery grey running shoes. Her golden hair, bleached lighter from the summer sun, had grown longer and it fell past her shoulders in natural soft curls. Meredith had parted it on the side and placed one small pink barrette at her forehead to hold it back. The sun was shining and they went out to the backyard to take Sam's picture on the deck beside the still blooming flower pots. She posed with her backpack over her right shoulder. Meredith snapped three pictures to make sure she had a good one.

Andy and Sam had been to the school last week with Sam's birth certificate and registered her as Samantha Aries Schaefer. In talking with Sam about this, she was pleased to be able to have her old name back. She seemed to understand that it was okay now to use it as her mother would no longer be worrying about being found.

****

Meredith was in the home care nursing office discussing some teaching opportunities for one of the nurses when the receptionist paged her, a rare occurrence; she usually just took a message or gave the caller a voicemail. When Meredith heard the page, she quickly returned to her desk and called the receptionist, who told her she had an urgent call from the school and that she would connect her. Meredith's knees went weak and her stomach started to roll.

"Mrs. Taylor, this is Mr. Hallaway, the principal at Canalta School."

"Yes, is Sam okay?" Meredith knew something was wrong, she could feel it in her stomach.

"We noticed Sam was missing after recess. Do you know where she might be?"

"God no, I have no idea." Her thoughts raced. *Someone has taken Sam; she would definitely not leave school on her own.* "I think we better call the police immediately."

"Okay, I will do that right now. Could you come to the school?"

"Yes, I'll be right there."

Meredith told one of her co-workers that Sam was missing at school and raced out to her car. She got to the school at the same time as two police cruisers. *Oh my god, what has happened to Sam?* Her legs were shaking and her pulse was racing as she parked her car and raced into the school.

They met in the principal's office. Sam's teacher, Mrs. Dufour was there too. She had been on the playground during recess, but had been distracted by the break-up of a fight between two grade four boys. She never noticed Sam was gone until after classes resumed. Sam's desk, at the front left, was empty. She asked Rilla and Holly what happened to Sam and they said she had left with a lady in a dark-blue car. Even though the girls indicated she went willingly, this astute teacher had reported the incident to the principal.

Mr. Hallaway introduced Meredith to Sergeant Willis and Meredith asked Mr. Hallaway to call Andy.

"Mrs. Taylor, do you have any ideas as to who may have picked Sam up from school?" Sergeant Willis asked."

"Oh god, not Auntie Colleen again," Meredith gasped under her breath as she held one hand over her mouth.

Sergeant Willis heard her and asked, "Who's Auntie Colleen?" Meredith quickly explained the relationship between Colleen and Sam's deceased mother.

"How much danger do you think Sam could be in if she is with this Colleen?"

"I don't know, I just don't know. But she must not be thinking straight to have kidnapped Sam. She had to have known that Sam's mother wanted us to have custody of Sam. Since we don't know what her motives are, I think we have to assume Sam is in danger."

"Okay, that's good enough for me. I want to issue an Amber Alert as soon as possible. I'll need a description of Colleen and her car and do you have a recent picture of Sam?"

"Yes, I took one this morning before I brought her to school. I will have to go home and print it."

Mr. Hallaway was back with them. "Andy's on his way." Meredith felt dizzy and nauseated. Her thoughts were swirling and she couldn't concentrate.

Mrs. Babcock, Sam's grade one teacher, was brought in to give a description of what she remembered about Colleen from last May. Holly and Rilla were interviewed separately by the police and gave their descriptions of the car and the woman Sam had left with. They both indicated again that Sam had been happy to see the woman and left willingly. This confirmed for Meredith that it had to have been Colleen who took Sam as she would not have gone willingly with a stranger.

By the time Andy arrived, Meredith was trembling with fear. She got up to meet him coming in the door and said, "Oh Andy," and fainted into his arms. When she regained consciousness, she was lying on the floor with Andy bending over her, holding cold wet paper towels on her forehead. She could see him but his voice seemed far away. The room was swaying as if she was riding on a high swing. The floor was pulling away from her feet, then the ceiling swooped toward her and darkness fell. When she regained consciousness a second time, Andy had her feet elevated on several staff jackets and she managed to stay conscious.

The sergeant had left to give his report to the Amber Alert and the Canada-wide RCMP information systems. He indicated that they may be looking for a woman named Colleen. Squad cars would be out on all major highways looking for a dark-blue sedan.

As soon as Meredith could stand and walk, the Taylors went home, printed the pictures of Sam that Meredith had taken before school, and then delivered them back to the police. Then Andy took Meredith home to wait. She lay on the sofa while he made some calls. He knew he had to call Aaron first but he hesitated while he gathered his thoughts.

"Aaron, how are you, son?"

"Okay Dad. I'm hanging in there."

"I'm afraid I have some bad news. Sam has been taken from the playground at school. We think it was Leanna's friend, Colleen, that took her."

Aaron was silent; he needed a few seconds to digest what his father was telling him. "What? Why on earth would she do that?"

"We don't know but we do know that she helped Leanna look after Sam for several months before she and Leanna dropped her off at our house. Maybe she wanted Sam to live with her. We just don't know, Aaron."

"Oh my god, this is awful, Dad. Have you called the police?"

"Oh yes, they are in the process of putting out an Amber Alert, but we don't have much to go on. Only Sam's two friends, Rilla and Holly saw it happen. They said Sam was happy to see this woman and went with her willingly. They were able to give a vague description of the car as a dark blue sedan. And they said the woman was slim and had short brown hair. This is the same description Mrs. Babcock gave when she saw Sam talking to a woman on the playground several months ago."

"What? When did this happen?"

"It was last spring. Later, Sam told us Colleen had come to visit her at school. Your mom took a picture of Sam this morning before she left for school and we have given that to the police. That's it, that's all we know."

"My god, Dad, this is just awful. What if I never get to meet her now?"

Andy was lost for words and hesitated. "I know, Aaron, your mom and I are beyond worried. The worst part is we can't do anything except sit and wait."

"I can't believe this, Jess and I were talking just last night about maybe coming up to visit you and Mom and Sam. And now... oh god, I can't believe this! This Colleen, she won't do anything to harm Sam, will she?"

"We hope not but we don't really know for sure. Aaron, I'm sorry, I have to go now, I have a few more calls I have to make. But I'll call you again soon, okay."

"Okay, Dad."

Andy felt awful saying goodbye but he simply didn't know what else to say to Aaron. Next he called the manager at the health unit to let her know what was happening. Then he called Wendy, then Arlene.

By noon, the news media started running the Amber Alert and Sam's picture was front and centre. This made Meredith crazy. She started yelling, "Damn you, Colleen, haven't you people done enough to us yet? I hate you, I hate you. Our dear Sam, where are you, where are you? Ohhh, I hope you're safe, I hope they find you."

Andy held Meredith until she stopped shaking. He put on some soothing music and made tea but she couldn't drink. The waiting was dreadful.

Aaron called. He had seen the Amber Alert and he was crying. Through his tears he stammered, "Dad, this is the first time I have seen a picture of my daughter. She's beautiful and I may never get to meet her now."

"We can't give up hope, Aaron; surely they will find her. They have to find her!"

"I have a very bad feeling about this, Dad."

"Don't give up hope, Aaron." Andy didn't know what else to say. "Are you at home?"

"Yes, I called Jess right after you called. We're both here."

"We'll let you know as soon as we hear anything, okay?"

"Okay, Dad."

Andy was so relieved to hear Jessica was with Aaron.

At 4:00 PM, Arlene arrived to try to comfort Meredith. She stayed with her while Andy, on the advice of Arlene, went to the doctor's office hoping to get some tranquilizers before closing time.

At 5:30 PM, the sergeant called. On the way home from work, a woman who lived twenty-three kilometres north of Dawson Creek saw an abandoned, dark-blue sedan on the side of the road. The road was a dead end and only used by two farm families in the area. She had been listening to the *Amber Alert* on the radio and called in on her cell. On arrival, the police discovered there was no identification left in the car but they used the license plate to discover it had been rented to a Rosemary Grant in Vancouver. It seemed that Sam and her abductor had disappeared into thin air. The road was fairly straight for one half kilometre, leading the police to believe a small plane or helicopter could have easily landed on it.

"We found some small tire tracks in the dry sandy gravel that looked like they could have been from a small plane. It appeared to have made a turn on the road to take off in the direction from which it landed. We alerted all air traffic control systems immediately and Canadian and United States airlines have been instructed to watch for a woman with Colleen's vague descriptors and a seven- year old girl of Sam's description. Her pictures have been distributed."

Andy looked at his watch. "That plane could have picked Sam and Colleen up over six hours ago!"

"Yes, this is definitely not good news. I'm so sorry, Andy. We'll keep looking but we have certainly lost the trail."

This latest information sent Meredith into a frenzy. Arlene managed to convince her to take two tranquilizers and got her to lie down again while she went to heat up some soup. Meredith refused the soup, saying her stomach could not handle anything right now. She took a few sips of cold water and curled up in a ball on the sofa. The Ativan took over and she was asleep in one half hour.

****

Aaron called for the third time to ask if there was any news. Andy took the call in the office away from Meredith. Aaron wanted to know if he and Jessica should fly home. Andy discouraged them, saying, "What could you do here? We just have to wait. We have to wait this out."

"God, Dad, this makes my refusing to meet her seem so selfish and self-centred right now. I'm totally disgusted with myself."

This was not a reaction Andy was expecting. *Oh no, our son does not need any more reasons to add to his guilt.* "Aaron, you did not do this, you had no control over this. Give yourself a break."

"But Dad, what if I never get to meet my daughter now? And if she had been staying with us, maybe this would not have happened."

"We can't think the worst, we have to believe we will find her. And Aaron, this most likely would have happened no matter where Sam was staying. Her abductor was obviously intent on doing this and it would not have mattered if Sam was with us or with you."

"Okay, Dad, please call as soon as you hear anything." Aaron hung up and fell into Jessica's arms in despair.

At 8:15 the phone rang and Andy answered it.

It was Pastor Felix. "Sorry to bother you, Mr. Taylor, but I just saw the Amber Alert about a seven-year old girl being kidnapped from school in Dawson Creek. Her name is Samantha Schaefer. I have to ask, is it Sam, Leanna's daughter?"

"Yes, I'm afraid so."

"I'm so sorry to hear that. Is there anything at all that I can do?"

"Only if you have information that could result in new leads. The police are at a dead end already."

"If only I did...Leanna said nothing about her friends; in fact, I thought it odd that there didn't seem to be any friends in her life."

"Well, if you think of anything at all, would you please call Sergeant Willis at the Dawson Creek RCMP detachment?"

"Yes, yes, I will do that. How is Mrs. Taylor doing with this?"

"She's beside herself with worry, as we all are."

"If there is any way that I can be of help, please let me know."

"Yes, of course, we have your number, Pastor."

At 9:00 PM, they had heard nothing more. Andy encouraged Arlene to go home. Meredith was still asleep so he lay back on a recliner chair beside her, covering himself with an afghan. Meredith woke up at 11:00 PM and went to the bathroom. She changed into her pyjamas and went downstairs to wake Andy and get him to come to bed. Once she was in bed, she couldn't sleep again. She went back downstairs and took two more *Ativan*.

Andy called Sergeant Willis first thing in the morning but he had no news of Sam. Knowing there was absolutely nothing they could do, Andy and Meredith both decided to go to work for a while. At work, Meredith couldn't concentrate and she hated being there because everyone was stopping by to ask what was happening and give their condolences. At least she managed to put "out of office" messages on her voice mail and email indicating she would be away until further notice. By 10:00 AM, she went home, grief stricken and exhausted. Sitting in her recliner trying to rest, she began to feel disembodied, like she was floating just above herself. This scared her and she got up to make some tea. Thinking that she was losing her faculties, she called Andy and asked him to come home.

Jessica called while Meredith was waiting for Andy. Aaron hadn't gone to work and was beside himself with worry and guilt. His regular counselling session was today and she would be taking him. He needed it more than ever.

****

At about 11 AM, Sergeant Willis received a call from Leanna's lawyer. He too wanted to confirm that the little girl in the Amber Alert was Leanna's daughter. He let Sergeant Willis know that he had never met Colleen but he did know she was Leanna's closest friend. He confirmed that Leanna had directed in her will that custody of Sam be given to the Taylors. And he revealed that Leanna thought Colleen would not make a good parent for Sam as she did not have the patience or the capacity to love a child unconditionally. After the call, Sergeant Willis began to have a sick feeling that Sam was in more trouble than he originally thought. *I won't reveal this information to the Taylors, they don't need to hear this.*

CHAPTER 26

The News Media
September 7

On day four, they still had absolutely nothing to go on. The police were making guesses as to what had happened; how the kidnapper had gotten away with Sam without a trace. Guesses, that's all they were. They had no leads, and no other witnesses except for Holly and Rilla and the farm wife who had first spotted the abandoned car on the rural gravel road. Sergeant Willis was honest with the Taylors. He said he believed Colleen had escaped the country and he had no idea where she had taken Sam. He admitted he was getting pressure to end the Amber Alert, but he was pushing to keep it going as long as he could.

The local, provincial, and federal media were all trying to get an interview with the Taylors. So far, they had refused, worried that it would cause more of a spectacle than it would be of benefit. Sergeant Willis suggested that, for some people, it is helpful to share their grief with the world. But Meredith just couldn't bring herself to go there yet. Underlying her own feelings of privacy were those of Aaron and Jessica. She was afraid that the press would dig and dig until they discovered the nature of Sam's conception. She feared that would lead Aaron into further despair.

When Sergeant Willis called to find out if there had been any further developments, he talked about a local reporter that he trusted to report only the facts, no sensationalism. "Meredith and Andy, I think you would find relief in telling your story to Mike. I have found him to be very sincere and caring. And, somehow, maybe this would give us a new lead."

Finally, Meredith relented and Andy supported her decision. "Okay, we'll talk to him but he needs to know it has to be brief and factual. Otherwise, I know I will break down with emotion."

"Alright, I will have him call you this morning."

As soon as the call ended, Meredith regretted her decision and her thoughts started to take off again. "I'm scared, Andy, I don't know if I can do this."

"Meredith, I tend to agree that sharing our heartache could be helpful. Let's just see how it goes...okay? Maybe something we haven't thought of yet could come out that would be helpful." He paused. "I can do all of the talking if you want me to, but you can interrupt me anytime you feel ready."

"That's just it, I will never be ready. Talking about it just reinforces that it's true. I still don't want to believe it. I know that's crazy but it's where I'm still at, Andy. I know I have to move past this denial but it's like my mind won't let me."

The telephone rang. Andy answered it. It was the reporter from *The Peace River Block News*. "One moment, Mike, I will get my wife to listen too." He held his hand over the receiver to tell Meredith who it was. "What do you think, dear, are you ready to do this?"

Meredith let out a guttural sigh and took a few seconds to respond. "He sure didn't waste any time, did he? Okay, maybe this will help me move forward."

"Mike, I have you on the speakerphone."

"Hello Mrs. Taylor, thank you for agreeing to speak to me. I would like to come to your house this morning so we can talk in person. Will 10:30 be okay with both of you?"

Andy and Meredith looked at each other for support. "What do you think, dear, will 10:30 be okay?"

She was still in her pyjamas. She noted that this would give her forty minutes to get herself together. She nodded her head reluctantly.

CHAPTER 27

———

Sam Becomes Brandy
September 5

Colleen believed she genuinely loved Sam, wanted the best for her, and was entirely convinced that it would be best for Sam to be with her. After all, she had spent time with her since the moment Sam was born, she had been in the delivery room with Leanna, she frequently babysat for her, and all three of them had gone everywhere together.

For the five months prior to Sam arriving at the Taylors, Colleen had moved in with Leanna and taken over Sam's care. She desperately wanted to be Sam's mother now that Leanna was gone and disagreed wholeheartedly with Leanna that Sam would be better off with her biological father's family. She felt a pang of guilt for going against her long-time friend's dying wishes but it was balanced by her anger at Leanna and she was certain she was doing the right thing.

She had used a fair bit of Leanna's money that had been willed to her to arrange for the successful kidnapping of Sam, and that was weighing heavily on her conscience. But she was thoroughly certain she was acting only out of love for Sam, not because of her own needs for lifelong companionship, something that had eluded her too. This was, she thought, one of the most powerful reasons why she and Leanna had become so close. But Leanna had never bent to Colleen's sexual persuasion.

Sam was excited to see her Auntie Colleen and had been more than willing to go with her. Colleen had told her that she wanted to show her something really neat. Sam was a bit hesitant, telling Colleen that she had to be back in class in a few minutes. Colleen responded saying, "It's okay, Sam, I talked to your teacher and she knows you'll be away for a while."

The small plane ride was exciting for Sam, so she soon forgot about getting back to school. She was enthralled by everything she could see on the ground and how small it looked. And flying through the few clouds that were in the sky kept her entertained. "Auntie Colleen, it's like flying through white fluff."

"Yes Sam, sweetie," Colleen smiled at how well things were going so far.

When Sam told her she was hungry, Colleen got some sandwiches, fruit and bottles of juice out of her shoulder bag for lunch. Shortly after eating, Sam said, "Auntie Colleen, I have to pee really bad."

"That's okay Sam, we are going to land in just a few minutes. You can pee then, just hold on for a few more minutes."

True to her word, the small plane landed on a country road with trees on both sides. There was a dark-colored van and a driver waiting just off the road on an entrance to a small opening of trees. Colleen took Sam behind the trees and helped her squat to pee and wiped her off with a tissue from her purse. Colleen squatted to relieve herself too. Then they quickly got into the van and the driver drove down a few country roads until they came to a highway.

"Auntie Colleen, where on earth are you taking me? I don't think I like this plan. I want to go home!"

"Don't worry, Sam, we're almost there!"

"Almost where?" Sam asked, sounding exasperated.

"It's a surprise, you will really like it."

"I don't want a surprise anymore, I want to go home!"

"Just wait, Sam you will really like this surprise more that you can ever imagine! I brought a couple of books for you to read. I know you love reading. Here you are, this will keep you busy for a while."

Sam took the books begrudgingly and began to read. In about ten minutes, she was asleep, lulled by the purring of the motor and the hum of the tires. She woke up just as the van stopped at the airport. She was a bit disoriented when they entered the airport—disoriented and scared. She held tight onto Colleen's hand following her from place to place.

Just before they boarded the plane, Colleen took Sam into a washroom and helped her change her clothes. Sam protested, "But I like my other clothes better. Gramma bought them for me to start school."

Just hearing the word Gramma, Colleen's irritation started to build and she jerked Sam's arms around to fit them into the long sleeves of a plain blue tee shirt. "Sam you need to be dressed properly for where we're going." Colleen grabbed and twisted Sam's silky golden-brown curls into a knot and pinned them securely.

"Oouuch! Ooouuch! That hurt, why are you being so mean?" Sam pulled her head away and moved back one step, hitting her head on the wall of the cubicle they were in. Colleen moved forward and covered Sam's hair with a plain navy-blue ball cap.

"But I hate hats," Sam protested loudly.

Colleen took a deep breath, managed to gather her wits and calm down slightly before they left the cubicle. *Thank god, there is not another soul in here to hear Sam's protests.* "I'm sorry Sam, but we are in a bit of a hurry to catch this plane." She grabbed Sam's hand securely, unlocked the cubicle door and quietly walked with her to the security area. By the time they were through security, the handicapped and parents with small children were already boarding and a line was forming for other passengers. They quietly slipped ahead of the queue, checked in, and walked up the ramp into the plane.

Once on the plane, Sam was getting suspicious and confronted her. "Auntie Colleen, are you taking me away from my gramma and grampa?"

Colleen knew she couldn't keep Sam in the dark forever regarding her plan and there was no going back now. She still felt confident that Sam would be happy about living with her. "Yes, Sam, it's just you and me now, isn't that great? We'll have the good old times back. I love you so much, Sam, sweetie." As she spoke, she was imagining an idyllic mother-daughter relationship. Sam's inheritance had certainly crossed her mind too, but she didn't know yet how she would get her hands on it.

"I love you too, Auntie Colleen, but I really, really love Gramma and Grampa. They are so much fun and they're my family now. My mommy wanted me to stay with them. I think I should go back. I want to go back, pleeeeease Auntie Colleen," she pleaded.

Colleen was livid with Sam's attitude and her anger began to percolate. She tried to keep her voice hushed. "Sam, I have cared for you and your mother for a very long time now and this is the thanks I get?" Sam's face remained determined but she said nothing. "I can't believe this. I have risked everything and spent..." Sam recognized Colleen's anger and her eyes started to fill with tears. Colleen stopped herself and caught her breath. *Don't ruin this now.* She looked around to see if any of the other passengers were listening, took Sam's hand in hers and started again, trying to sound upbeat. "Sam, we are on our way to Colorado Springs. I have bought the neatest house there for the two of us. Your bedroom is so cute, wait tell you see it. This is what I want to show you. I have even checked out the schools and found just the one for you. I've met your teacher and she's expecting you, dear. Oh Sam, sweetie, everything will be just fine when we get there, you'll see."

Sam's eyes remained wet, and tears started to spill down her cheeks. "But my gramma and grampa are going to be very worried about me." And I love my school in Dawson Creek. I have two really good friends there..."

The pitch in Colleen's voice elevated again. "Sam, they don't really love you like I do; they were just being kind to you. And your father, their son, still has not even come to meet you. He doesn't want you, can't you see that?" Her voice escalated. "Can't you see that?"

Sam started to cry. Not feeling very sure of herself, through her sobs she said, "That's not true. Gramma said he lives very far away and he is real busy working so he couldn't come yet. She said I just needed to be patient."

The stewardess stopped and asked what was wrong. Colleen spoke quickly, saying, "Oh, it's nothing, she's just missing her dad."

Sam and Colleen had boarded this American flight only thirty minutes before the international airline alerts had been made so the stewardess suspected nothing. After she left, Sam confronted Colleen again, "You lied to the stewardess, Auntie Colleen."

"Well, what was I supposed to say, Sam, that I kidnapped you and you want to go home?" Colleen knew she needed to keep her cool. That had not been a smart thing to say.

"Did you.... kidmap me?"

"No, for god's sake, Sam, your mom wanted me to look after you when she couldn't anymore. I rescued you and I'm just following your mom's request."

****

Sam said no more. Somehow, she knew that Auntie Colleen was lying about everything. She was trying to remember her Gramma's words. *I will always be your gramma, my dear.* Her tummy felt sick. She slumped in her chair, feeling helpless and uncertain. She refused all the refreshments the stewardess offered and remained quietly defiant and glum for the whole trip.

****

Colleen was jittery as she rented a car at the airport under the name of Karen Carter. This is who she would be known as from now on. She had learned the art of changing names and identification from Leanna. All it took was money and a good lawyer. She had arranged for a bogus passport and a school record for Sam under the name of Brandy Carter.

Sam was teary-eyed and it made Colleen more anxious. Already she was beginning to wonder about the wisdom of her plan. It was late and she was on her way to a motel close to the airport for the night. Then they would be on their way to Colorado Springs, about seventy kilometres from Denver. They pulled up to a motel that Colleen had chosen on her first trip to Colorado Springs.

"Okay, Sam, this is where we're staying for the night. You stay here while I go and get a room." Sam considered getting out of the car and running away but it was dark and she was scared.

To avoid notice and be certain she had a room, Colleen had made a reservation. She prepaid for one night, returned to the car with the key to the motel room, and parked right in front of the door. It was dark and quiet. She wanted to get Sam into the room without anyone seeing her. She hadn't been able to waste much time earlier trying to change Sam's looks, because she had to get her across the American border and onto the flight to Denver as quickly as possible. In the morning, she would cut Sam's hair very short.

Once in the room, Colleen instructed Sam that it was time for bed. "But I don't have any pyjamas and I don't have Buddy."

"Oh yes, you do, look in this suitcase. I packed it just for you, Sam," she said, trying to sound light-hearted and organized. *I will have to start Sam with her new name in the morning.* "Aren't these sweet? I know your favourite color is pink."

Sam gave her a disdainful look. "Not anymore, I like purple now and I can't sleep without Buddy," she said with finality." She was thinking of her treasured, mostly purple quilt that her gramma had made and given to her.

"Well, I guess you are going to have to tonight. I'll buy you a new teddy bear tomorrow," Colleen responded impatiently.

"I don't want a new teddy bear, I *want* Buddy."

"Well, I'm sorry Sam, but we can't go back and get Buddy. Here's your toothbrush and some toothpaste. Now pul....lease get ready for bed."

Sam grabbed the pyjamas, toothbrush, and paste and headed for the bathroom without looking up. She slammed and locked the door behind her.

Oh boy, this isn't so easy without Leanna here to say, listen to your Auntie Colleen, dear. She turned on the television and tried to find a sitcom. After ten minutes she spoke. "Sam, what are you doing in there? You must be done by now. Please come out so I can use the bathroom." There was silence. *Crap, what do I do now? This was supposed to be fun. Sam and I together as mother and daughter at last.* Colleen decided to wait it out. She turned off the television, lay on the bed, closed her eyes, and tried to rest. When she woke up, it was 3:00 AM. Panic set in. She turned over and looked at the other bed. Sam was there, sleeping quietly, lying on one pillow and hugging the other one. "Thank God," Colleen said under her breath. She didn't sleep again, vowing not to let Sam out of her sight.

Colleen was up early and had already cut and dyed her own hair red. She had dyed it red for her first trip to Colorado Springs, then dyed it back to dark-brown on her return. She didn't want to raise any suspicions anywhere. At 8:00 AM, she woke Sam and asked her to get up. Sam groggily stumbled to the bathroom and relieved herself. Remembering how mad she was, she stomped back to her bed, tumbled back in and pulled the covers over her head.

Colleen spoke in an artificially calm voice. "Sam, I'm going to cut your hair this morning. Please get up and sit over here."

A muffled voice came from under the covers. "I don't want my hair cut. Mommy and Gramma like my long hair. They both said I have such sweet curls." She pulled down the covers and looked at Colleen, defiantly. "You look weird today, how come your hair is that funny red color?"

"Sam, as you pointed out yesterday, I kidnapped you, but really it was to rescue you from your father's family who don't really love you so you could have a happy life with me. If the police find us, I could be in big trouble. I'd probably go to jail and then you would have nobody to look after you. I risked everything for you. Remember, your mommy is dead, Sam, gone forever. All you have now is me and, if I go to jail, you'll be all alone."

"I'll go back home to Gramma and Grampa. They'll look after me and they do so love me. They said they did!" She was starting to cry again.

"Sam, do you know how far from Dawson Creek you are? How would you get home with no money and no help? You'd be living on the street all alone with nothing to eat. Now... *please*... get yourself over here right now and let me cut your hair."

Sam didn't move, she was thinking about Colleen's threatening words.

"Sam, this is not funny. You need to make this work or you will have nobody to care for you." Colleen went over to the bed and pulled Sam to the chair and started cutting. She was angry and rough.

"Ouch, you're hurting me." Sam whimpered.

"Well, then, behave and cooperate. By the way, you have a new name this morning. From now on, you will go by the name, Brandy Carter. So, Miss Brandy, stop your crying and hold still or you will get a bad haircut." Colleen grabbed a chunk of hair and gave it a sharp pull.

Sam tried to stop crying and held her head up.

"So...you are Brandy and I'm your mother, Karen. But I want you to call me Mommy. Don't you ever call me Auntie Colleen again." Sam was quiet but her thoughts weren't. She was trying to synthesize everything Colleen was saying and she was getting very frightened.

Colleen had not anticipated this reaction from Sam and was certainly not prepared to cope with it. Her nerves were frayed. She had thought Sam would be thrilled to see her and to go with her. She admonished herself for not thinking of this possibility. *Sam was always so cooperative and loving when her mother was around. Why is she behaving this way? This is not how it's supposed to be. And I'm turning into a mean and nasty kidnapper, not the heroine rescuer I had imagined myself to be.* Colleen did not like what she saw happening. Already, her lack of parenting skills was becoming apparent.

Colleen stopped at a MacDonald's drive-through for Egg McMuffins, orange juice for Sam, and coffee for herself. Then they were on their way to Colorado Springs. When she had been there two weeks ago, she had purchased a small bungalow and some furniture and had talked to the school about registering Sam. She thought it would look less suspicious than just showing up out of the blue, and she wanted to have everything organized for Sam. She thought she had been very clever in dying her hair red for the trip, and then back to dark-brown when she returned. She was sure she was covering all the bases.

Sam did not eat her Egg McMuffin or drink her orange juice. Colleen tried to involve her in some conversation and practice their new names. "Brandy, we are going to go directly to our new house to have a look around and decide what we absolutely need to buy so we can manage for the next few days. I know we need some sheets and blankets for the beds. What else do you think we'll need? Remember to call me Mom when you speak."

Sam pressed back into her seat with resistance and her lower lip came out ever so slightly but she said nothing. She was scared but she was also very angry. Colleen knew she would not be able to take her to school if she was like this. It would be far too risky. She was developing a whopper of a headache and was beginning to feel trapped in what was becoming a very difficult situation. *How could I have been so stupid as to not anticipate that maybe, just maybe, Sam would not want to come with me? I have to figure out a way to turn this around.*

CHAPTER 28

Waiting
Sept 15

Memories of the last ten days were vague and mixed up. Meredith wondered at times if she was losing her mind, developing Alzheimer's Disease. Her mother and four of her mother's siblings had died of it. She thought maybe the stress was just accelerating the inevitable. She and Andy were trying to keep to a normal schedule, going to work, shopping, cooking supper, cleaning up dishes, washing, ironing. It was Saturday morning and they were trying to read the newspapers while having their morning coffee.

Her workdays had been a blur and Meredith knew she had not accomplished much. She was in a stupor most of the time. She just hoped she hadn't forgotten any important details for the two compression dressing therapy workshops she had organized for next week. She couldn't concentrate on the newspaper and her eyes drifted to the window, the same window she had glanced out of when the doorbell rang on the day of Sam's arrival.

Meredith's thoughts drifted over the time she and Andy had spent with Sam. The fears, the challenges, the exhaustion, the ambivalence; all had been worth the love and laughter Sam had brought into their lives for the last five months. She knew that if she never saw Sam again, she would not regret one minute of the time she had been blessed to spend with her. *Sam has given us much more than we have given her. She has added so many new dimensions to our daily life. I wonder if Aaron feels relieved. Relief is definitely not what I'm feeling.* She felt like she had a turbulent river roaring through her head from front to back, and in her gut, she felt a profound sadness.

Meredith knew that Aaron was continuing with his counselling. He had been thrown for another loop when Sam disappeared, once again blaming himself. But the counsellor he was seeing weekly was obviously good at what he was doing. Aaron was making excellent progress again. Meredith had talked to Jessica yesterday and gotten an update. He had received just five weeks of counselling and his flashbacks had stopped. He was still having occasional nightmares but he and Jessica were dealing with them. He was managing better at work, despite his self-blame about Sam's disappearance. *Maybe it's easier for him because he never met her.*

Meredith went upstairs to the bathroom, wandered into Sam's room, and picked up Buddy and the quilt she had given Sam. "Sam, are you okay, dear? Are you happy? I'll bet you miss Buddy terribly." She started to cry...

Andy heard her and came upstairs. "Meredith." He came over, sat on the bed beside her, and put his dependable arm around her.

She leaned into his warmth. "Oh, Andy, I know I have to let her go. She's not coming back, is she?"

He didn't answer. What could he say? He just sat and hugged her tight until her body stopped heaving with despair. "Let's make some breakfast, dear." He took her hand and led her down the stairs.

As Meredith was making breakfast, she had trouble concentrating, and as usual, her thoughts drifted. "People come into our lives for a reason, Andy. Why did Sam, with her wisdom beyond her years, come into ours? And why did she leave again? It doesn't make any sense."

"No, dear, it doesn't," he quietly agreed with her. Andy was helping with breakfast and he could see that Meredith was still tortured by her thoughts. It broke his heart because he didn't know how to help.

They sat down to what Meredith usually thought of as a scrumptious weekend breakfast of bacon and eggs, hash browns and fresh fruit. But she had no appetite. She pushed her food around on her plate, picked up a piece of bacon and took a bite, then had a piece of potato. That was it. She got up from the table with her coffee and returned to her chair.

She imagined Sam being spirited away under false pretences and she wondered if Sam was missing them as much as they were missing her. She didn't want to remember Leanna's words but she kept hearing in her head what Pastor Felix had read, "As I reviewed the possibilities for Sam, it didn't take me long to decide that she had to be with her father and his family..." Meredith's thoughts tormented her. *Why didn't Leanna want to give custody of Sam to Colleen? It should have been an obvious choice.* This made her shiver with fear. Andy kept eating but he thought to himself that it was time for Meredith to see her doctor.

On day six the Amber Alert had ended. Mike's article for the paper had not produced any more leads. They hadn't heard from Sergeant Willis for several days. The press had stopped calling. To them, Sam's kidnapping was old news already. But for Meredith it was like a raw, bleeding ulcer on the surface of her heart that she thought would never heal. And something was nagging at her. Somehow, she knew

Sam was not okay. She could feel the presence of a negative energy hanging over her like a dark cloud. She closed her eyes and tried to conjure up a picture of Sam. But all she could get was a dark silhouette with a light behind it; she couldn't see Sam's face clearly enough to know if she was happy or sad, excited or scared.

Andy brought her back to reality. "Meredith, what are we going to do today? We should make a plan of some sort so can we keep ourselves busy."

"Yes," she said, despondently, "we definitely need something, something active...but what?" *I know Andy is struggling too but he seems to be doing much better than me.* She remembered her friend Arlene's caring words; "Meredith, don't you dare let this make you sink into a depression." Meredith knew she had to get on with her life and she had to quit taking the Ativan her doctor had prescribed for her. She would endeavour to manage without it today. She attempted to think positively about how much simpler and easier life would be for Aaron and Jessica now that Sam was gone. *Maybe, somehow, in some quirky way, this is for the best. I must find the strength from somewhere to pull myself up.*

She could hear Andy on the phone. He was making arrangements with Arlene and Dave to go golfing after lunch. Meredith got up from her chair and went upstairs to get ready for the day.

CHAPTER 29

Sam's Depression
Sept 21

Colleen kept Sam at home for the next ten days, hoping that spending time together would put them into a natural rhythm. They shopped for all the household items they needed. She was sure that Sam would get excited and involved in decorating her room when they shopped for paint, wall hangings and curtains. Instead she remained adamant that she didn't care what color her room was because she didn't like it anyway. "I don't like this room, I want Wendy's room with the flowers and the butterflies and all the pictures of her family... my family."

Colleen was furious but she ignored this comment. While she was painting Sam's room, Sam watched television, read some books, and moped around. She started napping in the afternoon, which was very unusual. Sam had not done that since she was three. She looked despondent all the time, even when she was asleep. Colleen took her to a couple of movies she thought Sam would love and even that didn't raise any interest or excitement. Sam's emotions were flat and she fell asleep during both of the movies. She was eating very little and Colleen could see she was getting thin.

On Saturday morning, September 15, Colleen told Sam she would be starting school on Monday if she could remember to call her Mommy all weekend and if she could show some appreciation and respect for what Colleen was doing for her. Sam wanted to start school—wanted to get away from Colleen during the day, so she tried hard to behave better. This lifted Colleen's spirits a bit, thinking again that this was just going to take some time.

On Friday at noon, after Sam's first week in school, Colleen received a call from her teacher. "Ms. Carter, it's Sue Berkstrom calling."

"Yes, you're Sa... Brandy's teacher." Colleen lost her calm and almost called Sam by her real name. She tried to sound concerned. "Is Brandy okay?"

"Well, yes, she isn't hurt or sick or anything. But I am worried about her. I have noticed a couple of the other girls trying to befriend her but she rudely rejected both of them. And she doesn't seem to be able to concentrate in class. I have checked her school record and this does not appear to be characteristic of her. I am wondering, has your recent move to Colorado Springs been traumatic for her?"

"My goodness, no, she's been fine at home," Colleen lied. "Thanks for calling to let me know though. I will try to find out if something is bothering her at school."

"Alright then, please get back to me if there is anything I can help with. We could refer her to the school counsellor if necessary."

"Oh no, please don't do that yet," Colleen responded nervously. "Let me talk to her first."

Oh god, when is this going to end? Colleen complained to herself. *Sam talking to a counsellor could be disastrous. I'll have to have a word with her when I get her home.* Her nerves started to jump immediately. *I can't let Sam start talking to a counsellor. I can't believe this. It's been two and a half weeks of hell already. She's not worth it. She's driving me crazy. What the hell am I going to do?* She desperately wanted to open a bottle of wine. Maybe she would; she usually didn't drink at all until after Sam was in bed. She reasoned that she had two and a half hours before she had to pick Sam up from school. One glass wouldn't hurt.

When Colleen picked Sam up, she had calmed down somewhat but her nerves were constantly at the edge lately.

She faked a cheerful demeanour. "Hi Brandy, how was your day?" "Okay," Sam offered, begrudgingly.

"Is that all you can tell me?" Colleen's ire was already building.

Sam didn't answer. She had thought going to school would be better than being with Auntie Colleen all the time but she didn't like this school, the teacher was mean, and the other girls were stupid. She hated it. Sam was depressed.

Colleen decided to wait until she got home. The silence between them was thick. Sam stared out the window, away from Colleen's mean look.

Colleen prepared a snack of cheese and crackers for Sam. "Brandy, come to the table, I'd like to talk to you." Sam let out a huge displeasing sigh, put her book down and walked slowly to the table.

This put Colleen at a disadvantage already. *Damn this kid, I don't need this irritation.* She decided to be direct, no smoothing over the facts like Leanna used to do. Colleen always did think Leanna babied Sam too darn much. "Brandy, your teacher called today. She's worried about you. She says you're rude to the other girls and you aren't concentrating on your work."

Sam didn't answer. She took a small nibble of cheese.

"Is this true, Brandy?"

Sam persisted with her silence.

"Brandy, I asked you a question." Colleen's anger was starting to soar and a hot reddish-purple color began to rise along her neck.

Tears welled in Sam's eyes as she blurted, "The other girls in my class are stupid and I hate my teacher. She's mean to me. She keeps asking me questions I can't answer."

"Well, maybe if you listened in class, you'd know the answer!" Colleen spun, walked away into the living room and sat down. She had had enough. She sat there for a few minutes, returned to the kitchen, and caught a glimpse of Sam looking dejected, shoulders slumped, still at the table, her snack intact on the plate except for the cheese nibble.

Colleen poured herself another glass of wine, taking the bottle to the living room with her. She drank the whole bottle and fell asleep watching television, not giving another thought to the sad little girl sitting at the table.

In the morning, Colleen woke up with a terrific headache, her mouth parched, as if it was filled with fuzz from the clothes dryer. She sat up slowly, rubbing the back of her stiff neck. Suddenly she realized what had happened, and despite her throbbing head, raced to Sam's room. Sam was sleeping in her clothes on the top of the bed, the teddy bear Colleen had purchased thrown on the floor in the corner, nose against the wall.

My God, what have I done and how am I going to get out of it? This is not going to work. She wandered to the kitchen. Sam's snack remained on the table, the cheese dried up and curled at the edges. Colleen realized that Sam probably had not eaten anything since noon, that is, if she ate her lunch at all. She checked her back-pack and found the untouched lunch.

Colleen returned to the living room and lay on the couch, sensible thinking eluding her. She got up again, poured herself a large glass of water, and sat at the kitchen table, staring out the bay window at the rain until she drank the whole glass. The dark clouds that were

286

moving swiftly with the wind matched her mood perfectly. There was a storm brewing outside similar to the one in Colleen's head.

Slowly, as her dark thoughts swirled around her wildly, Colleen began to realize she did not have what it takes to parent a child on her own. She thought she had been doing just that in the last few months of Leanna's life before Leanna went to the palliative care unit. But if Colleen was truly honest with herself, all she had been doing was the physical tasks. Leanna had still been doing the most important aspects of the parenting; the loving, the listening, the guiding, the giving and receiving of true affection. In amongst the dark clouds, she began to realize her friend had been right. *I do not have what it takes to be good parent.* She whispered to herself, "My dear friend, I am so sorry for what I have done. I should have listened to you. You always were the wise one. But how can I undo it now? How can I go back?" She got up, got herself another glass of cold water and began to develop a plan.

CHAPTER 30

A Change of Heart
Sept 22

Colleen was still deep in troubled thought when she heard Sam's light footsteps on the floor going from her bedroom to the bathroom. She jolted upright and went to the kitchen, got a third glass of cold water and sat down at the table for a minute. When she heard Sam on her way back to her room, she headed in that direction too. She stopped at Sam's door and watched the frail little figure tumble back onto the bed.

"Sam," she said quietly.

Surprised to hear her name, Sam turned to look but her stare was sad and vacant, her eyes cloudy and sunken.

Quietly again, from the door, "Sam, I am so sorry, I have made a terrible mistake. I should never have taken you from your grandparents. You are so right, they do love you. Do you still want to go back?"

For the first time since she and Sam were in the light airplane that had taken them across the border, Colleen saw Sam smile; a weak, tentative smile, nonetheless, a smile.

"Yes, pleeease, Auntie Colleen, can I?" she replied in a half-scared voice.

"Sam, I have been thinking a lot in the last two hours. I need to find a way to get you back to the Taylors."

"Oh, Auntie Colleen, thank you, we can find a way together, I know we can." Sam's smile widened into the all familiar grin, somewhat emaciated but definitely Sam's grin. Her two front teeth, late by average standards, were just half-way out. She had not started to lose her baby teeth until a week after her seventh birthday.

"Okay then, why don't I make breakfast while we plan?"

"I'll help you," Sam volunteered. Colleen noted this was the first enthusiasm she had seen from Sam since they were on the plane to Denver. She knew she was definitely making the right choice, despite the consequences.

Both in the crumpled clothes they had slept in, Colleen and Sam made bacon and eggs, toast and jam, the first meal Colleen had seen Sam eat with enthusiasm since she'd picked her up in Dawson Creek. Sam downed a second big glass of orange juice, then asked for a banana. Her appetite was back. As they ate, they planned.

"Sam, I need to get you back to your gramma and grampa's without being caught by the police. That way, they will see I am returning you of my own volition."

"What does voli... mean?"

"Sorry Sam, that's a pretty big word for you. It just means I am returning you willingly. That way, they will hopefully go easy on me, not put me in jail, I hope."

Sam seemed to understand. "Auntie Colleen, I'll tell them you just made a big mistake. It will be okay, you'll see," she reassured confidently.

Colleen was amazed at how quick Sam was to forgive. She hoped others would be able to do the same.

"Okay Sam," she said with a half-hearted laugh, "I will call the man who gave us the plane ride to see if he can arrange for a plane to pick us up at the Colorado Springs Airport." *This will cost me a pile of money again*, she thought to herself, *but I don't dare use the airlines and go through customs.*

On Monday, Sam and Colleen made three flights to get home, Colorado Springs to Great Falls, Great Falls to Edmonton, Edmonton to Dawson Creek. The pilot went through customs in Edmonton but didn't declare his passengers. Colleen and Sam laid low while the plane was being refuelled. Under the name of Karen Carter, Colleen had arranged ahead to pick up a rental car at the Dawson Creek Airport. They arrived at the Taylor's address at 7:00 PM on September 24. As they drove up to the house, Sam was excited beyond description, bouncing in the car, straining against her seatbelt. But Andy was in the neighbour's driveway talking, his back to the street. Colleen drove right by.

"That's Grampa, Auntie Colleen, stop, stop, let me out now."

"No Sam, I can't. We'll wait until Mr. Taylor goes inside. Don't panic, dear. Sit still."

"But, but…"

Colleen cut her off. "Sam, I can't let them see me. Don't worry, we'll swing by again in a few minutes."

****

They were eating supper in the family room while watching the news when the doorbell rang. Meredith looked at Andy. He hesitated, gave her a quick smile, then got up to answer it. "Sam, my god, it's you, you're here," he exclaimed loudly enough for Meredith to hear as he picked her up and embraced her. Hugging her to him, he did a full circle spin.

"Grampa," she giggled as she hugged him fiercely."

Meredith jumped up, almost spilling her wine and ran for the door. She could hear Sam's excited voice, "Grampa, I missed you." They were hugging tightly and Sam could just barely see Meredith over Andy's shoulder. "Gramma, Gramma."

Andy turned halfway around and Sam's arms flew out toward Meredith. "Oh my god, Sam, it is you! You've come back to us!" They were all together, clutched in a tight three-way hug. "I can't believe you're really here."

Meredith released her grip first, standing back ever so slightly. "Let me see you, Sam. My goodness, you're thin and your hair is so short." *My god, she's thin, her eyes look enormous, her round rosy cheeks are gone and her hair is dull.* She put her hand on Sam's short curls and Sam reached out for her again. Meredith's eyes overflowed with tears. "Gramma, don't cry, I'm here, I'm back." Andy passed Sam to Meredith. He noticed there were no suitcases this time and walked out onto the driveway to see if any vehicles were on the street. By then, Colleen was well on her way to the police station to turn herself in. Andy followed Meredith and Sam inside and closed the door against the cool fall air.

Meredith went down on her knees, put Sam's feet on the floor and hugged her again. She gave her a kiss on her forehead, cupping her thin little face with both of her hands. "Oh Sam, we have missed you so very much and we've been so worried about you."

Sam smiled.

"And your teeth have grown."

They both laughed.

"I know, Gramma, I missed you too, that's why Auntie Colleen finally brought me back. I couldn't live without you. I didn't want to eat. I hated it."

Auntie Colleen—that brought Meredith back to reality. "Oh Sam, was it her that dropped you off at our door again?"

"Yes, she's on her way to the police station to turn herself in," she said in such a grown-up way. "She kidmapped me but she changed her mind when she saw how sad I was."

"And she's going to the police station right now?" Andy asked, unbelieving.

"Yes, she said the police will probably call here to make sure I'm okay."

"I suppose they will, Sam," Andy said, amazed.

Meredith didn't care. She was still hugging Sam and looking her over. "Sam, my little sweetheart, are you hungry?"

"Yes, I sure am!" Meredith gave her one more tight loving squeeze, feeling her thin frail body, and put her down, took her hand and walked to the kitchen to get her some supper.

Meredith took her eyes off Sam for three seconds to look in the fridge for the same leftovers she and Andy were eating. When she looked back, Sam was gone. She instantly felt the blood drain from her upper body and her knees started to buckle. She quickly sat down on a chair by the table. *Sam's return is a dream, I was dreaming.* But she could hear Andy on the phone talking to Aaron about Sam, his excitement bubbling. Her head felt like it was full of cotton. She managed to get up and stagger into the living room where Andy was sitting, talking, eyes and voice full of laughter. Andy was certainly real. She sat down. Then she heard Sam coming down the stairs, and then coming toward her. Meredith's vision was blurred from tears but Sam was there, holding Buddy and her quilt under her left arm, running toward her, sweet giggle ringing dull in Meredith's ears.

Sam stopped in front of her. "Gramma, what's wrong? You look sick."

At Sam's presence, Meredith roused from her faint quickly and put her arms out to Sam, pulled her up on her knee, and squeezed her firmly, convincing herself that she was real. "Sam, my sweetie," she said shakily, through her tears, "I looked in the fridge and then you were gone. For a minute, I thought I was only dreaming that you had come back. I got really scared again but you're truly here, aren't you?"

"Yes, Gramma, I'm truly here," she giggled.

As soon as Andy was off the phone, an RCMP constable called to confirm Colleen's story. Andy talked to him briefly, indicating that Sam seemed to be okay, thin but okay. The constable indicated that they would be holding Colleen in custody at least until the initial hearing. "Mr. Taylor, I think you should have Sam checked by a physician to make sure she is okay."

"Yes, I hadn't thought about that yet, but I guess it would be a good idea." "We will wait until morning to release this news to the press. So they will likely be calling you then. Do you have any questions?"

"None that I can think of right now, Constable, thanks for calling."

While Meredith and Sam were getting some supper for Sam, Andy asked, "I guess I should call Wendy and Ian too, huh?"

"Oh yes, you better at least give them a quick call right now."

Sam's ears perked up. "Are you going to call my daddy too?"

"Yes, Sam, he's been very worried about you and I already called him." Andy answered.

"You have?" she questioned.

"Of course, he's your dad, my dear. He was incredibly relieved to hear you're back with us."

"Okay," she said, unconvinced, and went back to helping Meredith.

After Sam was tucked into bed with extra love and fanfare, Meredith and Andy walked down the stairs together. At the bottom, they stopped and gave each other one of their favourite full body hugs, long, warm and loving. Their relationship was like the roots of two carrots wound around each other. Andy took her hand and they sat together on the loveseat. "Meredith, I will never again complain about how our life has changed. That girl belongs in this family."

"Yes, dear, there's nothing like a 'kidmapping' to change one's heart for the better, hey?" They both laughed. "Leanna was right, Sam is definitely a gift, a very 'precious gem' gift." *I wonder if Aaron will ever be able to call her a gift.*

They sat in silence, holding hands, until Andy spoke. "Meredith, what will we do with the press tomorrow? They are going to want pictures and an interview. How are we going to handle that?" The phone rang before Meredith could answer.

Andy got up to answer it. "Dad, Jess and I have been talking. We want to come next weekend to meet Sam. Will that work for you and Mom?" Aaron sounded more determined than Andy had noticed for a long time.

"That sounds wonderful. I don't think we have any other commitments, Aaron, just a minute, let me ask your Mom." Andy told Meredith what Aaron was asking. Meredith couldn't think of any downsides to this idea except she did have some trepidation about more new experiences for Sam right now. "Sure, Aaron, we would love to have you come this weekend. What time do you think you will get here?"

"We'll both take Friday off. If we pack Thursday night and leave first thing in morning, we'll be there by suppertime. That will give us Friday evening and all day Saturday. We'll have to leave right after breakfast on Sunday. What do you think?"

"Sounds like a great plan. We'll look forward to seeing you on Friday. We were just about to discuss how to handle the press tomorrow. We'll try our best to leave you out of it again."

"Thanks Dad, as always, I appreciate your thoughtful caring. I hope you can do that but, if you can't, I think I am much more able to deal with it now. So don't worry about it. See you on Friday."

"Aaron and Jessica will be here on Friday?" Meredith asked, unbelieving.

"Yep, they will be... for supper. What do you think?"

"It's absolutely wonderful that Aaron finally wants to meet Sam. It seems her 'kidmapping' has changed quite a few hearts, hasn't it, dear." They both laughed.

"We've been wanting this for months. But now I do wonder how much more excitement our dear Sam can handle in such a short time. I hope she will be okay with this. Sam has been waiting so long for this, I sense she has developed an indifference to her dad. She is going to have to deal with the press tomorrow too. And speaking of the press, I want to limit Sam's exposure to Mike only, Andy. I know he will handle this with care. He was so good when we gave him the story of Sam's disappearance."

It was hard for both Meredith and Andy to find sleep. There was so much happening again. They talked for a long time.

"We have to make an appointment for Sam to see the doctor. We should call and make an appointment tomorrow. I'll do that first thing in the morning."

"Yes, and when I told Aaron we would try to keep him out of the press again, believe it or not, he seemed like he didn't even care anymore. I think he is truly coming to terms with this whole thing, Meredith."

"Wow, wonders never cease. He and Jessica are going to be shocked by how thin Sam is. I think we should prepare them for it. I'll have to try to fatten her up with all the things she loves. I think she will gain her weight back quite quickly but not in four days." Meredith could hear Andy's breathing slowing. He was starting to drift off. "Oh Andy, the relief I feel tonight is exhilarating. I have been so exhausted but

I think my energy is already coming back. How can you sleep with all this excitement?" There was no answer. Meredith got up and took a sleep aid she had purchased from the health food store. She could tell she really needed it tonight. She told herself it was okay because she wouldn't need her Ativan anymore. *What a day it has been. What a roller coaster ride our family has been on for the last six months. Oh Sam, I am so happy to have you back, you sweet, sweet child. And your daddy is finally coming to meet you. Aaron, this is going to be alright. The roller coaster is slowing down a bit but the ride is not finished.* She was asleep in twenty minutes.

CHAPTER 31

———

Aaron and Jessica Meet Sam
Sept 28

In the morning, Andy was awake first, and he quietly slipped out of bed and left the bedroom, silently closing the door behind him. From the bathroom, he could hear Sam reading to Buddy. Despite his efforts at being quiet, Meredith heard him and joined him in the bathroom. He put a vertical finger to his mouth and indicated for Meredith to be quiet. They both stood there holding hands and smiling at each other as they listened. Andy spoke first, "Music to my ears, dear."

"Yes, I think I've never heard anything sweeter," Meredith whispered. "We have to tell her about Aaron's call last night. Should we do that now, before breakfast?" Andy nodded and they walked together into Sam's room, each one taking a seat on the bed beside her. Sam looked up and gave them her winning grin.

"Good morning, Sam," they said in unison.

"Good morning, Gramma and Grampa," Sam echoed.

Meredith started, "We have some very good news for you this morning."

Andy took over and told her about Aaron and Jessica's plan to come on the weekend. "Sam, your daddy does not want to wait any longer to see you. He got very scared when you disappeared and was worried that he may never get to meet you."

She bent forward and gave Andy a hug, then Meredith. Then her feet hit the floor. As she was running to Aaron's bedroom, she asked loudly, "Can we go look at their picture?

"That's my daddy and Jessica when they got married, right?"

"That's right, Sam. They were married two years ago."

"How long ago is that?"

"That was about when you were in kindergarten."

"Wow, do they have any other children?"

"No but they are expecting a baby soon." Meredith responded cautiously, wondering if this would bother Sam.

Sam looked like she was in deep thought. "Do you think they will like me, Gramma?"

"Oh Sam, what's not to like about you? Of course, they will love you, my dear." Meredith laughed but Sam looked troubled.

"When will they get the baby?"

"Oh, not for quite a while yet. Not for at least three months. Three months is the same as twelve weeks or eighty-four days. Let's count eighty-four days on our fingers so you can see how long it is." Sam, Meredith and Andy all held up ten fingers. "Ten, twenty, thirty, forty, fifty, sixty, seventy, eighty, and four."

"That is a long time. How will they know when the baby is coming?" Meredith took over and explained in her experienced way about having babies. In her public health nursing days, she had taught "too many to count" sex education classes in elementary, junior high, and high school. Sam took all this in with curiosity and enthusiasm.

After breakfast, they hadn't heard from the press yet. Andy went to work and Sam retreated upstairs. Meredith decided to give her some time. She cleaned up the dishes and called in to work to tell only the manager that she wouldn't be there, explaining that Sam had suddenly been returned last night. She asked her to keep this news in confidence until it came out in the press.

Meredith and Andy decided not to send Sam back to school for the rest of the week. They thought she had quite enough excitement for a while; and, besides, Meredith was not ready to let her out of her sight yet. When she went upstairs to get dressed, she found Sam in Aaron's room again. Meredith had turned one end of it into her office where she had a large dark walnut double pedestal desk and a grey two drawer horizontal filing cabinet. There was still a double bed, bedside table, and a dresser on the other side of the room. Sam was lying on the bed, propped on the pillows and shams with Buddy and her quilt, staring at Aaron and Jessica's wedding picture on the wall across from the foot of the bed. She had not heard or seen Meredith so she stood behind the edge of the doorway, eavesdropping.

"What do you think, Buddy, will we like my daddy?" She waited for Buddy's imaginary answer. "Are you scared to meet him too? He looks nice though, doesn't he?" Meredith's tears were back again. She was certain she hadn't cried so much in all her life as she had in the last six months. She waited quietly. "Buddy, I think I'm going to let you meet him first and see what you think. Okay?"

Meredith decided it was time to interrupt. She dried her eyes on her pyjama top and stepped forward, visible from the bedroom door. "Oh Sam, there you are, are you ready to get washed up?"

Sam looked up at Meredith, her tears flowing too. She wiped hers with her quilt and got up from the bed, leaving Buddy on the pillow, carefully covered with the quilt. "Okay, Gramma." she said, her voice quiet and forlorn. "I'll leave Buddy here to think for a while."

Meredith's heart cracked again. It must look like a very badly shattered windshield by now. She wondered how it could keep beating. The next rock thrown would surely finish it. *Sam has had so much to deal with in her young life already. How can I help her through yet more traumatic events?* She bent down, gave her a warm hug and whispered in her ear. "Sam, it will be okay. Your dad has loved you from afar. He is always thinking and asking about you," she exaggerated. "Now come and let's talk about what we're going to do today while we get dressed."

Meredith and Sam decided they would go grocery shopping first. All the major grocery stores in Dawson Creek offered ten percent off on Tuesday so Meredith liked to do the bulk of her shopping for the week on Tuesday. She was looking forward to going early today instead of fighting the after-work crowds. They both went downstairs to get the grocery list ready. Meredith glanced out the window and noticed a *Peace River Block News* van pulling up at the curb. Half expectedly, the phone rang. "Mrs. Taylor, this is Mike from your local paper. We understand Sam was returned to you last night. How are you and Andy and Sam doing?"

"Oh Mike, we are overwhelmed with happiness. And thank goodness, Sam is okay."

"Yes, I can only begin to imagine your relief. I'm so glad to hear Sam is alright. The kidnapping must have been horrendous for you."

"My god, yes, both Andy and I and our whole family were devastated. I can't begin to tell you how relieved and grateful we are."

"This is such a positive human interest story. The whole world will love to hear it. Would you be kind enough to grant me an interview?"

"Yes, we know we should do that. People are going to want to know and you want your story. But I don't want to do this alone. Please wait until I call Andy to come home from work."

"Okay, I would be most grateful if you didn't talk to any other press until I get the story first."

"Yes, Mike, Andy and I appreciated your sensitivity when Sam was kidnapped. You will be the *only* press we talk to. Just please wait until Andy comes back from work."

"Okay, thanks, Mrs. Taylor." Mike was young and energetic and had been very compassionate at the time of Sam's kidnapping. Meredith and Andy had truly appreciated his style of reporting—only the facts as they developed, no speculating.

Sam was listening. "Who was that, Gramma?" By the time Andy got home, Meredith had explained to Sam what was happening. She seemed okay—excited but okay. Mike gave them five minutes, and then he was ringing the doorbell.

"Thanks, Mr. Taylor, for seeing me."

"No problem. Come in, Mike."

Mike conducted a comprehensive interview, asking questions of each of them. It was obvious Sam's truthful and prolific account of her experience delighted Mike. "This is an amazing story, and it's mine. I can't believe it! Thanks, Sam." She smiled graciously at him.

He took pictures of all four of them, including Buddy and Sam's quilt. Thrilled to get this incredible scoop, he extended profuse thanks and best wishes. The story would be released in the *Dawson Creek Daily News* at 4:00 PM. Meredith and Andy knew they were in for a deluge of calls and visits afterwards. But they were determined to stick to one press release. They would avoid all other calls. They knew other networks could pick up the story from the *Canadian Press*.

Andy returned to work and Sam and Meredith went shopping, determined to keep a low profile. They ran into one of Meredith's co-workers and had to answer a few questions. Meredith told her she could get the details from today's paper. She heard a couple of older women whispering and looking at them but they didn't approach.

The check-out clerk was a young high school girl who paid no attention to them.

****

Meredith and Sam passed the next two days successfully, keeping as low a profile as possible. The people of Dawson Creek were mostly kind bystanders, smiling knowingly at them. Meredith took Sam to her office and introduced her to a few people. She hadn't done that before. Sam was delighted to see Deidre, who had big hugs for her and told her to come and visit Bailey, her dog, real soon. "She misses your attention, Sam."

On Thursday morning, Meredith had an appointment for Sam with her physician. He had followed up with Sam after Meredith had taken her to emergency for her broken arm so he knew her well. When Dr. Samuels entered the examining room, the delight on his face was obvious. "Sam, how good to see you again. I hear you have had quite an adventure. How are you doing?"

She beamed back at him. "I'm just fine now that I'm back with Gramma and Grampa."

"Well, let me have a look at you." He picked up one of her thin little arms and gave it a soft rub. "I think you have lost some weight, young lady."

"Yes, I have, I didn't feel like eating when I was with Auntie Colleen," she replied matter of fact.

Dr. Samuels looked at Meredith for answers and she explained what had happened. Then he established from both of them that they had no other concerns about what happened while Sam was away. "Okay, I'm going to order some blood tests and I would like to see her again in two weeks to do a weight check and make sure she is recovering as expected. Does that sound okay to you?"

"Absolutely, I think that's a good idea. I believe Sam is fine but we need to make sure."

At breakfast on Friday morning, Meredith reminded Sam that Aaron and Jessica were coming to visit for the weekend and would be here for supper. At first Sam was very quiet, non-reactionary. She kept eating her cereal and didn't respond. It was almost as if she hadn't heard them. This worried Meredith. *I hope she will be her usual happy self for Aaron and Jessica's visit.* She desperately wanted the meeting to go well but she understood that Aaron was still an unknown entity for Sam. *I wonder what Sam is thinking about? She seems bothered by something.* She decided to distract her.

"Sam, how be if you help me make some extra special suppers for your dad and Jessica for the weekend. His favourite foods are meatballs with mashed potatoes and lots of gravy, spaghetti and meat sauce with lots of hot spices and banana cream pie."

"She perked up immediately. "That's funny, Gramma, because I like all of that too. Let's make all of it."

"Well, you know, you are his daughter, there are bound to be some similarities, my dear."

"I guess so," she said with a tentative smile, her new front teeth reflecting the light from the kitchen window.

First they made meat sauce for Saturday. While it was simmering, they started on the meatballs. When the meatballs were cooking in oven, they started to make the banana cream pie. Meredith explained that the pie had to be made in three stages, first the crust, then the sliced bananas and the filling, and last, the whipped cream. While Sam was carefully stirring the vanilla sauce for the pie, Meredith was holding on to her and the pot to prevent an accident and she said, "Sam, did you know that we are multi-tasking?"

"What does that mean, Gramma?" Sam was back to her usual curious, lively self again.

Meredith explained, ending with, "This is what women do all the time. We are way better than men at multi-tasking." Sam giggled and stirred faster and Meredith took a quick and pleasant little trip down memory lane, remembering her cooking moments with Wendy.

Shortly after 5:00 PM, the doorbell rang and Andy went to answer it. Meredith glanced out the window to see Aaron's truck in the drive-way. "Sam, they're here." Sam was sitting on the couch with Buddy and her blanket, reading, having a quiet time.

Meredith met Sam at the entrance and they stood behind Andy as he opened the door. Meredith felt Sam clinging to her leg. Andy gave both Aaron and Jessica a big hug and backed away. Aaron kneeled down on the step and with a huge smile said, "So this is Sam whom I have heard so much about. I am so very glad to meet you, young lady." He held out his hand. Sam hesitated but Aaron was patient. Finally, she stepped forward and held Buddy in front of her, "This is my good friend, Buddy."

Aaron took Buddy's paw and shook it gently, smiling kindly at the bear, "Glad to meet you, Buddy." Then Sam moved forward cautiously and Aaron put out both of his hands. She slowly moved into them and he hugged her carefully and briefly, taking in the fresh scent of her hair and the frailness of her body. He let her go and turned to Jessica. "This is my wife, Jessica, Sam." Jessica knelt down on the step too and offered her wide-open arms, her smile beaming at Sam. Again, Sam moved cautiously toward Jessica and accepted her brief hug. Jessica released her and Sam backed away toward Meredith, smiling shyly at both of them. Aaron and Jessica each gave Meredith a warm linger-ing hug.

"Well, come in... Sam and I have been cooking all day for you."

Aaron looked directly at Sam, smiling, and asked, "What have you been making, Sam? It sure smells good in here."

"Gramma and I have made all your favourite stuff," she said decid-edly, quickly losing her shyness.

"Really, and just what is all my favourite stuff?" He kneeled down again, waiting for Sam's answer.

Meredith shared a knowing look with Jessica while Sam was telling Aaron what they had been cooking. *This is going well.* Jessica asked if she could help. Aaron and Andy retreated to the living room. Sam and Buddy cuddled up to Andy in the loveseat, content to listen to her grampa and her daddy talk.

****

The weekend passed pleasantly with no hitches. Saturday was a bit chilly but Aaron and Sam went for a long bike ride, Aaron borrowing Meredith's bike. They all played cards and taught Sam how to play Thirty-One. By the end of three rounds, Sam was getting very quick at adding the numbers. After supper, she read her favourite book, *The Coyote who Swallowed the Flea,* to Aaron and Jessica. When Meredith told her it was time to get ready for bed, she asked Jessica to help her.

While Jessica and Sam were upstairs, Aaron said "God, is she a sweet kid, and smart! Now I understand what you've been saying, Mom. I had suspicions that you were exaggerating just to make me feel better."

"Aaron, you know I would never do that."

He smiled, questioning her.

Meredith eased into a different subject. "Jessica is looking great. Her pregnancy certainly seems to be agreeing with her."

"Oh yeah, she says she feels better than ever, Mom. We are both so excited. It's damn hard to wait nine months to see what you are going to get though." They all laughed. Aaron was truly his old jovial self again.

"Mom, Dad, Jess and I have had some discussions about Sam coming to live with us. We do want to assume responsibility for

307

parenting her but we have decided to wait until after the baby comes. Is that okay?"

"Oh Aaron, it is the only reasonable rational thing to do. You and Jessica still need time to get used to your new baby, your parenting role, this is huge stuff, dear. And Sam needs some time too, for her life to return to normal. We need to go slow with this."

"But we're both so concerned about you and dad, this can't be easy for you, looking after a seven-year-old."

Andy responded, "No, Aaron, it's not... and it has changed our life and our retirement plans dramatically, but we're enjoying our time with Sam and we're managing just fine. I think Sam should complete her second year of school here. That will give you and Jessica plenty of time to get used to your new baby. You need to make sure this is what you want to do."

Meredith added, "I think we should come and visit you for a weekend sometime soon and let Sam get used to your house too."

"That is an excellent idea. We need to set a date tonight when Jessica comes downstairs."

CHAPTER 32

———

Visiting Aaron & Jessica
October 13

Sam returned to school on Monday morning, and Meredith went with her to her classroom. When Mrs. Dufour saw Sam, she bent down and gave her a big hug, tears in her eyes. "Mrs. Taylor, I was so relieved to hear Sam was back. I felt terrible about not seeing..."

Meredith held up her hand and interrupted. "Don't even go there, my dear. You had absolutely nothing to do with this, you are faultless, Mrs. Dufour. You cannot be everywhere and see everything."

"Well, thank you," she said, unsure of herself, "but..."

"No buts, Sam is back and all is well. That's all that matters." Meredith looked across the classroom. Rilla and Holly greeted Sam with excitement and the three of them were soon over in the corner looking at the new classroom hamster like nothing had happened in between the first day of school and now. Meredith smiled, took Mrs. Dufour's hand in both of hers and shook it briefly, giving her a reassuring smile. "You have a great day!" Then she quickly turned and left, knowing Sam was safe now. Driving to work, Meredith thought she had never felt better or more energetic.

****

Aaron and Jessica invited Andy, Meredith, and Sam to Calgary for Thanksgiving. The nine-hundred-kilometre drive from Dawson Creek to Calgary was long but delightful. The fall colors were at their peak and the sun was shining over Alberta's famous azure-blue skies. September had been a cool, wet month and the harvest had been delayed. But now the countryside was alive with fall harvest activity, field after field occupied by combines, grain trucks, swathers. The yet uncut golden grain was moving in waves across the fields, swayed by the light breeze. Wendy had once told Meredith that this was her favourite season because the sky was at its richest, deepest blue during the fall. When Meredith looked at the sky, she didn't have to wonder if this was true. She pointed this out to Sam, who was in the back seat with Buddy, her books, and pencil crayons.

The ten-hour trip seemed to go amazingly quick. They played games, sang songs, ate snacks, stopped for bathroom breaks and read. Meredith looked up and was surprised to see the city of Calgary coming into view as they crested a hill. "Sam, look, we're almost there, that's Calgary up ahead."

Sam looked up from her book and stretched to see. "Wow, it looks big!" The city sprawled out before them, much of it visible from their high vantage point, seemingly going on forever.

"It is, dear, over a million people live there."

"How many people live in Dawson Creek, Gramma?"

"Only eleven thousand. Here, let me write both numbers on your paper for you so you can see the difference."

"Wow, that must be a lot!"

"Yes, dear, Calgary is the biggest city in Alberta, the fourth largest city in Canada." Sam lapped up information like this and loved to repeat it to whoever was interested. She was an insatiable learner. Meredith suspected she would be repeating these demographics to Aaron and Jessica sometime on the weekend.

As they pulled into the driveway, Sam exclaimed, "Is this where they live?" The two-story house with attached garage looked so inviting to Meredith.

"You bet it is, we're here, Sam," Andy answered, already opening his door to get out and stretch.

"Wow, it's nice, I like Daddy's house." Aaron opened the front door. "There he is, there's Daddy." Sam was out of the car and running up the sidewalk into Aaron's open arms. She had claimed him as her own. Andy and Meredith smiled widely at each other, their joy spilling from their faces. They walked up the sidewalk with both trepidation and excitement.

After all the hugging, Meredith patted Jessica's tummy and said, "Oooo, this baby has grown."

Sam was immediately interested. She remembered that Aaron and Jessica were expecting a baby and she couldn't contain her questions, having trouble waiting for the answers. "Is it going to be a boy or a girl? Will it be my brother or my sister? Where will it sleep?"

"Well, come right in, Sam, and we will show you the baby's room," Jessica cooed. "We have it all ready."

As Sam was getting all her questions answered, Meredith watched her son and daughter-in-law. Jessica was radiant, glowing with her pregnancy. Aaron looked stunningly handsome and confident again, his iridescent blue eyes sparkling with mischief. She noticed Aaron had gained most of his weight back and his smile was warm; that familiar family grin. *God, it's good to see him looking like his old self again.* Quick memories floated by Meredith from when she had been pregnant with Aaron.

"So, Mom, how are you doing?" He gave her another big bear hug and Meredith felt the weight of the world lift from her fractured heart as he squeezed her in his arms.

"I'm doing just fine, Aaron. How about you and Jessica?"

"Oh, we're both doing great. I'm just on maintenance counselling now, once a month or as needed. Maybe one more session and I will call it quits."

"That's wonderful, I'm so happy for you, my son." They smiled and hugged again."

Sam was delighting everyone with her enthusiasm. She was enthralled with everything in the nursery. When Aaron took her suitcase and led her to her newly decorated room, she put Buddy on the bed and covered him with her quilt, telling him this was his room too. She loved Jessica's tabby cat, Zoey and Zoey lapped up Sam's attention. They were soon the best of friends.

After supper, Meredith and Aaron did the dishes while Jessica and Sam shared the reading of several books and Andy watched the news. Aaron and Jessica had purchased some books and games for Sam and had changed the furniture and decor in their spare bedroom. Aaron told Sam that it was her room for whenever she came to visit. The room was pink and yellow, the bed covers were soft and full of feminine ruffles; the furniture was white and feminine with lots of shelves for Sam's stuff. She was tickled with delight.

One step at a time, Meredith's heart was slowly mending from all the previous cracks. Each time she witnessed Sam doing something with or talking with Aaron or Jessica, she could literally feel the healing going on inside her. The cracks in her heart were mending, her bowels were slowly relaxing into nice soft curves, and her brain was unfolding from its twisted form.

She and Andy had been relegated to the family room to sleep on the sofa bed. Once they had settled in, she commented to him, "I can't ever remember feeling more satisfied in my life. I am sure I must have felt this happy when you asked me to marry you, dear, or when each of our own children arrived. But never more satisfied. So much has happened in our lives this year, it's almost unbelievable."

"Yes, it's been quite a soap opera, hasn't it?"

Meredith was already asleep, snugly tucked into the dependable curves of Andy's warm body.

****

Aaron was having his proverbial trouble sleeping tonight but it was excitement and ecstatic thoughts that were keeping him awake, not nightmares. At supper, he had been watching Sam and, for a second, he envisioned what she must have looked like as a new baby, then as a toddler. He knew she was becoming part of him, part of his family. It was beginning to feel like she had always been there. His thoughts amazed and tickled him. He turned over, fluffed his pillow and snuggled into Jessica, finally managing to quiet his brain activity, allowing him to drift off into comfortable slumber.

CHAPTER 33

Andy's Retirement
Oct 20

Andy's retirement had been looming over the Taylors and Meredith had given it very little thought until they returned from Calgary. Next weekend, they were scheduled to fly to Vancouver for Allison and Dave Saunders' daughter's wedding. Ever since the Saunders had moved to Victoria, both couples had spent their summer and winter holidays together. Their friendship was one of a kind. It was Saturday, only four days before they had to leave again, and Meredith was finally beginning to think ahead about it. She had talked to Wendy about looking after Sam while they were gone. But she felt so uncertain about leaving her—not because Sam would be reluctant; she loved to spend time with Wendy, Ian and the boys. Meredith questioned whether or not she herself could stand the separation.

The kidnapping had taken its toll on her nerves and she knew she was feeling far more protective than necessary but she couldn't seem to shut down her fears. They had to leave on Wednesday as they were also attending a wine and cheese pre-wedding party that evening for the wedding couple. Then they would travel to Victoria by ferry on Thursday for Andy's official retirement send-off on Friday, then back to Vancouver for the wedding on Sunday. It all seemed a bit too much to handle. Last year, she would have had no problem coping with this type of weekend itinerary. She thought Andy had been a tad edgy and figured it might be due to the finality of his retirement rather than his concern for leaving Sam or the numerous weekend commitments they had.

This morning at breakfast, she and Andy explained to Sam what was happening and she was quite excited about seeing Wendy, Ian, and the boys again. She had not seen them since she had miraculously been returned to the Taylors' only a month ago. Sam was just fine with the idea and Meredith planned to talk to Sam's teacher on Monday to warn her that Sam would not be in school from Wednesday to Monday. She hated the thought of doing this since Sam had missed so much school already and had only been back for three weeks. But life goes on and commitments must be met. *Where is that burst of renewed energy I experienced on the first day that I dropped Sam off to school feeling like life was back to normal? Just what is normal anyway? I'm really not sure anymore. Life still seems so darn complicated.*

With Andy's expert online help, Meredith had managed to purchase a shower gift for the bride and a wedding present online at *The Bay* in Vancouver—thank goodness for wedding registries. Meredith had felt a bit guilty for not shopping for the perfectly selected gifts but she desperately needed to be frugal with her time. And taking gifts on a plane would only increase the complexity of their travel. She urgently needed "simple" right now. At her age, looking after Sam and working remained a huge challenge. She felt Sam needed a great deal of nurturing and that was the most important task at hand. No matter what, she would be there for her ever-so-precious granddaughter who had been through so much in such a short time. Meredith spent all the time she could spare with Sam, giving her lots of opportunities to ask questions. She'd thought her mother's death would come up again sometime but it hadn't yet.

Meredith was amazed at how pragmatic Sam had been when talking about her time spent with Colleen. Sam's words floated through Meredith's grey matter. *"Auntie Colleen said my mommy wanted her to look after me, but I didn't believe it because she had lied to me about other things. Besides, I remembered that my mommy told me I should stay with my gramma and grampa until she could come and get me."* Sam's understanding of human nature was quite something. Meredith wondered if Sam still had not internalized that her mother was dead and would never be coming back. Sam had gone on to talk about missing Buddy, hating school, and not being able to eat. *"What I hated most was when Auntie Colleen cut my hair and changed my name to Brandy. Gramma, I felt like I wasn't me anymore."*

With all these thoughts floating around in her brain, Meredith was feeling like she was deserting Sam at a crucial time in her life. When she expressed these worries to Andy, he said Sam would be fine, that all was obviously going well with her. But Meredith wondered if, underneath the surface of Sam's contented demeanour, something might be brewing. Her reluctance to leave Sam and her need to be there for her husband at a critical life passage was creating some opposing forces in her head and her heart again. Those partially healed scars were threatening to break down and cause a volcanic eruption of nerves and blood and tissue inside her chest. Feeling anxious, Meredith headed off to school with Sam on Monday morning.

"What's the matter, Gramma? You don't seem very happy today."

"Oh Sam, I'm sorry. I'm really quite fine, just concerned that we have to leave you on Wednesday to go to Vancouver."

"But I'll be fine with Auntie Wendy and the boys, Gramma, it will be fun. That's silly for you to worry about that!"

Meredith's tears were at the brink. "Sam you are so wise for your years and I know you're right, but I can't quite get my head around it. I don't like leaving you."

Sam was smiling. "Well then, you will just have to phone me often and I'll tell you how happy I am."

Meredith laughed in spite of herself. "That, I will surely do, my dear." She reached over and squeezed Sam's knee.

"Mrs. Dufour, I'm so sorry but I'm afraid we have to take Sam out of school for four days as my husband and I have to go to Vancouver and Victoria this week." She sighed apologetically and went on. "We'll be taking Sam over to my daughter's in Grande Prairie for the time that we're away."

"Oh, Mrs. Taylor, don't worry about Sam missing school. She is completely caught up already from her last absence and she picks up on her learning tasks so quickly. Four days will not create even the smallest ripple for her. Don't worry one minute about this. But I will certainly miss Sam. Now that is something you should worry about." She laughed, indicating she was joking and she waved her hand at Meredith. "You go and have a wonderful time. I hope it will be at least somewhat restful. You probably need it."

"Well, thank you, thank you so much for making this easy. I was concerned about her missing more school."

"No worries there, Mrs. Taylor, I assure you, it won't create a single ripple."

"Okay then, she will be away Wednesday through Monday, returning on Tuesday morning."

"Got it, I will write it in my registry. Thanks, I'll see you when you get back."

Meredith felt a wave of relief washing over her on her short drive to her office. Mrs. Dufour had been very reassuring. Maybe now she could concentrate on work, packing, and getting her mind ready to go. As soon as she got to her desk, she decided to check in with Wendy about their plans.

Monday and Tuesday flew by. Wednesday morning, Meredith, Andy, and Sam were in the car early driving to Grande Prairie. Winter was threatening an early arrival with the first snowfall during the night. A luxurious white carpet covered the Peace Country except for the highway. The snow had melted on the asphalt and the road was clear. The stubble from the grain crops was poking through the snow, picking up the morning sun and glowing gold. The bark of the aspen trees glistened silver. Sam was quiet in the back seat, enthralled with winter's first display of diamonds, sparkling everywhere; in the fields, in the ditches, on the boughs of grass bent over by the weight, on the tree branches, on the power lines. The elegant aspen branches were bent slightly with the fine lines of snow clinging on top of them. The spruce branches were hanging much lower, laden with heavy clusters of snow and diamonds. As the sun demonstrated its increasing warmth and a slight breeze began to build, diamond clusters started to fall from the power lines and aspen branches. Meredith had grown up in the Peace Country and she and Andy had deliberately sought out jobs here after finishing university. On mornings like this, she was grateful for the intense beauty of where she lived.

Wendy and the boys met them at the airport and, as soon as the boys saw Sam, they came running over and took their turns excitedly telling her what they had planned as she bent over and gave them both a big hug. Wendy caught up with them and gave Sam a long, warm hug. Andy was right again. Sam would be fine in Wendy's loving, capable hands.

As they waited in security, this scene was replaying in Meredith's head and she smiled at Andy and hugged his arm. "So Andy, this is it for you—we are on our way to your retirement party. How are you feeling?" *It's time I thought about my husband for a change.*

"Good, Meredith, good, I can hardly wait until this is over though. You know how I hate to be the centre of attention."

"Yes, my humble, sweet husband, I do." Andy always played down his worthiness and his accomplishments but Meredith knew he was greatly appreciated in his work circles.

"You know what the best part is," he said. "I am going to have you all to myself and we are going to have a fantastic weekend. And, boy, do we need it!"

"You said it. I'm looking forward to it too. I'm going to rest and relax and think about you and Allison and Dave and their daughter's wedding and you and you and you."

"That sounds good to me. And no more worrying, Wendy's got it all under control."

"Yes, she does!" Meredith said emphatically, working at convincing herself.

Once Meredith was on the plane, she was finally able to relax. Andy was holding her hand and she looked up at him, thankful again for his organizational skills and his supportive ways. He always managed the details of their trips and vacations, making sure the car was properly maintained and ready, or booking flights, hotels, rental cars, purchasing travel insurance, renewing passports. He did it all. This was one of his jobs in the division of household labour.

Andy took out his book and began to read. Meredith was comfortable with only her thoughts. She let him read for a short while but she wanted to talk. "Andy, at times like this, crossroads in our lives, you know how I love to reminisce. Do you remember when we first met? At the Tuck Shop on the campus. God, you were handsome." She smiled gently at him and he put his book down willingly. "Remember, I was with another fellow and we joined you and two other aggies." (Agricultural Students)

He humoured her. "Oh yes, dear, how could I forget?" "There was an incredible magnetism, a compelling attraction between us, I can

320

still remember the strength in it. We began to snatch glances at each other, both of us knowing the inappropriateness of our flirting, both unable to stop ourselves."

He picked up her hand and squeezed it. "You were so cute with your curly golden-red hair poking up in all directions, your grin, I loved your grin...and your bright blue eyes, such lively eyes."

"We fell in love that day, Andy, that's what started it all."

"Yeah, and I knew you were dating Gene. I didn't know what to do, he was my classmate and my friend."

"But we both knew, didn't we, without even talking?"

"Yep, that moment in time was a definite revelation." He bent over and gave her a quick kiss. As they looked forward, the stewardess walked by and gave them both a grin.

****

The ferry ride to Victoria was relaxing and the movement of the ferry in water was lulling them both into pleasurable relaxation. The pre-wedding wine and cheese party had been held at the same hotel that everyone was staying at, so Andy didn't have to drive and had taken on his share of wine, keeping up to Dave, the father of the bride. Meredith smiled as she thought about the party, the conversations, the anticipation of the wedding. Then she turned her attention to her husband. "What are you thinking, Andy?"

"Oh, I just hope they keep it simple. I told Helen I didn't want any fanfare so she promised a simple luncheon."

"My dear, you are so sweet, I love your modesty."

Andy had worked for the Ministry of Agriculture and Fisheries for fifteen years and he had given it his best. But he was quite happy to be giving up all the political and bureaucratic frustrations. He knew he would have to find other work, at least part time, to keep him busy, but right now, he just wanted to rest for a while, take time for some peace and quiet, and enjoy the outdoors. He planned to do a lot of hunting with his friends this fall. He loved the "bush" as he called it.

Once they were settled into their hotel, they called Wendy and talked to Sam. All was well there. Andy took Meredith out for supper to a wonderful little Greek restaurant, The Periklis, that he had eaten at on previous trips to Victoria. He was thrilled to be able to share it with Meredith this time. The food was all locally prepared and quite authentically Greek. Andy ordered a bottle of red wine recommended by the waiter and some tzatziki with pita bread for an appetizer. Meredith had never tasted such delicious tzatziki and she sopped up more than her share. For the main course, they had chicken souv-laki with spanakopita and rosemary-garlic roasted potatoes. Finally, they shared two desserts, wine-poached pears and cherry-chocolate baklava. Between the wine and the incredible food, they were both stuffed. They walked to the hotel, holding hands, swinging arms, gig-gling like a pair of teenagers, and feeling inconceivably wonderful. They were both in bed and asleep by 9:30.

Andy had to attend a final meeting in the morning. Meredith was still in her P.J.s as he gave her a quick hug and kiss. As she got herself ready for the day, Andy's touch still present on her skin, she thought of how addicted she was to his caress, even after all these years. When she was ready, she wandered down to the mall to shop. It was only three blocks from their hotel. She would meet Andy at the office just before lunch. She was quite thrilled to have a big-city mall to shop in. Dawson Creek offered all the amenities but it was nice to have big-city selection to choose from for a change. And having two and a half hours all to herself to shop was a rare and welcome privilege.

Their hotel was perfectly located three blocks from the mall and one and a half blocks from the Ministry Office. After her shopping trip, Meredith changed her clothes, put on a fresh coat of lipstick and headed out to meet Andy. When she entered the building, the security guard sitting behind a big desk looked her way, as if to say, "And who are you?"

"Hello, I'm Andy Taylor's wife. I'm just waiting for him to join me for lunch."

"Okay, have a seat," he said with no expression. He looked down at his desk, didn't give her a moment's notice. In a few minutes, Andy and six co-workers arrived. He proudly introduced Meredith as his lovely wife, making her feel special as he always did. All eight of them headed to the restaurant where six more co-workers and the deputy minister joined them. Andy's manager had honoured Andy's request to keep it simple. After the meal and many jokes about retiring, Andy was honoured with flattering words from several of his co-workers and the deputy minister, who presented him with a Meritorious Service Award signed by the premier, the minister and the deputy minister.

It was all over within an hour and a half and Andy and Meredith were able to catch the 3:00 PM ferry back to Vancouver for the wedding. Sailing time was about one hour and forty-five minutes. They chatted and laughed about Andy's retirement luncheon and tried to plan their time in Vancouver. They would have the evening and most of the day tomorrow as the wedding didn't start until 5:00 PM. Once they settled in their hotel, they wandered over to Davie Street to find a restaurant for supper.

The weather was mild and it wasn't raining, somewhat of a treat for Vancouverites. They had experienced even more rain than usual over the summer. It seemed the whole city was out enjoying themselves. The streets were crowded and people were bumping into each other frequently as they passed. Andy and Meredith were uncomfortable with the crowds of unfamiliar and sometimes very strange-looking people. They held on to each other tightly. Some of the many restaurants were quite empty and a few were crowded with patrons waiting in line to get in. It was easy to tell where the good food was.

Andy refused to wait in line so they kept walking all the way down to English Bay. They had both eaten at the Boathouse before and were hoping it would not be so crowded. The restaurant was full but they were still seating people in the bar where you could get the same food as in the restaurant. Disappointed, they decided to accept the bar. It was very noisy, the waitress was over extended, the service was haphazard, and the food mediocre. They were reminded of why they liked to live in Dawson Creek, big-city life was definitely not for them. After supper, they headed back to their hotel room, relaxed for a while with the television, and were asleep by 9:30.

The next morning, they had breakfast at a nearby Smitty's and walked over to Robson Street, another favorite spot for Vancouverites. By 11:30 AM, it was just as crowded as Davie Street the night before. The sun was shining again and people were out enjoying it. They did some window shopping and eventually found a Greek restaurant they were vaguely familiar with and had a late lunch. They walked back to their hotel for a rest before getting ready for the wedding.

"God, Andy, this trip is making me feel old. A trip to *Vancouver* used to be exciting but I can't say I'm enjoying it this time. Maybe I'm just tired."

"I think were both tired, Meredith. I will be so happy to get home."

****

Their flight landed at Grande Prairie at 2:30 PM on Sunday. Wendy and the boys and Sam were there to meet them. Sam saw Andy first and she ran full speed toward him, almost bowling over a small, frail, elderly woman. She leapt into Andy's arms and reached for Meredith, grinning from ear to ear, exposing her beautiful new front teeth. In the last month, they had finished their descent and made her look so much more grown up, strikingly white, perfectly-formed teeth, too big for her little girl face. "Gramma, Grampa, I'm so happy you're back. I missed you! Did you have a good time? Was the wedding nice? Can I see all the pictures?" *Bubbly, vivacious Sam,* Meredith thought, relieved to see her so happy.

"Yes, yes, and yes, Sam. We had a wonderful time but we missed you so much. Did you have a good time with Wendy and Ian and the boys?" Meredith asked.

"Oh yes, we baked cookies and did puzzles and went swimming and biking. AND, we had more snow. We all had to shovel it off the driveway so we could come and meet you."

Over Sam's shoulder, Meredith could see Wendy grinning, the boys hanging back and waiting their turn for a hug. Meredith wondered if they felt pre-empted by Sam. She needed to make sure she fussed over them too. It had been a wonderful, event-filled weekend but both Andy and Meredith were so glad to be back. They thanked Wendy profusely, said goodbye to the boys and were quickly on their way home to sleepy, comfortable Dawson Creek, no traffic, no crowds, familiar faces everywhere, all the comforts of home. People had been asking them lately, "So when you retire, are you going to move south?"

Their answer was definitive. "Oh no, we'll be staying right here and hope to be more involved than ever in our community."

CHAPTER 34

———

Christmas with Sam
December, 2007

November in the Taylor house was uneventful, at least in terms of what the previous months had turned up. That didn't mean that it wasn't busy. In early November, Andy and Hugh and some other friends always did a fair bit of hunting. The Peace Country has plenty of wild game; deer, moose, elk, Canada geese, ruff grouse, so plentiful that the farmers have great difficulty keeping their grain and hay from getting trampled and eaten. The geese eat the grain as it's lying in the field in swaths, waiting to mature and dry for combining. This is a superb menu for them to fatten up on before they fly south. The deer are so abundant, it is not unusual to see ten or fifteen in a field at dusk or dawn and they are always a road hazard. Moose are not quite as much of a nuisance for the farmers as they like to stay in the bush but they do travel and cross highways regularly. They are an even worse road hazard because of their size, often reaching over a thousand pounds. They have longer legs, placing their body mass at the height of an average car's windshield.

Most of the farmers are quite happy to have hunters come onto their land to help control the populations. Andy and his friend Hugh were out for the first week of the hunting season and managed to get a doe deer, a young male elk, and a young male moose, all three of which produced excellent meat.

Once the hunting was over, Andy was at loose ends. Meredith came home for lunch one day and he told her he had just purchased a pair of cross-country skis for Sam. He said he was taking Sam skiing on the weekend and Meredith could come with them if she wished. She laughed. "Andy, you are a case. Thank goodness for Sam or you would have nothing to do." It was Andy who had been picking Sam up from school since his retirement and taking her to her skating lessons on Monday and Thursday. He basked in her successes, delighted at how well she was doing with her skating. Her coach told Andy that she was a "natural."

By the time December arrived, Sam was getting excited about Christmas. It made Meredith mad that the Christmas retail hype started right after Halloween. She wanted to downplay the consumerism as much as possible but it was darn hard in the current milieu. The immediate family had decided a couple of years ago to draw names for Christmas but Colby and Dylan were not included because everyone wanted to get something for them. Now Sam would not be included in the draw either and she would get way too much, at least in Meredith and Andy's mind. The older they got, the less they needed and the less they spent and the more they hated to spend. They had been in a saving mode since Wendy and Aaron finished university and were out of their pockets. They recognized they were becoming old and miserly but they couldn't help themselves. For them, it was simply part of the march of time.

It was hard to get into the groove of Christmas. Meredith knew she had to pump it up a bit for Sam's sake. Sam and Wendy were two peas from the same pod when it came to Christmas. It was all about giving. Meredith spent quite a bit of time shopping with Sam, helping her purchase stocking stuffers for everyone. When she didn't know what to get for Ian, Meredith told her to call Wendy. When she didn't know what to get for Aaron, Meredith told her to call Jessica.

Andy commented, "That girl is soon going to be talking on the phone as much as Wendy does." It was comical listening to the seriousness of her phone discussions. Meredith and Andy stole secret glances at each other, exchanging knowing smiles.

Two weeks before Christmas, when Meredith was tucking Sam into bed, she asked, "Gramma, can we invite Auntie Colleen for Christmas?"

Meredith was as stuck for words as she had been on the day Sam arrived. She hesitated, and then said, "My goodness, Sam, I never would have thought of it. Have you been thinking about your Auntie Colleen?"

"Yes, I think she might be very lonely without me or my mommy. She might be all alone for Christmas, Gramma."

Meredith and Andy had not yet discussed with Sam what they knew about what was happening to Colleen. They wanted to distance both Sam and themselves from the terrible ordeal she had put them through. They knew she was still being held, pending her trial for kidnapping. "Sam, your Auntie Colleen is in jail waiting for her trial and is not allowed to come out. Do you know what a trial is?

"No."

"Well, it's when Auntie Colleen will be taken to the courthouse, something like where we went to get custody of you. She will have a lawyer who will tell her side of the story. There will also be a lawyer called the prosecutor who will tell how bad Auntie Colleen behaved when she kidnapped you and how that affected you and us. They will both tell their side of the story to the judge and a jury of people chosen to make a decision on what to do with Auntie Colleen."

"But I already told the police that Auntie Colleen just made a big mistake, Gramma. What do you think the judge will decide?"

"That's a good question, Sam. I don't know but I think they may go easy on her since she did return you to us," she reassured.

"When will we be able to see her again?" Meredith could tell the issue of Auntie Colleen was not going to go away. Sam would be determined about seeing her again. Auntie Colleen had been a huge part of Sam's past and it was apparent she had already completely forgiven her. She marvelled again at Sam's sweet innocence and the generous nature of her heart.

"I don't know but it may be quite a while. The activities of our court system move very slowly. Now... let's read, you need to go to sleep."

"Do you think I could phone her in the jail and wish her a Merry Christmas?"

"I don't think so, Sam, but it is very generous of you to be concerned about her. Now let me read to you." Meredith started reading before Sam had time for another question.

"Andy, you will never guess what Sam asked tonight as I was tucking her into bed." Meredith repeated the essence of her conversation with Sam.

"Oh god, Meredith, surely we won't have to deal with this woman again?"

"I don't know but Sam is determined and she is not likely to forget. And, for certain, you and I and Sam will be asked to testify at her trial."

"Testify, yes, but this is a preposterous idea...to consider letting Sam visit with her kidnapper."

"Why not? She's not likely to take Sam again."

"I can't believe you're even considering this. After all we went through. You don't know what that woman may be thinking."

"That's true but, for Sam's sake, we may have to reconcile with her."

"No way! We will be keeping Sam as far away as we can from her."

Meredith said no more but she knew they had not seen or heard the last of Auntie Colleen.

****

Wendy, Ian, and the boys would be arriving late Christmas Eve as they were going to spend the evening with Ian's family. Aaron and Jessica were staying in Calgary to celebrate with Jessica's parents as Jessica was getting too close to her due date to travel.

After Aaron and Jessica had come to visit Sam the first time, they had formed the habit of calling every Sunday. Both of them always asked to speak to Sam. Listening to Sam talk to them was heartwarming. In the beginning, they had prompted her to tell everything about her week; now she was getting very good at it and didn't need any help. It was like she had saved it all up to tell her dad and Jessica.

When Aaron called on Christmas Eve, Sam jumped up and ran for the phone. "That must be Daddy, I'll get it." She didn't even wait to see if it was Aaron. She picked up the phone and started talking. "Hi Daddy, it's Christmas Eve and we're all waiting for Wendy and the boys to get here." Then she was quiet and serious. Finally, she spoke. "I hope it's a girl. I want a baby sister for Christmas, Daddy." Meredith and Andy's ears perked up. "Okay, here's Gramma."

"Mom, we've just arrived at the hospital. Jess's contractions are six minutes apart. She said to tell you she's starting to have some "show," whatever that means. I have to go; I'll call again as soon as I can." He had no time for questions or goodbyes. His voice was filled with excitement and worry.

After Meredith and Sam filled Andy in on the news, Sam had a million questions. "How did they know it was time to go to the hospital? How does the baby come out? How can the baby breathe in there?" And finally, with a worried look she asked, "Gramma, do you think Daddy and Jessica will still love me as much when they have a new baby?"

"Absolutely, Sam, Grampa and I had Aunt Wendy first, then we got your daddy. When he arrived, our hearts just opened up and made room for him too, right beside Wendy." Sam's worried look dissipated and she was on to more questions.

Meredith finally managed to tuck Sam into bed at 10:15. Wendy and Ian arrived at 11:30, each carrying a sleeping boy over their shoulders, already in their pyjamas. Once the boys were tucked in, Meredith and Andy spilled Aaron's news. They hadn't heard from him since 7:30 and Meredith felt like she was sitting on a thousand thumbtacks. Andy poured everyone a drink and Meredith brought out the snacks she had prepared after tucking Sam into bed.

They had just settled into the family room with their drinks when the phone rang. "Mom, we've got a baby sister for Sam. She's so beautiful and so tiny. I cut the cord and I've held her already."

"Wow, what a Christmas present for all of us, Aaron."

"Yeah." They're cleaning Jess and the baby up right now. Jess was so fantastic, what a trooper! Tell Dad he has a 7 lb. 12 oz. gorgeous, red-headed granddaughter. I've got to go."

For a moment, Meredith was speechless. But she recovered quickly. "Sam has her baby sister, a seven pound, twelve ounce redhead! Aaron was so over the top excited." Meredith held up her glass for a toast. "Here's to Aaron and Jessica and their new baby. What a memorable year it has been!"

CHAPTER 35

Sam meets Emily
Jan 16, 2008

Emily was three and a half weeks old and Meredith hadn't seen her yet. She was beside herself. All the emailed pictures just weren't good enough. In fact, it made her yearn for more. When Wendy had been admitted to the hospital to have the boys by caesarean section, it was an emergency because she had developed Helps Syndrome, a condition of pregnancy that is much more common in multiple births and puts both the mother's and the babies' lives at risk. Once the obstetrician made the diagnosis, he told Wendy and Ian to go directly to the hospital and he would meet them there immediately.

After Ian called Meredith at work to let her know what was happening, she went straight to her co-workers and said, "Wendy's having her babies, I have to go NOW." She called Andy and they were on the road to Grande Prairie within twenty minutes. When they arrived, Wendy had just been rolled into surgery and they waited with Ian, his parents, and his brother and wife. They were there to see their grandsons when they came out of the operating room and saw them again in the neonatal intensive care nursery a half hour later. Since then, Meredith literally got withdrawal symptoms if she went more than three weeks without seeing them. She would get edgy and have a hard time concentrating on her work.

"Andy, it's been over three weeks since Emily was born. We have to go and see her this weekend." It was Meredith's first chance to get away from work for a four-day period.

"Where did that come from so suddenly?"

"I don't know, I've been so busy with my hectic January schedule, I finally had time to think. We have to go this weekend or we may not see her until Easter."

"Okay, you call Aaron and Jessica and see if it's okay with them and I'll check the five-day forecast." Travel in the Peace Country and anywhere in Alberta can be treacherous in the winter. Snowstorms can blow up quickly and the temperature can drop twenty degrees or more overnight.

In the morning, Meredith arranged for Sam to be away from school for Friday and Monday and they were on the road to Calgary at 8:00 AM on Friday morning. It was still very dark in the Peace Country; sunrise was not expected until about 9:20 and Sam went right back to sleep. The sun rose under crisp clear skies and the temperature was minus twenty-six Celsius. The roads were clear and Andy made great time, arriving at Aaron and Jessica's at 5:30, despite four bathroom breaks and a quick dinner at McDonald's in Whitecourt.

As they got closer to Calgary, Sam was beside herself. She asked Meredith so many questions. "Will I be able to hold her?"

"Of course you will, but you will have to stay seated while you hold her on your knee."

"Okay, but how much does she weigh?"

"She weighed seven pounds and twelve ounces when she was born but she...

Sam interrupted. "How much is that?"

"Well, let me think...do you know how much a pound of butter weighs?

"I guess so."

"Okay, think about seven pounds of butter, Sam."

"Seven, that's quite a bit! I think that's a lot more than my doll weighs. Does she eat anything except milk?

"Nope, that's it, and it's Jessica's milk. Emily drinks by sucking from Jessica's breasts."

"I know that, Gramma! But it seems kind of weird, don't you think?" She didn't wait for the answer. "How much time does it take to look after a baby? Can I change her diaper?"

"It takes all day and all night to look after a baby. When she sleeps, Jessica will sleep but Emily might wake up every two to three hours for more milk."

"Oh my gosh, Jessica must be ex...haus...ted!"

"You said it, Sam. That's why we have to be as much help as we can be while we're there. Jessica will be tired and we need to look after her while she looks after Emily."

"Will Daddy and Jessica have any time for me?"

"Yes, Sam, I think your dad will have plenty of time for you; but Jessica might be pretty busy." Meredith thought this question was the most important one. She made a mental note to let Jessica and Aaron know Sam's concern.

As soon as they pulled up in front of Aaron and Jessica's house, Sam was out of the car and racing ahead to ring the doorbell. Aaron answered it quickly. He swept Sam up into his arms and she put hers snug around his neck. Time or the arrival of Emily had not cooled their relationship one bit. Their hug lingered and he kissed her on her cheek. When he finally set her down in the entry, he turned to Meredith and Andy. Sam kicked off her boots, threw off her jacket, and ran up the stairs where she heard soft sounds coming from Jessica and the baby.

****

Jessica allowed Meredith and Sam to hold Emily after every feeding until she had been asleep for at least a half hour. Emily was a dream-come-true baby, contented after feedings, already sleeping six to seven hours at night. Her golden-red hair was just like Aaron's when he was born but his new hair came in blonde. Favoured speculation for the weekend was whether she would be a blonde or a redhead. Sam didn't care. She loved her and was so careful with her, wanting to know every detail regarding her care. She followed Jessica around like a puppy, observing and asking questions. And with careful help, she did manage to change Emily's diaper a few times.

Meredith and Sam did a fair bit of meal preparation while Andy and Aaron did the dishes so Jessica could get the rest she needed. She was doing well with breast feeding but Meredith knew that, around three to four weeks, new babies have a significant growth spurt and start demanding more milk. Jessica needed her rest and Meredith had definitely informed everyone of this.

When both Jessica and Emily were up, Meredith made sure they took loads of pictures of her and Andy with Sam and Emily, of Aaron, Jessica, Emily, and Sam and of just Sam and Emily.

The weekend was over far too quickly for Meredith and Sam. Andy was okay; he was always anxious to go home after being away for a while. The Southern Alberta weather was cooperating again. It was clear and calm but cold, still minus twenty-seven Celsius. But Andy had checked the weather for the northern part of the province and it looked like a snowstorm was brewing in the north. Andy discussed this cold front that was coming down from Alaska with Aaron and Meredith. "We may run into a storm north of Whitecourt. Vicious winds and heavy snow are expected."

"Oh, oh, maybe we shouldn't leave today." Meredith was much more cautious about travelling in inclement weather than Andy and she certainly would not be unhappy to stay another day.

Aaron looked concerned. "You're all more than welcome to stay. But if you think you should go, have you got all the winter gear and food you might need in a storm?"

"Are you kidding, your mother has an over-the-top survival kit in the car all winter." Andy laughed and said they better get going. "Who knows, we could have a storm come in over the Rockies overnight and the south will be inundated with snow tomorrow. We will keep an eye on the weather developing up north. We can always get a hotel in Whitecourt if it's looking too bad to travel."

"Okay, Dad, but you better stay in touch with us and let us know how you are making out."

"We'll definitely do that. Meredith will call you every once in a while."

Emily was already down for her morning nap by the time they were ready to leave. When Aaron and Sam hugged goodbye, they were both teary-eyed. While still hugging him tightly, Sam asked, "When are you coming to see me again, Daddy?"

"We are hoping to come up to Gramma and Grampa's for Easter, Sam. That's only two months away. Can you wait that long?"

"I guess so," she said hesitantly. "But I will miss you lots!"

"And I will miss you, my little sweetheart! But we will call you every Sunday. And you will be a very busy girl with school and your skating. It will be Easter before you know it."

By the time everyone had hugged everyone else and said their goodbyes, Andy had packed the car and was getting edgy. "Okay, Meredith it's time to go. We have a long road ahead of us."

"Yes, yes, I know." She turned to Jessica and gave her one last hug. "Thanks so much for everything, Jessica. We both love you like our own daughter, you sweet girl." Holding her tears back, she quickly turned and took Sam's hand and led her to the car.

The trip started out well. From Calgary to Red Deer, the wind was blowing from the west and the snow was drifting across the road but not accumulating on it. The road cleared from Red Deer to Edmonton. Then just north of Edmonton, they caught up to the storm. The wind was blowing again and the snow started to accumulate on the sides of the highway. The radio was warning drivers to stay off the road unless travel was absolutely necessary. The storm worsened so quickly, the snowfall was heavier and the wind was relentless. The traffic did thin a bit but the big transport trucks were the worst problem. They kicked up so much snow with their tires.

After Meredith saw the fourth vehicle in the ditch, she was getting worried. "Andy, what are you thinking? Should we get off the road soon?"

"Yes..., if the storm doesn't let up by the time we get to Whitecourt, we better stop. Man o man, the snow wasn't supposed to start until north of Whitecourt."

"Thank you, dear, I definitely..." Meredith didn't get to finish her sentence. She saw the oncoming car skidding toward them and felt Andy making an avoidance move that put him into a skid. They did a one-eighty half circle and landed in the ditch, tipped almost halfway on their side and facing the wrong way.

"Shit, shit! Damn stupid driver! What the hell?" Andy looked back and saw that the other driver hadn't even stopped. "What an idiot!"

Meredith looked back at Sam. "Are you okay, dear?"

"I think so... what happened?"

"We're in the ditch, Sam. Grampa had to avoid another car coming toward us and we went into a skid and landed in the ditch. But...it seems we are all okay, thank heavens."

"I need to check the exhaust to make sure it is clear of snow so we can keep the car running." It was Andy's door that was the most blocked by the snow. He pushed as hard as he could and he couldn't open it.

"Maybe I can get out and check." Meredith pulled on her winter jacket, mitts and boots, pulled up her hood and tried her door. It was heavy to push open because of the angle but she managed to squeeze out. The snow was hard and deep, up to her crotch. As she tried to move forward in the crusted snow, she broke through and fell into it head first, face plant in the snow. She had difficulty getting upright again but she managed to reach the back door handle and used it to pull herself up. She pulled off her mitts to wipe the snow from her face. Bracing herself on the side of the car, she moved forward slowly. Once she got to the back of the car, she could move more easily in the tracks made by the tires. The exhaust on her side was just barely clear but she had to dig a hole with her mitts to clear the one on the driver's side. The snow was packed and hard so it wasn't easy.

Making her way back to the front door was not quite so hard as she had loosened up the snow a bit. While she was struggling to get the car door open again, a big truck stopped on the road beside them and the trucker came over to help. "Are you okay, Ma'am?"

"Oh yes, I'm fine, we're all okay. My husband couldn't get his door open so I have just managed to clear our exhaust pipes."

"Okay, good, at least you can keep warm now. I think I may be able to hook onto the back of your car and pull you out. You get back in and stay warm." He pulled the car door open with ease.

"Thank you so much. I am ever so grateful."

"No problem, I'll go and get my chain and shovel and see what I can do."

Andy had clambered over to the passenger's side and was climbing out of the car to help the trucker. Meredith moved out of the way for him then climbed back into the warm car. She checked on Sam and saw that Andy had covered her with the blanket they always carried in the back seat.

"What's happening, Gramma?"

"This very nice trucker is going to try to pull us out of the ditch, Sam." Meredith expected more questions but Sam was quiet. She looked worried. "It's okay, dear, we are going to be just fine. Why don't you read your book for a while?"

It took about fifteen minutes for Andy and the trucker to clear enough snow away from the frame under the back of the car to find a solid place to hook the chain on. Andy opened the door and told Meredith to get into the drivers' seat and put the car into reverse. Then he got into her seat and closed the door. The trucker moved forward slowly until he could feel the chain was taunt. Then he started pulling a bit harder. Slowly, the car groaned and began to move backwards through the tracks in the snow and then back up onto the shoulder of the road. Both Meredith and Andy breathed a huge sigh of relief.

"Okay, I need to trade seats with you and get the car turned around facing the right way." They both jumped out at the same time and met at the front of the car. The trucker was there too. "I'll wait for you to get turned around and check your car out to make sure it's okay to drive."

"Thank you so much for your help. What is your name, sir?"

"Fred Strand."

"And I'm Andy. This is my wife Meredith."

"Happy to meet you both." As they shook hands, he asked, "Where are you headed?"

"We are on our way to Dawson Creek but I think we will get a room in Whitecourt for the night."

"That's exactly what I am planning to do. This is a pretty crazy storm. It came up so suddenly—I wasn't expecting it this soon."

"Same here, we thought we would have no trouble getting as far as *Whitecourt.*"

"Okay, you get turned around and back on the road and I will follow you."

"Well, thanks again. Here, let me give you something for your help." Andy pulled a fifty-dollar bill from his pocket and was handing it to him.

"Oh no, I don't need anything. I'm just happy to help." He was already walking away and waving.

"Wow, nice guy, hey?" Meredith commented.

"Yeah, guys like that are few and far between. Let's get going."

As they were pulling into Whitecourt, Meredith said, "God, Andy, we were lucky that trucker came to our rescue. We could still be out there in the ditch waiting for a tow truck, maybe even all night."

"Yeah, it sure could've been much worse!"

****

Even though Aaron and Jessica were so busy with Emily, as promised, they still called every Sunday, mostly to have a visit with Sam. Meredith managed to get every detail out of Jessica as to how Emily was doing. It was a tremendous emotional struggle for her to be so far away. The whole family was planning to come for Easter but that was a long wait. With Sam in school and Meredith still working, time did fly by.

On Wednesday and Thursday night before Good Friday, Meredith and Sam were busy bees, getting food ready for the weekend. Even though Meredith had a good supply of baby toys from when Colby and Dylan were babies, Andy decided he had to take Sam shopping for a few more. She came home delighted with what they had found and had to show all of them to Meredith. "And just look at this, Gramma, look at what this ball does when you push it. It blinks colored lights and plays soft music."

"Wow, that's pretty nice, Sam, I think Emily will really like it!"

On Friday night, after Sam, Colby, and Dylan were in bed, Aaron and Jessica gathered everyone for an announcement. "So, Mom, Dad, Wendy, and Ian," he said with a big grin on his face, "Jessica and I want you to know that we are planning to adopt Sam. We wanted to give you lots of notice, especially Mom."

"Oh, Aaron, I knew this was coming. Sam should definitely be with you and Jessica, that's very clear in my mind but my heart...." Meredith was having trouble talking. "God, I love that child, as I love all my grandchildren. But she has been such a huge...part of Andy's and my lives for the last year."

Aaron got up and went over to hug his mother. "I know, Mom, that's why we wanted to give you lots of warning. We won't take her away from you until after the school year ends. That way, all of you will have plenty of time to get used to the idea."

"Aaron, we are all so happy for you and Jessica...and I know Sam will thrive with you." Meredith was still choked. Are you going to tell her tomorrow?"

"Yes, we will."

"Gosh, bro, you and Jessica have already caught up to us with two kids! And here I always thought you were a little slow!" At that, they all laughed.

No one was shocked by the news, just a bit dazed for a few seconds.

Finally, Andy spoke. "Well, I guess it's time to hide the Easter eggs for Sam and the boys."

EPILOGUE

Friday, July 18, 2008

"Hi, Mom, you're not going to believe this. Is Dad there, can you get him on the line too?"

"Yes, just a minute...okay, Dad's on, what's the big news, Aaron?"

"Well, you knew we were going to Vancouver this weekend to see Leanna's lawyer, didn't you?"

"Yes, we remembered."

"So...as Leanna indicated in her letter, she left a trust fund for Sam but we had no idea how much. I had pretty much forgotten about it altogether until Dad reminded me at the adoption proceedings. Well...get this, we will be receiving a cheque every month until Sam turns eighteen."

"How much?" Andy asked.

"Are you both sitting down?"

"Yes," they answered in unison.

"Would you believe $4000.00 a month for a total of $48,000 a year until her eighteenth birthday. This adds up to a grand total of $528,000.00. And the amount increases at the rate of inflation. Then, when she turns eighteen, as long as she's going to school, her trust fund will give her $50,000.00 a year in four equal instalments, adjusted again to inflation. I can't believe it. Jess and I are still in shock."

"Wow, this granddaughter of mine is going to need some coaching on how to use her money," Andy added. Meredith knew Andy would consider this at least partly his job.

"Sam is not to be told about this money, any of it, until she turns eighteen. Then she is only to be told about the $50,000.00 a year her mother has provided for her post-secondary education for up to seven years. She will find this out in Leanna's letter to her. There was another letter to us too."

"What did it say?" Meredith queried hesitantly, wondering if the letter was upsetting.

"I'll get Jess to read it to you. Mom, I'm so glad we decided to adopt Sam first before going to see Leanna's lawyer. I would have always wondered if the money had been an influence on our decision. And...this $4,000.00 a month will go to you and Dad, retroactively for the past year, nice bonus for your kind-heartedness, hey?"

"Oh my goodness, and I'm glad we didn't know about it until now too. I would have also wondered if it had affected your Dad's and my decision to take Sam in."

"We get $48,000.00?" Andy questioned.

"Actually, you will be getting a cheque in the mail for $56,000.00, it was almost fourteen months, Dad."

"Well...that will be a nice little bonus for our retirement investment fund. Do you know how much is in the trust fund to cover all this and how much will be left when Sam turns twenty-five?" Andy asked.

"Nope, we don't find that out until she's twenty-five. When she turns eighteen, the letter for her from Leanna will be delivered to us. Leanna wants us to be present when she reads it as she wants Sam to have our support when she finds out about her conception. When she turns twenty-five, she will receive a second letter in the mail from Leanna's lawyer, advising her of her remaining inheritance. She will get part of it when she's twenty-five and the final instalment when she's thirty. I'm guessing Sam is going to be a wealthy woman."

"Where on earth did Leanna get all this money? I know it certainly wasn't from her job as a nurse," Meredith questioned.

"Apparently, when her parents died in the car crash when she was twenty-two, the inheritance she received was substantial."

"Well, it seems she must have looked after it well," Andy observed.

"Yeah, no wonder she could afford to hire private detectives to check us all out. How else did she know so much about our family?"

"And the letter, Jess, are you going to read it?" Meredith asked.

"Yes, it's not very long."

Aaron and Jessica

> *As indicated in my first letter to you, I have established a trust fund for Sam so that she will not be a financial burden to you. I am aware that, financially, you are doing well yourselves and probably don't need it. But I have the money and it needs to be used for a worthwhile cause. As Sam's mother, I can't think of a more worthwhile cause than her. My lawyer will lay out the conditions of the trust for you.*
>
> *My only request to you is that you don't spoil Sam with too much. I want her to know the value of money and managing what she has. Money and material*

things will never make her happy. Only your love, her friends, and her personal achievements can do that.

I know this to be true. That is why I never spent any of my inheritance until I became ill. Since my parents died, I have made my own way, not wanting to even touch their money. My childhood was a constant reminder of what money does to people.

I want to thank you and your parents again for taking Sam into your family and giving her a loving home. I know without a doubt that I made a good choice when I chose her father.

Leanna

"Oh my goodness, that's quite a letter. How are you and Jessica feeling about all of this, dear?"

"Well, it has certainly given us another new perspective on Leanna."

"Yes, she was pretty darn sure of how things would turn out, wasn't she? I wonder if she had an alternate plan in case we didn't come through for her," Meredith mused."

"I guess we'll never know that, Mom!"

****

"Oh Andy, what is Sam's life going to be like as an adult? I don't like that she's likely going to be wealthy. That can make your life crazy."

"Meredith, are you going to be worrying now about something that will be happening when we are dead and gone?"

"But Andy, I'm already thinking about how this money will eventually set her apart from her parents and her siblings. That's not a good thing!"

"Let it go, dear, let it go. We don't even know if there will be a substantial amount left when Sam is twenty-five. Let's go to bed." He got up and offered her his hand.

"Okay, okay, but what will happen when Sam finds out the truth about her conception, when she reads Leanna's letter? She will find out when she's eighteen, Andy. What then?" How will she feel about herself and her family and how will it affect the way she chooses to live her life?"

He didn't answer.

Meredith was quiet for a few minutes while she and Andy tidied up the kitchen. "My god, I will be seventy-one by then and you will be seventy-five. I hope we are still here to help her through that."

"What will we be able to do by then? Life will be so different and we will be so out of touch with Sam's reality."

"We will have to make every effort to stay relevant in her life, Andy. She is going to need us *more than ever* when that happens! And remember when I said to you a while ago that people come and go in our lives for a reason. Sam has changed our lives forever, made them richer, more exuberant. Still, I don't think we know yet the whole reason why she has come to us."

With these thoughts lingering in the air, they headed up the stairs.

ACKNOWLEDGEMENTS

My thanks and appreciation go out to all the wonderful people who helped me with this book. My whole family has been extremely supportive and encouraging. My husband helped me with computer issues and did some of the research for me. My son Darcy helped me with some computer issues that were beyond my husband's ability to help.

I want to thank two of the people I interviewed, Kathleen Kennedy from Child Protection Services in Dawson Creek and Brent Neumann of Neumann Counselling Services.

Several people read my book in the early stages when it was not nearly finished yet. Heaps of thanks go out to my daughter Beckie and my daughter-in-law Renee, to my dear friends Sheila DeCosta and Lynn Haugen and my nurse friend Claire Kirk. Their comments gave me the encouragement I needed to continue.

My cousin and friend Corinne Nowoczin, did an amazing job of editing my finished draft, enabling me to clean up my punctuation, word use and spelling. Her attention to detail was meticulous.

A local author, Fran Kimmel, read my finished version and gave me some invaluable suggestions to improve some areas.

The local Writers' group that I belong to has been instrumental in motivating me to finish my book.

Without the enduring help and encouragement of many of the above people, I never would have been able to complete my manuscript and get it to print. To them, I am forever grateful.

BOOK CLUB DISCUSSION QUESTIONS

1. Meredith and Andy have worked hard all their lives, saving money for retirement. How does Sam's arrival affect their outlook on their future and contribute to the upheaval in their lives?

2. Why is it so easy for Meredith and Andy to accept Sam into their family?

3. Is it fair of Meredith and Andy to expect their son to assume responsibility of Sam?

4. What do you think about Meredith realizing she was already spiritually connected to Sam before she was born and this influenced her to make a baby quilt?

5. What do you think of the psychologist's approach to helping Aaron begin to see things differently?

6. How do you feel about Leanna after reading her letters to the family? Is she a criminal or just a victim of life's circumstances?

7. When Sam is kidnapped by Colleen, how do you begin to feel about her? Is she justified in taking Sam after she had spent so much time looking after her while Leanna was ill?

8. Sam's kidnapping is a turning point for Aaron. He begins to think differently about Sam and realizes he has missed

an opportunity to know his daughter. Do you think Sam's kidnapping is critical to Aaron being able to accept her into his life?

9. What do you think will happen to Sam when she finds out how she was conceived? Is there a good time in her life for this to happen?

10. How can her family help her through the tough knowledge of her conception?